FROST BOUND

Published by Renegade Publishing

Cover Art Selkie

Editing by Oceans Edits

Proofreading by Red Ink Ninja and Maddie

ASIN: B0DRDZMMGW

Paperback: 979-8-33483-6098-6

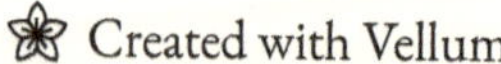 Created with Vellum

To those who are over men:

Let's choose monsters instead.

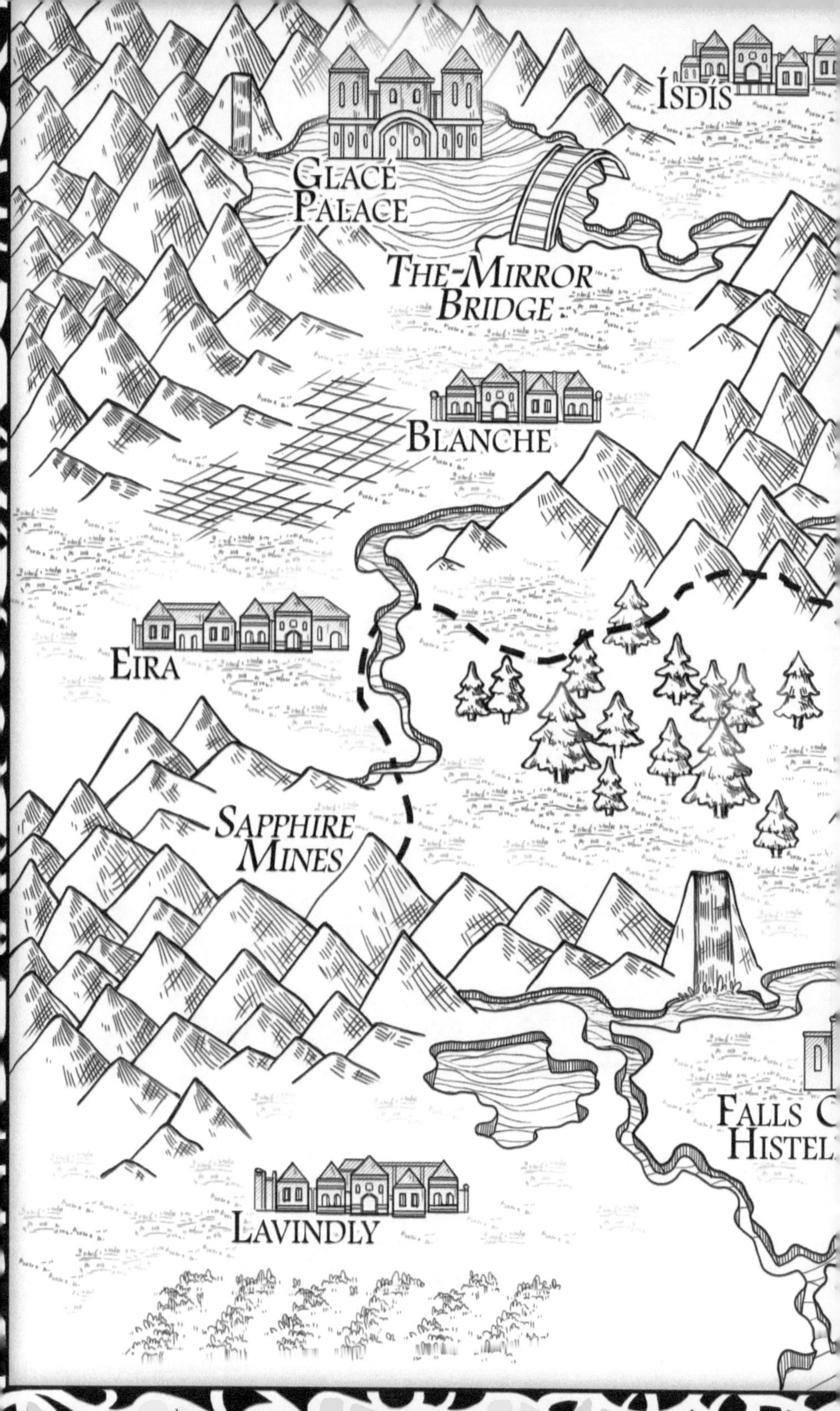

ÍSÐÍS
GLACÉ PALACE
THE-MIRROR BRIDGE
BLANCHE
EIRA
SAPPHIRE MINES
FALLS O
HISTEL
LAVINDLY

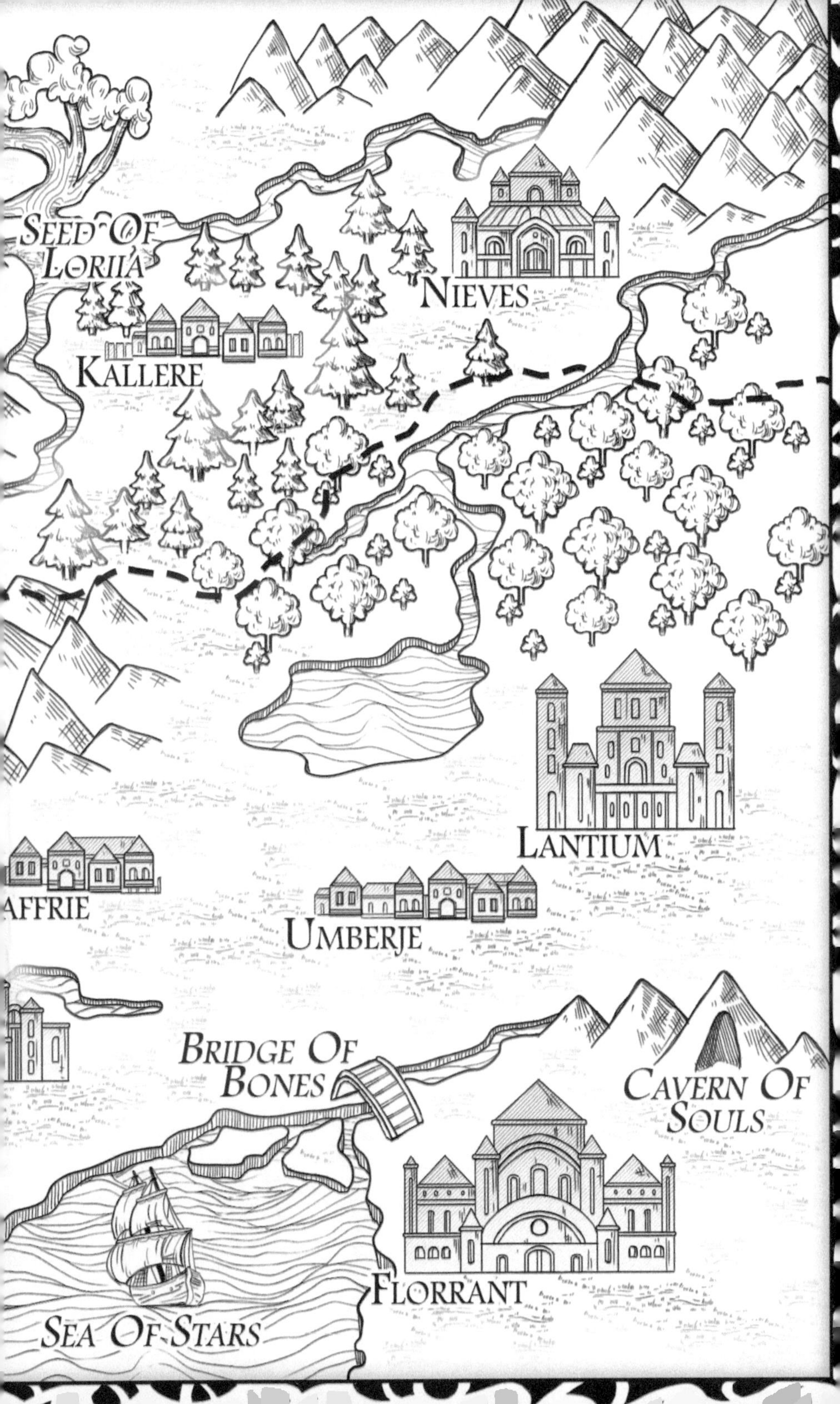

SEED OF LORIIA
KALLERE
NIEVES
LANTIUM
AFFRIE
UMBERJE
BRIDGE OF BONES
CAVERN OF SOULS
FLORRANT
SEA OF STARS

SYNOPSIS

Dahlia Skysinger has managed to survive the underworld of Astera her whole life through clever deals, selling her voice, and never staying in one place too long. When her little brother is caught stealing from the crown, Lia is forced to make a cruel bargain with the royals.

Her life for his.

To regain her freedom, Lia must impersonate the princess, marry the monstrous frost giant king, then spy on and . . . *kill* him.

Taking a human bride is King Neve's last chance to secure peace for his people. Promised a frail mortal princess he could lock away and forget about, the last thing he expects is a woman with a sharp tongue and a reckless amount of courage. Lia might be the key to avoiding war, but he doesn't trust a single word that falls from her pretty lips.

And so the wicked game of trickery and survival begins.

But what happens when an assassin starts to have feelings for her target, and a king's icy heart begins to melt for his little human bride?

Book One of The Entangled in Trickery Series

Also By Frost Kay

Rebel's Blade

Crown's Shield

Siren's Lure

Enemy's Queen

King's Warrior

Warlord's Shadow

Spy's Mask

Court's Fool

Prince's Poison

The Aermian Feuds Collection

Kingdom of Rebels & Thorns

Queen of Monsters & Madness

Reign of Blood & Poison

DOMINION OF ASH

(Post Apocalyptic Fantasy)

A Spire of Lies

A Kiss of Shadow

A Touch of Mayhem

NEVER MISS A BOOK RELEASE.

Get exclusive giveaways, bookish news, review copies, and a free gift upon sign up by subscribing to Frost Kay's newsletter:

https://www.frostkay.net/book-loot

Glossary

Common Loriian words:
Reilleve - queen
Reillov - king
Niliave - wife
Niliov - husband
Loviaye - bride
Valles - female (human or giant)
Vallos - male (human or giant)
Nonnae - a healer
Nonnaette - a healer's apprentice
Haunt - the Frost Throne's elite warriors
Mommar - mother
Povvar - father
Saloes - human
Caern'ye - shoulder horns of highborn giants
Seittae - Please
Jiaell vei - Thank you
Lo bietelle - I'm sorry

Lo kaeye vei - I love you
Tue - Are you
Araevve - stop
Daemiir - sleep
Sei - yes
Niv - no
Lae - my
Vei - you
Lo - I
Bentai - curse for a woman
Jaivelle - a singing gem
Lysterm - black iridescent dye native to Loriia
Astrylle - snow owls that bond with warriors
Germals - color changing fish
Dimedon - huge bear like creatures
Rukhal - a stag like creature

CHAPTER ONE

DAHLIA

BEING POOR REALLY WAS THE WORST.

Dahlia lifted her chin higher as an aria spilled from her lips, all the while slapping away the oaf's hand just to her left. The bloody sod wouldn't stop pawing at her skirt and touching her right ankle. Any touch to her legs made Lia want to claw and kick. Anything to hide her shame.

Keep it together.

She smiled at the drunken crowd in the large, dimly lit tavern, and continued to play her part as the mysterious traveling bard. People were always intrigued by the mysterious. In truth, Lia was just your average young woman trying to keep her family fed.

The last note fell from her lips and the men and women cheered, some slamming the bottom of their tankards against the tables. Lia smiled, her stomach cramping as a serving maid passed by the small stage with two bowls of stew and crusty bread. Gods, when was the last time she'd had a proper meal? Two days? Three?

She reached for the cup of water on a stool to her left and took a sip, praying it would settle her empty stomach. Just a few more songs until she'd finish her set, then the barkeeper had promised some dinner for herself and her brother.

Speaking of her brother...

Dahlia scanned the room, searching for Cosmos' familiar mop of dark strawberry-blond hair. Her lips thinned when she didn't find him. Where was the little devil? He was not supposed to leave his chair tonight with so many of the Giver's Recurrence in attendance—the slum lord's elite bruisers. The thug's men usually didn't leave their little kingdom of Wicked unless on a job. What were they up to tonight?

Mentally, she kicked herself. During her performances, she lost herself to the music, something Cosmos well knew. He sometimes used her distraction to sneak out and spend time with friends ... if you could call them that. He'd fallen in with the wrong crowd in the last year, and she couldn't pry him from them. Lia growled underneath her breath. When she found her brother, she would skin him.

A large palm settled against her ankle once again, meaty fingers encircling the delicate bones.

He'd picked the wrong day to bother Dahlia.

Rotating her hips, Lia glared down at the man grinning up at her and kicked him in the forearm with the left foot of her pointy-toed slipper. She'd had them reenforced with metal for occasions such as these. He dropped her ankle and howled, clutching his arm. She yanked a dagger from the secret pocket in her dress and dropped into a squat, pressing the sharp tip into the man's belly. His dark eyes widened comically.

"Keep your hands to yourself," she hissed softly. "Or I will gut you like the pig that you are." The leather ring woven through the fingers of his right hand caught her eye, and her scowl deepened. Not only a worm but a philanderer. "Maybe I should find your wife and tell her what you've been up to."

He turned paler and leaned away from her blade. "I meant nothing by it. It's just a little fun."

"It's only fun when both of us consent to it. What you were doing was not innocent," Lia practically growled. "Be gone with you."

He scrambled from his chair and disappeared.

Good riddance.

Dahlia slowly stood and stowed her blade. He was a degenerate and a bully, to be sure. She hoped he minded his manners from here on out, but that wasn't likely. At least this was the last night at The Bawdy Bessy for a few weeks, so if he got any ideas about exacting revenge for the slight, she'd be long gone.

Straightening her skirt, she stepped back into the center of the small, raised stage and began clapping her hands and stomping her foot to a slow, rhythmic beat. Soon the whole tavern joined in, and Dahlia opened her mouth and sang.

Only a few more songs and then she could eat.

Hopefully, her stomach wouldn't devour itself in the process.

✳ 3 ✳

By the time she'd finished for the night, Dahlia was hot and sweaty. Her heavy fall of reddish-blonde hair stuck to the back of her neck uncomfortably. She waved to her well-wishers and scooped up the meager coins that some of the patrons had tossed into the basket at her feet. It wasn't much, but they would be able to buy two-day-old loaves of bread. And from her earnings tonight, she'd be able to pay off the last of their debt to the Giver.

Lia shivered just thinking about the creature whom they still owed gold.

She coiled her hair up on top of her head and pinned it in place as she wove through the rowdy crowd toward the bar top. It killed her that they'd been desperate enough to seek the Giver's help in the first place. They hadn't borrowed much, but the interest had buried them. They'd needed the money for Cosmos' medicine, which he couldn't do without or his fits would emerge, leaving him writhing with his eyes rolled back into his head.

She remembered her mother taking Cosmos and herself to the temples as children. That didn't last long once they'd seen one of her brother's episodes and had glimpsed the mottled skin of her legs. Dahlia swallowed hard; she could still see the clerics screaming at her mother that she'd birthed the offspring of darkness. Dahlia scrubbed her palms along her biceps to ward off the sudden chill that ran down her spine. Even now, she was terrified of anyone who wore the amaranth robes of a cleric. They'd burned one too many people in the name of light.

Lia caught the eye of the barkeeper and jerked her chin toward him. Viro was a tall, thin, older man who looked like a stiff wind could blow him over. That was part of his power. People underestimated him, but she'd seen him knock out four men double his size and half his age. He was not someone to mess with, which was why she liked performing at The Bawdy Bess. While there were lechers every so often, he kept them in line. It was one of the few taverns in which she felt safe.

Her eyes slanted to the Recurrence sitting at a table in the back. *Almost* completely safe.

Viro placed two bowls of steaming meat and vegetable stew before her with a whole loaf of fresh bread.

Dahlia shook her head and pushed the loaf of bread away, despite how her mouth watered. "We didn't agree on bread, and I can't afford it."

The barkeep's eyes narrowed, and he stubbornly pushed back the bread. "It was slightly burnt. I couldn't sell this. Take it. Every time I see you, you're paler and thinner."

Heat burned in her cheeks as she held his gaze, her fingers twitching against the bread. He pitied her. A few years ago, Lia's pride would have kept her from accepting such a gift. And a gift it was. The loaf didn't have a bit of char on it.

"Thank you," she murmured, giving in for the sake of

her brother. She swore he had a hollow leg with as much as he needed to eat.

Viro gave her a sharp nod, the tension on his face easing some. The older man didn't smile often but this was as close to satisfied as she'd ever seen him. "Eat, and then I'll settle your payment."

Dahlia bit her bottom lip and glanced out the window. It was far beyond dark, and she didn't want to wait any longer to visit the Giver. Their debt was due by sunrise. "Can you pay me now?"

The barkeeper nodded and dug into his pocket. "I can do that. May I ask where you're off to in such a hurry?"

She debated telling him a lie, and decided it was smart if at least one person knew where she was going. "The Giver."

Viro stiffened, and glanced around the tavern, his gaze resting on the Recurrence before slapping the coin into her open palm. She quickly hid it in one of her secret pockets. There were way too many pickpockets in their city.

"Lass, you should know better than cavorting with that miscreant." Disproval dripped from his words. "He's a monster. One of *them*."

Lia hid a shudder and shrugged. "I had no other choice." She balanced the bread over the top of one of the bowls and pushed it back toward him. "Will you keep this in the back for Cosmos and give him a message for me? I lost track of him during the set. I am going to eat and then visit the Giver. I'll be back for him later tonight."

Viro now outright glared down at her. "You're going alone?"

"I know how to protect myself." To a point. It wasn't as if she was some great warrior, but she'd picked up some skills over her travels in the last nine years. Enough to get her into trouble. "I'll be back before you know it."

The barkeeper grunted before holding up one finger. "Don't leave before I come back."

She shrugged and dug into her stew. Flavor exploded across her tongue as she tried to savor the soup. It was just too good. The veggies were sweet, the meat tender, and the broth salty. Just as she gulped down the last bit, just short of licking the wooden bowl, Viro moved back to her. He placed a tiny canvas bag on the bar before her.

"Take this with you. If you run into any trouble, just toss a little of that at your attacker, or dip your fingers into it and smear it across their face."

She eyed the bag. "What is it?" *Please don't be poison.*

"Ground chiles from the south. Don't get any near your own eyes or you will want to tear them out to stop the burning for about twelve hours."

That sounded horrible. Carefully, she placed the little spice bag into her pocket. "Thank you once again. I'll pay you back." Lia didn't know how, but she would try.

"No need. You bring me more customers than any other bard in the area." He plucked her bowl and spoon from the counter and turned away. "Be careful."

"I will."

Steeling her nerves for the task ahead, Dahlia retrieved her threadbare cloak from the paneled wall, tossed it over her shoulders, and slipped outside. The air held a chill, signaling that fall was soon to be gone for the year. She lifted her hood over her hair and avoided as many people as possible as she made her way down to Wicked.

Lia avoided puddles of unmentionable liquids on the cobbled lane and breathed through her mouth to try to filter out some of the wretched stench that permeated the edge of the area. Brothels, peepshows, and gambling taverns filled the rookery. Whatever your diversion or perversion, the Giver supplied it. She crept along the street, trying to avoid attention, but from the way the hair stood up at the base of her neck, she knew she was being watched. The Recurrence was always creeping around, surveying the Giver's personal kingdom.

Upon reaching the Giver's palace—a gentlemen's club that no real gentlemen would ever enter—she inhaled deeply and fortified herself for what was to come. Stars, she wished she had Cosmos. While he was only fourteen, the boy was nearly six foot tall, and scared off interested men just by scowling at them.

That was a selfish thought. She'd never bring her brother anywhere near the monster of the slums. The half-blood frost giant struck terror inside her every month she had to pay down their debt. Each time she stared into his soulless black gaze, all she could see was the Haunt as he beat her mother half to death. A shudder wracked her body, but she pushed through it.

Time to get this over with.

She pulled a king face card from her pocket and held it up to the guard at the door. The rough-looking man nodded to her and opened the sturdy door to the brothel.

Lia kept her expression placid, and just barely kept her nose from wrinkling at the scent of rose perfume, sweat, spirits, and sex. She quickly strode down the gaudy, low-lit corridor, and kept her eyes straight ahead. One time in the past, she'd made the mistake of looking into one of the rooms, and it still haunted her to that day.

Her pulse sped up as she reached the double mahogany doors at the end. Two Recurrence dressed in livery guarded the door. It was a joke, really, an attempt to make his thugs look more civilized. They were animals in lace protecting a monster parading as a king.

Shoving her thoughts away, she once again held up the card, and they let her inside. Dahlia didn't hesitate to go inside the Giver's repayment chambers. Hesitation was weakness in this world, and she wouldn't be seen as their prey.

She'd never be prey again.

She blinked hard at the bright lights. It always threw her off. The proportions of the furniture were wrong, just a bit too big and angular. Torches lined the walls, and two fireplaces crackled on either side of the gilded room. Every surface seemed to shine with gold. She focused on the Giver, who loomed behind his immense desk, smiling, fangs bared.

Her pulse sped up, but she kept calm. He might be half frost giant, but he wouldn't eat her. At least not today. She still owed him a debt. If there was one thing she knew about him, he was greedy.

He waved a large light-blue hand at one of his plush scarlet seats and she barely managed to suppress a flinch.

"Please sit. We have much to talk about." His smile widened and it sent ice through her veins.

Gray skin, black claws, blood...

Dahlia shut down the memory trying to surface and strode farther into the room. She stumbled when she caught sight of her brother tied up and kneeling beside the Giver on the floor, his brown eyes filled with tears.

"I'm sorry," Cosmos whispered.

Her knees wobbled and threatened to give out. She placed a hand on the velvet chair to steady herself before once again meeting the Giver's gleeful black gaze.

"What is this?" she rasped, feeling like the world was about to collapse upon her.

"This is a sentencing, my dear. We'll discover what your brother's fate is together. Isn't that exciting?"

CHAPTER TWO

NEVE

Three months earlier

"You must take a *loviaye*," Olwen declared. The king's oldest friend tapped his claws along the crystal table between them, a smirk pulling on the scar that cut across his cheek and into the left side of his bottom lip.

The newly crowned king of Loriia had known this was coming. Neve's advisors had been hounding him to secure the frost kingdom with an heir since the last assassination attempt. His claws clicked faster against the carved wooden arm of his throne in frustration. They still hadn't figured out who'd sanctioned it.

Astera. Vergllos. Beltisse. It could be anyone at this point.

Although he'd planned this discussion, Neve still felt

nauseous at the idea of taking a foreign bride—a *loviaye*. Especially one that was *saloes*—a human, someone so different from himself—small, breakable, pitiful, *dangerous*. There wasn't an honest human among the kingdoms he'd visited when he was a child. It was why he'd lost his *mommar*.

The king locked his emotions down, feeling the tell-tale stir of rage at the long-past injustice.

"I agree with you." He nodded to his cousin, Eyri, who was scribing the meeting. "I've held the throne for a year. It is time I take a *niliave*." He paused. "A *human* wife."

His council erupted with cries of surprise and dissent around the rectangular table. He waited it out and smothered his flinch when his sister's voice rose above the din.

"You cannot be serious!" she shouted. "That is the stupidest thing I have ever heard. You hate *saloes*."

Neve clenched his teeth and took a deep, calming breath. His sister wasn't wrong. They shared the same opinion of the Asteran people as a whole, but to blatantly question him outright in front of his advisers was inexcusable. Her heated remarks would make him look weak, and that was something he could not afford. The kingdom was on the brink of civil war with their own clan lords, and with the Asterans pressing in along the border ... he had to make this sacrifice, and the council needed to side with him. For everyone's sake.

Shut Lumi down now.

He leaned forward in his chair. "Do you want your kingdom to fall into war and ruin?" Neve asked softly, his voice as hard as steel.

Her lips pressed together, turning a pale blue from their normal navy. "No, of course not, but..."

"That is what will happen if we do not forge a truce with the humans of Astera." He scanned the councilors in the room with a stern glare. "We have waged war for hundreds of years with the *saloes*, and it has gotten us nothing but a small mine to the south, widows and orphans, and hatred. This stops with me. Our people must move forward or we will not survive, and we might as well hand ourselves over to Astera's greed now."

Lumi swallowed hard and crossed her arms, disgust rippling across her face. "You would wed a human, bring one of those monsters into our home after what they did to our *mommar*? What they did to you?"

His black claws scratched against the wooden arms of the throne. Even after all these years, Neve could still feel a phantom throbbing in his shoulders—where his *caern'ye* used to be. They'd maimed him by sawing off his shoulder horns and leaving him for dead. It was the least of his torture at the humans' hands, and a bloody miracle he'd survived; his mother hadn't been so lucky.

"She is precisely the reason why this needs to be done." The words were necessary but painful to say. Saying he loathed humans was too pale of an expression for the deep-seated rage, pain, and bitterness he harbored. But he was the king; he couldn't afford to think like his sister did. He had a kingdom to rule, a people who needed trade to survive—trade that needed to go through Astera.

He would marry the little *saloes* wretch, place the princess in the tower, and pray she was as sickly as his spies reported. With any luck, he'd never have to see her after the wedding. "As much as we'd all like to invade Astera and take it by force, it's not possible. We all know how the Battle of Kallere ended." He exhaled heavily. While frost giants were larger and more skilled in battle, humans bred like rabbits and had greater numbers. It made for an evenly matched battle, which led to far too many casualties. *So much death.* He'd lost two of his brothers and his father.

"The only path forward is a peace treaty." The words tasted like ash on his tongue. He wanted to curse at the universe for serving him such a fate.

His *povvar's* closest councilor, Eira, brushed her snow-white hair from her face, her dark gaze looking pensive. "I agree with you, *lae reillov.* But I do have a question. What makes you think they will even entertain such a deal? They only have one legitimate child, from my recollection."

Neve smiled for the first time, revealing just a touch of fang. "Our spies have reported that Queen Allium detests her daughter. The princess is kept cloistered in her own wing of the castle, and has no contact with the court."

"And you're not worried she has some defect?" Eira asked, arching a white brow in question.

"I know she does. The queen revealed a tidbit to one of her lady's maids, one who happens to be in the pocket of one of our spies."

"They hate us," Lumi challenged. "They could marry the Asteran princess off to anyone."

His smile widened mercilessly. "True, but the Asteran crown is deeply in debt. While they were able to continue farming despite the blight of the last few years, they didn't hold up several of their trade contracts. Astera's coffers are empty. They scraped enough together to fulfill some orders for their eastern customers, but they've left their own people to suffer and starve. I have a feeling they'll be glad to sell their daughter off to the highest bidder. Anything to stall a growing rebellion amongst the people."

"Even to so-called monsters?" Lumi spat.

"Especially monsters. The queen is calculating and vain. Allium knows the value of royal blood, and we are the only ones who can afford it."

Bacti, a male with lavender skin smiled, but it wasn't nice. "What of the clans? They expect you to take a bride from the people to unite us. They will not take it well when you choose a foreigner over their highborn daughters."

Neve had thought of this. "I will take their daughters as the queen's ladies-in-waiting. It's one of the highest positions a *valles* can be offered."

Bacti nodded. "Very good, sire. Seems like you've thought of everything."

It took everything inside of Neve not to twitch. There was something about Bacti that rubbed him the wrong way. They'd grown up together, and were friends of a sort ... but he didn't trust Bacti, not like he trusted Olwen.

"What of an heir?" Olwen asked, a smirk on his cocky face. He laced his fingers across his stomach and leaned back in his wooden chair, which groaned under his muscle and weight. "There's never been a half-blood on the Frost Throne in all our history."

Neve narrowed his eyes at his closest friend but

answered the question nonetheless. "A valid question. We all know it is possible for humans and giants to breed, but the survival of the mother is low. Depending on the state of the princess, we may have to enact the concubine edict to secure the Frost Throne."

Lumi snorted and crossed her arms. "I'm sure Flyka will love that," she grumbled underneath her breath.

His former love, Flyka, still hadn't spoken to him since he told her of his plan three weeks prior. He'd be lucky if she'd spit on him if he were on fire, let alone be his concubine. If Neve was honest, he prayed it wouldn't come to that. He'd been raised in monogamy, and had no desire to venture outside of those bonds, even if the idea of laying with a human turned his stomach.

"I will make sure the kingly line is continued one way or another. That is all that is important," he replied.

"Peace and trade are all fine and good, but what will this alliance do for us?" Warrin, an old, silvering warrior asked. "*Saloes* are greedy, and they breed quickly. Do you have plans on letting them cross the border and settle in Loriia? Is it worth the risk?"

Running a hand through his blue-black hair, Neve sat back in his throne. He'd anticipated this. "I have no immediate plans on letting Asterans immigrate into our kingdom. They must prove themselves trustworthy first. I'm under no illusions that this truce will be easy for either side. There are centuries of hatred and violence on both sides. Peace and trade aside, I hope to procure part of their harvest each year." He held his hand up as Warrin opened his mouth to speak. "While we can support our kingdom now, there's no guarantee that the blight or some other disease could affect our crops in the future. Astera can grow things we cannot. This alliance is worth the risk."

"Then am I to draft a letter to the Asteran monarchy, *lae reillov*?" Eyri said, pushing a thick pair of spectacles up his azure nose, black eyes blinking. His studious cousin was quite the scholar and secretary.

The king scanned his council, but all stayed silent. A begrudging agreement.

He dipped his chin in assent. "So be it. I would like to see a draft tonight."

"Yes, *lae reillov*," Eyri replied softly.

"Thank you."

The king stood from his throne and his advisors rose quickly and bowed, their closed fists resting between their hearts. Neve rounded his throne and strode out of the crystal throne room. His back teeth ground together as a pair of light slippered steps followed him. He'd had a feeling his sister would follow him. While Lumi had said nothing at the end of the discussion, she'd been fuming in her seat.

"Not now, Lumi," he growled, his boots slapping against the stone floor. Still too close to the council room. Noise traveled in the stone hallways beneath the palace. His council would be able to hear every word they spoke.

"I will not be silent when you're acting a fool," she hissed back, her voice echoing in the arched corridor.

Qov.

He spun around and grabbed his sister by the arm, pulling her into an empty armory room. Neve slammed the wooden door shut.

He rounded on Lumi. "You cannot speak that way to me."

She scoffed, tossing her braids over her left shoulder. "Just because you're *reillov* now doesn't mean I won't stop acting like your older sister."

"I'm not asking you to. But godsteeth, Lumi, I can't afford to have you oppose me so publicly. Too much is at stake. We need to be seen as a united force, or one of the great houses could see us as weak and decide they want the throne for themselves. Civil war would break Loriia and leave us ripe for the Asterans. Beltisse is content for now, but Vergllos is playing along the edges of treason."

"I'm just so angry!" she shouted, waving her hands, the sleeves of her black dress flapping wildly like a demented raven. "I don't want to have one of those scorpions lurking about the palace. They took everything from us." Tears filled her eyes. "You're welcoming the enemy into our home."

"Do you think it doesn't bother me?" he growled, his own rage at the situation licking up the back of his neck. "That it doesn't sicken me to think about taking a human as my life partner? Even the idea of touching her cool body or looking into her pale gaze disgusts me." Neve ran a hand over his face. "I feel vile thinking and praying that their damaged princess doesn't survive long after the contracts are signed."

Lumi covered her trembling mouth as one tear dripped down her cheek. "You just seem so calm and collected all the time. Like you don't care about what they've taken from us."

His shoulders throbbed again, and he hissed, closing

his eyes for a moment. "I was the one who was attacked, Lumi. *Tortured.*" He opened his eyes. "I watched our *mommar* die in *my* arms as a child, choking on my own blood and pain. How could you ever think such a thing?" His voice was raw—old memories and agony clawing up his throat. "I hate them."

His sister pulled him into a hug, her head resting against the mangled remains of his *caern'ye* on his right shoulder. "I'm so sorry."

"It's okay to be angry with me, but it must be in private. I will always be your little brother, but I am now your *reillov*. Whether we want it to or not, it changes things. I need you to support me on this. It is the only way I'll survive what I must do."

Lumi pulled back and met his gaze. "Our die is cast then?"

Neve nodded. "Let's pray luck is in our favor."

CHAPTER THREE

BASIL

Three months later

The king and queen of Astera were going to kill him.

Basil nodded to the guards outside the throne room and smoothed his hands down the pink silk of his doublet, wiping the sweat off his palms. The letter in his pocket practically burned a hole in his chest as the guards opened the ornately carved doors. His heart thundered as he briskly walked toward the two towering amber thrones at the end of the massive room. Each of his steps echoed off the vaulted green marble ceiling.

Death. Death. Death.

That's what his monarchs would order as soon as he offered them the treaty the Loriians had sent.

He stopped at the bottom of the steps and knelt,

bowing deeply to his sovereigns. The courtier kept his eyes trained on the bottom step, grimacing as a bead of sweat fell from his brow onto the pristine floor.

"Rise," King Randa commanded, his tone equal parts bored and irritated.

Basil rose and swallowed hard, pasting a practiced smile on his face. One that had kept him alive for many years. One had to learn how to trick, lie, and persuade in the court of Astera.

"I have news from Loriia, your majesties." He pulled the letter from his breast pocket and cursed how his hand trembled from nerves.

Queen Allium rolled her hazel eyes and held her hand out for the correspondence, the numerous gems decorating her fingers twinkling in the light. "We don't have all day, Basil. Give it to me."

He scrambled up the steps and placed the sealed parchment in her hand before quickly backing down the stairs, well out of reach when the king's inevitable rage consumed him.

The queen read the missive silently, her brow becoming ever more furrowed, her pale fingers crinkling the paper. "This must be a joke," she hissed, glaring at Basil over the top of the letter like it was his fault.

"Don't keep me in suspense, my love. Just what do those frost giants propose?" The king waved a hand toward his wife. "Read it to me." He leaned onto his throne and slung a leg over the armrest, the portrait of negligent power.

"I'm not your secretary," Queen Allium sniped, glaring at her husband.

"You are my queen, and you will do as I ask," King Randa retorted with a smirk, brushing a lock of auburn hair from his cheek.

She glared at him, her fingers tightening on the letter. Basil began to sweat even more. The last thing he needed was for them to get into a fight and then turn it on him.

"I will read it for you," he offered, proud that his voice didn't shake.

The queen narrowed her eyes at Basil, tossing her silky black hair over her shoulder. "No need. I can handle a simpleton's task."

A dig at him, but at least it had dampened the brewing argument between the king and queen.

For now.

"The Loriians propose a truce." The king snorted but the queen kept reading. "They want to put the past bloodshed behind us and move toward a more prosperous future."

"And how does the new Frost King suggest we do that?" King Randa asked, playing with one of his gold bangles. "Our kingdoms have been at war for centuries."

Basil inhaled slowly and clasped his hands behind his back to keep from trembling.

"Marriage."

The king dropped his foot to the floor and straightened in his throne. "What did you say?"

Queen Allium held out the missive to him, which he snatched from her fingers. He quickly scanned the letter, his hands beginning to shake.

"Those monsters want our daughter?" he growled, brown eyes sparking, "They dare suggest such a thing after they killed my own mother? How dare they!" He tore the treaty in half and tossed it into the air.

Basil tried not to cower as the king scooted forward in his seat and stabbed a finger at him. "Who do they think they are to ask such a thing? Presuming that we'd ever give up our flesh and blood to those blue devils."

"I believe the new king is earnest," Basil managed to get out. "He wishes for peace. As the last of his father's line, if he fails, his kingdom will fall into civil unrest." He licked his lips. "Did you see what he offered as a gift of good faith?"

"We don't need their gems and metals," Randa growled. "If I want them, I'll take them by force. Retrieve the mines they stole from Astera five hundred years ago. It's insulting that they'd offer such a thing."

Queen Allium placed a hand over her husband's and ignored the wrathful glare he turned on her. "The harvest has not been strong for four years. How will you feed an army to invade?"

"Mercenaries."

"That's a good idea, my love." She petted the king's sleeve as if soothing a wild animal. "But how will we pay them with no gold?"

Basil watched the queen. She held the real power. While the king wielded brute strength, she ruled with cunning and mercilessness. It was the queen one really had to look out for, or you'd find a knife in your back as soon as you turned around.

"Then what do you propose? Give our only daughter to those monsters?" the king yelled, his anger reverberating throughout the room.

"I would never do such a thing."

Basil kept his expression neutral. The queen hated her daughter. If the rumor was true, she'd tried to kill the child when she was just a baby because of her birthmarks. The court had never seen the girl in person. She'd been cloistered in a tower away from all prying eyes for her whole life.

"But there are always other options." She smiled, and it sent a chill down Basil's spine. She leaned her elbow on the armrest, and placed her chin in her palm, bright red nails tapping against her cheek. "I think it's time we speak to the Giver."

Basil blanched but recovered quickly. The Giver was a known murderer, peddler of drugs, and trafficker of people.

And the king's bastard son. One the queen had never invited to set foot into the palace.

She smiled at Basil, but it held a cold and ruthless edge. "Please extend our invitation to our ... son. We have plans to make."

Taking that for the dismissal it was, Basil backed away from their thrones, hands held out almost in supplication.

As he reached the doors, the king spoke. "As you well know, Basil, keep silent. If any whispers or rumors reach our ears of our discussion, it will be your head."

Basil bowed. "Of course, Your Majesty."

He stepped from the throne room, his back soaked in sweat. The doors clanged shut but his anxiety didn't lessen. He needed to visit the Giver and pray that whatever the king and queen were up to wouldn't get him killed or throw their kingdom into another war.

❋ 27 ❋

Chapter Four

Dahlia

Present Day

A sentencing.

The Giver's own form of justice where he acted as judge, jury, and executioner.

Lia swallowed hard and forced herself not to collapse in despair. She held the monster's black gaze and tried to think through the panic. The Giver always negotiated. If he wanted Cosmos dead, he would have acted already. He wanted something from her. Just the thought alone was enough to make her want to throw up. Over the last year as she'd made payments, he'd hinted at making other arrangements where he took more than just her coin.

Her stomach rolled but she steeled herself. She'd do whatever was necessary to protect her brother. It was her fault Cosmos was without their mother. It was Lia's responsibility to sacrifice whatever it took to take care of him.

Green eyes fading, cooling blood, a trodden leaf crown…

Exhaling slowly, Dahlia shoved her fear and the past down deep and sat in the velvet chair. Despite her long legs, she couldn't touch the floor, her feet swinging as if she were a child. It was … off-putting. She crossed her legs and lifted her chin to disguise her unease. "What is he accused of, Giver?"

He *tsk*ed. "Giver. That's no way to address a friend. Please call me Adder."

A poisonous snake. What a fitting name for such a creature.

And why share his name now? They'd been meeting for well over a year. Just what was he up to?

She dipped her chin in acknowledgement. "Adder, what exactly is my brother accused of?"

"Theft."

Her brows furrowed. "I see." Cosmos had a great many flaws. He could be impulsive and trusted too easily, but he wasn't a thief. How did she say that without offending the crime lord who could break her neck as easily as a toothpick? "May I ask who is accusing him and what witnesses you have?"

Adder laced his fingers on the top of the desk, a smile twitching at the corner of his lips like he knew a secret that she didn't. "I am the witness."

Godsteeth. "You?" She slanted a glance to her brother. *What have you done?*

"Yes. It seems a few of your brother's friends learned

of one of my lucrative operations. They thought no one would notice if some gold went missing." His sinister chuckle caused the hair to raise at the back of her neck. "I *always* know what is going on in my side of town. Your brother was the lookout and never saw me coming." She flinched as Adder patted her brother on the top of his head. "He was the only one not to run. It's the only reason he's not dead like the rest of his friends."

Her stomach heaved and she placed a hand over her navel. All of those children ... murdered. She blinked to keep the tears from falling, and stared at her glassy-eyed brother, who was trying to be brave but was scared. He may have grown in size, but he was still a little boy to her.

Keep it together.

"What are you planning to do with him?" she asked, her voice wavering just a little.

Adder pushed out of his seat, bypassing her brother, and rounded his desk. He sat on the edge of the desk, blocking her view of Cosmos. He was positively huge as he loomed over her, and that was saying something as she was tall for a woman. She tipped her head back to keep her gaze on him, her nails digging into the armrests and sinking deeply into the fabric.

His black gaze tracked the movement, a predator through and through. "I have a problem, my sweet Dahlia. In normal circumstances, I'd string him up with the rest of his lot." Her heart seemed to stop. "But I feel like that is not enough. They all tried to steal from *me*—their Giver. It was too bold. What if others get the same idea?"

She licked her lips and began carefully: "I know stealing is wrong, but they were just starving kids, not a rival gang. Hasn't there been enough punishment already?"

Adder arched a black brow at her. "You believe your brother should go without any repercussions?"

"No, but I don't believe torturing and killing youths will gain you anything." Her pulse raced as she waited for him to react to her blunt words.

"This is why I like you, my sweet flower. You're so very practical. On this we can agree. Killing your brother would not gain me anything. *But* sending him to the crown for his crimes would put gold in my pocket."

She stiffened. The dungeons of Florrant were a living hell. "You mustn't."

"I feel as if my hands are tied, Dahlia. In fact..." He gestured to Jekket, another half-giant, who hauled Cosmos from the floor. She slipped from her chair as the Recurrence guard dragged her struggling brother from the room. Her jaw clenched when Jekket winked at her just before he closed the door behind them. Stars, she hated him. Lia stared at the exit, feeling as if her chest were about to cave in. Fighting would be futile, but she still wanted to try.

Be smart. Keep calm. Don't lose your head.

Large pale blue fingers clasped her chin and forced her attention to the demon who'd stolen her brother away. He brushed his thumb along her bottom lip and Lia jerked away, almost tumbling back into the chair. Her hand dropped to the chile powder hidden beneath her cloak.

"Why?" she rasped, trying to get her emotions in check, just stopping before she dipped her fingers into the spice. "What do you really want?" Everything was a game to him.

"That is the question I've been waiting for you to ask." He placed his palms on his desk and leaned back, stretching out like a lazy cat. "You have a decision to make that could save your brother."

He was dangling Cosmos' freedom in front of her to see if she'd bite. Lia didn't want to engage him, but she needed information. "What are you offering me?"

"Such a clever girl." Adder chuckled, eyeing her in a way that made her wish she were wearing a shapeless fur coat. "I have been entrusted with a special task that I believe you can help me with."

"What is it?"

"Show me your legs first and we'll go from there."

How did he know? Her body flashed hot and then cold. "M-m-my legs?"

"No need to be shy." He gestured at her skirt. "Let me see them."

Dahlia trembled as she grabbed fistfuls of her skirt and slowly lifted it. Bile burned at the back of her throat as the warm air caressed her calves. She stopped when the hem reached her knees. It was far enough that he would see the blotchy, patchwork pattern of her skin. Humiliation burned her cheeks as silence stretched between them.

She hated that allowing someone to look at the splotches of different colors on her legs made her feel lacking. Defected.

Like an oddity or animal in the traveling fair.

"Have you seen all you needed to see?" she asked, her voice tight. There was one blessing for her disease. It had kept away the unwanted attentions of men. Maybe it would repel monsters too.

"I've only seen one other person like that," the Giver murmured, still staring at her legs. "How did you come by it?"

"Born that way."

"Interesting." He blinked out of his stupor and waved a hand at her skirts. "I've seen enough. You'll do, my sweet flower."

Godsteeth, she hated that nickname. "What do you mean?"

Adder clasped his hands together. "I am to meet with one of the king's men on the morrow. I will need you to accompany me."

"As a paramour?" She could play his floozy as long as she didn't actually *become* his lover.

"No, you're too special for such a thing." His smile became smug. "Allium is going to hate this."

Who was Allium? "And my brother?"

"As long as you return on the morrow, he will be kept safe from the crown's dungeons. But if you run or try to rescue him in any way..." He flashed his fangs. "Well, then you'll both wish you hadn't crossed paths with me. Death would be a pleasure."

Finally, a truth. "How do I know I can trust you?"

"Oh, Lia, you can't, but you don't have much of a choice, do you?" He straightened from his desk and pressed a kiss to her cheek, his lips overly warm. "See you tomorrow." With that, he rounded the tall table and began shuffling papers.

Dahlia stared at him, feeling her anger rising. He'd

threatened what was left of her family and then went about his night like it was nothing. She shoved her hand into her pocket and pulled out the coins she still owed him. Lia slapped them down onto his shiny desk and waited until he met her gaze.

He arched a brow. "That isn't nearly enough to bribe me."

"I'm not bribing you. It's the last of what I owe. My debt has been paid."

A smug smile. "And here I thought you forgot."

"Not on your life," she retorted. "I will not be in your debt any longer."

"Never say never, my flower," he said, brushing his fingers over the back of her hand, leaving a chill in their wake.

Dahlia jerked back. "What time should I arrive for our journey?"

"Right after sunrise. Now get some rest. You have a big day tomorrow."

As if she could sleep.

It pained her to leave her brother behind. Everything inside her cried out to go in search of him. But even if she did manage to find Cosmos, they'd both be lucky to survive. He'd be alright for one night. Adder wanted something from her and that was the only leverage she had. All she had to do was show up and her brother would be free. With their debt paid, they could finally leave the city and travel with the theater troupe. Leave the Giver's rot behind.

Only if you survive tomorrow.

A grim thought that was all too true.

CHAPTER FIVE

NEVE

"WHO SENT YOU?" NEVE BELLOWED IN THE human's face. The man didn't flinch.

A professional assassin, then.

Disgusted, he tossed the tied-up man back into the flimsy chair and paced toward the door. Three hours of interrogation and still nothing.

"Take him away," he growled.

Two of his Haunts peeled away from the walls of the small inn room and dragged the assassin out. The door clicked shut and Neve sighed, waiting for the trio of *I told you so*'s from his closest friends. He brushed his nose with the back of his hand, hoping it would erase the scent of the man from his mind.

"Who wants to go first?" he asked, turning to face Olwen, Eyri, and Flyka.

Flyka tossed her silvery white hair over her shoulder,

all the while glaring at him. "If you'd been sleeping in this room, you'd be dead." She leaned back against the far wall, the faded floral wallpaper making her gray skin look garish.

"You of little faith." Neve nodded to his cousin, Eyri. "Are you alright?"

Eyri nodded from the foot of the bed and gingerly touched the bandaged wound on his chest. "It will heal quickly. It was just a scratch."

Olwen scoffed and pushed away from the low-burning fireplace. "It was a bit more than that. It was thirty stitches by my count." He crossed his thick arms and raised a black eyebrow at Neve. "You think our precautions were over the top now?"

Neve swiped a hand down his face, rubbing at his chin. When they'd suggested he change rooms with his cousin, it seemed extreme. They'd been traveling in Astera for only two days. No one knew their route but his inner circle. He'd begrudgingly agreed only because Flyka was so adamant, and she'd threatened to knock him out and move him herself.

He locked eyes with his Haunt; she stared angrily back. Hurt lurked in her eyes. Neve had done that. He'd hurt this passionate, strong woman. Another mistake that would keep him up at night. He should have known better than to get involved with her. At the time, he'd been a prince and she one of his Haunts. He needed to marry royalty, and she was forbidden to marry. Even without the *saloes* bride separating them, they would have never worked.

"It was a wise suggestion," Neve admitted. "Once again, I am in your debt."

"It is our duty to protect you," Flyka replied woodenly. "You owe us nothing."

Olwen snorted, his eyes crinkling at the corners. "Always the dutiful soldier. You might do this for duty, but I do it for the favors."

Neve rolled his eyes. Olwen had been his best friend since they were children. He'd never cared about the advantages that being close with a prince could bring. Neve could be himself with Olwen. No judgment. No expectations. Just friendship.

Eyri adjusted his spectacles and smiled teasingly. "Favors such as floral-scented soap?"

Olwen fluttered his lashes. "I would do *anything* for soap from the south."

The two began to natter on, and Neve's attention drifted back to Flyka. She watched Eyri with a soft smile. His Haunt only ever showed that soft side to Eyri. Neve glanced at his cousin, who gestured animatedly with one arm. Eyri was goodness and light. He saw the world in a positive light most of the time and it uplifted people around him. Part of Neve wished his cousin wanted the throne. He would have made a good *reillov*.

"My lord?" Flyka's voice called.

He turned back to her. Once again, she was the queen of ice. She rarely showed Neve her soft side. It was part of what had attracted him to her in the first place. She understood him—the way he wasn't overly emotional, his drive and competitiveness. His life hadn't been simple, and ruling giants wasn't easy, as he'd seen of his father's time as king. Someone was always coveting the throne, and people would do almost anything to attain power.

"Yes?" he said, moving to her side. He leaned his back against the wall, their shoulders touching slightly.

She didn't move. Maybe she'd forgiven him.

"You cannot be casual with your safety."

"I know."

"You are the last true king, with no heir." Her jaw tightened. "I still struggle with why *you* had to come fetch the *saloes*, but I supported you."

Neve nodded. He'd honestly been surprised when she volunteered to come with the delegation to secure the princess. "You know why I had to come. How could I expect the people to accept this marriage if I wasn't following our customs? Things must change."

"As you say, *lae reillov*." She swallowed hard.

"Speak your mind," he murmured.

She turned to face him, turmoil creased into her forehead. "I understand that, but other arrangements could have been made. You are in too much danger, and the Frost Throne should not have been left unattended."

"Lumi is responsible."

"She is, but she's not you." He warmed at the compliment. "We cannot change the situation we are in, but I would ask you to trust my judgment when it comes to your protection. Eyri will continue to impersonate you until we reach Loriia. You'll go by your middle name Arun." He opened his mouth to speak and shut it when she gave him a stern look. "No questions asked."

"You know I trust you with my life, Flyka. Nothing has changed."

She studied his face as if looking for a lie. "Hasn't it, though?"

Neve's chest tightened. "*Lo bietelle.*" I'm sorry.

"You have nothing to be sorry for. We both knew this was to be the outcome." She shifted on her feet, a very un-Flyka thing to do. "We need to find the road back to friendship. I don't like this murky area of unease."

The tightness in his lungs eased some. "I as well."

She gave him a small, crooked grin. "Then it's settled. The past is the past and you'll listen to your Haunts from here on out."

"You mean you?"

"Who else?" She nodded to the door. "I believe it's time for sleep, my lord. You'll sleep with the other Haunts, and behave until we pass the Loriian border once more."

"As my lady Haunt commands," he said. Not that he would get any sleep. "What of the assassin?"

Flyka smiled, fangs exposed. "He'll enjoy our hospitality until we can return him to his monarchs, of course."

Chapter Six

Dahlia

THE TREK TO THE PALACE WAS A SOMBER AFFAIR.
Well, it was on her side.

The bloody Giver hadn't stopped spouting off
random facts as they passed through the city. He'd even
had the audacity to loop her arm through his like they
were lovers out on a morning stroll. In a swirl of dread and
fear, Dahlia had allowed it, not daring to prod the
temperamental snake. She needed to keep her head.
Cosmos' life depended on it.

The slums gave way to family homes and then the
markets. The circular maze-like cobbled streets looped
over each other, gradually getting wider. Fancy inns and
restaurants bracketed the road, all bustling with well-
dressed workers off to do their masters' bidding.

She tried not to stare too hard at the massive homes
that held highborn men and women. Lia had only ever

come this far into the capital city of Astera once—and it was at night. The architecture was stunning, almost enough to distract her from the task at hand.

Almost.

All too soon, the palace loomed before them, the soaring outer wall jutting from the ground like bleached white bone. Lush green vines hung over the edge of the wall, softening it a touch. She had the feeling that once she entered the walls of the royal palace, she'd forever be trapped in games she had no business playing.

Adder noticed her attention on the plants. "Did you know the plants are flesh eaters and poisonous?"

She blinked slowly. A drunk soldier had once told her as much, but Lia had never put any stock into it. She squinted at the top of the wall once again, noticing a few soldiers.

"How do they not get sick?" she mused to herself.

"Immunity. The crown puts them through a rigorous set of ... well, let's call them tests to make sure they're fit."

A shiver of foreboding swirled in her belly.

Torture. He meant torture.

Lia held her breath as they crossed the drawbridge, her gaze straying to the lotus flowers in the moat, and pausing on the golden eyes that glittered from the murky water below.

The Giver leaned down to whisper in her ear: "Did you know those beasties survive on live human flesh?"

Her stomach churned. "Live?"

He patted her hand. "Don't feel sad, sweet flower. They were traitors. They deserved it."

Her knees wobbled beneath her skirt, and it was all she

could do not to tear her arm from Adder's and run. She took slow, steady breaths as they entered the bailey. It bustled with servants, farm workers, and castellans. The air held the scent of iron, fresh bread, the stables, and exotic flowers.

It was almost enough to make her want to throw up.

A nondescript man approached them and exchanged words with Jekket ahead of them. The half-giant nodded to the Giver. They changed their direction, and instead of going through the gatehouse, they veered toward the brewery. No one spared them a glance as they entered the small, warm building smelling of hops.

"Where are we going?" she braved to ask, as they wove through copper stills.

"You'll see soon enough." Adder tightened his grip on her hand, his touch a bit too rough. She winced and nodded to the man they'd been following when he opened a plain wooden door, revealing a wide stone corridor. It looked like a gaping mouth ready to gobble them up. Her skin prickled as they walked into the enclosed space. Their party was silent, and time seemed to stretch out with each clack of their heeled boots against the marble floor.

Her pulse leapt when another simple door appeared at the end of the long hallway. Jekket opened it, and the Giver halted for a moment, his black gaze wandering over her face. "Be silent unless spoken to, and make sure you think before you speak. You're smart, Dahlia. Don't do something stupid that will get your brother—or yourself —killed, or I'll be very put out."

"Just what are we walking into?" she whispered.

"Victory, my flower. Sweet victory."

That didn't bode well.

Words fled her as they stepped through the door and moved through a curtain of lush ivy.

Pure opulence surrounded her.

She gaped open-mouthed as she took in the grand splendor of what appeared to be a solarium. White marble columns with copper streaks carved like trees stretched toward the arched ceiling that was studded with gold stars. Two mirror fountains ran down opposite walls and collected into crystal clear pools with pale sand bottoms and colorful fish. The air was scented with the lilies that grew in bright clusters around the room. Chaise lounges littered the solarium in intimate corners, like a warm invitation.

"Close your mouth, Lia. We don't want our hosts to think us simpletons," Adder commented, his tone teasing.

She snapped her mouth closed with a blush. "I didn't think we were coming inside the *actual* palace." How'd he even manage to get inside? Her gaze strayed to the door they had passed through, now hidden behind a wall of ivy. "I shouldn't be here," she muttered.

"Hush, and do compose yourself." He released her arm, and she felt a thread of panic. What was he doing? "You're exactly where you're supposed to be."

A footman peeled away from the door and nodded to them. He pressed on a vein of copper on the wall, and it slid to the side, revealing another secret doorway at the end of the room. Adder sauntered through the solarium like he owned the place and slipped through the doorway. She hustled after him, not willing to be left alone. She frowned and slowed next to the fountain as she spotted a serpent the color of blood coiled up at the edge of the water. It struck one of the fish and slithered away with its prey.

Godsteeth, Lia hoped she wasn't the fish in this situation.

"Hurry up," Jekket growled behind her. His hand brushed along the curve of her hips, making her jaw clench. He'd always been too touchy, with a violent temper on the side.

She brushed off his hand and slipped into another dark corridor, but this one led to a spiral staircase. Dahlia trudged up behind the Giver, her gaze latching on to his right hand. His fingers clenched into a fist, and then released over and over as they ascended the staircase.

A nervous tic. That didn't bode well.

She studied Adder from the back. Lia had visited him every week for over a year to pay off their debt. Never once had she seen him this formally dressed. Every inch of him was covered from neck to boot. She frowned. It was as if he was trying to hide his lineage—which was odd considering it was part of the reason he had such a fearsome reputation. Everyone knew Loriians were monsters, and Adder played it up.

Her thighs burned as they climbed four stories of stairs. They reached a platform where an older man awaited them, dressed in so much white lace it made his red face look like a tomato set on a doily.

"Basil," Adder commented.

"Giver," Basil replied with a short bow, one the Giver did not return. "They are ready for you." The man's keen eyes swept her from head to toe. "I see you have brought them a gift."

Dahlia's eyes widened. They'd better not be talking about her.

"I have."

Stay calm. Stay calm. Stay calm.

Basil *tsk*ed. "Let's hope it is enough." He opened yet another plain door and swept inside. "Your Majesties, may I present the Giver."

Dahlia gasped, and Adder shot her a frown before stepping out of sight. Jekket nudged her forward, and she pressed backward, not wanting to move. Why would he bring her before the monarchs? What could they want from her?

He was going to get her killed.

"Move it, or I will drag you in there myself," Jekket growled, his hot breath washing over her.

On wooden legs, Lia stepped into the room, keeping her eyes on the floor. She'd heard of people being executed for less. Her mind conjured up the image of the creatures in the moat. That would not be her fate today.

Carefully, she shuffled farther into the room, studying her surroundings from the corner of her eye. A blush tinged her cheeks as she spotted the provocative paddles and strangling contraptions along the walls. She'd glimpsed some of the devices at the Giver's brothel before.

He'd brought her to the royals' pleasure room.

"Kneel," the guard behind her hissed.

Lia dropped to her knees, attempting to make herself the smallest she could. Maybe if she held still, she could blend in with the floor.

Stop gawking, breathe, and listen.

"What a delight it is to see you again, Allium," the Giver purred to Lia's left.

Dahlia's eyes rounded as she stared at the plush colorful rug depicting writhing bodies. It was racy to be sure, but Adder had used the queen's first name. No one did that and lived. The queen's last lover had been strung up outside the palace walls for calling out her name just once, or so the stories had gone.

He was going to get her killed before she could save her brother.

"It's Your Highness to you," the queen snapped.

Lia winced, and bowed lower, her neck aching with the movement.

The king chuckled, the sound grating on her already raw nerves. "Come now, darling, don't be so hard on my son."

My son.

The words rang in her ears, even as her jaw dropped. Had she heard that right?

"He may be your son, but he is not mine," the queen hissed.

Sweet stars, Adder was one of the king's many bastards.

Lia's mind spun.

No wonder he'd never been arrested or executed for his many crimes. Bloody curses, the royals could have given him the slums. Just what was she tangled up in?

Nothing good, that was for sure.

"Come now," the Giver cajoled. "You know I view you as the mother I never had."

Dahlia schooled her expression and tried to blend into the floor. There was definitely too much sarcasm in his tone.

"I tire of this trivial conversation," the king drawled. "He's only here for one reason. Have you managed to procure what we asked for?"

"I believe I have, Your Highness. Has Basil apprised you of the situation?"

"He has," the king replied. "Bring her to us. I'd like to get a good look at the creature."

The Giver's boots entered Dahlia's vision. "Time to shine, my flower."

He took her trembling hand, and she stood, still keeping her gaze on the ground, loose hair falling along her cheeks. Adder guided Lia forward until she could just make out the edge of a rose-colored gown shot through with gold to her right, and shiny black boots with sparkly gold buckles to her left.

"She's well trained, I'll give you that much," the queen commented begrudgingly. "The mousy little thing hasn't lifted her gaze from the floor since she entered the room."

"Only the best for my lady stepmother."

"Not on your life, mongrel."

"Enough!" the king's voice cut, sharp as a knife. Dahlia flinched, and the Giver's fingers tightened painfully around hers for a moment. A warning. "I can barely hear my own thoughts listening to you two bicker. Let me get a proper look at this girl." A pause. "You may rise."

The Giver squeezed her hand again, this time much more gently. Lia gritted her teeth and forced herself not to yank her hand from his. The situation was precarious as it was. Slowly, she straightened, eyes lifting to take in Astera's monarchs. Her first impression was that the queen was stunning in a cruel, sharp sort of way, while the king was a pompous windbag. The monarchs looked like two primped peacocks. Lia took in the finery of their outfits and had to swallow her disgust. Their jewelry alone could feed the city for years.

The king scooted forward in his seat, scrutinizing her. His dark gaze flicked to Adder. "It's a fair likeness, I'll give you that. Almost uncanny." The way he smiled was a mirror of the Giver's. Godsteeth, it was eerie. "The hair alone..." He brushed his hand over his thin mouth as if in thought. "You've done well, my son."

Adder seemed to stand a little taller. Just what had he done well at? Why was she here?

"Not so fast, my dear," the queen interjected. She pushed a black curl from her shoulder and lifted her chin, her honeyed eyes gleaming as she stared down at Dahlia. A shiver snaked down Lia's spine at the malice and knowing that glinted in the queen's gaze. "We have yet to see the markings."

Lia blanched, and she tugged her hand from the Giver's. She bit her bottom lip as it trembled. How did they know about her legs? She stared hard at Adder until he met her gaze.

"Show them," Adder commanded softly with a nod toward her skirts.

Everything inside her rebelled at the idea of showing them her greatest shame, but there was no other option. Lia wouldn't even make it out of the room if she bolted.

There was a much bigger game afoot, and she was just a pawn.

With shaking hands and heated cheeks, she grabbed handfuls of her rough-spun skirt and lifted it inch by inch. She forced herself not to curl in on herself as she exposed her legs to their scrutiny.

The king whistled, drawing her attention. His lip was curled in disgust that made her feel only a foot tall. "Blood and bones, it's enough to turn your stomach. Hideous."

Heat pressed at the back of her eyes, but she blinked it away. It was just skin. A condition she'd been born with. Not a disease. Then why did their words hurt so much?

Others have said worse. Don't crumble. Just survive.

"We've seen enough," the queen said. Lia quickly dropped her skirt. "What is your name?"

"Dahlia, Your Highness," Lia replied, looking to the royal who watched Dahlia like she was a succulent fruit.

"No family name?"

"Only self-proclaimed. My mother was from one of the traveling bard clans, so it's Skysinger."

"I see." The queen smiled, but it seemed almost mocking. "So floral. How plebian. And yet fortuitous. I was once enamored with flowers myself. Well, dear Dahlia, I have a proposition for you. It seems your brother is in a bit of trouble with the crown."

So the Giver hadn't kept his word. She swallowed down her bitter words and kept her focus on the queen. An outburst would do no one any good.

"He's a good boy," Dahlia said softly. "Made the wrong friends."

"I'm sure he is, but the law is the law," the queen

crooned. "You know stealing has never been tolerated in Astera. It's a serious crime. Your brother's life is in the balance."

Lia's stomach dropped to her feet. "His life?"

"Indeed. While execution is too harsh, serving a few years in the Asterium fields is well within the rights of sentencing."

No. To serve as a harvester in the hallucinogen fields was a death sentence. The pollen of the flowers burned the lungs, eyes, and skin. Most of the workers went blind first, then numb, and eventually drowned in their own blood. It was a gruesome, painful death for the rare jewel-like dye. With her brother's health in the state it was, he wouldn't make it more than a fortnight.

Lia darted a glance to Adder, but he was watching the queen. There was no one here to save her. She only had herself.

"It is, Your Highness," Lia stated woodenly.

"But he is very young for the field, and sickly from what I hear," the queen drawled. She smiled, and it cut right through Lia as if she could see every fear she had. "That does not have to be his fate. We could be lenient."

And there was the bait. Dahlia held the queen's gaze. "He's my last living companion, Your Highness. His heart is my heart. What will you have of me?"

The queen laughed, and it grated Lia's ears. "So very bright. You'll do just fine." Her blood-red lips curled. "We need a spy in the Loriian court."

Loriian. *The frost giants.*

Lia blanched, her palms sweating. "Me?"

"You."

"But I'm not a spy."

The queen waved a hand. "We need you to watch, listen, and write to us. That's not too difficult, is it?"

It sounded simple, yet it was anything but. When her troupe had traveled near Loriia's border, she'd seen the traitors staked at the kingdom's edge. A warning for any humans passing into their realm without permission.

She swallowed hard. "Why me?"

"You're the perfect fit. Now, will you accept?"

"I will ... if it spares my brother." The words were difficult to get out past the fear. "And that is what my lady requires of me." A tactful add-on.

"It is. I assume you're learned?"

"I am." The words felt wrong in her mouth. "My mother taught me well."

"Perfect. Then your training will be short." She looked to her husband, who'd stayed silent, observing the interaction. "What say you, my lord?"

The king grinned. "It seems we have it all in hand. Basil will handle your training. You will stay here until the envoy comes for you. You're dismissed."

Dahlia bowed low, hardly knowing what she'd agreed to. She shot a look at the Giver, who smiled lopsidedly at her and winked. Stars, she hated him.

With slow steps, she moved toward the man they called Basil. He held the hidden door open for her, a fake smile on his face.

"Oh, and, sweet Dahlia?" the queen called. "Behave and work hard, will you? Or your brother goes to the fields."

Chapter Seven

Dahlia

She hadn't seen Cosmos in two weeks. Each day that passed she grew more terrified. Where did they have him? Was her brother being fed? Was he warm?

The questions haunted her.

Dahlia leaned against the frescoed window frame and stared at the dwindling sunset. The colors seemed to lack luster, or maybe that was due to her mood.

Even Adder hadn't deigned to visit. She thought for sure he'd show his slimy face to gloat in his triumph. But nothing.

Servants came and went. The only face she knew was Basil.

He appeared in her room—or cell as it was—each morning with an itinerary. She asked for Cosmos every day but was met with Basil reassuring her that he was whole. Words were a tricky thing. Whole could mean that they hadn't cut off his head but that he was in pain, suffering, starving. Her mind found new ways to conjure nightmares each time the sun sank low.

The guilt was enough to drown her. While there wasn't much choice when it came to the queen's request, Dahlia had been stuffed to the brim and pampered beyond anything she could have imagined. The silent servants even bathed her in milk each night. Exposing her body to strangers had been harrowing, but the maids never even batted an eye at the markings on her legs. They just scrubbed until Lia's scalp burned and her skin turned pink. They'd done their best to erase any mark of hard labor from her hands and feet.

Dahlia sighed and glanced at the full-length mirror, her lips turning downward.

She hardly recognized herself. She looked like a highborn lady—nothing like the traveling bard who couldn't afford even a burnt loaf of bread. Her only solace was the books she found in the bottom drawer of a side table. It had been a long time since she'd been able to read. The monarchy had banned most books as dangerous to the morals of their kingdom.

Dahlia glared at her reflection. What rubbish. She saw it for what it was. Control, not safety.

Turning away from the looking glass, she moved toward the adjoining rooms of the suite, following the soft murmurs. More than met the eye when it came to the queen's task. Lia could have easily gone with the retinue as a servant, so why all the fanfare? They were trussing her up like a sacrifice.

It made her uneasy.

She paused in the doorway and observed as servants carried in garment after garment, Basil cooing and clucking over each one. Some made the cut and were placed in decorative wooden trunks, the others sent away. Lia's eyes rounded as Basil opened a silk bag and pulled out a strand of autumn sapphires. They only ever had been found in Northwestern Astera, the part the Loriians had seized hundreds of years ago. How did the monarchy get their hands on those?

He hummed, dropped them back into the bag, and tossed the strand into the nearest trunk. She gaped, staring at Basil in shock. How could he be so careless with something so valuable? And why were they going into her trunk? The sapphires were not for the likes of her, acting highborn lady or no.

"Basil," Dahlia said sharply, pushing into the room. The steward glanced away from a particularly stunning green velvet skirt. He smiled, but it never reached his eyes as he tracked her approach.

"Yes, my lady?"

She glared at him. "That is not my station, and allowing you to call me that is against the law." One she could be flogged and imprisoned for.

"Your case is different. You need to get used to it."

"Why?" she pressed, hands on her hips. "What is going on?"

"You will be told when it is necessary."

The sleepless nights, the terror and worry for Cosmos, and all the secrecy pushed Dahlia over the edge. "No, you will tell me now! I won't stay in the dark any longer."

The maids froze, and Basil blinked slowly. He waved

his hand, gold rings flashing, and the serving women filed out of the room, the last one closing the door with a soft click. Silence stretched between them. Her chest rose as she tried to take calming breaths.

Basil stared at the closed door for a long moment before meeting her gaze, all traces of the faux amiableness gone. "You need to get a hold of yourself. Your outbursts could get us both killed."

Lia glared at the steward. "One outburst. *One.* I've been very affable despite no new information on my brother, all the fittings, the classes, and the beauty treatments that hurt more than help. I've kept my temper under control. I've kept my head down, but that..." She pointed at the silk bag haphazardly cradled on a crinoline dress. "...makes no sense, and screams danger. I've never heard of any highborn owning autumn sapphires."

"That's because you've spent time with the wrong people."

She gritted her teeth and forced out, "I'm not ignorant, as I have proved so far. Sapphires like those haven't been traded to this kingdom in five hundred years. Only royalty would have access to something that valuable or that old. Why would the queen send those with me?"

"You assume they are for you."

She paused, eyes still focused on the bag. If they weren't for her, and she was meeting an envoy... "A trade gift?"

"It's not my place."

"Make it your place," she growled, exasperation coloring her tone.

Basil studied her. "I suppose you have demonstrated

yourself to be an intelligent young woman, except for that recent outburst."

"Thank you, I think."

"I will tell you this much." He crossed his arms, the lace at his sleeves fluttering. "You need to play your part perfectly or you and your brother will be executed."

That wasn't anything new, but hearing it out loud was enough to make her feel a little faint. "The sapphires, Basil. Explain them to me."

"They were a ... gift for you," he drawled.

"From the monarchy?" She didn't believe it. The gems were a statement.

"From the Loriians."

Her stomach dropped. Lia wavered and placed her right hand on the striped divan to keep from falling over. "And why would the giants send *me* something like this?"

"Because you're not impersonating just any highborn, but the heir of Astera."

He said it so matter of fact, like he was commenting on the weather, not the bloody fact that she was supposed to pretend to be the reclusive princess.

"Why?" she rasped, slumping onto the couch. "Impersonating royalty is a death sentence."

The last time she played princess lead to death and pain. This time would be no different. She could feel it in her bones.

"This was sanctioned by our majesties themselves."

As if that meant anything. The law still held. "If I was ever caught..." She swallowed hard. The Loriians would make her wish she was dead. And if she failed the king and queen? They'd have her hanged for treason. Or worse. "Godsteeth."

"Then don't get caught."

"But why?" Lia sputtered. "Why not send the princess?" Wasn't that what royalty did? They sent ambassadors back and forth to foster good spirit. Although she didn't know what good spirit the frost giants had. They hadn't crossed the Asteran border unless it was to wage war.

"She's the only heir."

Dahlia blinked slowly. The only legitimate heir. "So … I am to go in her place."

"Yes. Which is why it is imperative for you to keep up your etiquette studies." Basil clapped his hands together. "Not that you'll need them amongst those barbarians, but at least you'll make our kingdom look good."

This was way bigger than she anticipated. "When will the envoy be here?" she asked.

Basil brushed some lint off his velvet doublet. "Three days' time."

Not nearly long enough. How did they expect her to impersonate someone she'd never met? Lia squeezed her eyes closed, a headache starting to throb at her temples. "I want to see my brother."

"That's not possible."

"Make it happen," she replied firmly, eyes locking on Basil.

Whatever was on her face wiped all superiority from his own. "You're making a dangerous demand of me."

She shrugged. "It seems I've already made a deadly

deal with our queen. I want to see my brother safe and secure before I leave."

"He'll be fine."

She scoffed. "And I'm supposed to trust you?"

"What else are you going to do?"

What was she going to do?

Fight, her mind whispered. *Run.*

Neither would work.

Negotiate.

"Basil, the successfulness of this ruse rests mostly upon your shoulders, no?"

He squinted at her, straightening. "My queen has tasked me with your care."

"And if I make a mistake ... you will also pay the price." A small twitch. A confirmation. "So we're partners really, aren't we?"

"Getting the handle of being a royal so soon?" he sniped. "If you want to play games, I assure you I've been playing them much longer, lass."

She doubted he'd ever been this desperate.

"I'm not playing with you. You want me to succeed and be obedient. I want my brother safe and out of the queen's clutches. Dear Basil, I believe you're the man who can make that happen."

A little praise never went wrong.

He pursed his lips and cocked his head. "I'll see what I can do."

"Do that." Dahlia rose from the divan and strode toward the bedroom, thankful the skirt covered her shaking legs. "We have three days until I'm collected. I want him out sooner rather than later. Tomorrow, even."

"You'll owe me," Basil called softly. "And my prices can be steep."

"You're no worse than the Giver."

She screeched to a halt as the monster himself grinned at her from the chair next to her bed. Just how much of their conversation had the Giver overheard?

"Hello, my sweet flower," Adder crooned, snapping one of her books closed.

Dahlia glared at the halfling. How the devil did he find that? "Get out."

"That's no way to treat an old friend," he crooned, rising from the chair. He tossed the book onto the seat and casually strolled toward the window as if he owned the place.

He was no friend of hers. Lia exhaled slowly, barely keeping her poisonous words to herself. The Giver never just showed up out of the goodness of his heart. He wanted something. She needed to keep her cool.

"It was my understanding that *friends* don't lie and use each other," she gritted out, not able to keep the anger out of her voice. She bustled to the chair and picked up the faded blue book, brushing her fingers over it tenderly. "But I admit I am curious as to why you're in my room now."

He *tsk*ed, his onyx gaze flickering to her face. "Your room? How quickly you've settled into your new abode. They even put you in the royal suite, glass ceiling and all."

Florrant was known for the spired glass ceilings in the center of its palace. Dahlia had seen them gleaming in the light from afar, but had never dreamed of experiencing them in person. The first night she had hardly slept. It was as if the black night sky was trying to swallow her whole.

Adder faced her fully and leaned a shoulder against the wall. "As for the lying and using bit, it happens all the time, dearest. You can only count on yourself."

Despite her resentment for what he'd done, she felt a small flicker of pity for him. She placed the book on her side table and walked toward the door. She didn't like the idea of being trapped in this room with him. "That's a very bleak view of the world."

His lips thinned for a moment before he covered it with a smile. She'd gotten to him. It was only there for a moment, but she'd seen the unhappiness in his eyes.

"It's only the truth," he said.

"As you see it," she replied.

They stared at each other for a long moment. Today had been a deadly revelation—one that could lead to her destruction. She didn't have the time or energy for his games.

Fatigue weighed down on Lia, and she rubbed at her eyes. "What do you want?"

"To offer you a deal."

"One you'll just break again?"

"Come now, you don't really think I had a choice in the matter? Who am I to the king and queen of Astera?"

"Their son," she said dryly.

The Giver shook his head and pushed away from the wall. "*His* son."

He walked past her to the buffet and pulled the stopper out of a glass decanter. Her nose wrinkled as he took a swig straight from the bottle.

"And what does that mean?" she murmured.

"It means that there is an order for things. Everyone has someone above them pulling the strings. Everyone is leashed."

"You look pretty free to me."

The decanter dangled from his thick fingers, and he gestured toward Dahlia. "As do you, my flower. You're staying in the royal quarters in the Asteran palace, dressed in fabrics I'm sure you've never even been able to touch before, eating foods you'd never be able to afford. You could walk out that door with two of the candlesticks and live as a wealthy woman for the rest of your life. And yet you stew and read books that are *illegal*."

She curled her fingers into fists. "First of all, you know I can't leave Cosmos. Nothing is ever that black and white. And second, the books came with the room."

"I'm sure they did. There are different rules for those wealthy enough to afford them." He arched a brow. "You are *making* a choice to stay. You're not trapped."

His logic was flawed, and yet it struck a dissonant chord within her. Lia grasped the bottom of her neck, feeling like the air was too thin. "Why are you here?" she whispered.

"To offer your brother safety while you're away in Loriia."

So perhaps he had listened in to her conversation with Basil.

Hysterical laughter burst out of her. "You? You're the one who put him in this situation in the first place."

Wrong thing to say. Bullies never want to be blamed or be held accountable for their actions.

His expression darkened to a deeper blue and his fingers tightened on the bottle. "Your brother tried to steal from me first. These are the consequences of his actions, not mine. As for the queen ... well, she's a conniving wench who always tries to foil my plans." His face morphed into a deranged smile. "But I will get the best of her this time, which is why I need you." Goosebumps broke out along her arms as he stalked closer. "We'll steal your brother right out from underneath her."

"What do you mean?" she rasped as he brushed his thumb along the edge of her jaw.

"You look so much like her," he murmured.

"Like who?"

"Like my *sister*."

The princess.

"So you knew the whole time..."

He scoffed, dropping his hand. "I'm in the business of secrets, my flower. Of course I knew. And that's exactly how we're going to get your brother out so the queen doesn't do something we will all regret while you're gallivanting with frost giants."

"You think she would send him to the harvest?"

"The queen does whatever makes her feel best in the moment. Right now, I've won the battle, and she doesn't like that. She'll try to strike back at me."

"Leaving Cosmos in the crossfire..." Unfair, but reality.

He grinned. "Now you get it." Adder took another swig from the decanter before turning on his heel and placing it back on the buffet. "The night the envoy arrives will be the day we strike. The monarchy will be too busy with the foreign delegates to pay much attention to who is in their dungeons."

Dahlia filed that information away. Basil would have to get Cosmos out before Adder made his move. It would have to be tomorrow or the day after at the least.

The Giver approached her once more and cupped her cheeks, his skin slightly warmer than her own. "In three days' time, one of my men will come for you. We'll need you for a distraction." His eyes sparkled. "It will be your first big test to see if you can pull off the princess ruse."

Lia pulled out of his grip, and he winked at her.

"I'll see you soon, flower. Mind your manners."

And with that, he walked out of her room, greeting Basil jovially.

Dahlia closed the door behind her, locking it before leaning against the wood. She closed her eyes and thumped her head on the door. There was no way out but through. Through one mistake, Cosmos had thrown them into the fire.

Her brother.

The Giver.

Basil.

The princess.

The envoys.

The king and queen.

Too many opponents.

One too many secrets.

Lia's heart raced and she began to pant. Dropping to her haunches, Lia put her head between her knees as she tried to calm herself. She began counting to a hundred, attempting to match her breathing with the cadence of her counting. When her pulse no longer pounded in her ears, she lifted her head.

One thing at a time, her mind said.

Protect your brother, her heart pleaded.

Don't break your promise to your mum, her guilt cried.

Don't lose yourself, her soul whispered.

Dahlia had a feeling that what she thought or felt didn't matter.

This was a matter of survival.

Chapter Eight

Dahlia

Basil was moving too slowly.

They only had one more day until the delegation arrived from Loriia, and Cosmos was still in the dungeons. The pompous man assured her it was all taken care of, but she didn't believe him. Not until she saw her brother with her own eyes and held him in her arms.

Dahlia had managed to bribe a maid to trade dresses, and had the uniform hidden underneath her mattress. She'd even gotten a few of the servants to open up about the palace. She offered them a few treats or spirits, and with a cleverly worded question or two, Lia gathered enough information to create a mental map of the area around her.

The dungeons were surprisingly close to the royal quarters. In her mind, she'd imagined the king and queen would like the criminals to be as far away from them as possible. It seemed that the queen had a taste for blood, and liked to visit the prisoners to exact their punishment.

The wretch.

It also seemed that no one knew what the princess looked like. The Asteran heir only had two servants who attended her, and both were mute due to the queen's cruelty.

Her cruelty knew no bounds, it seemed.

Lia waited until all the servants left for the night before closing the door to her bedchambers and locking the door. She quickly stripped and dressed in the servant's garb before creeping over to the far wall, opposite the western windows. It had taken her four hours the day prior, but she'd discovered the secret door the Giver had used to enter her room. She'd even been able to explore it last night. It had been nerve-racking, but worth it.

The secret corridor ended near where she suspected the entrance to the dungeons was. Plus, she only had to make it across one intersection of hallways once she left the relative safety of the hidden hallway. Last night, she didn't see any guards posted nearby from the peepholes.

Dahlia pressed the slightly raised notch on the molding of the wall and the door swung inward on silent hinges. Nerves danced in her belly. She never did anything without a plan, but Cosmos' time was up. Lia needed to get him a message before he was spirited from the palace.

She picked up one of the copper trays full of treats from earlier, making sure to balance it on her palm before she entered the dark corridor.

Carefully, Lia shut the door behind her, leaving the shabby hallway lit only from the filtered light of the peepholes. One of the saucers rattled, and she grabbed the other side of the tray to keep it steady. It would ruin everything if she dropped the bloody thing and someone heard it.

In no time, she reached the end of the hallway. She paused at the door and peered out through the crack. No one was in the curtained alcove. Lia pressed her ear to the door and listened for what felt like an eternity.

Nothing.

It's now or never.

With her heart in her throat, she adjusted her grip on the tray to one hand and flicked the metal latch with the other. The door swung toward her and she stepped into the alcove, slippers silent on the polished stone.

The discreet door swung back closed with a soft click.

She'd made it outside her rooms without anyone noticing.

Dahlia approached the deep red curtains and paused right before touching it. She listened, her ears straining for any sound. *Nothing.*

This was the part that scared her the most. Stepping out into the light.

It took her longer than she wanted to admit to gather the courage, but Lia swept aside the heavy curtain and into the corridor.

No soldier seized her. No servants questioned her. No queen to capture her.

Just an empty hallway and a night sky above her.

Swallowing hard, Lia put one foot in front of the other, gaining speed. All she had to do was walk and mind her own business, not draw attention. She flinched as a male servant rounded the corner and headed straight for her. She kept her eyes forward, fingers tightening on the tray.

Please don't speak to me. Please don't speak to me.

He smiled, but passed by without incident.

Lia exhaled through her teeth. Her steps slowed as she reached the intersection. She veered right, going toward the center of the palace. At least that's where she thought she was going. A pair of soldiers were stationed at the end of the hallway, copper armor gleaming in the lantern light.

She kept her head held high, enough so she didn't look like she was cowering, but not high enough that she looked like a haughty servant looking for attention. They stared right through her. They probably saw dozens of servants come and go each day. Nothing suspicious about her.

Dahlia reached the shiny onyx stairs and began the descent. The glass ceiling of the palace drew farther and farther away as the spiraling staircase slowly consumed her. Hallways branched off at each level and still she continued down. The air chilled as she finally reached the bottom of the staircase. A long hallway stretched out before her, completely encased in obsidian.

The flames from the lanterns danced along the slick walls, creating a hellscape. She shivered, and forced her feet forward. Two soldiers stood at the end of the hallway, a lotus-shaped doorway behind them.

It didn't fit. It was too pretty.

Lia pasted a small smile onto her face and slowed as she reached the men. She held out the tray and glanced down shyly at the floor. "My lady bids me to bring you something sweet." Dahlia held her breath, waiting to see if they'd take the bait. If the queen was down here as often as the servants had led her to believe, Allium must favor some of the men as well as her bloody pastimes.

The soldier on her left cracked first, reaching a gloved hand out to pluck a raspberry tart from the tray. "Please send Her Majesty our thanks."

Lia smiled and lifted the tray toward the soldier on the right, who seemed to be studying her. "Can I tempt you with something sweet?" A double entendre. She hadn't met a man who didn't like a provocative twist of words.

Her statement did the trick. A trickle of interest entered his gaze. He slowly took a date cake, his gaze raking down her body. "I do have a sweet tooth."

She forced a giggle out. "So do I."

"Maybe we'll have to explore our taste for sweets together." A blatant proposition.

"Perhaps..." she drawled. "I can't keep the others waiting. My lady expressed her desire for me to thank you all." Lia stepped between them.

"Hold your breath," the flirty one called. "It stinks down there. And continue to the very end. The men are at the back."

She hustled down one more flight of stairs. With each step, the stench grew worse. Her eyes watered, and she choked back a gag as her slippers touched down on the grimy stone floor.

No more flowers or shiny obsidian.

Just rows of bars and cells and filth.

Oh, Cosmos.

She crept down the aisle, feeling sick at the state of the

people in the cells. None called out to her, but cowered against the back walls of their cells, eyes downcast in fear. She frantically scanned each person, looking for her brother's familiar mop of hair, his freckled face.

Steeling her nerves, Dahlia slowly approached a right turn in the hallway. She didn't know what lay on the other side. More guards to be sure. All she had to do was keep her calm. The sound of boots against stone ahead caused her to freeze. Her fingers clutched the tray.

Did she push forward or run back the way she came? Neither seemed like a good idea, but staying frozen in the dungeons seemed even worse.

The only way forward is through.

With wooden steps, she moved forward and swung around the corner with a smile painted on her face. Lia skidded to a stop as she came face to face with Basil and her brother. She gasped, barely managing to keep the treats on the metal tray.

Basil glared at her. "What are you doing here?" he hissed.

She didn't answer, and stared at her brother. He was dirty, and thinner than the last time she'd seen him, but he didn't look broken. His clear gaze didn't look to be in pain.

"Cosmos?" she whispered.

He swallowed and gave her a lopsided smile. "Hullo, sis."

She took one step forward to hug him, but Basil held his hand up. "Don't you dare. There are too many eyes on us right now."

Lia tore her attention from her brother and peeked

around Basil's arm. Sure enough, two guards were watching the exchange. "Don't leave the dungeons without me," she hissed. "I'll be back soon."

Basil's lips thinned, but he gave her a small nod. He pushed past her, towing Cosmos along.

Dahlia put extra sway in her hips as she approached the guards. A little distraction never hurt anybody.

They, too, took goodies from her tray while murmuring thanks and little else. The back of her neck prickled as she walked away from them. Would they call out for her to stop? Could they see right through her ruse? She wanted to run.

Keep slow steps. Don't speed up.

Lia sighed as she turned the corner and spotted Basil and Cosmos waiting for her in a puddle of darkness. She hustled to meet them. Shoving the tray into Basil's hands unceremoniously, Dahlia yanked her brother into a hug. Tears sprang into her eyes, and she felt how thin he was. How could he have lost so much weight in so little time?

"Are you okay?" she whispered, pulling back to cup his gaunt cheek.

He laid a dirty hand over her own. "I'm fine, Lia."

"Did they hurt you?" she asked, scanning him from head to toe, running her hands over his arms and sides, looking for injuries.

"No. Just not enough food."

"I'm sorry," she murmured, feeling guilt for all the meals she'd eaten since arriving at the palace. She hugged him again, slipping two silver spoons she'd stolen from her room into his pocket.

Cosmos gave her a half-smile, eyes twinkling. He knew

what she'd done. "Not your fault. I only have myself to blame. I'm the one who is sorry." He eyed her. "Are you okay? How are you here? Please tell me you didn't make any deals with the Giver."

She swallowed hard. Lia had done something worse.

"While this is all touching," Basil bit out softly, holding the tray out, "we don't have time for this reunion. We need to get him out of the palace before the window closes."

Dahlia glanced at him before snatching a treat off the tray and giving it to her brother. He stuffed the whole thing in his mouth. "You were never going to let me see him."

The older man rolled his eyes. "Would you rather have seen him or known he was safe?" He huffed out an irritated sigh. "Say your goodbyes. *Later*, we'll be discussing your actions when you've gotten back to your rooms."

Basil stepped away, giving them some semblance of privacy.

Lia clutched her brother's cold hands and lowered her voice. "Go visit Viro. Make sure you lose Basil's escort, and do not go anywhere near Wicked. Keep your head down. The Giver will be looking for you once he realizes you're gone." She paused, waiting until her brother nodded. "I have a little coin and your medicine hidden in our room at Viro's inn. Take it and leave the city. Head north to Lantium. You can find work in the maple fields."

"I know," he whispered. "You've had me memorize our escape route since we arrived in Florrant. Where will you meet up with me?"

Her throat tightened. "You'll be on your own for

awhile. It will take me some time to catch up. Play your music. Earn coin, and move on quickly."

"No." Cosmos shook his head. "We stay together. We've never left each other behind." His voice cracked.

She gave him a brittle smile. While she planned on disappearing once the envoy passed the Loriian border, anything could go wrong. "Don't worry about me. I'll catch up in a few weeks. You'll hardly even know I'm gone."

Cosmos glared at her. "You're not telling me everything."

"There's not time to argue, you stubborn boy. Please do this for me?"

He swallowed hard. "Are you going to be okay?"

"I always am."

His gaze flitted to Basil and back to Lia. Lowering his voice he asked, "What if I have a fit?"

"Keep to yourself as much as possible." She squeezed his hands. "Take care of yourself. I love you."

Her brother cleared his throat. "How long do I wait?"

"If I don't make it by spring, make your way into Fierre."

"I don't speak Fierran."

"It's easier to learn than Loriian, and you'll be able to blend into the crowd better. I will find you. I promise."

Basil held out the tray like it was something dirty. "Time is up."

She took it from his hands, feeling sick. It felt like she was giving up her own child. One look at her brother's face was enough for her to school her expression. He needed to see her confident or he'd never leave the city, leave Lia behind.

Basil scowled at her. "You know your way back, I presume?"

"Yes."

"I'll meet you there in a bit. We need to have a little chat." The words were completely innocuous, but set her on edge. "Give us five minutes before you come up."

Cosmos pressed a kiss to the top of her head.

"I love you," she whispered.

"Love you too."

She leaned against the bars of the nearest empty cell and watched as her brother walked away. Had she done enough to prepare him for the world? Had she fulfilled her promise to their mother?

All she knew was that they were both alone now.

And safety was nowhere to be found.

She left a treat next to each cell until all the treats were gone. She wished she had more for the rest of the prisoners, but it was the best she could do. Her heart pounded as she ascended the stairs and passed the entrance guards. She tucked her head down and walked forwards, not meeting their eyes.

Just before she reached the next set of stairs, the flirty guard called. "If you give me a few, sweetheart, I'll meet you in the kitchens."

Glancing over her shoulder, she gave him a smirk. "I'll see you there."

His low laugh followed her up the next staircase. Her steps sped up once she was out of eyesight and earshot. The guard would be highly disappointed when he arrived at the kitchens and she was nowhere to be found.

Voices echoed above Dahlia and she paused, frowning. They sounded familiar. Lia closed her eyes and listened for another few seconds.

Haughty. Cold. Feminine.

Queen Allium.

Cold dread settled in the pit of Lia's stomach. There was no way she'd be able to get past the monarch. She kicked herself. Forward or backward? Her legs wouldn't move.

The voices drew closer. Too close.

Move now.

Backwards it was.

Dahlia fled down the stairs. She darted to the right at the first landing, heart racing. The short hallway led to a large, circular, domed room lit by small decorative lanterns. Floor-to-ceiling plush curtains puddled on the stone floor. Divans and couches littered the center of the enclosed indoor pavilion.

The voices grew louder still.

She reached the first alcove and yanked back the curtain, only to hesitate. A bed. What if the queen's destination was this bed? Plus, there was too much light. Nowhere to hide.

Lia dropped the curtain and sprinted for the farthest alcove. Sweat dripped down the back of her neck as she slipped behind the fabric. Thankfully, this alcove was dark. She clutched the tray to her chest and tried to breathe shallowly. Her pulse leapt as she spotted the queen and her entourage through the crack between the curtain and the wall.

"I want this pavilion to be transformed into a state of decadence by the morning," Allium commanded.

"It will be done," a matronly servant commented, a firm line between her thick gray brows.

Dahlia backed away from the curtain as the queen moved out of sight, her voice drawing nearer. "Those bloody monsters ruin everything! To arrive early is beyond rude."

Arrive early?

Lia stepped back onto what felt like someone's boots. She frowned, brows furrowing. What the devil was that? Glancing over her shoulder, Dahlia squinted into the dark, making out a shape.

A statue. It was just a massive statue.

She blinked up at the naked, masculine chest and pierced nipples bathed in shadows before rolling her eyes. Only in the Asteran palace would she find something so crude and barbaric.

"Get this place cleaned," the queen seethed right outside the curtain. "I will not have our enemies believe we're simpletons incapable of cleanliness."

Dahlia's attention snapped back to the flimsy textile separating herself from the monarch. It waved as someone passed it.

She drew farther back, her back brushing against the

statue. There was nowhere to hide. Dahlia hugged the tray close to her chest.

Please don't let her find me.

The air changed and the hair along the nape of her neck rose a moment before a huge hand closed over her nose and mouth. She released a little squeak and tried to surge forward. A tree-like arm banded around her middle and jerked her back into a hot, hard body, knocking what little air she had from her lungs. The tray dug into her ribs painfully, caught beneath her attacker's arm.

She clawed at their forearm with her fingernails, desperate to escape. Their breath skated across the top of her head.

"Don't fight or I'll kill you," a deep, terrifying, heavily-accented voice hissed in her ear.

Chapter Nine

NEVE

THIS WAS NOT WHERE HE WANTED TO BE.

The tiny *valles* in his arms flailed and scratched at his forearm with her blunt, clawless nails.

It was pathetic.

As if she could get away.

He cocked his head, tracking the sound of the queen and her entourage.

They were right outside the nook. If Neve didn't get the human under control, they'd both be exposed. And that was something he couldn't afford.

"Don't fight or I'll kill you," he growled softly in her ear, her language feeling uncomfortable on his tongue. While he'd learned their common tongue as a child, it wasn't often that Neve had spoken it.

She froze, terror perfuming the air so much that his eyes watered.

Godsteeth, he hated that stench, but at least she believed him.

He pulled the *valles* farther into the dark, easily dragging her away from the partition. He loomed over her, scowling as she managed to wrap her fingers around his pointer and middle fingers, yanking with all her strength.

Did she really think he'd let her go that easily just for her to scream?

Her cheeks hollowed beneath his palm and the female began to struggle harder. His claws flexed against her cheek, one pricking the bottom of her left earlobe. Iron tinged the air, along with another dose of fear.

Neve rolled his eyes and tipped his head back to stare at the ceiling. Now he'd have to contend with the scent of her vile blood. Humans were just the foulest...

He flinched as a soft, fleshy wet tongue licked across his palm. His grip loosened enough for her to wedge eight of her fingers between her cheeks and the top of his hand.

His lip curled upward is disgust.

Saloes were vile.

The female sucked in a ragged breath. "My nose," she whispered. "Need to breathe."

Neve blinked slowly down at the *valles*, particularly at the way his hand wrapped around her tiny, pale face. He'd been suffocating her. His fingers flexed. Part of him wanted to cut off her air again just so she'd pass out but not enough to kill her. At least then he could leave her in the alcove and slink back outside to meet up with his men.

A muffled. "*Please.*"

There was something in her tone about the way she pleaded that made him hesitate.

Hesitation was always a mistake and yet ... he didn't tighten his grip.

He tilted her head back so that she was staring up into his face, tears dripping from her wide fearful eyes. Eyes that unnerved him with too much color—her white sclera opposite of his black. Little flecks dusted her nose and cheekbones, standing out against her creamy complexion. She looked like the dead. Sallow and dull.

"Close your eyes," he commanded softly.

She obeyed immediately, shaking in his grasp.

A smug grin tipped up the corner of his mouth. Neve wasn't worried about her seeing his face—human eyesight was poor compared to Loriian, especially in the dark. But he certainly didn't want to stare down into her off-putting eyes.

He turned his head and listened to the progress of the queen. She'd almost reached the corridor leading from the pleasure hall. Soon enough, he'd be able to leave the *valles* behind.

She sniffled and he glared down at her.

"Be quiet."

She nodded, exhaling heavily against his palm.

Neve shuddered. An odd sensation that he didn't like one bit. It made the hair along his arms rise.

He shifted, his left hand flexing on the female's rounded hip. *Valles*—human women—were soft, nothing like the angular strength of the frost kin females. If his princess was anything like this woman, how would he be able to bed her? Neve grimaced. It would be an unpleasant event to be sure. That's if he didn't break her first.

Then again...

He mentally slapped himself. A death like that would be unfair to the princess and scarring on him. Better to leave the princess to die in the tower he'd prepared for her.

Tears seeped underneath his palm, wet and sticky.

Enough is enough.

He could barely hear the queen and her sycophants any longer. They were at least two hallways down. Time to play the beast.

Neve traced one of his claws over her pallid cheekbone. "You will be silent about my presence here, won't you?"

The *valles* nodded, her eyes still squeezed closed.

"I hope so or I will find you." He released her mouth and wrapped his fingers around her neck. The human's pulse thrummed against his thumb like a little bird. Neve squeezed once, just enough so that her breath stuttered. "And I *always* keep my promises."

She swallowed hard and gave him one sharp nod.

"Now be gone with you and don't turn back."

Neve released her roughly and she stumbled forward. The little female crashed through the curtain, not looking back. He sighed as he listened to her flee from the alcove, slippers slapping against the stone floor.

Good riddance.

Rolling his shoulders, he glided out of the alcove and straightened his cloak. Maybe he'd do just a little bit more exploring before he returned to his people.

Discover just what secrets the humans wanted to keep from him.

Chapter Ten

Dahlia

It was a miracle that she made it back to her room.

Dahlia hugged a satin pillow to her chest and sang softly whilst she sat on the floor of the spacious wardrobe, eyes glued to the door, waiting for the monster to find her.

When would the demon come for her? She could still feel his whispered threats crawling along her skin.

Duck and cover, for the beasts now roam. Escape now quickly, don't lead them home.

Don't tarry, don't tarry, my dear little one. You are not alone and the danger is gone.

How long had she been hiding? Time warped, and all she could do was rock and count to shut out the fear—the memories.

Vacant eyes, blood, Cosmos.

Sleep and dream for the day is naught. Stars will keep you while fear is fought.

Don't tarry, don't tarry, my dear little one. You are not alone and the danger is gone.

If the monster was coming for her, she didn't want to see it. Pressing her forehead to the tops of her knees and closing her eyes, she fought against her memories and lost.

Nine Years Earlier

Sometimes Lia hated being an older sister.

She loved her younger brother Cosmos but some-times, just sometimes, she wished she could go out without having to worry about him. With her mum always working, Lia had to take care of her rambunctious little brother, and it was ... annoying. He was constantly sticky, hungry, and making a mess of things.

Dahlia sighed and sat on the edge of the fountain in the center of town. She longed to go play with the other girls, but none of them wanted a dirty little boy around, which meant Lia had to follow her brother everywhere as he ran with other littles his age, played in mudpuddles, or collected bugs.

She scuffed her bare toes along the dirt between the old cobbles of the street and glanced toward the snow-capped mountains that loomed above the little town. Her mum said soon the ground would be covered, and they'd have to wear boots again.

She couldn't wait. Winter was magical.

"Lia, come play with us!" Her head snapped up and she smiled at Maege. The little girl waved her light blue hand in a *come here* gesture.

Dahlia shook her head and kicked her buckskin-covered legs. "Mama is harvesting today. I have to mind Cosmos."

Maege frowned. "He's playing with the other boys. Come weave crowns with us. We're going to be princesses."

She glanced over her shoulder at Cosmos. He was right there in the square playing marbles. It wasn't as if she was leaving him. They were in the same area. Maybe they could both play.

"Okay," she said slowly, hopping down from the fountain. Lia padded over to the girls and waved shyly. "Hi."

A chorus of hellos and fanged smiles greeted her. Maege patted the spot beside her and Dahlia plopped down, taking the vine her friend offered. She once again checked on her little brother, who hadn't moved from his spot. Some of the worry left her as she tied the vine into a circle and began to weave fall leaves into a crown with the other girls.

She'd just attached a small acorn at the front when the sound of horses and jangling armor met her ears.

"Haunts!" Maege yelled.

Everyone bolted upright. Dahlia scrambled to her feet, crown in hand. She scanned the square as people ran in all directions. Her stomach dropped when she couldn't see her brother. Her mum was going to be so mad. She always said to hide if the ghost-like soldiers began searching the village.

"Cosmos!" she screamed, dodging adults as they snatched up their children and ran. "Cosmos!" Her heart pounded in her ears; she could barely breathe as she searched the square. The horses thundered closer.

"Not fair!" she heard her brother cry.

Frantically searching, Lia spun in a circle, until she spotted Cosmos near the tanner's, fists on his hips, red-faced. She sprinted through the fountain, ignoring the cold water, and leapt over the other side, skidding to halt behind her brother just as he tried to shove the bigger boy, Wallin, with skin the color of the sky. He didn't move, but a nasty look crossed his face, and he punched her five-year-old brother in the face. Cosmos toppled back, crying immediately.

Crimson trickled down his face, and something hot wiggled in Dahlia's chest. She dropped her crown and brushed her brother's tears away, patting his nose with the end of her tattered dress. "I know it hurts, but we need to hide."

"Haunts?" her brother sobbed.

"Yes." She pointed to a stack of barrels. "Go! I'm coming too."

Cosmos climbed to his feet, still crying softly as he ran to the barrels and hid.

"Run, you big baby," Wallin yelled. "The ghosts are coming to get you, and there's no place to hide."

Lia slowly faced the boy one year younger than her. Wallin was a bully through and through. Her mum said the reason he was so mean was because his parents hadn't taught him to love all different kinds of people. But Lia thought he was mean because he liked it.

He stood a head above her even though she was older. He flashed his fangs at her and made a shooing motion. "Run back to your papa." A pause. "Oh, that's right. You don't have one."

The heat in her chest tightened. "I do. He died."

"You're lying. My papa says that he ran away because he didn't want to be a papa."

Her face flushed and her fingers curled into fists. "That's not true. You're the liar."

Wallin leaned closer. "He left you because you're a pathetic, colorless human."

Her control snapped.

Lia swung, her fist connecting with the boy's cheek. He cried out and grabbed for her, but she darted beneath his arm and kicked the back of his leg. Wallin crashed to his knees, and she jumped on his back, knocking him flat to the ground. Lia pulled his black hair, her knees digging into his spine.

"You're a liar and a bully and a—"

"What is this?" a scary voice growled.

Dahlia froze, blinking out of the red haze that had descended over her vision. She trembled as Haunts surrounded them, white armor gleaming despite the cloudy sky. Her fingers tightened as a pair of black eyes studied her from the top of a huge shaggy horse with sharp teeth. Wallin whimpered, and she came back to herself. She scrambled off of the boy. The boy climbed to his feet, crying.

"What happened here?" the scary Haunt barked.

"She attacked me because I won the game," Wallin cried.

Lia frowned. "That's not true. He cheated and hurt my brother."

"Where is this brother?" another Haunt demanded, his black eyes narrowing in his pale gray face.

Dahlia stiffened, but kept her mouth shut. Haunts stole human children, her mama said. She shivered under the dark gazes of the huge monsters surrounding her. Cosmos had to be safe. He was her responsibility. She glanced at Wallin, who also didn't say a word. His story would be proved a lie if they found her brother.

"Gone," Lia commented.

"You wouldn't lie to us?" the scary Haunt asked, his pale fingers flexing on the reins. He hopped off his mount and grabbed her by the front of her dress. He hefted her into the air.

"N-no, sir," Lia managed to get out, holding on to his arm while her legs kicked the air. He bared his long fangs in her face and she blanched, tears welling in her eyes.

"This is what happens when we let them mingle among us. They cause pain and suffering," he said. "Time for a lesson." He lifted his other hand and Lia whimpered, scrunching her eyes closed as she waited for the blow.

"No!" her mama's voice shouted. "Leave her alone! She's just a little girl."

Lia yipped as the Haunt dropped her; she hit the ground too hard, falling to her rear. She started to cry as her mother hung on the scary Haunt's arm, glaring up at him. Lia screamed when he hit her mum and she dropped onto all fours. She scrambled toward Lia and yelled when another Haunt kicked her in the gut, toppling her onto her back. Her head made a sickening crack against the stone, and yet she still crawled toward Dahlia, until she caged the girl beneath her body.

"Mama!" she sobbed, clinging to her rough-spun dress.

"It's okay, my sweet," her mum slurred, the pupils of her eyes looking weird. She almost looked like a Haunt, her eyes were so black. "I love you. We'll be okay..."

The blows kept coming until her mother collapsed, curling around Lia.

Lia continued to cry, pressing her face into her mum's chest.

"Human scum," she heard someone say, before a wet glob hit the side of her neck.

They were spitting on them, but she held still as her mum made a faint shushing sound. A whip cracked, and then the clatter of hooves started.

The Haunts were leaving.

They lay like that until the square rang with silence. Lia's tears dried and itched on her face. She raised her head and stared at her mama. Blood dripped down her face.

"Mama?"

"*Leph*," she wheezed, her gaze focusing on nothing. "*Teg leph.*"

"I don't understand." She scooted back and her mum cried out in pain. "I'm sorry, Mama." Something wasn't right. "Help." She barely whispered it for fear of the Haunts coming back.

"*Leph*," her mum repeated, and began to shake.

Lia stood, fear pumping through her. She searched the area for someone, *anyone*, but no one was around.

In the middle of the square lay her trampled crown.

Her mother wheezed and seized on the ground.

This was Dahlia's fault.

All because she wanted to be a princess for an hour.

"Dahlia!"

She jerked and cringed back against the wall, the fabrics around her rustling. Lia stared at Basil, who stood in the doorframe of the wardrobe with his hands on his hips. Her heart thundered and nausea swirled in her gut.

"What the devil are you doing?"

Lia blinked slowly at him. Hiding, that's what she was doing. And reliving the horrors of her past. Didn't he know monsters lurked in the castle? That they'd come for her?

The steward threw his hands in the air and stomped over to her, shoving aside all the garments around her. Dahlia wrapped her arms around herself, feeling exposed, like a raw nerve. He reached down and pulled Lia to her feet. His brows slashed together as his gaze swept her face.

"You look like death."

"Thanks," she croaked. Fatigue crashed down upon her as she tried to pull out of the nightmare that threatened to suck her back in.

"What happened to you?" he questioned, suspicion in

his tone. "Were you discovered? Did you expose us?" When she didn't answer, Basil grabbed her by the biceps and shook her. "Answer me!"

"No..." She shook her head. "Only the ghosts of my past came to haunt me." Bane and blood, she was tired.

He harrumphed. "We all have ghosts, sweets. Now is not the time to let them bother you. Too much is at stake." Basil lifted a lock of her hair and squinted at it. "Despite your little adventure last night, I was able to get your brother out of the palace." He sniffed. "No thanks to your meddling."

Dahlia rubbed her forehead. "Last night?"

"Yes, *my lady*," he emphasized. "It's well into the day. The whole palace is in an uproar due to the fact the envoy arrived early, and they don't plan to stay even one night."

Her stomach dropped. "What?"

"That's why I am late." He pulled her from the wardrobe out into the light of her bedroom. "I've arranged for your things to be packed and sent along."

Lia glanced at the ceiling. The gloomy sky hovered just outside the domed glass roof. Not a good omen. The weather seemed to reflect her mood. "My things?"

"Yes, you silly girl. You'll travel with the Loriian delegation, and your trunks will follow behind you."

"So what now?" she asked woodenly as Basil hustled her into the bathing chamber.

"We dress you properly, and ready you to leave with the envoy."

Dahlia swallowed hard, feeling faint. "Are they as scary as everyone says?" She hadn't been able to see anything in the dark, but she felt how the giant had loomed over her like a demon ready to devour her. All she could see was the Haunts in her memories as they beat her mother.

Basil paused, meeting her gaze. "They are ... different."

Translation: terrifying. "I don't think I can do this."

"You must. What are a few claws and fangs?"

Lia shuddered. "Monsters."

"Maybe, but..." His gaze trailed to her legs and then back to her face. "What are a few monsters against a witch?"

"I'm not a witch."

"Could have fooled me."

She closed her eyes and centered herself. All she had to do was get through the meeting and the next few days of travel. Once the delegation had passed the Loriian border, she'd disappear and meet up with her brother. She'd take him and flee the kingdom.

Duck and cover, for the beasts now roam. Escape now quickly, don't lead them home.

DAHLIA COULDN'T BREATHE AS SHE DESCENDED A grand staircase of pure copper. Fear wrapped around her throat like a serpent. Basil strode ahead and waved a hand at the doorkeepers. The two liveried men opened the elaborate double doors, revealing the throne room within.

Lia paused at the bottom of the stairs and pressed a hand to her belly, the hard corset unforgiving beneath the emerald gown. The maids had cinched her so tightly, it felt as if her ribs creaked with each movement. After the last few weeks of being subjected to the fashions of court, Dahlia was thankful she didn't have a drop of highborn blood.

She stared at the profile of the queen, who hadn't looked in their direction. Queen Allium was like a diamond—glittering, cold, and hard. King Randa was another matter altogether. He leaned forward out of his great amber throne, his gaze roaming all over her. Inwardly, she winced. No father would look at his daughter in such a way. If the king wasn't careful, he'd ruin the ruse just by looking at her.

Or show just how depraved he actually was.

The steward waved his hand at her, his expressionless mask in place. Dahlia could take a lesson or two from him. He transitioned with his crowd. While Basil portrayed himself to be an addled fop, she had a feeling he was more calculating, and savvier than anyone knew.

Pushing her shoulders back, she glided forward, her eyes on the ground in submission. Playing princess or not, Lia wouldn't get her head cut off for raising her eyes in insolence. From beneath her lashes, she caught glimpses of soaring columns, gilded frames, and emerald marble. She paused at the bottom of the dais and curtsied, nary a wobble in the movement. Her thighs cramped as she held the stooped position, waiting for the monarchs to bid her to rise.

"Rise," King Randa commanded.

Slowly, Dahlia straightened, still keeping her eyes on the ground. Her lungs labored for breath, but she tried to pull in slow, even sips of air.

"My love," the king commented. "Look what our dear Basil has done."

"You mean turn a commoner into a royal? It's repugnant, and yet ... she's perfect." Queen Allium's tone was begrudging.

Lia didn't feel any pride at the compliment. Looks were only skin deep.

"Let's see if she's truly ready. Look at me, Dahlia."

She peered up at the queen, a little queasy. Allium reminded her of a spider sitting upon a throne, ready to devour her. Dahlia fought back a shudder as she got a good look at the thrones. Large insects were trapped perfectly inside the amber like little trophies.

Like how they'd trapped her.

The queen smiled but it was chilly. "I assume you know the stakes if you should fail...?"

"I will not fail." *I'll run.*

Allium hummed, her blood-red lips pursed. "My king, what do you think?"

Randa pushed his ginger curls from his face and grinned. "I think she knows what is at stake should she fail."

Thank the fates that Cosmos was out of their grasp. Once she crossed the Loriian border, she would disappear, reconnect with her brother, and flee south. There was no way they could stay in Astera, but they could start over. They would be free.

The king grinned, but it was more of a baring of his teeth. "I like you, Dahlia. Our spies have said that you've been very obedient and have kept to yourself since your arrival in our home. Your silence made me curious.

Quiet people can't always be trusted, can they, my dear?"

Her heart thumped harder in her chest. Had they discovered her brother's disappearance already? She didn't dare look at Basil. She kept her attention focused on the king, maintaining her blank expression.

He clicked his painted nails against the armrest of his throne, his smile smug. "I had my son do a little digging. It seems Cosmos isn't your only family member, is he?"

Her stomach dropped. *No.*

Lia's mind whirled and her fingers sank into her gauzy green skirt. He couldn't know about their mother. She'd never told a soul about...

"It seems you've been hiding your dear old mum in the northern countryside."

A lump rose in her throat and the air felt thin. How did they find out? Even Cosmos didn't know that their mum still breathed.

King Rada's smile widened. "I can see from the gleam in your eye that you've been weaving a tangled web of lies, dear child. Just know that your secret will stay safe with us —your mother will stay safe as long as you do what you are told. If not..." He drew a line across his throat. "...we will relieve that foolish creature of her existence."

Spots danced across Dahlia's vision, and she wavered slightly. Basil clutched her left arm, squeezing a bit too hard. A warning.

Get a hold of yourself.

"You'll be a good girl, won't you?" the king crooned.

Lia found herself nodding as she tried to tamp down the panic. Every time she thought she'd crawled out of the hole she found herself in, Dahlia found herself deeper down. When would the dirt start raining down?

"Good. We have another task for you." The king's smile turned predatory. "We wish to be apprised of your movements, and any ... discoveries ... you make while visiting Loriia."

"What should I be looking for, Your Majesty?" she said, throat dry.

"Anything that will help us."

"I will do my best."

"I'm sure you will," Allium said. "But that is not all. That kingdom has caused problems for us for a long time. We wish to be rid of this new king and his presence in our lives. You will do this for us."

Dahlia's lips parted but she managed to keep in her gasp. They wanted her to assassinate the Frost King. She glanced at Basil, but he stared straight ahead like he listened to murder plans all the time. For all she knew, maybe he did.

"Will that be a problem?" the king asked, syrup coating his tone, but not able to hide the glee and malice in his gaze.

"No," she all but whispered.

"Excellent. I know this won't be an easy challenge, but I'm sure you'll use every single *asset* of yours to the fullest."

Translation, seduce the Frost King if you must.

Lia wanted to throw up.

"Don't worry, Dahlia. I will send you help. Just keep an eye out for our spy."

"Who is it?"

Allium smirked. "Now, now. Let's not get greedy. What if you fail immediately? We can't let you ruin all our plans."

By failure she meant Lia's death.

She waved a hand to Basil. "Give her our gift."

Basil produced a box with a simple emerald ring. "Hold out your hand."

Slowly, she held out her right hand and Basil slipped the jewelry onto her middle finger. Lia stared at the ring. "Thank you for the gift." Why would they give this?

"It's more than the sum of its looks, darling," the queen preened. "Press the stone."

Lia followed the command, and the emerald top swung open, revealing a tiny hidden compartment with a wickedly sharp needle in the center. Her stomach dropped. A poison ring?

"A little something to help with the job. Make sure you have contact with the king for ten seconds. Nothing more, nothing less."

Her mind scrambled. There were so many things that could go wrong with this situation. "Can they scent the drugs?"

"No," the king supplied. His smile turned gleeful. "We've had it tested several times."

She hid her disgust. *On who?* Lia closed the ring.

"Now that's done and over with..." The queen gestured to her left. "...come stand next to me. It's time for you to officially meet the mongrel delegation."

Basil stepped away from Lia; she lifted her skirt and ascended the dais to stand beside Allium's throne, her legs shaking slightly.

They expected her to murder the Loriian king. A giant. He'd wring her neck before she even got close to him.

"I do have one question. What name am I to go by?"

"If you remember our prior conversation, I was once very taken with the floral." She waved her hand lazily. "I thought of myself as a romantic in my youth. As it happens, the princess shares her middle name with you. That's how I knew you'd been sent to us."

Only through trickery and betrayal, not by fate.

"Her middle name is Dahlia?"

"Yes, you stupid girl. That is what I just said, isn't it?"

Lia bit back her retort and nodded. "Yes, my lady."

The queen glanced up at her. "Prepare yourself, little flower. The monsters are afoot. Try not to look too shocked and terrified when they enter or I'll be *very* displeased." A pause. "Also, they brought their *king*." Dahlia's eyes widened. The Frost King hadn't left his kingdom since he'd been crowned. "I believe he wishes to assess you before he brings you into Loriia. Don't mess this up!"

"Yes, my lady," she replied softly, keeping her attention on the doors straight ahead with the ring heavy on her finger. Yesterday had terrified her, but it mostly had to do with the dark, the threats, and the surprise. Today, she knew what she was in for.

"Bring them in," King Randa commanded.

CHAPTER ELEVEN

NEVE

HE MADE THE ASTERAN MONARCHY WAIT TWO hours for them.

While the alliance would be good for the kingdom, he didn't appreciate having an assassin sicced on him the moment he entered the country. The bloody human monarchy could wait.

It was with immense satisfaction that he arrived with his Haunt dragging his would-be murderer. Flyka, Olwen, and himself all surrounded Eyri, who took the lead. Neve hid his smile at how his cousin chafed under the royal black regalia. As a whole, Loriians ran hot. They wore little clothing, but *saloes* had delicate sensibilities.

They crossed the immense elaborate throne room and paused far enough back that the human monarchs weren't leering over them. He scanned the room. The princess was nowhere to be seen.

Curious.

"Welcome, King Neve," Queen Allium said, her gaze sweeping over them. "We didn't know you would be attending."

Olwen, Flyka, and Neve all dipped their chins in respect while Eyri stood tall, pretending to be *reillov*. It gave Neve an extra layer of protection, but also time to study the humans. It was a blessing he and his cousin looked so much alike—apart from the spectacles.

His cousin arched a brow and gestured a hand toward their prisoner. "Is it?"

"Yes. Somehow, you're both early and late," the queen stated sharply. "Impressive to say the least."

"I aim to please," Eyri replied. "But it seems I do have some unpleasant business we need to attend to."

Neve tossed the gagged, tied-up man to the floor and crossed his arms. The assassin groaned but otherwise stayed silent.

King Randa cocked his head. "What is this?"

"A gift," Eyri replied, his tone hard and haughty—everything they expected of a king. "It seems you might have lost one of your men."

Neve studied the king, who showed no indication of knowing the man. *Interesting.* His attention moved to the queen, who had a faint smile upon her lips. Amusement at their theatrics? Or something else?

"I've never seen that man before. Just what are you implying?" the king asked, his tone dangerous.

"Nothing," Eyri replied with a smile. "Just that one of your humans attacked my men and I don't appreciate it.

Especially when we've come here in good faith, as you requested."

"How dreadful and shocking," the queen said, her tone dripping with false concern. "I'm surprised your men didn't slay the brigand."

"It was not our place to take that which is not ours," Eyri replied. "I would not anger my new ... ally."

Allium's smile thinned. She didn't like being reminded that they were all bound now. "How thoughtful. I am horrified by this turn of events. We give you his life as recompense, as is your custom, I believe."

So the queen had done her research on their laws.

"Let it be done." Eyri waved Neve forward.

It was quick. Neve never liked to linger and extend death. The assassin never even cried out.

He wiped his bloody knife on his trousers, like the barbarians the humans expected them to be, and stepped back into the protective circle. He stowed his knife and noted how closely the queen was watching him. Her perusal made his skin itch. Like she was seeking a weakness.

She wouldn't find one. Even if he internally cringed at the red blood now staining his breeches.

Their man bled out onto the floor, and yet the king and queen didn't flinch. They were used to violence, then. Maybe even delighted in it.

That was an unsettling thought. But not surprising for the *saloes*.

"Shall we move on to our next line of business?" the queen asked.

"My thoughts exactly," King Randa cut in, sitting

back in his puny throne like a spoiled princeling. "All our treaty requirements have been met but one."

Eyri nodded to Flyka, who strode forward with a frosted glass box in her hands. She handed it to the dandy-looking human at the base of the dais who stank of nervousness. He opened the box, checked the goods, and nodded once to the king.

They'd requested three vials of the black weeping *lysterm* dye, Loriia's most expensive export. The flowering trees from which the dye was derived only grew in Loriia's harsh northern lands.

"Now where is the woman?" Eyri asked, adjusting his spectacles. "I want to see the princess."

The king and queen exchanged a glance.

"Come meet our friends, daughter," the king called.

A petite figure stepped from behind the queen's throne and took King Randa's outstretched hand. Neve froze as he got a good look at the *valles'* face.

It was the female from the day before. What trickery was this?

He shot a glance to Flyka, who was already watching him. His lips thinned, but he turned back as Eyri approached the dais and held his hand out for the tiny creature. She trembled slightly as she released her father's hand and slowly descended the stairs, flowy green skirts pouring down the step. She stopped when she was eye level with Eyri, still two stairs from the bottom of the dais. His cousin took the human's pallid hand in his own, engulfing it, and placed a kiss on the back.

"A pleasure to meet you, my lady," he heard Eyri murmur.

Neve glared at the *valles*, studying her face in the light of day. Was she a decoy? He stared hard at the king. Their coloring was similar—hair, skin, eyes—even the nose shape. He squinted at the queen. He saw nothing of the queen in the princess. Maybe that was why the queen hated her so much?

While he didn't find humans appealing in the least, he could see that the queen was classically what the humans called beautiful. She was almost pixie-like. And while the princess was tiny—she was clearly a larger *valles* compared to the queen. Broader hips, lusher curves, taller.

Taller. He scoffed. She barely reached his nipples, if that.

"It'll be a pleasure to have you in my home," he heard Eyri say.

The little human stared at him with wide, off-putting eyes, and gave his cousin a small smile. "The pleasure will be all mine, my lord."

Neve doubted that.

Time to get out of the serpent's lair and back to their kingdom. They'd already received the Asteran bride gifts in the last week. All that was left was to secure the princess and her things.

He couldn't quite call her his *niliave*—his wife—even though they'd been married by proxy over a fortnight prior. She was a stranger, one that was necessary but unwelcome all the same. *Valles* she would remain.

Eyri coaxed the princess down the rest of the dais, her gaze sliding to the dead man. She blanched but covered it quickly. It seemed the princess didn't share her parents' love for violence.

His cousin towered over the princess as he bowed over her hand. "It will bring me great joy to show you our kingdom. I must return immediately. Your effects will follow behind us once we depart."

The princess pulled from Eyri's grasp and turned to the dais. She curtsied low. "I will take my leave. With your permission, your majesties."

The queen stood from her throne and floated down the stairs to embrace her daughter. She clasped the princess by the cheeks and pressed a kiss to her forehead. "Do us proud and go with our blessing."

Allium tipped her head back to peer up at Eyri. "Take care of our daughter, Frost King, or the last war will look like child's play."

A nice little threat. How cute.

Eyri took the princess' hand and pulled her gently away from her mother. "I don't take kindly to threats, but as she's your only child, I will excuse your actions. She will be safe."

Neve kept his expression serene. A lie. She was a means to an end. Nothing more.

Allium smiled, but it was sharp and deadly. "I expect so. Write often, daughter."

"I will ... mother."

She would not. Neve wouldn't have any Loriian secrets being spilled.

Human blood would be spilled first.

CHAPTER TWELVE

DAHLIA

DAHLIA SOAKED IN HER FIRST BREATH OF FRESH air as the horses were saddled. She was finally out from beneath the Asteran monarchs' control, and yet she felt like the danger had only grown.

"My lady?" the Loriian king's accented voice washed over her.

She spun to face the giant, her pulse hammering faster. He was at least seven feet tall and all lithe muscle. Her gaze snagged on the set of wicked horns that curved from each of his shoulders.

Natural weapons.

Blood. Screaming. Black eyes.

"They are called *caern'ye,*" the king offered softly, pushing his spectacles up his deep blue nose.

Lia blinked hard to dispel the memories. A blush

tinged her cheeks in embarrassment. "I didn't mean to gawk, my lord."

The king smiled, flashing a long fang that made her breath catch. Frost giants were predators incarnate. He could tear her throat out in a second flat. Luckily for her, she doubted they would hurt the Asteran princess in her own kingdom. In fact, the king seemed almost downright affable. But she didn't trust it. They were enemies. Restrained aggression practically teemed in the air.

A shiver skated down her spine as she felt eyes upon her once again.

Dahlia peeked over her shoulder and locked eyes with the frost giant who petrified her the most. His narrowed black gaze seemed to be pinned on her since she'd stepped out from behind the throne. If looks could kill, she would be dead by now. He clearly wasn't a fan of humans, by the perpetual snarl he cast her way.

Shiny phthalo blue and black braids hung around his face as he bent to tighten the saddle. Long, tapered ears peeked out, proudly studded with black gems and spikes. His movements were quick and efficient, and somewhat angry.

As if he could feel her attention, he glanced her way. Lia stood stock-still, like a hare scented by a wolf. A low growl rumbled in his chest, and she jerked her eyes away. No need to court trouble. She'd stay far away from that one.

"You do not need to fear us," the king murmured.

"I don't," she replied, fixing a bored smile on her face. The wind whipped past her, cutting right through her gauzy court dress. Even the embroidered cloak Basil had thrown over her shoulders seemed unpractical for the morose weather.

You need to fear me.

The emerald ring felt heavy on her finger.

He tapped his blue nose. "I can smell it on you."

Embarrassment crested first, and then horror. How was she to hide anything from the giants if they could smell her emotions? Lia wrapped her arms around her waist, clutching her cloak a little tighter.

You're fine. Just shove your feelings deep down. You've been practicing for years.

"I apologize, my lord," she managed past the lump in her throat.

He smiled, which, to be honest, was still frightening. Lia hid her flinch. At least she thought she did, until the king's grin faded.

"You do not have to apologize for your feelings, my lady."

"I do have to apologize for my rudeness though." She stared at his chest and frowned. His fine black embroidered shirt was open all the way to the waistband of his trousers. A dark blue nipple peeked out as he attached a bag to his saddle. No piercing. Well, he hadn't been the one to threaten her in the dark, she noted absently. "I've not been out in the world, truth be told, and I've never been in the presence of giants." A truth and a lie. "Your appearance is quite fearsome. I'll work on my reactions. I meant no offense. Please forgive me."

The king chuckled, tucking a navy-blue strand of hair behind his long, pointed ear. "There is nothing to forgive.

We both are... how do you say it? In this together. I have only been in the company of two *saloes* before."

"Saloes?" she asked, nose crinkling in confusion.

"It means *human* in Loriian."

"Saloes," she repeated, the word flowing off her tongue. She cocked her head in curiosity. "How did you meet them?"

"Both tried to kill me."

That was sobering. Dahlia didn't know what to say to that.

Soon, I'll be number three.

Awkward silence stretched between them.

The king cleared his throat and gestured to the biggest horse she'd ever seen. "I assume you can ride, no?"

"Yes, my lord." But nothing that bloody big. The horse was easily nineteen hands tall. Straddling the beast would be a challenge. Her thighs were already crying out in pain at the thought of the long ride ahead of her.

He nodded and turned his back. "Then I will have my man Arun help you find your seat."

"That's not necess—"

Dahlia gasped as an enormous pair of hands settled on her waist from behind, his fingers overlapping. She hadn't even heard the monster approach. The giant tossed her up onto the mount and she latched on to the horse's mane, almost falling off the other side. She blew her hair out of her face and straightened. It would have really hurt to fall off the other side.

She whipped around to curse out the devil, but found herself almost eye-to-eye with the blackguard who kept throwing glares her way. If there was one thing Dahlia hated, it was bullies. She shuddered, trying to hold his pitch gaze. It was like peering through the gates of hell.

"That was unnecessary," she clipped out.

He blinked slowly, his lips thinning, but otherwise said nothing.

Despite her fear, she jerked as she noticed how haphazardly her skirts were strewn about. Frantically, Dahlia tugged at the dress to make sure it covered her legs. Luckily, she'd worn hose beneath the gown, but the need to hide her legs was ingrained in her.

She struggled for a moment, and yelped when the giant yanked her skirt down, his claws tearing through the delicate green material. Dahlia reflexively kicked at him, and he caught her booted foot. Fear swirled in her gut as he bared his fangs, a hair-raising growl that caused her to lean away from him. The brute dropped her foot and grabbed the front of her dress, jerking forward so they were eye-to-eye.

"Watch yourself, *valles*," he hissed, the words heavily accented.

His voice rang in her ears, overlapping with the memory of the threat the night before. Dahlia began to shake, and the blood drained from her face. This was the giant who'd threatened to kill her. He looked as if he wanted to rend her limb from limb.

"Let go," she managed, hating how his claws held on to the top of her corset, his claws pressing between her breasts.

"Arun!" the pale female giant barked from atop her own mount.

The bastard released the top of her dress, and it took

everything inside Lia to straighten and not cower. He hissed, and then stalked away. Her fingers clenched hard against the reins. If this was how one got treated as a princess, she couldn't imagine what it would be like as a regular Asteran. She glanced around, noting that it was a sea of shaggy horses and blue-skinned beings. She would be well and truly alone. The king had denied any human servants to accompany her, leaving her alone with the giants. It was odd that a princess would travel without her own servants or protection.

The female giant sidled up to her and Dahlia swallowed hard. Between the female's silvery hair and pale gray skin, she looked like every horror Lia had dreamed since the attack on her mother all those years ago. It was like life had been breathed into her nightmares and been given a body.

This one was a Haunt. One of the king's famed warriors.

She'd known it the moment she'd stepped out from behind the queen. There would be at least one. She'd prepared herself for it during the two hours they'd waited for the Loriian delegation. It wasn't any easier.

The Haunt considered her. "If you think he's bad, he has nothing on me."

Dahlia knew that firsthand. The Haunts had destroyed her family with cruelty and violence. "Understood."

"Do you?" the female asked, her words less accented than Arun's. This one dealt more with humans. Lia didn't know if that made her more wary or slightly comforted.

"Yes."

"Do you know what I am?"

A murderer. "One of the king's champions."

"I am his blade, his heart, vengeance, and shield. There is nothing I would not do for my king."

Message received. The Haunt wouldn't hesitate to kill Dahlia if she stepped out of line. It was laughable that the female giant perceived her as a threat. What was she compared to the Frost King? Sure, she could handle herself with a bow, and a dagger on occasion, but that meant nothing when dealing with real-life monsters. She could barely look at the king without wanting to run screaming in the other direction.

But the Haunt was right to be wary. Dahlia had been tasked with their destruction.

"And I am just an honored guest who wants the same things as your king."

Another lie.

That seemed to smooth some of the giantess' feathers. Lia didn't want to cause trouble for the king. All she needed to do was keep her head down until she could formulate a plan and get to her mum and then Cosmos. The politics of kingdoms was of no consequence to her. The plan to flee as soon as they crossed into Loriia would no longer work now that Queen Allium knew of her mother. Dahlia's heart clenched. Her mum had been through so much already. She couldn't allow her to suffer anymore.

"As you say," the Haunt replied. She lifted her chin and nodded toward the drawbridge. "You first, my lady."

Dahlia pulled up her flimsy hood and urged her mount forward, following the Frost King. She gazed impassively down at the creatures peeking out of the moat water almost dispassionately. They didn't terrify her like they used to. They were trapped as much as she was.

She released the breath she held when they reached the other side, the clack of hooves against stone ringing around them. Lia sat tall and scanned the area out of habit. Nowhere had ever truly been safe. Especially as a young woman traveling with a little boy.

Her gaze snagged on a man leaning against a nearby building to her left, his hat drawn low over his face. There was something about him...

He lifted his chin and she stiffened.

Jekket.

He gave her a toothy grin and a tip of his hat that made her straighten in her seat. Why the last-minute goodbye? Was it a promise of retribution? A warning from the Giver? A taunt to make her feel off-kilter?

Her horse whickered and she loosened her hold on the reins. Jekket disappeared down the alley like smoke, but it did nothing to soothe Dahlia's nerves.

The Haunt sidled closer, her attention pinned to the alleyway. "He seemed to know you."

Lia schooled her expression. "Probably just some vagabond looking for an easy mark."

"Your fear says otherwise."

"I am surrounded by frost giants. Anyone would be terrified of you."

The giantess grinned. "You're right. How lucky for you."

They wound their way through the city as night approached. The storm gathered above them and Lia prayed that it wouldn't break any time soon. Their group reached the enormous arched Bridge of Bones. The white stones stuck out from the canyons and land around it like bleached teeth. Even though it was sturdy, there was something about being suspended so high in the air that unsettled Lia.

Farmers hustled across the bridge, their wagons trundling along. She grimaced as she glanced toward the edge. The canyon was deep, ending in a large river that fed into the Sea of Stars. Legend had it that the monarchy threw traitors off the cliffs to feed the sharks below in the estuary.

The wind rose, whistling through the deep canyon below. Dahlia closed her eyes and let her horse lead, listening to the haunting melody of the wind. Music could be found in almost anything. It was her solace in times of trial and fear.

"*Tue daemiir?*" a deep, somewhat angry voice asked. *Arun.*

"No, her heart is racing too fast," the giantess replied.

Dahlia's eyes snapped open, and she turned left to the female giant, ignoring the one looming to her right. She knew the scary one was Arun. "What is your name?"

The giantess cocked her head and answered slowly. "Flyka."

"You can hear my heartbeat?"

"I'm trained for such things." She smirked, then her smile widened. "I even heard your pulse increase in reaction to my fangs."

Lia pressed her lips together. Even if she could hide

her emotions, they were still able to read her body. It was bloody unfair. "It's nice to meet you, Flyka."

"Is it?" the giantess asked as they neared the end of the bridge.

Speak only truth. "I've always liked the idea of traveling and new cultures. Books have been an escape. It's a privilege to interact with a culture that many will never get the chance to spend time with." *Privilege* was a stretch, but it made Flyka sit a bit taller. The female seemed to like the compliment. Lia would store that away for later.

Some of the tension released from her shoulders as they reached solid ground once more. The road forked in three ways.

Northeast toward the city of Lantium.

West to Saffrie.

South to Lavindly.

Please go north. Please.

Even if she couldn't meet up with her brother, maybe she'd pass him on the way? It was a dream, but she had to hold on to it. Dahlia glanced over her shoulder at Florrant, praying Cosmos had gotten out of the city. She turned back to the road and sighed in relief when the bulkiest warrior veered north.

Perhaps the stars had heard her pleas.

Lightning crackled across the sky, thunder following. Droplets of water began to fall from the clouds.

Or maybe she was as cursed as she'd always been.

Chapter Thirteen

Neve

The farther he traveled from Florrant, the more he regretted his decision of taking a human *loviaye*.

They'd only been on the road for seven hours when the princess began to wilt like a sick flower. Humans were *so* weak. He cursed underneath his breath when she slumped even lower in the saddle. Neve had wanted to make it closer to Loriia's border before stopping. He'd been gone long enough, and Flyka had spotted several men tailing them. He didn't want to deal with more assassins.

Sighing, he edged up next to Eyri, who kept wiping rain from his spectacles.

"We need to stop for the night," he said in Loriian.

His cousin squinted. "So soon? I thought you'd want to put more space between us and Florrant."

Olwen slowed so his pace matched their own. "What's the plan?"

"We stop in Umberje for the night. This way, we can choose where our followers catch up with us. Preferably with the princess tucked in for the night."

His best friend chuckled. "Hiding her from the truth of what backstabbing creatures her family really are?"

"No." He didn't care what she thought. "I don't want her to accidentally be killed before we get into Loriia."

"But her death is acceptable if we're in our own kingdom?" Eyri asked, arching a brow.

"It's less dangerous for us *if* such a thing were to happen in Loriia." He nodded to Olwen. "Will you go on ahead of us and find a suitable place?"

His friend pursed his lips. "I don't like leaving you behind with so little protection, sire."

"I'll be fine."

"As you say." Olwen flicked the reins and his mount picked up speed, soon disappearing from view.

The rain continued to fall, but Neve welcomed it. It helped soothe the fire raging within. He'd been uncomfortable in Astera. It was much too hot for his taste.

"You're angry," Eyri commented, water droplets rolling down his spectacles. "Why?"

"The consequences of my decision are dawning on me."

"She doesn't seem so bad."

Neve's brow furrowed. "You've known the little mouse for all of ten hours."

"She hasn't complained once." Eyri shrugged. "I heard that *saloes* don't like rain."

He opened his mouth to argue when a haunting melody reached his ears.

Crying to the stars but they don't hear my plea.
A darkened night, one whisper away from breaking.
Fighting for life but no one hears me.
Light is just a figment of imagining.
Death is calling but I cannot pay his fee.

The hair along Neve's arms rose at the spellbinding aria that poured out of the princess. He'd heard nothing like it before. How did something so powerful come from an entity so small? He shivered, and he blamed it on the rain dripping down his spine.

"Fire and ice," Eyri whispered, looking over his shoulder. "Who knew *valles* could sing like that? It's beautiful."

Neve grabbed a hold of himself and slowed his horse until the human caught up with him. She huddled in her fancy cloak, only her lips and nose visible in the dark night. Her song rose to a crescendo.

"Enough!" he yelled.

She jerked, the hood of her cloak turning in his direction, her ballad cut short. It made something inside his chest ache.

"Are you so foolish?" he barked in the common tongue. He'd never quite mastered it like Flyka or Eyri. The words felt clumsy.

"I'm just singing."

"We are in enemy territory, traveling with not one but two royals. You are giving our ... how do you say it? Position away."

"And our horses do not?" she quipped back, voice thready. "Or *your* shouting?"

"The rain drowns out their sounds, and you…" He shook his head. He did not need to explain himself to her. "Be silent."

"Please," she snapped, a little more heat in her voice. "*Please, my lady.*"

He stared at her. She thought him nothing but a servant. Neve didn't have to yield to this *valles*.

And yet, noting the way her lips had pressed into a thin line, he'd made her angry. Good, then he wouldn't suffer alone. Neve had a part to play. He swallowed down the curse curling on his tongue. "*Please*, princess, stay silent so you do not put everyone's lives at risk for the sake of your amusement, *my lady*," he said, pouring every bit of arrogance into his tone instead.

Her mouth popped open, a little puff of hot air escaping.

"Something you must say?" he pressed.

"Not to you." In an instant, all traces of ire were gone. Only frigid compliance left.

For some reason, he didn't like it. And that made no sense.

Olwen had procured two rooms for them at an inn on the outskirts of Northern Umberje.

Neve assessed the building as they arrived. It was a bit rundown, but if trouble arrived on their doorstep, it would be easy to dispose of the evidence. He led his horse right outside the stable and swung down from the saddle, his boots landing in a puddle. He pulled his bedroll off the horse as a young child stumbled out of the dimly lit stables, rubbing his eyes. Flyka cut him off and handed him a small bag of coins before giving him instructions for their horses.

He frowned as he spotted a couple embracing each other, their lips locked together. Neve practically gagged. Mouth mating was not a Loriian custom. It was a disgusting human practice. Godsteeth, he hoped the *valles* never tried something like that on him.

Eyri jumped down as well and frowned, his attention on the couple, then moving to the princess. "Are you going to help her?" Eyri muttered in Loriian.

The princess was untangling herself from her soggy cloak and dress while appearing to figure out the best way to climb down. It was utterly ridiculous. Every movement she made seemed uncoordinated and stiff.

Neve crossed his arms. "She specifically told me not to touch her, so no, I will not be helping her."

He continued to watch the spectacle as she swung her leg over the horse and stared at the ground. A smile curved the corner of his lips. Just what would the haughty princess do?

His amusement fled when she pushed away from the horse and dropped to the ground. Her knees buckled and she took a step, tripping on her skirts. The *valles* pitched forward, hands outstretched. Without a thought, Neve caught her elbow before she fell face-first into a deep mudpuddle. His fingers curled around her dainty forearm, noting how his hand engulfed it. It was almost comical.

"I've got it," the princess muttered.

She was standing, pale face tilted up to him, cheeks and nose an alarming shade of red. It bothered him just how much her color changed.

The princess coughed, the color in her cheeks deepening.

Neve released her like he'd been burned, and she swept past him with all the dignity of a drowned rat. Just how long had he been staring? He followed her, making sure to kick the mud off his boots before entering the inn. The inviting warmth of a fire welcomed him into the space. The room was long and rectangular, with a bar at the very far end. Olwen waited for them, holding the keys in his hands, no innkeeper to be seen.

The princess left a trail of water behind her as she walked to the hearth and held her hands out to the fire. Neve winced. How could she be so close? Even from here, it was warm. Sweat started to bead on the back of his neck.

"How do you want this to go?" Olwen asked in Loriian as Neve reached the bar.

Neve blinked at his best friend. "What do you mean?"

"Flyka won't be leaving your side, per her oath, but the *valles* should not be alone with a male that is not her family or husband." He pursed his lip, his long scar puckering. "Even though you've been married by proxy in *saloes* custom, the marriage rites have not been completed in Loriia."

"So concerned about the princess?"

Olwen shook his head. "No, but I can sense she's on the verge of losing it, and I don't want to deal with a royal tantrum."

"Fair enough." Neve rolled his neck. "Put Flyka, myself, and the human in one room, and you and Eyri take the other."

Olwen whistled. "I don't like you with just one warrior."

"You don't think I'm enough?" Flyka asked, joining their conversation.

"No, but you have more than one royal to care for now," Olwen pointed out. "You'll have both the *reillov* and our future *reilleve*'s lives in your hands."

Future queen.

It echoed like a bad joke in his ears. Had he really thought this through?

Flyka nodded. "You're right. We'll all stay in the same room, and set the other one up as a decoy."

Movement from the corner of his eye caught his attention. Eyri stood beside the princess, whispering softly to her. He frowned at his cousin. What was he doing?

Neve cleared his throat. "My lord? Your room is ready."

Eyri nodded and held his arm out, gesturing for the princess to go first. She curtsied, and then strode toward their group. Flyka climbed the stairs first, followed by the princess and Eyri. Neve's nose twitched as she passed him, a delicate scent hovering in her wake. He rubbed his nose, trying to dispel the smell, and followed her up, Olwen hot on his heels.

Neve hid his smile at how his friend grumbled about tiny human spaces. It would be nice to be home soon, where none of them would have to stoop to get through doors or worry about the support of any given chair.

Flyka unlocked the door to the room and gestured for the *valles* to enter. The princess moved straight to the small fire and crouched before the hearth, seeming to ignore everyone. Neve assessed the room. It was large enough that they would all be able to sleep. His gaze moved to the bed. Undoubtedly, the princess would want it, which was fine. It wasn't as if anyone would fit in it except a *saloes*.

"What are you doing, my lady?" Olwen asked, leaning his shoulder against the wall nearest to the door.

Neve glanced at the human as she tossed more wood on the fire from the rack. "Building the fire."

"It's already sweltering in here."

"I'm freezing," she muttered, her odd eyes narrowing. "How are you not cold?"

"Frost giant," Olwen replied, with a smirk and a wiggle of his brows.

She blinked hard and dismissed Olwen, unlacing her dripping cloak. The *valles* pulled it from her shoulders to hang it next to the fireplace.

Neve flinched, and ignored the choked sound from Olwen's direction.

The green dress she wore was almost transparent and clung to her curves. It was vulgar, unnatural, and ... something else.

Tracing the line of her figure made him want to fidget. To fit his hand to the flare of her hip.

Qov.

Neve crossed his arms and looked away. He froze as he watched his inner circle gawk at the human. Eyri showed curiosity—ever the scientist. Flyka seemed to be searching for weapons, and held two of her fingers out. Two hidden weapons. *How cute.* And Olwen—well, his best friend held a gleam in his gaze that Neve wasn't quite comfortable with. It seemed the human form appealed to his friend.

Olwen caught his glare and shrugged sheepishly.

"We should all get some rest," Eyri said, breaking the silence. "You may have the bed, my lady."

The princess put her back to the fire and Neve blinked slowly. He could see her breasts. Well, most of them. It was difficult to look away from the oddity. The women of his culture weren't as endowed as humans. Breasts were to feed their young, nothing more. The *valles* pushed up and out of an undergarment that looked like a shield strapped to her body.

The human crossed her arms over her chest, effectively ending Neve's gawking. "Thank you, but that won't be necessary. I'll take a bedroll by the fire, my lord. I'd like to be near the heat after the ride we just had." She smiled softly at Eyri. "Thank you kindly for the offer. Enjoy the bed."

Her attention turned to Flyka. "If you could show me to the privy, I would be most grateful."

Flyka arched her brows at Neve in question. He nodded, and she gestured to the door. "Let's go."

The two females hustled out of the room, closing the door behind them.

Olwen whistled. "I've always wondered what those humans have under all their layers. Not as displeasing as I thought it would be."

Neve scowled at him. "I doubt she missed your perusal."

His friend shrugged. "Chalk it up to curiosity, *lae reillov*. And all I have to say is that my curiosity is piqued."

Neve walked to the hearth and pulled his bedroll from its waterproof sheath, laying it parallel to the fire. "You can have her."

"You're giving her your bedroll?" Eyri asked, sitting on the edge of the bed.

Neve tossed his hands in the air. "Someone has to sleep in that bed, and she made it clear it wouldn't be her. So, Eyri, you're the shortest of us. You can sleep there." He held his hand palm up and wiggled his fingers. "Hand it over. I'm using yours."

His cousin groaned. "I'm going to have to sleep at an angle."

Olwen thumped his chest and eyed the bed. "There's no way that thing would hold my weight."

"And Flyka?" All three of them smiled at the same time. She'd be sleeping by the door. If anyone tried to get in, they'd have to go through her first.

Eyri tossed his bedroll to Neve. He laid his out near the window, opening it just a crack. The cold air brushed over his skin. He pulled his shirt off and hung it next to the fire. Next, he placed his boots and socks near the hearth. He crawled into his bedroll and stretched out while Eyri and Olwen both got ready for bed, before going to arrange the room next door. They returned and settled in, the crackling fire filling the silence.

Neve found himself staring at the door. The women had been gone for quite some time.

As if his thoughts had conjured them, the door opened and the princess and Flyka entered. He stared, his teeth grinding together. The little *valles* wore one of his shirts as a night dress—one that he'd given to Flyka a long time ago. It hung off the princess' shoulder, showing more pallid skin. She wore a pair of green hose beneath that clung to her like a second skin. Her vibrant rose-gold hair was braided back from her face. Her nose was still red, her lips a soft pink. *Saloes* coloring was bizarre. They changed colors like some of the *germals*—little fish that lived in the Lake of Glass.

She moved straight to the bedroll before the fire—his bed—and curled up in a tiny ball. The blankets shivered as she got comfortable. A sigh escaped her, and it made something inside his chest clench.

Neve turned his back to the human and stared at the wall before closing his own eyes.

Her comfort was none of his concern. She was here for one purpose and one purpose only.

Peace.

If such a thing were possible.

Chapter Fourteen

Dahlia

Dahlia bolted upright, disoriented and groggy as thunder rumbled above. She rubbed her eyes and brushed a few hairs from her face. Her breath sawed in and out as she tried to calm her racing heart. It was only a storm. She pulled the covers up to her chin as a cold breeze drifted through the room. Glancing over her head, she glared at the open window. It was bloody storming. Why the devil was the window open?

Crazy giants.

She closed her eyes and tried to sleep, but it wouldn't come. A deep snore came from her right. Squinting, she spotted the mountain of a giant sleeping peacefully on the floor, his chest rising and lowering with his powerful breaths. Olwen was his name. He snorted in his sleep again, the loud snuffling seeming to rattle the rafters. How could anyone sleep with all that racket?

Lia shifted slightly and winced. Her body ached something fierce. While she knew how to ride, it had been quite some time since she'd ridden a horse—let alone the fuzzy, giant ones. Straddling the great beast made her feel like a contortionist. The inside of her thighs were raw and aching.

She inhaled deeply through her nose and frowned.

Rosemary and cedar.

Dahlia lifted the blankets to her nose. Not those. She dropped the covers and sniffed the collar of the massive night dress. There it was. Her muscles loosened as she took another whiff. The scent was pure comfort. Whatever soap the giants used, Lia couldn't wait to get her hands on some. It made her mouth water.

Rolling onto her left side, she stared at the fireplace. The flames were long gone, the coals glowing softly in the hearth. Another spasm of pain shot through her, and she glanced once again at the window. It was still dark out. It was possible she'd only slept a few hours, if dawn hadn't broken yet. Rain pattered on the roof, and she stifled a groan. She prayed they wouldn't make her travel in the rain again. Even now, she could feel the stiffness in her fingers from the cold of the day's ride.

Olwen's snores somehow got louder, and Lia rolled her eyes. Despite how gritty they were, and how much she needed to sleep, she wouldn't be able to fall asleep with all that noise.

Quietly, she rolled toward the fire onto her hands and knees. Her back twinged as she began rolling up her pallet. She tied the thin cord around the bedroll and sat back on her knees before hauling herself to her feet. Goosebumps rose along her arms, and she smoothed her hands along her biceps to ward off the chill. Light flashed from the window, followed by another crack of thunder.

Lia stared at the king sound asleep on the bed. She spun the emerald ring on her finger. All she had to do was creep to the bed, poison the king for ten second, and then flee. Her stomach churned. Maybe she could beat Cosmos to the maple harvests.

What of the Haunts?

Sweeping the three giants slumbering on the floor, Dahlia knew she couldn't do it. She'd never make it out alive.

And it's wrong.

She crept to her cloak and slung it over her shoulders. It wasn't completely dry, but it wasn't soaking wet like it had been. Dahla tiptoed to the door, turned the handle, and pulled. The hinges creaked and she froze, glancing at the giantess sleeping behind the door.

Dahlia's pulse leapt as she stared down into pitch eyes, narrowed with suspicion.

A good thing you didn't approach the king.

She blew out a heavy breath and jerked her head toward the hallway. "Going for something to eat," she whispered. "I'll be by the fire."

Flyka nodded once.

Lia edged into the hallway and closed the door. It was highly inappropriate to go into a public space dressed in one's sleeping garments, but Dahlia was too hungry and tired to care. Plus, they were in Umberje—it was as rustic as it got in Astera. Surely, no one would begrudge her comfort.

You're a princess now.

With a grumble, she buttoned the front of her decorative cloak. It covered enough that no one would know the difference.

Following the scent of bread and bacon, she descended the stairs into the main area of the inn. A simple wooden bar stood to the right, and table and chairs to her left. Three large chairs surrounded the fireplace, their faded fabric looking more inviting than shabby.

A man slept at one of the far tables, his feet propped up on top, a hat over his face. Dahlia eyed him and wove her way through the furniture before standing in front of the fireplace. The flames danced merrily, and finally some of the chill fled her bones.

Dahlia turned her back to the fireplace when a woman bustled out of a swinging door to the left of the bar. The buxom woman paused, blinking her gray eyes at Lia.

"What are you doing up, love?" She placed her hand on her round hips. "Me husband said you only just arrived."

Lia smiled at her. "Couldn't sleep."

The innkeeper's wife shook her head. "I suppose not with the way the storm is carrying on." She held up a finger. "I have just the thing. You wait there."

As if she would be leaving the fire anytime soon.

The woman pushed through the door once again, leaving Dahlia to her own thoughts and rumbling belly. When was the last time she'd eaten? Not yesterday. Was it really before she'd seen Cosmos? She placed a hand on her cramping stomach.

The innkeeper's wife rushed back into the common

room carrying a cup of steaming tea, a thick slice of bread with honey and butter, and a knitted blanket slung over the crook of her arm.

"Into the chair with you, missy," the woman commanded. "From the looks of ya, it seems like a stiff wind could blow you over. That won't do with the company you're keeping."

Lia plopped down in the nearest chair, sinking down into the worn cushions. The innkeeper's wife handed her the cup of tea and she curled her fingers around the warmth with a happy sigh. There was nothing more pleasant than holding a cuppa on a cold day. The woman then set the bread on a small, dented side table beside the chair. She laid the blanket over Dahlia's lap and then stepped back, surveying her handiwork.

"That's better."

Lia smiled at the older woman. "Thank you, madam."

"Pssssh," the woman said, waving a hand. "Call me Birdie."

She took a sip of the milky tea and savored the cinnamon. "This is just what I needed."

"Just so," Birdie commented, nodding. "Well then, you eat your treat and try to get a little nap in that chair." She patted Lia's knee. "I'll be behind the bar folding sheets, so you'll be looked after."

Warmth suffused Dahlia. She loved when women womened. It wasn't a safe world for the female sex as a whole. Never would she sleep in a public place, but with Birdie around? Lia felt safe.

"Thank you."

"It's nothing, dearie."

Birdie bustled away in a rush of homespun skirts and began humming softly behind the bar. Lia tried to eat her bread slowly, but it was gone too soon, followed by her tea. Her eyelids felt heavy as she leaned her head against the wingback of the chair. Maybe she'd just close her eyes for a moment...

SHE ALWAYS KNEW WHEN SOMEONE WAS LOOKING at her.

Dahlia's eyes snapped open; blearily, she searched to her right and left. She stiffened when the giant to her right winked.

Olwen.

The Loriian had stuffed himself into the chair next to her. It groaned as he leaned forward, hands clasped between his splayed knees.

"So your tongue is pink," he murmured.

Lia snapped her mouth closed and wiped her cheeks for saliva. "What of it?" She must have been sleeping deeply. Even now she felt a bit foggy.

The beast opened his mouth and flicked his long, pointed tongue out. Dahlia stared. His tongue was black, with ridges. Unbidden, a memory from her childhood surfaced of a giant boy sticking his tongue out at her. She'd forgotten Loriians had black tongues. Lia shrugged and pulled her blanket up to her chest. *"Shocking."*

Olwen grinned, making him seem less intimidating.

"You don't seem shocked, my lady. In fact, you look decidedly unimpressed."

"What I was unimpressed with was your snoring last night," she retorted.

Don't let him get to you. Make friends. Collect information.

He looked affronted. "*Me?* I never snore."

Flyka materialized at Lia's right side. "You most assuredly do," she replied dryly. "It's a bloody miracle anyone got any rest." The giantess held out a plate with a flat cake, bacon, eggs, and maple syrup. "Break your fast, my lady. We must be on the road soon."

Dahlia took the food from Flyka without complaint and stared at the window past Olwen while she shoved the breakfast into her mouth.

It was still raining.

A shiver ran down her spine. She would need something heavier than the thin cloak she wore to survive the day. There was no way she'd be able to go through another trip like last night. She'd catch her death.

As if Olwen heard her thoughts, he leaned back in his chair, rubbing his chin. He scanned her from head to toe. "I think we need to outfit you with something more proper for the journey."

She nodded, swallowing the fluffy eggs. "Are my things with my mount?"

He pursed his lips. "Most of your effects were either sent ahead or are behind us with the rest of the caravan."

She mulled that over. Maybe she could trade her fine green dress for something sensible. Surely, Birdie would know of someone who would barter.

The door flew open and Arun ducked inside, looking angry as usual. The food congealed in her gut as she watched the menace approach with a bundle under his arm, the top of his head almost reaching the ceiling. Rain dripped down his cheeks and bare chest, but he seemed not to notice.

She forced herself to eat the last bit of meat despite her churning belly. One never knew when the next meal would arrive. Heat stained her cheeks once again as she caught Olwen studying her.

"What?" she groused, setting her plate on the empty side table. Had Birdie cleaned up after Lia's early-morning snack? She'd need to thank the woman.

"You eat like a warrior, my lady," he stated bluntly.

"What does that mean?" she asked, keeping her attention on Olwen and ignoring the glowering presence behind her.

"Swift and efficiently. Like someone is going to take your food."

He hadn't asked a question, but he was probing her. Apparently, some habits were hard to break, and playing princess wouldn't be easy.

Tell the truth. Mix it with a lie. The lie is the truth.

She brushed the crumbs from her lap. "In my culture, thin women are exulted above all else. You've met the queen. She has high standards." *Truth.* "She expects that in her daughter as well." She would let them draw their own conclusions from there.

Olwen crossed his thick, muscular arms across his wide chest and frowned. "What a stupid ideal. Every *valles* is different, and should be appreciated for her uniqueness, not punished for it."

His sentiment warmed Dahlia. He still frightened her, but she softened toward Olwen. Just a bit. "My beliefs exactly."

He smiled, flashing his fangs, and Lia swallowed, shoving down her fear, and returned his smile. The giant had shown her understanding. That wasn't something she had expected.

A bundle of clothes was tossed roughly into her lap. "Get dressed. We're already late."

Arun's deep, dark voice washed over her, and Dahlia just barely managed to hide her shudder. She clutched the parcel to her chest and stood, making sure to lay the blanket over the back of the seat with care.

She dipped her chin at Arun, not meeting his gaze. Not that it really mattered. She couldn't tell where he was looking anyway. His eyes were completely black.

Lia hustled away from the fireplace, waving at Birdie, who was still folding laundry. The innkeeper's wife returned the greeting and went back to her chores. The Frost King reached the bottom of the stairs and Dahlia curtsied.

He nodded to her and smiled, the corners of his eyes crinkling. "Good morning, princess. I trust you slept well?"

"As well as I could, my lord."

"Excellent." He walked by her to the group, standing out in his black regalia, murmuring a low hello to his guards.

Lia watched them for a moment. Arun's face turned in her direction and she fled up the stairs to ready herself for the soggy day.

Hopefully, the rain wouldn't be so horrid.

HOPE WAS A CRUEL MISTRESS.

Despite the rough-spun, sturdy dress and heavy cloak she'd been given, the water eventually soaked through. The weather had only gotten worse throughout the day. At one point, Lia had lain on the top of her horse, Anwen, and held on for dear life. The wind howled as they passed one of the biggest lakes she'd ever laid her eyes on, tearing at her cloak. White-capped waves crashed onto the pink sands, leaving foam behind.

She ducked her face into Anwen's mane to avoid the stinging pelt of the rain that seemed to be falling sideways. Her palms and fingers had stopped stinging hours ago. Dahlia didn't know how long they'd been riding, but they'd eaten the noon meal hours ago. All she wanted was a fire and her bed.

You can do this. You've been through worse. Just sing. Focus on the song.

Her fingers knotted in Anwen's mane and she began humming, her voice rumbling in her throat while the storm did its best to tear her from the horse.

The stars will keep you safe, little one,

There's no need to fear the dark.

The storm shrieked above; she clutched Anwen harder, her cheek pressed to the mount's mane.

Rise to the sky and take flight,
Embrace the night and soar.

A bellow.

Dahlia blinked slowly and lifted her head, squinting. Arun was thundering toward her, destruction written across his face. She yanked on the reins and stopped. He yelled and gestured, but she didn't make out his words. He was too far away.

The giant leaned over his horse and urged it faster, Olwen and the king behind him. The hair at the nape of her neck rose as she heard a huff. She straightened in the saddle and twisted slowly.

Her stomach dropped as she spotted a creature she had hoped never to cross paths with.

A dimedon.

The height of her horse and twice as wide, the creature bore down on Flyka. Shiny black fur rippled over its robust body. Flyka's mount kicked at the beast as it swiped its long claws at her. Despite its short legs, the creature moved quickly. It bared its long teeth that were nestled in a short snout.

There was no way the giantess would be able handle the beast alone, and the others were too far away. They wouldn't make it in time.

It's not your job to protect Flyka.

She's a Haunt.

Dahlia swung Anwen around and urged him toward the giantess, her heart pounding.

She couldn't just stand by and watch the giantess fight for her life, even if she was a Haunt. It was wrong to stand on the sidelines. Lia needed to help.

Chapter Fifteen

NEVE

HE'D MADE A MISTAKE.

Neve had assumed that Flyka could handle anything.

He hadn't counted on a bloody dimedon.

Rage fueled him as he raced toward his Haunt.

A curse flew from his lips when the *valles* turned her mount around and raced toward Flyka. She was going to get herself killed. The creature swiped at Flyka, catching her thigh. His Haunt didn't cry out, but pain rippled across her face as she tried to keep out of the beast's reach. His mouth went dry as the princess released her reins and pulled a slingshot from her cloak, holding on to Anwen with just her thighs.

She fired, hitting the dimedon right in the forehead. The creature snarled, its attention now on the princess. Flyka maneuvered her mount behind the beast, slashing at its hindquarters. It bellowed and charged at the *saloes*. The princess didn't slow and fired once again, hitting the dime-don. The bear roared as the projectile lodged in its eye. Horse and creature met. Anwen reared up, catching the human off guard. She scrambled for the reins and wasn't quick enough.

Neve's heart stopped as she tumbled off the back of the horse and into the mud and sand.

The *valles* didn't move.

Almost there.

He urged Alastor faster, and hissed out a breath when the princess pushed her hood back and crawled away from the prancing horse and snarling dimedon. He balanced in the stirrups just as the creature spotted the human on the ground. It released a roar and lunged.

Neve launched off Alastor and onto the dimedon's back. He yanked his sword from the sheath at his hip and stabbed the creature with all his strength. The beast cried out and shuddered, trying to claw him off its back. He didn't let go of the pommel, putting all his weight into the blade. The dimedon wobbled, and then crashed to the ground beneath him. Neve didn't move but held on tight, counting in his head. It was possible the creature was playing dead. They were intelligent.

Olwen, Eyri, and Flyka circled, their steeds prancing.

"It's dead," Eyri called, adjusting his foggy spectacles. "Its gaze has gone murky in its one good eye."

Neve pulled his sword away and slid off the dimedon's back, landing in thick mud. He held up his blade as he rounded the creature, his boots squelching with each step. His shoulders slouched as the cloudy eye stared sightlessly back at him. He stowed his sword and approached the animal. He ran his fingers around its broad head, searching for a marking. His lip curled as he found what he was searching for.

A circle with three twisting lines.

A brand. Qovving humans.

Neve cursed and ran his hands through his hair. This wasn't one of the wild beasts that were native to the area. It was an animal trained to hunt by scent that had been sicced on them. It made him sick. He ran his hand through the dimedon's wet fur and offered a few words to the beast.

"It wasn't your fault," he whispered.

He turned from the animal and looked to Flyka. "How bad is it?" he asked in Loriian.

"Manageable, but I need stitches." Silver blood leaked through her fingers.

They needed to be out of Astera *now*. "Can you make it another two hours?"

"I'll bind it tightly. I'll let you know if we need to stop sooner."

"Is she alright?" the princess called, slogging through the mud, her cloak covered in sand and muck.

Neve turned to her, fuming. He marched through the slop and the sleet. Towering over her, he pointed to the dimedon.

"This is what your people do," he spat in the common tongue. "This is your legacy."

She shook, staring up at his face in surprise, the little sprinkles across her nose standing out against her complexion. "Excuse me?"

He crowded into her space. "That animal was *sent* to find us. It was no accident."

The *valles* blanched, all color draining from her face. "That's not possible."

His upper lip curled and he snarled at the princess. She yelped and tried to take a step away, but he seized her upper arms, yanking her against his body and lifting her slightly. "You can't be so naïve. It is *branded*. That creature is trained by scent. It had Flyka's and yours. What do you think that means, *princess*? Would your family sacrifice you so easily? Do you have so little worth? What are you hiding?"

A fire lit in her strange gaze as she glared up at him. "And what of you? Is this little charade to get rid of the princess of Astera? By my accounts, we're close to the border."

"And what would you know of my kingdom?" He leaned into her face. "You know what I think?"

"What?" she spat, bottom lip trembling.

"That you're not so innocent after all."

She laughed right in his face. "And you are?"

He seethed, his fingers flexing on her biceps. His nose twitched when a tantalizing scent of ginger and amber and sugar teased him. Neve's mouth watered. He inhaled deeply, pressing a little closer to the princess.

It was her.

His enemy.

His little human *loviaye*.

He'd scented her like she was his proper mate.

Neve dropped her like he'd been burned. His hands

shook as he backed away from the human. He pointed a trembling finger at her.

"Get back on your horse," he commanded. "We leave now."

THE SLEET DID NOTHING TO COOL HIS HEATED skin or his temper. Every time he glanced in the *valles'* direction, he became angrier.

How could she have been so reckless? What was she thinking when she charged that dimedon?

Neve snorted.

Nothing, absolutely nothing.

Rage burned in his gut when he caught Flyka wincing and pressing a hand against her wound. He frowned at the silvery blood that dripped down her trousers.

They would pay.

Whoever had attacked them would wish they were never born. No one hurt one of his people without seeing the consequences of their actions.

"*Lae reillov?*" Olwen called.

Neve squinted at his friend through the sleet. "What?"

"I can smell the weather turning for the worse. We need to stop and find shelter now."

"We're almost to the safe house. Just a few more miles. We need to get over the border."

Olwen's lips thinned, but he dipped his chin. "As you wish."

THE WEATHER DID INDEED WORSEN TO THE point where he could hardly see in front of his horse. Sleet and snow pelted Neve from the heavens angrily, as if berating him for taking a human *loviaye*. There was no welcome to Lorriia. It felt like condemnation.

Some of the tension disappeared as he caught a glimpse of the old barn just ahead. He slowed his horse as Eyri sidled up next to him. Olwen rolled the doors open and waved his hand. Neve didn't need to press the mount at all. Alastor practically pranced into the barn. Eyri, Flyka, and the human followed.

Olwen wrestled the doors shut, cutting off the wind and snow. It howled outside as if raging at being thwarted.

Neve sprang from the saddle and shook the sleet from his hair. While he had no aversion to the rain, the snow tended to seep into his bones after a while.

He turned to Flyka, who lifted her uninjured leg over the horse and perched sideways in the saddle.

She glared at the ground, and he frowned. His Haunt never did well when she felt vulnerable.

"Do you need help?" he asked softly, the scent of sweet hay and wet horseflesh filling the air.

She shook her head and peered toward the door. "No,

Olwen will help me," she said a bit louder than necessary. "Tend to the princess."

Olwen strode toward them and helped Flyka off her horse. They limped to the side of the barn designed for living.

His mood soured further as he glanced at the bedraggled creature in the soaked brown cloak. Neve strode over to her, only catching a brief glimpse of her chin.

"Do you need assistance, my lady?" he asked through gritted teeth.

She hunched over farther, her cracked knuckles clenched against the reins. "No. I'm f-f-fine."

Her raspy voice made him frown. She sounded nothing like she had this morning.

He crossed his arms as she slowly lifted her right leg from the shortened stirrups and twisted to face him. She jumped from the saddle and stumbled upon landing, her cloak wrapped around her awkwardly. Neve lurched forward and caught the princess by the elbows before she fell on her face.

What was wrong with her? This was the second time he'd kept her from falling on her face.

Her bones were so fragile beneath her skin. His fingers flexed on the wet fabric of her sleeve. He could crush her so easily if he wasn't careful. Without his permission, his thumbs caressed the sides of her forearms.

"I said I'm fine." The *valles* jerked out of his grasp, almost falling once again.

Neve scoffed. "Clearly."

She tossed her hood back and scowled at him, her little blue lips turned downward. He blinked slowly. Blue lips?

Her lips had been pink before. Were humans really so changeable? Could they shapeshift as well? Was he discovering a human secret?

Even as the questions ran through his mind, he couldn't tear his attention from her mouth, pouty and bowed at the top with a fuller bottom lip. A low heat flickered inside his chest the longer he stared.

Blue looks good on her.

The errant thought jarred Neve out of his ludicrous musings. He took a big step backward, off-kilter. His hearts pounded in his chest as the princess ignored him and drifted toward the living area.

What the devil was that? Had he really been admiring the enemy?

There was something very wrong with him.

Neve tipped his head back to stare at the ceiling of the barn and rolled his shoulders.

It wouldn't happen again.

At least he hoped.

Chapter Sixteen

Neve

By the time he'd gotten himself calmed down, everyone had settled into the spacious living quarters. A fire roared in the fireplace, taking up almost the entire length of the wall to his right. The human stood there in her damp dress with her back to the fire. He quickly glanced away, not willing to stare at her any longer than necessary.

A copper bathtub sat in the corner near the hearth, with Olwen pumping water into it from the spout. Neve nodded to his friend and stepped inside, closing the door to the barn. To his left, three sets of rustic bunkbeds created an open-ended square that faced the fireplace. Flyka sat on the middle-bottom bed, cutting some of her trousers away from the gash with methodical strokes as Eyri unpacked some of the medical supplies.

Neve kicked off his dirty boots and went to them. He

knelt beside Flyka and took the blade from her shaking fingers. The stubborn female would never admit when she needed help. She grimaced at him but didn't try to take it back as he cut away the leather and picked threads from her long cut.

"You need stitches," he muttered.

Flyka pursed her lips. "But not from you. You're worse with a needle than Olwen."

"Hey," Olwen groused from his corner as he continued to pump hot water into the tub. "I'm a warrior, not a seamstress."

"That we can agree on," Flyka muttered.

Eyri lifted the needle and stared at the tip. "I read an article about a new way to stitch…"

"No," all three of them chorused at the same time.

While his cousin was a brilliant scribe and erudite, he was not a healer. They'd all been on the trial end of his experiments in the past and it never ended quite right.

"I can help," the princess interjected softly.

Neve looked to her. She clasped her hands in front of her and rocked back on her heels, looking a little sheepish.

"I'm good with a needle."

"What would a princess know of stitching wounds?" Neve retorted.

The sheepish look dropped from her face, replaced with determination and a touch of contempt. "What do you think princesses do all day? We *stitch*." She tossed her wet golden-red hair over her shoulder. "What's the difference between skin and fabric? It will close the same."

She walked to the washtub and dunked her hands into

the water. The *saloes* yanked her hands back and stared down at the water, then up to Olwen. "It's hot."

"Is that a question?" Olwen drawled, scratching at the shaved side of his head.

"How?"

"Underground hot springs."

"Amazing," she whispered, before pushing her sleeves up and scrubbing her hands up to her elbows. "Do you have a bowl and clean rags?"

Olwen handed them to her wordlessly. The princess filled the small bowl with water and strode across the room, rags in hand. She stood before Flyka, pointedly ignoring Neve.

It rankled, and he didn't know why.

"With your permission, I'll clean and stitch this in no time."

Flyka stared at the princess and gestured to her leg. "You can't do any worse than anyone else."

The princess knelt on the floor, despite the mud from Flyka's boots. She pulled off her emerald ring and tucked it into the pocket of her dress. She dunked the rag into the warm water and began dabbing Flyka's wound, cleaning it with sure but gentle strokes.

"Humans have red blood, not silver," the human commented, glancing at Flyka. "I wonder why that is."

"How the creator designed us, I supposed," Flyka muttered.

Neve leaned a shoulder against the bedpost as Eyri handed the human the threaded needle.

"Thank you, my lord," the princess murmured. She

lifted her arm and coughed into her elbow, glancing up once more at Flyka.

"No backing out now," the Haunt murmured, a taunt in her voice.

"Do you have something for the pain?"

Flyka held up a wooden flask and took a deep pull. "I'll be fine."

"Here we go," the *valles* muttered. She didn't hesitate as she held Flyka's skin together and began to close the cut. Neve watched as she made small, concise stitches, never wavering. He looked to Flyka, whose jaw was clenched. She breathed heavily, with short pants.

"This part will hurt," the princess murmured. "It's much deeper here."

The first stitch, Flyka paled, the second she wavered, the third she passed out, slumping against the mattress.

"Finally," the princess breathed, some of the tension in her shoulders easing. She focused on her work but addressed Eyri. "My lord, do you have honey or something like that for infection?"

"I do." He pulled a small, stoppered bottle from their emergency kit that they kept at all their safe houses and handed it over to the *valles* with a bright smile. Why the devil was he looking at her like that? "Thank you for your help, my lady."

"It's nothing. I'm the reason she was hurt in the first place. She was protecting me." There was heaviness to her voice that Neve didn't like. He rubbed his lower heart, and then brushed the emotion away. Her feelings were not his concern.

The group fell into silence as she worked. A sigh

escaped the princess as she tied the last knot and then carefully slathered the healing tincture over the gash. Eyri handed her the clean strips of linen, and she wrapped it around Flyka's leg before tying it off.

She sat back on her heels and exhaled slowly. "All done. Now we just need to get her into bed."

"I need you to move back first, my lady," Neve said gruffly.

She used the bunk to pull herself to her feet and edged out of the way.

Neve and Eyri arranged Flyka until she was situated on the bed. He stiffened when the princess edged herself between himself and Eyri, leaning down to fluff the pillow. Ginger and amber with a hint of sweetness teased his nose once again, and he held his breath. He caught Eyri's meaningful look and scowled. His cousin was going soft for the little *saloes*, and they'd only just met three days ago.

He eyed the *valles* as she brushed Flyka's hair from her face, pulled off her boots, and then draped a blanket over the top of her.

"She won't need that," he commented. "Her body will keep her warm enough, especially when healing."

"Blankets aren't always for heat. They're for comfort and safety sometimes. Right now, she probably feels vulnerable. A blanket will help that when she wakes."

"Why do you care?"

She pursed her lips. "A little kindness never hurt anyone." She pressed her hand below Flyka's collarbone and to the right, her brows furrowing.

"What?" Neve huffed.

"Her heart rate is wrong."

"Because we have two hearts, my lady," Eyri supplied, brushing a long strand of wet hair from his face, his nose crinkling in mirth.

The princess gaped for a moment before snapping her mouth shut. "It seems I've learned many new things about Loriians today." With that, she picked up the supplies from the floor, curtsied to Eyri, and retreated to the fire, where she murmured to Olwen in a low tone.

"Unexpected," Eyri mumbled in Loriian.

"It's odd that she did so well, no?" Neve replied, eyeing the little human. "By all accounts, she should not have been able to do that. Yet she stitched the wound like a seasoned battle healer. It doesn't make any sense."

"Maybe there's more to her than the crown? Sounds like someone I know."

Neve wrinkled his nose. "Don't compare me to that creature. My senses are telling me that she's hiding something."

Eyri arched a brow. "Maybe she is, but she's just one little *valles*, no?"

One tiny little female. Even so ... he had a feeling she would wreak havoc on his life.

Chapter Seventeen

Dahlia

All she wanted was to crawl into the steaming bath and warm up.

It was a bloody miracle that she'd been able to stitch up the giantess at all. Lia flexed her fingers toward the roaring fire, but they continued to burn. It seemed like the cold had settled in her bones. The tightness in her chest wasn't ideal either. Sickness was lurking in her lungs, she could tell.

"You stink," a growly voice stated, his rugged accent rounding vowels a human mouth could not.

Dahlia flinched, and glanced over her right shoulder at the brute who glowered at her from near the doorway. What had she done to get on his bad side? Since the moment she'd appeared in the Asteran throne room, he seemed to have it out for her.

Was it because of their first encounter? Did he think she would bring it up?

She rotated until her back faced the flames and stared him down. "I beg your pardon?"

He nodded toward the steaming bath in the corner. "Bathe."

Lia balked at the order. She glanced toward the giant with the long scar down his cheek—Olwen. He continued to pump hot water into the deep basin, looking utterly bored. Dahlia quickly scanned the room for a screen or divider for privacy.

Nothing. Did they expect her to wash with everyone watching?

Not on your life.

"No, thank you."

Olwen blew out a heavy breath. "Whyever not? Arun isn't wrong." He touched the bridge of his crooked nose. "You need to bathe."

"It's not proper," she replied tightly. Even if she were desperate enough to crawl into the steaming warmth the bath promised, there was no way she'd disrobe amongst a bunch of monsters.

Well, King Neve didn't seem so monstrous. She glanced his way, watching as his chest rose and fell in the slow breaths of someone in deep sleep.

"What does propriety have anything to do with washing?" Arun growled, pushing away from the door. "It's basic hygiene."

Her jaw dropped. "Everything. It's not seemly for a princess to disrobe amongst the other sex."

He scoffed, the strong line of his jaw ticing. "I forgot

about the stupid rules *saloes* hold themselves to." He reached over his shoulders and tugged off his tunic, revealing an expanse of smooth, muscled skin. "Fine, I'll enjoy the bath."

She stared at the scars that spread out like roots down each shoulder toward his pierced pectorals. Just what had happened to cause those? She didn't remember those from the time at the palace.

Her gaze trailed down his chest over his sculpted indigo abdomen, stopping at the waist of his trousers, where his claw-tipped fingers began to unlace them.

A blush raced to her cheeks, and she jerked her attention away, only to catch him staring at her as he began to remove his leathers. His words finally penetrated her mind.

He's going to bathe while we're all in the room.

Dahlia had never considered herself a prude, but she'd never been in a room with a bathing male. She spun on her heel and faced the fireplace, focusing on the flames.

The wet slap of his pants landed at her feet, and she closed her eyes, listening as the giant brushed behind her and stepped into the tub. He groaned, and more heat filled her cheeks when water splashed onto the stone floor.

He was really bathing while she was in the room. While everyone was in the room.

"You sure you don't want to stare a little more, *valles*? To help me wash my back?" Every word dripped with disdain and mocking. Maybe a touch of taunt. "Maybe use that rusty blade on me that you keep hidden?"

This is no way to treat a princess. Don't back down.

She bent to pick up his trousers and faced the tub

with a scowl. Arun leaned back in the tub, his arms bracketing the sides in a relaxed pose, his scarred knees popping out of the soapy water. It was a marvel how he made the massive tub look downright tiny.

Lia stormed closer to the tub and tossed his pants into the water. She kept her eyes on his expression and grinned inwardly as the smug smile was wiped from his face. Carefully, she clasped the edge of the basin and leaned over the edge, her damp locks brushing the surface of the bath.

"If you think for one second that you can order me around, think again." *Bastard.*

He reached out, curling a strand of her hair around his finger. "I would never presume to, *my lady.*"

Olwen snorted, and she tossed a glare his way. He immediately smothered his laughter, turning it into a cough. Dahlia's attention turned back to the bully in the tub. She dropped the fingers of her right hand into the water and drew a pattern in the oil that slicked the top from the soap. Neve followed her movements before tipping his chin up, his complete attention on her face as he released the lock of her hair.

A mistake on his part.

Lia cupped a handful of water and tossed it into his face. He sputtered as she retreated out of his reach, feeling victorious. "Wash your own bloody back."

It would be easy to stab Arun with her poison ring. He made it easy to hate him.

Instead she turned her back to him as Olwen snickered under his breath. Lia gritted her teeth as she moved away from the warm fire to the bunkbeds, fatigue riding her hard. Part of her wanted to pull the blankets from the mattress and sleep before the hearth, but she didn't want to be anywhere near Arun.

Instead, she pulled her outer dress off and hung it on the bedframe, left in only her damp undershirt and leggings. She quickly crawled into the bed, her back to the room as she snuggled beneath the blankets. Lia gritted her teeth as she trembled, pain and the cold threatening to make her teeth chatter together.

She hissed out a breath and curled into a tighter ball before rolling to face the room, her back to the wall. She felt too exposed the other way. She kept her eyes closed and ducked her head beneath the blanket to preserve her heat and to keep from seeing the brute bathing.

The inside of her thighs screamed. She was sure they were raw and bloody, though she couldn't check. Dahlia began to sing a song in her mind, and rocked gently, praying that she'd fall asleep.

Her eyelids lowered and a warm weight settled over her.

Just a little longer...

THE STORM DIDN'T LET UP FOR THREE DAYS.

Three.

Dahlia swallowed slowly, her throat burning like someone had dragged a rake down it. Her eyes watered, and she discreetly dabbed at her nose with the linen she'd filched from the bandages. Goosebumps ran down her arms and she rubbed at them. One moment she was burning up and the next freezing.

It was bloody inconvenient. This was not the time to be ill.

She couldn't afford to be weak among the Loriians.

Lia craned her neck and watched as Flyka flowed through a set of stretches like she didn't have a nine-inch cut along her thigh. Lia winced on the giantess' behalf and turned back to the fire.

No, she couldn't afford to be vulnerable. Especially since the wound didn't seem to slow the Haunt down at all. While she wasn't comfortable with Flyka, she'd warmed a little to the gruff giantess. She didn't let anyone boss her around. That was something Lia begrudgingly admired.

Dahlia scootched closer to the flames, pain ricocheting up and down her legs and up her spine. She stifled the whimper and dropped her chin to her chest, closing her eyes as she tried to work through the pain. Her limp, dirty hair fell around her cheeks as she hissed a slow breath out between her teeth.

The sound of ringing steel pulled her from her concentration. Dahlia glanced at the closed door leading to the barn and horses. The monsters were training. They spent most of their day out in the barn, only to come in once the sun set to hand out rations and then bathe. Arun the brute and Olwen the flirt as she thought of them, liked to tease her about it, but she was too tired and sick to care. Each night she crawled underneath her blanket, ignored the splashing of water, and prayed sleep would take her.

She winced and picked up a lock of her hair. She

needed a bath days ago, but didn't dare with so many witnesses around. The horrid pain on the inside of her thighs concerned her, as did the tickle in her lungs. Lia stared longingly at the steaming water in the bathtub.

If only.

Flyka plopped down next to Dahlia, startling her. She hadn't even heard the giantess approach. Flyka stretched out her long legs and leaned back on her powerful arms, sweat gleaming on her brow.

"How were your exercises?" Lia asked, her voice slightly strangled.

The giantess smiled and it sent a chill down Dahlia's spine. She still hadn't gotten used to the fangs.

"Getting better each day." A pause. "You could join me."

Dahlia grimaced. "Maybe one day. Travel takes the energy right out of me."

Flyka studied her in a way that made Lia want to squirm.

"You slept more yesterday and today." A statement that was more like a probing question.

"What else is there to do?" Lia countered. "We're trapped here."

"Not for long." The giantess glanced at the lone window. "The men have been clearing a path from the barn. We'll be leaving in a few hours."

Dahlia blanched and tried to cover it up when Flyka frowned. "So soon?" she rasped, her throat aching.

"Yes, but first we're going to bathe."

Her stomach bottomed out. "Excuse me?" Surely, they wouldn't force her.

Flyka rubbed her nose. "I can no longer stand your scent." Lia opened her mouth to argue when the giantess held her gray hand up. "I know *saloes* are touchy about nudity, but it is not so in my kingdom. You're now of Loriia. Our customs are yours. But..." She pushed up to her feet and stepped to the door. "I know that the *vallos* make you uncomfortable, so it will just be us *valles* bathing today."

Flyka yanked open the door, letting in frigid air that caused another bout of goosebumps to lift on her arms.

"Stay out if you know what is good for you," Flyka yelled into the barn. "We're bathing, and you don't want a dagger to the throat." The giantess slammed the door closed and offered the tiniest closed lipped smile.

That struck Dahlia in the chest. Flyka had noticed her discomfort with her fangs. That made her feel all of two feet high.

"I don't think the *vallos* will be bothering us," the giantess added.

"*Vallos*?" Lia questioned, the word rolling off her tongue.

"Males," Flyka answered, moving back to the washing basin and dipping her pointer finger into it. She grimaced and yanked her hand back. "*Vallos* for males, *valles* for females. And you can go first, princess."

"You're the one who sustained an injury."

The giantess lifted a brow. "It's too hot for me. I like my baths a little cooler." She held her hand out to Lia. "Come on, then."

Dahlia stared at Flyka's wicked claws, but slowly took her hand. The Haunt hadn't been anything but cordial since they left Astera. The giantess pulled her to her feet, and she bit her cheek to keep from groaning.

"You sure they won't come in?"

"Not on their life," Flyka replied.

Lia pulled off her thick socks, and then started on the ties of her skirt, letting it drop to the ground, leaving her in her leggings and a long-sleeved bodice. She grunted and pulled it over her head, only for her hair to get caught. Heat suffused her back and Lia froze as Flyka stepped close and untangled the strands.

Breathe. She's not going to hurt you.

The giantess hissed out a breath when she got the top bodice and undershirt free, and a heavy silence settled between them. Lia peered over her shoulder and flinched at the rage on Flyka's face. "W-what is it?" she managed.

"You've been traveling and sleeping in that torture device all this time?" The giantess began plucking at the strings of Dahlia's filthy corset. "It's barbaric. I can see where the bone has dug into your skin and made you bleed. What sort of garment is this? I should cut the ribbons and destroy it."

"Please don't. I need some sort of undergarment." Lia held the corset to her ample chest as it loosened, a sigh leaving her immediately. It was pure relief. "It's the undergarments of all *valles* in Astera," she said, trying out the word. "It helps corral our breasts and shape our figures."

Flyka snorted. "What nonsense. Your figure should not be shaped or changed. Each person should be as they are."

"A sentiment I wholeheartedly agree with." The corset finally loosened, and she held it closed and moved to the edge of the basin. "But my breasts tend to get in the way if they're not confined in some way."

"They are large. They would be a hinderance in battle."

Lia chuckled at the blunt statement. "I imagine they would. Not that I've ever seen battle."

Lia set the corset on the floor, making sure her back was to the door. She released the belt that held her sling and dagger, dropping them to the floor, then removing her ring and shoving it into the pocket of her skirt. Her nipples tightened in the cold air, and she wrapped her arm across them as she swung a leg over the edge and into the hot water.

Her toes burned and cramped, but it was manageable.

"What are you doing?" Flyka growled. "You need to remove your hose."

With a will of iron, Lia lifted her other leg into the basin and dropped into the water. She hissed out the agony that burned through her limbs. Stars dotted her vision, but she didn't pass out. The water reached the bottom of her chin, and her hair floated around her in the soapy water. One tear seeped out of her left eye, and she quickly dashed it away, before looking up at the giantess.

"I am not comfortable bearing myself to the world with strangers." She didn't let her gaze waver as she stared down Flyka. "Thank you for arranging a more private bath though," she added softly. "I've been cold for days."

The giantess shook her head. "I *know*. Your flat teeth chatter at night. It got so bad last night that Arun gave you his blankets to stop the racket."

Lia blinked. The mean giant that couldn't stand her

gave Lia his blankets? Why would he do that? Surely, it didn't bode well. His only interactions with her were cutting. What sort of game was he playing?

Flyka approached the tub with a bar of soap and a vial of what looked like perfumed oil. She handed the bar to Lia and poured the vial on the top of her head, kneeling beside the basin. She arched a brow at the Haunt. What was this?

"I'm not a lady's maid," the giantess said roughly. "But I had plenty of sisters to know how to wash a head of tangled hair."

Lia's eyes closed as Flyka gently detangled her locks and scrubbed her scalp. She almost moaned when the giantess ran her claws lightly over her scalp. It was bloody wonderful. The claws in her nightmares were used for slashing but the Haunt was so gentle. It made her shift in discomfort.

"Had?" she asked softly, opening her eyes to wash her arms.

"They all died." A brusque statement.

Dahlia frowned at the wall. "I'm so sorry." And she was. Losing Cosmos would kill her.

"Don't be. They died like warriors."

Lia pursed her lips. "Were they Haunts like you?"

"Yes. They died protecting our last queen when *saloes* invaded our borders." Her scrubbing turned a little rougher.

Saloes ... humans.

Dahlia twisted and bravely placed a hand on Flyka's forearm. The giantess paused her scrubbing and stared down at her. "I'm truly sorry." Losing family left scars on a person's soul. Her mum haunted her daily.

Flyka sighed, losing some of the tension in her body. "It wasn't your fault, princess." She gently shook off Lia's hand. "Now turn around so we can get you clean. You stink," she replied without any heat.

Lia spun back around and stared at her distorted reflection in the water. It seemed everyone had lost someone to the violence between Astera and Loriia.

And they will again if the queen has anything to say about it.

She dashed her hand through the water.

"Would you do anything for your family?" she asked softly.

The giantess paused, then began rinsing out Lia's hair. "I would do anything for my king and my family."

Dahlia nodded. So would she. Even if it meant tearing Loriia apart.

And the thought scared her.

CHAPTER EIGHTEEN

DAHLIA

IT ONLY GOT COLDER.

Flyka had been right.

They'd set out just as soon as her hair dried from the bath.

Getting onto Anwen had been a feat in and of itself, and then staying there without crying another. The shaggy horse bore each of her flinches with dignity, but only after she'd offered him dried fruit. He loved treats.

Each time Arun would toss an annoyed glare her way, Dahlia would dig down deep and pray for strength. There was something about the giant that made her want to prove him wrong. To be stronger than he expected from a human.

It took four freezing days to reach an enchanting city called Kallere. Four days of her delegation speaking mostly in Loriian. She asked questions when she could and gathered information, but she had a feeling they were playing games with her. Which was why they spoke predominately in a language she did not understand. It was isolating.

The only bright spots were the plants that stood out in bright contrast against the untouched snow, their flowers almost defiant in their beauty. Her favorite were the willowy trees with pale grey trunks and thin, limber branches dotted with dark bluebell-looking flowers. The delicate trees stooped in the wind almost like a man bowing to his dance partner, their swaying tips almost touching the earth in homage.

Then there were her conversations with the Frost King. He was incredibly bright and had a curious mind. Any time she asked a question about one of the resilient plants, he always had an answer for her. There was something about how his eyes sparkled behind his spectacles when talking about the flora, that tugged at her chest.

How was she supposed to kill him?

Maybe it was a good thing that envoy hadn't been incredibly welcoming. With each spouted fact about the Loriian countryside, she liked the king more. And it made it more difficult to contemplate her task.

Reaching Kallere was a relief, mentally and physically. It had charming little white frescoed homes that hosted rich timber supports that bisected the buildings. Slate roofs sparkled, making the place almost seem magical.

Her skin had tingled the entire ride through the city as giants stood in the doorways or along the road calling out in Loriian, tossing flowers and paper snowflakes at the king. They stared at her and whispered, sometimes touching her boots or legs.

Lia's nose was stuffy, her head feeling like it was filled with cotton, and she couldn't get warm. So it had been an unexpected joy to stop in a village outside of the city for the night. Not only did she receive her own room, a steaming bath, and proper nightgown, but a new set of white-trimmed leathers, a flowy skirt, and a bodice trimmed in warm fur. Dahlia had no clue how they knew her size. They were distinctly Loriian-made. But the thought didn't bother her as much. As long as she was warm, that was all that mattered.

She locked the door and barely managed to push an enormous trunk in front of it just in case someone got ideas about coming in. She stripped off all her clothing, hid her ring, and painstakingly removed her hose, the abused flesh sticking to the fabric.

It was a whole other agony to bathe with open wounds between her thighs. Lia finally let herself cry without anyone watching, her chest shuddering as all the fear, worry, and pain of the last few weeks crashed down upon her.

Had Cosmos made it to Lantium? Had he found a safe room and board? Was her mum still safe?

The questions plagued her at night.

A fit of coughing took her, to the point she gasped for air and her lungs rattled, causing her head to ache fiercely. She tipped her head back against the stone tub and stared at the ceiling, bubbles lapping at her chin.

Godsteeth, she was so tired. The rattle in her lungs was getting worse.

You need a healer.

She didn't dare say anything.

Dahlia closed her eyes and slipped beneath the water; all sounds muted. She held her breath and began reciting a song in her head—something she'd always done as a child. It helped her train to dive deeper when hunting for mussels in lakes as she and Cosmos traveled from city to city, performing for crowds.

Jolly good, darling, dance round and round,
You've nary been lost.
Set your heart free, don't look to the ground,
Spirals and dips.
Jolly good, darling, you're bound you're—

A muted crash, then hands seized her biceps, hauling her from the water. She sputtered and then screamed. She clawed at her attacker and opened her eyes, only for soap to drip into them.

"What the *qov* are you doing?" Arun's voice snarled at her. "Trying to drown yourself?"

"Soap in my eyes," she yelled, trying to rub at them. They *burned*.

The giant dropped her, and she sank back into the tub, rubbing at her eyes. Cold water sluiced over her head, and she coughed, still rubbing at her eyes.

"Stop rubbing," the giant growled. "Tip your head back." She did as he bid, squeezing her eyes closed as if that would remove the painful stinging. "Now blink."

It hurt, but at least he didn't drown her. He continued to pour a little water into her eyes until the soap stopped burning. She pressed her legs to the bottom of the tub and wrapped her arms around her breasts as he glared down at her, teeth bared.

Thank the stars for the bubbles. They covered her

body. Had he seen her legs? The water was deep enough that it should have at least covered her to the waist. Her relief was quickly overshadowed at the realization that he'd seen her whole top half.

Heat rushed into her cheeks. "What are you doing in here?" she barked, hating how he loomed over her.

He leaned down, his fingers curling around the edge of the stone tub. "Saving your life it seems."

"I was fine. How did you get in here anyway?" She leaned back and gaped at the door. It was splintered in three places, and the trunk was halfway across the room. "What the devil?"

"My sentiments exactly," he snapped, pulling her attention back to the massive angry male scowling at her. "Were you trying to kill yourself?"

"No!"

"Then what were you doing under the water for so long?"

She jerked. "How do you know how long I was in my bath?"

"I was assigned to guard you, and your crying and splashing stopped."

Tears welled up into her eyes. He'd heard her sobbing? Her gaze moved to his long, tapered ears. Of course he had. There was no privacy to be found among the Loriian. "I was testing how long I could hold my breath," she whispered, trying to keep her cool and not lose it. "It's something I've always done."

He pursed his lips and stared at her *hard*, like he was trying to see into her soul. "Your voice sounds different."

She blinked at him. "That's because I sucked in water

when you yanked me from the tub and then dropped a pitcher of water over my head!"

"I was trying to help you, *valles*."

Her brows lowered. "Don't you *valles* me! My name is Dahlia!" She was so tired of being called *princess* or *female*. She'd always prided herself on being calm and pragmatic, but there was something about Arun that made her want to scream and quite possibly throw something.

He cocked his head. "You give me permission to call you by your name?"

She rolled her eyes, and he jerked. Seems the big ol' bad frost giant was unsettled by her eyes.

The feeling is mutual, you big brute.

"Call me Lady Dahlia if you must." The tension in his face seemed to melt as his eyes ran over her once again. Embarrassment rose hot and heavy as his attention dropped to the water that rippled around her neck. She cleared her throat. "Now that you've ascertained that I'm fine, please leave."

He released the basin edge like he'd been burned, and backpedaled, pausing at the door. "I'll have dinner sent up to you, and more blankets."

With that, he spun on his heel and slammed the door shut. It shuddered on its hinges but held.

What had that been about?

A raspy cough escaped her. It didn't matter. All she needed to focus on was cleaning her thighs, getting a cup of tea down, and a good night's sleep.

Surly giants could go suck rocks for all she cared.

CHAPTER NINETEEN

NEVE

HE LED BOTH THE PRINCESS AND HIS *RUKHALS* TO
the tiny inn.

No, not the princess. *Dahlia.*

The beasts snorted and shook their heads, their long
ears flopping before perking up once again. Olwen stood
in the melting snow with a cheeky grin on his face.

"What?" Neve groused, tying up the two *rukhals*, who
immediately began to munch on the greens he'd left on
the ground for them.

"How does it feel to be wearing black again?" his
friend asked.

Neve rolled his shoulders, the ceremonial garb pulling
tightly across the back of his broad shoulders. "Uncomfortable." It was bizarre to be wearing royal regalia at all. It
wasn't something he wore except for formal occasions,
and those were few and far between.

One of the *rukhals* nosed his shoulder, its rounded downy muzzle looking for treats in his pockets. He smiled and turned to wrap his arms around the beast. "Looking for food already, old friend?" Neve patted Cessa's tawny coat.

Cessa lipped his braids and stomped one hoof, shaking his impressive set of antlers.

Neve pulled the apple from his pocket and held it out to the *ruhkal*. "Spoiled beastie."

A gasp came from behind him when Cessa took the apple from his hand. Neve spun around, snow crunching beneath his boots.

His breath caught and his stomach dropped.

Dahlia stood just outside the inn, in the white *loviaye* garb. The dress molded to her body. His mind flashed back to the tub the night before, at all the exposed flesh he'd glimpsed before she dropped down into the foamy water. He shook his head to dispel the image. He had never been curious about human bodies. He'd expected to be disgusted, and a part of him was, but the other half had been *intrigued*.

There's something wrong with you.

Dahlia shivered and pulled the white cloak closed, ending his perusal. The *valles* glanced at him, her strange eyes rounded in her fair face. He frowned. There were dark spots beneath her eyes and her nose was bright red. He'd noticed that her skin changed colors in the cold, but the princess had been indoors all night.

Dahlia approached him, her attention turning to Cessa, who crunched on his apple happily. She paused before him, her ginger scent mixing with the crisp air. He pursed his lips as he scented something florally and sweet. Her soap?

Soapy bubbles slipping down slick skin.

That way danger lies.

"You ride stags?" she whispered as if it would scare away the *rukhals*.

Neve glanced at Cessa, who eyed the princess with interest, probably wondering if she had another treat for him. "They are called *rukhals*," he found himself explaining. "They travel far better in the deeper snow than our horses. Much nimbler, albeit slower at times."

"Can I pet him?" she rasped, her voice throatier.

A smile tried to sneak onto his face, but he squashed it immediately. "Cessa is gentle to all." He stepped away so his *rukhal* could meet the *valles*. "Let him scent you first," he said gruffly.

"Hello, Cessa," she crooned, holding her hand out flat. His beastie crept closer and gave the princess two heavy sniffs. She held absolutely still as Cessa pressed a little closer. A soft tinkling laugh escaped her as she ran her hand along the *rukhal*'s downy nose. "Aren't you just a beautiful boy? Absolutely stunning."

Cessa leaned into her as she continued to pet his nose, then neck, and finally wide chest.

A bright smile bloomed across her face that made her eyes crinkle at the corners. For some reason, it didn't bother him as much. In fact, it was almost enchanting until it widened to show her flat teeth. He smothered his shudder. She hugged Cessa, pressing her temple to his neck, and crooned softly to the beastie while he snuffled her hair.

It amazed him how *saloes* could be so gentle to animals, and then completely ruthless to other beings in the next moment.

They cannot be trusted.

"*Rukhals* are noble beasts. They are not meant to be hugged." He flinched at the sneer in his own voice, but hardened his heart. Showing some affection to his *rukhal* didn't make her any less human.

She recoiled, smile completely gone, her cracked lips tugging into a severe thin line. Dahlia ignored him, and reached into her pocket to pull out an apple that had been split in half.

"He has already had an..." he trailed off as she fed Cessa the half of the apple, pressing a kiss to the top of his snout. She then moved to the *rukhal* he had chosen for her and fed that beastie a treat as well.

Without another word, she turned away from him and marched back into the inn. She nodded to Olwen before slamming the door behind her.

"That wasn't very ladylike," Neve muttered in Lorian. "A spoiled *valles*."

Olwen's brows rose, his smile crooked. "And the way you stole her wonder and joy away didn't have anything to do with her reaction?"

Neve shifted uncomfortably. "I cannot trust her."

His friend walked through the slush and clasped a hand on Neve's shoulder. "I don't disagree with you. Until she proves herself, we shouldn't trust her, but we don't have to be cruel."

"She is a *saloes*. You have lost as much as I because of their race."

"Aye," Olwen said, his brows furrowing. "But in the time we have spent with the princess, she's not been rude or cruel to us. She's taken our teasing with more grace than I would in her situation. Plus, we've ridden hard even though she's soft and our mounts much too wide for her to be comfortable. Not once has she complained. I can respect that. If we show some kindness, perhaps we will gain an ally, no? Isn't that the reason for your marriage?"

She was a task he needed to complete. That's all Neve had planned on. He hadn't planned on her fire, or resilience, or how much he liked to needle the *valles*. He'd expected many more fits along the way, and she'd been quiet, apart from her humming softly.

Except for when you provoke her.

"How do you think she will react when she finds out you're really the king and her new husband?" Olwen asked in Loriian, his face turning to the inn. "She's warmed up to Eyri quite well."

Everyone liked his cousin, including the princess. And it bothered him, just a touch.

"About as good as she reacted when I tried to help her mount the horse." He ran a hand over his thick braid, remembering how she kicked at him. "At least the pretending will be over after today. Then we can go our separate ways."

Olwen looked at him in surprise. "Do you really think it will be that easy? Surely, you've spent enough time with that *valles* to know she has fire that she keeps dampened. One wrong move and you could burn the palace down to ash."

The door to the inn opened and Eyri spilled out,

followed by the princess. She shut the door behind them, and Neve blinked slowly as he observed Dahlia shiver and reach for her hood, only to cough harshly. His cousin helped lift the hood over the *valles'* head, and she smiled up at him gratefully.

A string pulled taut in his chest. He rubbed the ache and then dropped his hand when Flyka appeared to his left.

"Are you ready, *lae reillov*?" she asked in Loriian. "For the ceremony?"

"As ready as I'll ever be."

He followed as Eyri led the princess to her mount and then moved away. She stared at the *rukhal*, her mouth slightly opening.

"There's no saddle," she muttered to herself. He curbed a smile when she planted her hands on her hips and squinted up at the beastie. "You can do this."

He moved a little closer, running his hand along Cessa's back.

Nova twisted his neck to look at the *valles*. She huffed and petted his nose. "Just what am I supposed to do, my lord *rukhal*?"

"Nova," Neve offered.

She blinked. "Excuse me?"

"His name is Nova."

"Oh." She gave the beastie a soft smile, one that was thankfully close-lipped this time.

Neve gave Cessa one last pat and then crossed his arms, ready to square off with the princess. He needed to lift her onto the *rukhal*, as it was part of the wedding ceremony.

"We ride without saddles."

Her jaw dropped. "No saddle?"

"None."

"Do you have ones for children?" she asked, a touch of hope in her voice. "When we traveled through Kallere, I noticed the older children were almost my own height."

"No."

Her shoulders drooped.

Neve clasped his hands together. "It's not so bad, princess. Nova is trained well. All you need is the slightest pressure and he will follow where you lead. You can hold on to his horns, and he won't mind. Plus, he's not as wide as the horses, so it will be easier on your short legs."

"Short legs?" she chuckled, which turned into a wheezy cough. "I'm tall for a *valles*, as you say."

He frowned. Neve didn't like the sound of that cough. Was there something wrong with her lungs? "What is wrong with you?" he demanded. "Are you sick?"

She flinched. "It's nothing. Just the cold air."

Her words seemed like a lie, but why would she hide an illness?

Perhaps it is what kept her hidden away in Astera?

Neve took a step closer, eating up the space between them. He stared down into her alien eyes, trying not to shudder at how the green and brown circle in the middle seemed to rove about without thought. "If you will permit me, I will help you mount."

She held her breath as she looked around him for someone else, but his Haunt had already mounted and moved away.

She exhaled heavily, and nodded.

Neve wrapped his hands around her dainty waist, his claws touching in the back. She weighed nothing as he perched her sideways on Nova, who pranced a little bit. He peered up at his *loviaye*, and frowned as he watched her wince and try to shift carefully.

"Are you in pain?" he growled.

"No," she replied, her face a mask of serenity.

A lie.

He inhaled deeply and paused as the scent of sweets and florals were stronger. What the devil was that?

"Am I expected to ride sidesaddle?"

"No." He inhaled again. Was it the soap?

"Okay. Then be off with you. I am alright."

She'd dismissed him. *Again.*

Neve bowed to her, his jaw clenched, and spun around to Cessa. He leapt onto the *rukhal*'s back and nudged him to turn around. He watched with keen eyes as the princess slowly moved her right leg over Nova's back. Her face never creased once, but perspiration shone on her forehead.

Were humans tired out so easily?

He grimly turned his attention away.

Just get through the day. Marry your valles *and be done with it.*

If only it were that easy.

Chapter Twenty

Neve

Nightfall approached, and with it his nerves.

Neve stared at the Olek Mountains to the northeast as the sun began to set.

They'd made good time on the *rukhals*. They were so close he could see the immense holy tree in the distance, and the hair rose along his arms. Only a few more minutes before he would lead his *loviaye* across the life-bringing waters and be bound to the *valles* for the rest of his life.

His hearts pounded at the thought, and his palms grew a little sweaty.

It was one thing to commit himself to this treaty, and another thing to follow through with it.

"I love this part of our land," Eyri commented softly. "It feels magical, festive."

Neve glanced to his cousin and tried to smile, but it

was forced. Nothing about this day felt magical or festive. In fact, an impending sense of doom hovered over him that made him want to bolt into the snowy winter lands.

Eyri looked over his shoulder and switched to Loriian: "I know she's not what you would have chosen for yourself, but at least she's not like her parents."

He grimaced, brows slashing together. "That we know of." The princess hadn't complained too much over the last week, but that didn't mean she was innocent. There was no way she was unscathed, being raised among such vipers, even if she had been cloistered.

"Do you really think that woman is a spy?" Eyri asked. "She's kept to herself. Not once has she tried to get into our good graces."

"Flyka." While he was appreciative for the *valles'* help, why had she done it? No one had known she possessed those skills. What did she expect to get out of the deal? Did she think it would endear them to her?

Eyri sighed. "What did she gain from that?"

"I don't know."

"You're always so suspicious."

"I have to be," he gritted out. "I can't afford to think any other way."

His cousin gave him a pitying look which made Neve bristle. He didn't need anyone feeling sorry for him. He was the bloody *reillov* of Loriia.

They fell into silence as the group pressed on toward the Seed in the distance. The tree grew larger the closer they got, the snowy lands around them bathed in the sun's fading light. The snow sparkled like a thousand gems, and he couldn't help but glance back at the *saloes*.

She'd pushed back her hood and was staring at the winter countryside, her lips slightly parted as if in awe. A thread of pride wound around his chest, and he sat a little taller. If his kingdom awed him every time he saw it, what must it be like for a human who'd never been to Loriia?

In fact, as far as he knew, only two *saloes* had visited the Seed in their history. It was something that they guarded fiercely. A holy place. The beginning of life for their kingdoms. Or so the stories went.

A rattling cough broke the peaceful silence, and he winced.

"Her cough has gotten worse today," Eyri commented in Loriian. "I asked her about it and all she said was that the cold air stings her lungs." His cousin frowned. "Does that sound right to you?"

Neve shrugged. "I don't know much about the human body, only that they have one heart opposed to our two. And that most do not like the cold."

"Well, our princess has seemed to weather our cold quite well."

He arched a brow. "Our princess?"

Eyri had the decency to look bashful. "You know what I mean."

Neve smiled at how his cousin squirmed on his *rukhal*. It was so easy to tease him at times. "I was just jesting."

"You don't do that much anymore."

That wiped the smile from his face. "The burden of responsibilities are heavy upon my shoulders." He didn't have time for frivolities. His carefree youthful past was well over.

"That doesn't mean you have to destroy yourself for your kingdom. It's okay to take a moment for yourself. To be yourself. No one is expecting you to be your father."

His heart pinched at the blunt but genuine advice. "I know," he rasped. "It's hard not to give my all when our kingdom demands it."

Eyri nodded. "Now you will have a wife too."

A *niliave*. A wife.

"Indeed." But for how long? He hadn't sussed out the reason the Asterans had given their only child to their enemy.

She coughed again, the sound wet. Maybe she had weak lungs? If so, she was not long for life; he'd help her go quickly and painlessly. He wasn't a monster.

He rubbed at his chest when it twinged uncomfortably.

He dropped his hand, and his expression hardened.

And if she was a spy ... she'd be executed as a traitor.

Either way, his wife wouldn't be long for this life.

THE ROAR OF THE RIVER GREW LOUDER AS THEY approached the life-giving waters. Neve stared at the crystal-clear aquamarine water, vapor rising into the air as shadows from branches of the Seed cast wicked-looking claws across the river and snowy banks. He clicked softly and Cessa stopped just before the river's sloping southern bank. He lifted his hand and waved to his people, who lined the northern bank, awaiting their king and his new bride.

They cheered, holding up their flickering lanterns. A symbol that his people would always be his guiding light.

He glanced to the west, noting the old stone bridge that led to the city. Dark green pine garlands dotted with pink flowers of the *vestrellaye* trees decorated the sides of the bridge, along with large lanterns.

The road that would always lead home.

Neve dismounted Cessa and nodded to his Haunts. He pulled his regalia off, leaving him shirtless. Next, he pulled off his boots and socks, shoving everything into his bag and pulling out his fur *sillovia*—the ornamental *caern'ye* cover—one that he'd share with his *loviaye* once they'd been bound by crossing the waters together. Lastly, he slid on the embroidered jerkin cuffs his *mommar* had stitched for his *povvar*.

A lump formed in his throat, and heat pressed to the back of his eyes.

I wish you were here with me.

He closed his eyes and took a moment to compose himself, the snow melting beneath the soles of his feet.

You can do this.

The snow reached his knees, but he hardly felt a thing as he faced the *valles*. The princess had pulled her hood back up and slumped over Nova. She looked like a wilting flower. He frowned, and curled his hands into fists. His people needed a strong queen.

Olwen clicked, and Cessa fell in line with the other *rukhals*.

He nodded to his Haunt as Nova approached him.

Neve held his hand out and gave the beastie a rub along his snout, pulling a dried date from his pocket. The mount lipped it off the flat of his palm, his large dark eyes seeming almost happy.

"There's a good boy," he murmured in Loriian. "Come." He clicked, and Nova began following him down the slope toward the river's edge.

"Why did you disrobe?" the princess asked, her voice hoarse. "And where are the rest of the delegation?"

"They're traveling to the bridge. We'll meet them there," he replied in the common tongue.

The chilly water lapped at his bare feet, but it wasn't too bad. He'd swum in far colder waters. Neve led Nova farther into the water when the princess gasped.

"What do you think you are doing?" she asked. "The bridge is over there."

"This is where we cross."

"Certainly not," she said, her voice going shrill.

Nova waded deeper into the water, and Neve clicked for the beastie to stop. He peered up at his human *loviaye*.

"This is part of the ceremony." He bowed before the princess as cheers exploded from his people. His hearts pounded as he straightened. He held out his hand. "Take my hand, *seittae*." Adding a please never hurt anyone.

She pushed back her hood and stared at his upturned palm like it was a snake. Neve waited, feeling the stares of his people keenly. The breeze picked up, brushing a few pinkish-gold strands of hair across her pale face.

Her eyes darted from him to the water, to his people, and back up the riverbank. His back molars ground together as he read her mind.

She is going to bolt.

Neve stepped closer and curled his hand around her calf. She jerked at his touch, but he ignored it, pulling until the princess slid toward him. He caught her around her tiny waist, and she hissed when he maneuvered her until she sat sideways on the beast's back. He took her left hand in his own and she tried to pull away. He growled, and wrapped his fingers around her wrist, holding out his left hand toward the water.

He could feel the dainty bones beneath her skin. He brushed his thumb along the rapid pulse there. "We need to cross. Do not worry. I will do most of the work. I just need you to hold on."

The whites of her eyes widened, and he flinched.

"No. I will not."

He gnashed his teeth, feeling like his fangs would snap off. "You don't have a choice. This is what must be done."

"You're trying to kill me," she spat.

He jerked. Why the devil would she think that?

Before he could respond, she clicked and nudged her heels into Nova. The *rukhal* lunged forward and to the side just as the princess yanked her hand from his hold. He shouted as the *valles* lost her balance and tumbled off backward into the river.

Chapter Twenty-One

DAHLIA

Her back hit the water first, then the icy barrage closed over her head.

Dahlia reflexively gasped and clawed for the surface, kicking her legs though they tangled in her skirts.

She burst into the air coughing and spewing water as the river pulled her downstream. Her eyes burned; her skin stung as if she were being pricked by thousands of needles. She locked her gaze on the bank, which was farther away than she remembered. Arun raced along the edge of the river, his pitch-black gaze locked on her.

"Hold on!"

The cloak snagged on something in the water below and she cried out when the clasp dug into her throat as the river feverishly tore at her legs. She gagged and tugged on the infernal clasp with numb, shaking fingers.

Stay calm. You can swim. Slow breaths.

The clasp gave, and she kicked to keep afloat as she was towed down the river, the cry of frost giants filling the air. Lia kicked hard and gritted her teeth as the weight of the skirt and boots threatened to pull her beneath the surface.

Her legs ached, feeling like giant blocks of ice moving in slow motion.

Get out of the water.

Her attention snapped onto Olwen, Flyka, and the king on the bridge. They dropped a rope from the stone railing.

"Grab the rope," Arun bellowed from the side, still trying to keep up with the swift river.

Dahlia scooped her arms through the frigid river, her limbs protesting each movement. She gritted her teeth and ignored the pain. All she had to do was grab the rope.

The river tossed her to the right and she scrambled, grazing a rock, her fingers seeking purchase along the slick stone, only to be tossed back into the rapids part of the river. Her breath fogged in thin clouds as she kicked harder, going at a diagonal to get in line with the rope.

The bridge rose ahead, and she lifted her hands, catching the rope. It slipped in her grip, and she wrapped it around her fist. Her body jerked to a stop, which was a completely different torment of its own. The river angrily tore at her, trying to suck her down. Lia growled, trying to hold on as the Haunts above began to lift her from the water.

Her limbs trembled and her whole body shook as she tried to hold on. Dahlia's eyes widened the moment her arms gave out. The rope burned faintly before it caught, jerking her right arm above her head. Agony exploded through her body and she screamed, crashing into the river in a tangle of limbs.

For a moment, she curled in on herself in the water, holding her broken arm to her chest.

Kick. Fight. Don't stop moving.

Her body was so tired. Lia kicked and tried to open her eyes, disoriented. Which way was up?

A firm arm banded around her waist and yanked her up. Dahlia broke the surface, sputtering.

Tears poured from her eyes as she clung to whoever had pulled her from the water with her good arm. She opened her eyes, gaping at the fearsome expression on Arun's face.

"We're too close," he whispered.

Her eyes rounded at the sharp boulder the river would dash them against. She closed her eyes, preparing for the pain. Her heart raced and her stiff fingers spasmed against his wet skin. She was going to die.

"*Qov!*" he yelled, startling her tired eyes open. He glanced down at her and spun a second before they crashed into the rock.

Her teeth clacked together, even though he'd taken the brunt of it. She stared up at his face—deep blue brows slashed together, fangs bared, and forehead wrinkled in pain. He groaned, panting hard.

"Don't let go of me," he panted as the river tugged them back into its furious rush, yanking them beneath the surface once again. His claws pricked her when he tightened his grip, but she felt no pain. Time seemed suspended, and her lungs started to burn.

Don't panic. Just a little longer. Hold your breath.

They broke the surface.

"Wrap your arms around my neck," he shouted over a distant thunder. "I will swim for the both of us."

She shook her head, her eyelids feeling extremely tired. "Can't," she slurred, her lips stiff. "My arm."

He cursed again, and hitched her tighter, keeping his hand secured around her waist. She stared up into his ferocious face as he began to swim against the river. Her chin dropped to his shoulder even though the water lapped at her mouth. She'd just rest for a little bit. The roar of the river chanted in her ears. She leaned her cheek against Arun's shoulder and stared at how the water narrowed, seeming like it came to a stop.

Waterfall, her mind whispered.

And yet Lia couldn't find it in herself to worry. All she wanted to do was sleep.

Movement in the sky caught her attention. A large owl swooped through the air, its feathers so white they were startling against the coming night. She felt her body giving out, her grip slacking.

"Come on," Arun growled.

They neared the edge, the water turning white and seeming like it curled in on itself as it tumbled into oblivion. They stopped moving, suspended in the angry river.

She watched as the water sucked at her legs, trying to drive her over the waterfall's edge. She knew she should be scared, but couldn't find it in herself to feel anything.

The enormous owl swooped closer, its golden eyes a startling contrast to its round white face. It seemed like it was telling her something.

A sigh escaped her. Finally, the cold was receding,

warmth creeping into her limbs. Maybe the river wasn't so frigid.

Her stomach lurched when they moved, only to get yanked suddenly. It went on and on until the water slipped from her lips, to her neck, and then chest. She tipped her head against Arun's neck, eyelids falling shut, the shriek of an owl and the thunder of a waterfall lulling her to sleep.

Just a quick nap.

The brute shook her roughly and slapped her cheek.

Lia laughed, but it was more of a gurgle as his penetrating, terrifying eyes focused on her face. "That didn't hurt," she slurred, her face feeling all wrong.

His lips turned downward and his brows slashed together, water dripping from his chin. "Don't close your eyes. Keep them open, *jaivelle*."

She cried out, a bone-deep pain shooting through her shoulder as he lifted her into his arms. He didn't know just how heavy her eyelids were. Her head lolled back, and she smiled as the sun retreated completely and one star winked at her, the outline of an owl above.

The sky blurred, and she closed her eyes as the wind picked up.

"Stay with me," a deep rumbly voice whispered.

Chapter Twenty-Two

He ran.

Olwen, Eyri, and Flyka fell in by his side. The crowd parted with gasps as he sprinted toward the city. His gaze flew down to the *valles* in his arms. Her lips were a stark blue against her pale complexion that seemed almost translucent. Little puffs of air came from her slack mouth, her eyelids almost closed, eyes rolled back into her head.

Qovving hell.

Neve shook her but she only groaned, limp against his chest.

The crowd thickened around the edge of town with little huts.

"Make way!" Flyka shouted.

Neve assessed the area. It was an hour walk to reach the Seed—the center of the city.

She won't make it that long.

"Your grandmother who is the healer still lives near here, no?" he huffed, glancing at Olwen.

"Yes."

That's all the confirmation Neve needed. He veered down a snow-packed road, and then up the main street of the village. He loped up the steps to the healer's home and barged in.

Olwen's grandmother and two of her *nonnaette* - her apprentices - squeaked in surprise at his intrusion. Warmth curled around him immediately, along with the scent of herbs as he made his way into the large room. *Nonnae* stood from her stool near the fire and met him midway, her attention scouring him, and then the *valles* in his arms.

"What happened?" she muttered, her lips thinning as she pressed the back of her black hand to his *loviaye*'s forehead.

"Our bonding didn't go as planned."

"She's too cold. Bring her to the fire." She hustled to the hearth and yanked a cot in front of it. "Lianna, Loshika, get the bath ready. We need to get this *saloes* warm *now*."

Neve followed her, water dripping down his legs, leaving a path behind him. *Nonnae* grabbed a pair of scissors and nodded to him. "Lay her on the cot. We need to get the wet clothes off of her."

He did as she bid, agony and breathlessness crashing over him at the movement. Neve pushed through it and knelt beside the cot. The old woman shoved a blade into his hand.

"Help me. We don't have much time."

A kernel of fear rooted in his gut as he cut the ties of the bodice. He placed the knife between his teeth and ripped the garment from her body. He frowned at the undergarment beneath it. "Is that bone?" he whispered to himself as he tugged at the tightly bound cage that seemed to be squeezing her breasts right out the top, leaving bloody sores near her armpits.

"Stop gawking and start cutting," *Nonnae* reprimanded, snipping the last of the skirt away. "Each minute could mean her life."

Neve sliced the top of the undergarment and then pulled the tight fabric apart. The rending of wet satin filled his ears. He kept his gaze averted as her breasts slipped free, and focused on her sleeves. While he didn't know much about humans, he knew they were prudes when it came to nudity. His wife wouldn't want him gawking at her body, even if it was in morbid curiosity and not desire.

A breath whistled out of his nose at the bruising around the shoulder of her right arm. A dislocation.

"*Lae reillov?*" Olwen's voice sounded behind him.

Neve curled over his *niliave*. Frost giants didn't care about nudity, but his little *valles* did. "Get out. Flyka, I need you."

He registered two sets of boots leaving as the giantess squatted next him. The door closed, cutting off the cold air.

"What do you need of me?"

"Her other arm."

Flyka got to work, carefully slicing off the other sleeve as Neve ran his claw gently over Dahlia's bruised shoulder.

A sharp breath pulled his attention to *Nonnae*, who stared at one of the *valles'* legs. His jaw slackened. Her legs were ... a pattern of different-colored skin. A puzzle of flesh.

"What caused this?" he whispered. Humans changed colors constantly with their emotions, but something like this? It didn't seem possible.

Nonnae's gaze flew to his for a moment, her hands resting near the human's knee. "I'm not sure, *reillov*, I've never treated a human before."

"A witch?" Flyka offered.

The healer *tsk*ed. "There's no such thing in any land, only charlatans."

Neve glanced away as *Nonnae* continued to cut the trousers from the human to stare at her face. Just what sort of creature was she? Just whom had he bound himself to?

"*Qov*," the healer muttered.

"What?" he asked, still staring at Dahlia's face, particularly the dots on her nose.

"Infection."

"From the water?"

"Her thighs, my lord."

This time he did look. His gorge rose as he got a good look at the mess that was her inner thighs. Flesh peeled away as the healer gently tugged at the soaked bandage that was stuck to the skin, blood and pus sullying the linen.

"How did this happen?" the healer hissed.

"I'm not sure. She's been stiff on the journey, but I attributed it to her being a *saloes*." Shame pricked him.

Nonnae chuckled, but it wasn't nice, pushing her black and silver braid from her shoulder. "She was limping because she was so *qovving* saddle sore. It was a bloody miracle she made it so far." A *tsk.* "She must have an extremely high pain tolerance and a will of stone."

Neve looked away as the healer continued cutting, and glanced at Flyka, who frowned fiercely.

"I should have known," his Haunt whispered, guilt in her tone. "She never took off her pants around us—even me. I thought it was human propriety."

"It's not your fault." It was *his.* She was his charge. He unbuckled the thin belt hanging on her bare waist, pocketing her old dagger, slingshot, necklace, and ring. "Her injury rests on my shoulders alone."

"Not to break up this guilt session, but it's time for you to make amends, my lord, and take care of your wife. She needs a bath, and you'll need to climb in with her," *Nonnae* murmured.

He gently lifted his *loviaye* from the cot, cuddling her body close to his, making sure his claws and fingers went nowhere near her wounds on the inside of her thighs. Neve followed the healer into the next room, where a natural stone pool stood in the middle. Steam curled off the surface, and he broke out in a sweat just from the heat of the room alone.

Nonnae gestured to the pool. "In you go."

The first step into the tub burned, the second scorched, and finally he stood in the waist-deep water. He stepped to the edge and the healer knelt next to him, brushing a wet lock of hair from Dahlia's cheek.

"Make sure you have a good hold on her. She won't like this bit."

Neve lowered the *valles* into the water until it reached the bottom of her chin. She came to life with a scream that made his ears ring. She struggled in his arms, wailing about burning. He held her tight, his jaw clenching at the sobs that wracked her body.

"I'm burning alive," she cried out, eyes glassy.

He pressed a kiss to her hair and held her tighter. "It's okay, *jaivelle*. You're okay," he crooned, rocking slightly as she continued to cry and thrash.

Her cries and sobs turned into bone-rattling coughs. Her body slowly warmed, and then the shakes began. Dahlia's flat teeth chattered so hard he thought they would fall right out of her mouth.

"That's enough," *Nonnae* commented. "We need to set her shoulder, and then get her warm and dry. Her lips are still blue."

Neve stood, lifting the *valles* out of the water, and she began shivering harder. Water sluiced down their bodies as he once again followed the healer to a small room to the left. The heat from the roaring fire was almost smothering. Flyka waited next to a mattress on the floor in front of the fire, and what seemed like a hundred blankets.

"Hand the *saloes* to your Haunt, *lae reillov*. I need to get a look at you," *Nonnae* commanded.

"I'm fine."

"I'm sure you are, but you won't be much help to your bride if I can't check on you. I can see you hiding your pain."

He reluctantly handed the princess over to Flyka who,

with the help of the *nonnaette,* toweled off the shuddering princess. Neve stood still, dripping water onto the floor as the healer inspected his back, her claws running softly along tender spots.

"No internal damage," she muttered. "Only large bruises and a few fractured ribs. Did you inhale any water?"

"A little."

"I'll give you tonic to help with lung health, then." She stepped away, pursing her deep purple lips. "Strip, *lae reillov.*"

He reached for the laces of his leathers. "Why?" With the heat of his room and body, they would soon be dry.

Dahlia screamed, and his eyes snapped to her over his shoulder. The *nonnaette* stepped away from Flyka as she placed the princess' arm back down. They'd reset her shoulder.

"Your mate needs body heat," *Nonnae* replied, answering his question. "You're her best option so that she doesn't lose any fingers or toes."

He blanched, but wiped the look from his face when the healer bared her fangs at him. Neve didn't need to be told twice by the old crone.

Neve divested himself of his pants and stalked to the nest of blankets on the floor, naked. Sweat beaded on the back of his neck and forehead at the blazing heat from the fire. He took a towel proffered by the *nonnaette* with a broken claw and dried off quickly. He then lifted the covers and scooted in, jerking when her freezing body touched him. A hissed breath escaped between his teeth when he pulled her back flush against chest, his *sorav* aching so much he pulled his hips away from her rounded buttocks. She whimpered again and he cursed, forcing himself to press his whole body to hers despite the pain.

A moan escaped her as she shook in his arms. Dahlia tucked into a ball, and he curled around her, trying to touch as much of his skin to her as he could. She was so bloody cold. And *tiny*. It triggered his protective instincts. He ran his thumb soothingly across her dimpled navel, tucking her feet between his thighs.

Nonnae dropped to her knees in the nest, holding a cup in her hand and began to try to get the liquid into the princess. He watched silently as the healer patiently fed the human small sips. He inhaled deeply, his nose twitching with the scent of the ice spirits.

His brows rose. "Something so strong?" Most giants couldn't handle more than a few sips.

"She needs it to heat her from the inside." The healer set the cup aside and placed her fingers on the inside of Dahlia's wrists. "I'm not sure how fast her heart is supposed to beat," *Nonnae* huffed, frustration twisting her lips. "But I think hers is too slow. I don't like it."

The *nonnaette* with a pockmarked neck stepped forward and held out a long metallic cylinder with a tapered middle. The healer pulled back the blankets and gestured to Neve. "Turn her onto her back so I can listen to her breathing."

Dahlia moaned and shivered harder, but her eyes stayed closed. *Nonnae* bent over the *valles* and placed the metal cylinder just above each breast.

"Now her back."

Neve rotated the human carefully onto her belly so

the healer could listen there. He scowled at all the bruising and scratches along her fair skin. When had those happened? He arranged Dahlia back into his arms as the old woman leaned back, scowling.

"She's sick." It was said like an accusation.

"From the water?"

"No, there was already liquid in her lungs, *lae reillov*." Her eyes narrowed on Neve. "Did she show any indication of sickness on your journey?"

"She grew paler the longer we traveled, and she had dark smudges beneath her eyes."

"The princess has been coughing," Flyka added. "And she was cold all the time."

Neve nodded. "Her nose was red. Does that mean anything?"

Nonnae pursed her lips, and placed her hand over the *valles'* forehead. "They are not as physically strong as we are, but I believe humans don't tolerate the weather like we do either. What were the traveling conditions like?"

"Rain, sleet, snow." *The usual.*

She winced. "I think extended exposure to such weather can kill a *saloes*."

He blinked slowly at *Nonnae*. "The cold will *kill* my *loviaye*?"

"*Extended* exposure." She pushed back from her knees and onto her feet, gesturing to the *nonnaette*. "My apprentices will clean her thighs and dress the wounds. I know a *vallos* who had a human wife before she died. I'll send for him."

"How did she die?" he asked, already knowing the answer.

"Birth."

"I'll do it," Flyka piped in, taking a step toward the door.

Nonnae pointed a knobby finger at Flyka. "Don't think I can't see you limping either. Send my grandson for him. He'll know the *vallos*. Then sit down until one of us can look at that leg."

Flyka nodded once before disappearing from Neve's view. He grimaced as Dahlia continued to shake. "What do I do?" he asked, helplessness crashing over him.

"Keep her warm and pray that she survives until I can get some answers."

Chapter Twenty-Three

The shivering eventually stopped.

And the fevers raged.

Then came the hallucinations.

Neve sat on a low stool near the fire, his hands clasped between his legs, elbows on thighs. It was well into the night, and yet he couldn't sleep.

It had been four days since their wedding. Four days since any clarity had entered the *valles'* gaze. Four days since she'd glared at him.

Sweat dripped down his back and he reached back and pulled his black linen shirt off, laying it over his left knee. *Nonnae* kept the room sweltering. She said the human needed it. It would help break the fever. She needed to sweat out the sickness.

The princess thrashed, tossing her blankets off, legs

splayed awkwardly. Neve grunted as he stood from the stool and edged around the mattress on the floor.

His gaze paused on her wrapped thighs, smelling strongly of herbs and honey. He closed his eyes in shame. He'd never forget the sight of her thighs. Neve couldn't imagine the pain she'd been in. When had it started? Their very first night in the rain?

He opened his eyes as he knelt on one knee and tugged down the shift one of his people had given her. Even now people camped outside the hut, praying for his *loviaye*.

Neve had expected to be met with open hostility at taking a human bride. But it seemed his people near the Seed had accepted it. They were tired of war. Everyone was.

He huffed out an angry breath. No one had told him that prolonged exposure to the rain, sleet, snow, or cold, could cause illness. The conversation with the widower of a human wife had been enlightening and concerning.

Humans would get sick if they got too hot or cold. Extended exposure to the elements caused death, or loss of limbs. A narrow birth channel meant death. They'd had to cut the babe from the *vallos'* wife. The change of color in their skin expressed emotion, as did the way they moved the colorful part of their eyes.

"You should have told someone," he growled down to the *valles*, her eyes twitching behind her thin closed eyelids.

As if you made it easy.

He grunted, and pulled the blankets back over the top of Dahlia.

Her eyes flew open, staring sightlessly at the ceiling,

before turning on him. The pupils were blown wide, and the stench of fear filled the air. Her mouth gaped open, and she screamed.

He hated these dreams the most.

Neve held his hands up. "It's okay, Dahlia. You're okay. I won't hurt you." She stilled for a moment, and he tensed at her wild-eyed look. "Don't do it."

The little human bolted, clumsily scrambling from the bed. He slowly climbed to his feet as she wobbled in front of the flames.

Please don't fall backward. Seittae. *Please.*

She pitched forward, running for the door.

Neve intercepted and caught her around the waist. She swiped at his face, so he tossed her over his shoulder, his ribs protesting, before stalking back to the bed. Her fists pounded weakly against his spine, but the blows didn't hurt.

The fight left her as quickly as it came.

She went limp on his shoulder, and he carefully lowered her into the bed as sobs escaped her. "I want my mum," she cried, fat tears rolling down her gaunt cheeks.

Her plea tugged at his heart. There were so many times in his life he'd wished for his *mommar*.

The door creaked open, and he craned his neck to see *Nonnae* watching them.

"I've got her," he murmured. The healer nodded and closed the door as he turned back to the princess. "It's okay. You're not alone."

She blinked up at him, no recognition, but calmer just the same. "I'm scared of the monsters."

"I'll protect you," he found himself saying. "There are no monsters here."

Her attention shifted to the fire. Her breathing increased, and a wet cough sputtered from her lips. "They always come for me. Always. Fangs, horns, death in their eyes."

She spoke of Loriians. *He* was one of the monsters from her dreams.

"They wouldn't dare harm you," he whispered. "They are there to protect you, to fight for you. They are your champions. You are their *reilleve*."

He started to pull the mess of blankets back up when she seized his hand, her fingers only wrapping around half of his wrist, her emerald ring catching in the firelight. He followed the limb back to her creased face. "Don't leave me to the darkness."

Neve stared at her distraught heart-shaped face and made a choice. He lifted the covers and slid in next to her. She released a shuddering breath but burrowed into his chest. He stared down at her golden-red hair, his arm held in the air. He laid his arm around her waist and cupped the back of her head, before laying his head down. She was burning up, her breath and skin, leaving his own feeling tacky, and yet he didn't move. Over her head he watched the flames, and tried to regulate his breathing, running his claws through her wild, sweaty hair.

Her fluttering pulse slowed until all the tension fled her body, a soft snore escaping her.

What are you doing?

He closed his gritty eyes.

Probably making another mistake.

Chapter Twenty-Four

Dahlia

She woke with her lungs on fire and her throat feeling like it had been torn to shreds.

Her head ached, and she squeezed her eyes shut harder.

It felt as if she'd gone on a bender for days and then had been beaten with a club.

A groan escaped her. She shifted, pressing farther into the warmth that blanketed her entire back. She blinked one eye open, and a blurry hearth swam into view, the flames dancing merrily.

A fire.

Lia lifted her right hand and winced, setting it back down on the thickly knitted blankets. Her shoulder didn't like that and her palm was bandaged.

Where was she? How did she get here?

The stags, the trip, and the river...

She sucked in a sharp breath. The last things she remembered was Arun, and wanting to sleep.

Something tightened around her waist and Dahlia stiffened. She slowly glanced down to find a blue, muscled arm draped over the curve of her hip, a clawed hand pressed possessively to her belly. Her pulse leapt and she forced herself to peek over her shoulder.

A scream burst from her lips.

Eyes as dark as hell popped open and locked on her a moment before the giant sprang up, caging her in with his body. A blade appeared in his hand while he scanned the room.

Arun.

Dahlia stared at his jawline and tried to wiggle away. His attention turned to her and the snarl on his lips disappeared. He sighed, and sheathed his blade before rolling away from her. Lia sat up quickly, the world spinning for a moment, before she yanked the blankets up to her chin, as if they could shield her from him.

"What are you doing?" she rasped, her voice almost gone. Screaming hadn't been her best idea.

He climbed to his feet, all feline grace, and moved to the window, sunlight pouring in. She gaped at the mottled bruises that covered his entire back. How had that happened?

"I asked you a question," she stated, trying to put some command into it, but falling short.

The frost giant faced her and leaned back against the wall, crossing his arms over his muscled chest that led to a tapered waist. Heat filled her cheeks, and she jerked her gaze back to his face.

"How are you feeling?"

The question surprised her.

"Like I've been put through the wash, dragged across coals, and beaten by a club," she rasped, coughing. Her chest *ached*. It was as if she were trying to breathe through a wet rag.

Arun walked to a stool and plucked up a cup that had been set on it. He prowled around the mattress and squatted down, holding the cup out as if he would help her drink. She jerked her head back and held out her hand.

They stared at each other for a long moment before he silently handed over the rounded wooden cup. Her hand shook as she brought it to her mouth, sloshing some of the liquid onto her chest.

"Stubborn *valles*," he whispered under his breath before his warm hand settled over hers. He cupped the back of her head with his other hand to steady her. Warm savory liquid flowed over her tongue and down her throat. It felt like heaven. She took another gulp, and mewled when he pulled the cup away.

"Just a little at a time. You haven't been able to eat. We need to get something into that stomach of yours first or you'll vomit."

She watched him as he stood and walked back to the stool. Why was he here instead of Flyka?

He placed the cup on the floor next to the stool, his bruises once more on display.

A vague memory from the river surfaced. A rock.

"You took that blow for me." If she had hit the rock, it would have killed her. She scanned his face as he straightened and took a seat on the low simple stool. "Thank you, Arun."

"That's not my name."

Lia frowned, fingers sinking into what felt like woolen covers. "What do you mean?" The king, Flyka, and Olwen, had called him Arun. "Of course it is."

Unless it was a nickname?

He placed his hands on his knees and leaned his angular jaw on one hand. "I have something to admit to you, my lady."

My lady. If he was using an honorific, it must be bad.

"Our people have been enemies for centuries. When I wrote to your parents, I was shocked when they replied so quickly."

That's because they're greedy. Lia kept that thought to herself. And he wrote to Allium? Was he some sort of scribe too?

He straightened and rolled his neck, his blue-black hair shining in the light from the lone window. "While a peace treaty between our kingdoms was the goal, I didn't trust the Asteran monarchy."

She blinked at him.

He waited as if she would defend the king and queen.

"That is very wise. A few traded goods and a piece of inked paper does not make a friendship. It is always wise to be cautious but innocent," she admitted.

The giant cocked his head. "My thoughts exactly. Which led to my deception."

Her stomach sank and her mind raced through possible scenarios. Had he discovered the truth? Or had the treaty hidden some sinister agenda?

They're going to torture me for information I don't have.

They plan on holding me for a ransom they won't get.

They will kill...

"Loriia needs to be protected at all costs. The king is the kingdom."

"Every kingdom needs to be protected," she drawled. What was he getting at?

Arun looked her straight in the eye. "I am the king."

She stared at him, before bursting into laughter, which led to another round of painful coughing. Once she'd managed to curb the fit, she wiped her watering eyes. Lia flinched at the seriousness on his indigo face. A sinking feeling rose in her gut.

"I don't understand, Arun..."

"Arun is my mother's clan name." He straightened on the stool, holding his chin high. "My name is Neve Arun Winterborne, King of Loriia, Blade of the Frost Throne. The *vallos* pretending to be me is my cousin Eyri."

Lia swallowed hard, not believing her ears. Just what sort of game was he playing?

You can beat him. You've dealt with the Giver.

She took a moment to really study him.

He'd always seemed more proud and edgy than the rest of the delegation. Chafing even at using her fake honorific. Each time she tried to put distance between them and put him in his place, he came back more willful.

If what he said was true, the Asteran monarchs expected her to spy on *this* giant? To cause upheaval in *his* court? To kill *him*?

You'll never get close. He'll kill you first.

"Why tell me this now?" she whispered, her tongue sticking to the roof of her mouth. She fiddled with the emerald ring still blessedly on her finger. "You know I'll be returning to my family once my stint among your court is over. This information will start a war. Why tell me?" It didn't make sense.

His brows lowered, making him look even fiercer. "Returning home?"

Fear curdled her stomach. Why did he look surprised? "Yes, when my trip is over, I will return to Astera." Unless he'd lured the princess of Astera to Loriia for another reason. Unless he'd guessed the truth that she was really a spy, an unwilling assassin.

"No, *niliave*, you will stay here indefinitely."

A lump rose in her throat and the world spun. There wasn't enough air. "Why?"

"Because you are the *reilleve, lae neilave*."

Those words sounded familiar. "What does that mean?" she rasped.

He crossed his arms. "You're the queen, my *wife*."

Chapter Twenty-Five

DAHLIA

WIFE. WIFE. *WIFE.*

The word marched through her mind like a chant until all she could hear was that condemning word. The frost giant watched Dahlia closely as she took large gulps of air, coughing between them.

This couldn't be right.

Queen Allium wouldn't have sent her this unprepared, would she?

Do anything to secure trust. Use your assets.

Was this what the bloody queen was alluding to? It couldn't be true. How was the marriage even legal? Dahlia wasn't the true princess, she was an imposter.

She shook her head, but her mind screeched to a halt.

The sapphires.

Those jewels had haunted her. It didn't seem right that the delegation would give them to her as a gift. They were veritably priceless. It didn't seem likely that the giants would have given them to her as a gift of peace, but as a bride gift?

It made perfect sense.

Her heart pounded and she coughed, trying to breathe. Dahlia doubled over for a moment.

Randa and Allium sold you to the monsters.

She shuddered and slowly stood on the bed, wavering on her feet, with the blankets still clutched in her fingers. The room swam, and she ignored the giant watching her reaction all too closely. Lia grounded herself, warmth from the fire licking at her calves.

She froze.

No.

Ever so slowly, she looked down.

Her legs were bare.

Lia blanched, and stumbled backward off the mattress against the wall, dragging the covers with her.

He knew.

Arun—no, the Frost King—rose from the stool, uncoiling like a serpent, his entire focus on her. "What exactly are you implying? That you did not know of the betrothal?" His tone was dripping in darkness and danger.

She edged toward the door to her right, his attention never wavering from her. "I was told *nothing.*" *Only that I am to kill you. Poison you.*

The tiny room seemed to close in on her and the air much too hot. She couldn't breathe. Lia needed to get out now.

He cocked his head as she neared the door. "Do you

really think you're going to get away? Run away from this situation?"

Her hand curled over the knob. "I won't stay. I *can't* stay."

Dahlia yanked open the door as he rushed her. She threw the blankets at him as she slipped out the exit and into a large open room. Three startled giantesses gazed back at her from her right. Lia lunged for the door on the left that looked like escape.

All she had to do was get outside and then she could ... she could...

Her feet left the floor and her back slammed into a hard warm surface. Lia coughed hard, and she scratched at the bare blue forearms wrapped around her.

"Let me go!" she hissed, kicking uselessly at the giant holding her in the air.

"Never. We must speak."

Lia reached out a trembling hand to the oldest female, with gray streaks in her black hair. "Help me."

The older female placed her hands on her hips. "Put the *reilleve* down. She's in no condition to be tossed about by the likes of you."

"She was trying to escape." His voice rumbled along Lia's spine.

"Well," the female pursed her lips, "I don't think the *valles* is that foolish as she's only in a shift and is ill. Am I right, *reilleve*?"

Dahlia swallowed hard, her throat aching. She slumped in the king's grasp. "I just need some air." The room was spinning, and she couldn't *breathe*.

"And you shall have it." She gestured to a cot near the

window. "My lord, if you'd be so kind as to set your *niliave* here."

Tears burned in her eyes as she continued to wheeze, her lungs squeezing painfully. The king's grip loosened, and the world wavered as he wrapped an arm around her back and caught her behind the knees. She didn't even feel embarrassed as the angry giant stomped across the room carrying her like a princess. Lia expected him to drop her like a sack of potatoes, but he gently set her on the cot next to the window and stepped away.

She tucked her legs beneath her shift, and leaned her cheek against the glass pane, her breath fogging up the window. How was she supposed to escape now? What would happen to her mother? Did they really expect her to assassinate the king? *Her husband?* The world blurred.

Her breath came faster, and dots swarmed her vision.

"What's wrong with her?" a deep voice asked.

"Panic, *lae reillov.*"

"What do we do?"

"Hold your wife and I'll get the window."

Lia jerked as large, muscled arms curled around her and pulled her loosely into the king's embrace. Her gaze latched on to the old giantess who cranked open the window. Cold air rushed in, crisp and clean. It stung her lungs and cheeks, but Dahlia welcomed it.

The female sat at the end of the cot and laid a knitted blanket over her leg. She then set her deep purple hand over the top of Lia's foot before patting it. "That's it, *valles.* Take slow sips of air." Her chin lifted as her attention shifted to the hovering male behind Dahlia. "Keep your breathing steady, *reillov.*"

The rhythmic thumping of his hearts was a constant staccato behind her. Lia closed her eyes, feeling like she was ready to fall apart.

Sing.

A dark melody bloomed in her mind.

Duck and cover for the beasts now roam. Escape now quickly, don't lead them home.

She began to mouth the words.

Don't tarry, don't tarry, my little dear one. You're not alone and the danger is gone.

Despite her breathlessness, a low hum vibrated in her throat. The words of her mother's song spilled from her lips as she opened her eyes. A sea of cool toned skin, white snow, and warm brown huts stood outside.

Sleep and dream for the day is naught. Stars will keep you while fear is fought.

Don't tarry, don't tarry, my little dear one. You're not alone and the danger is gone.

The people turned to face her, but she didn't see their faces. Dahlia repeated the song as her heartbeat slowed, and her breathing with it. The last note cut through the air and hovered in the quiet before she was able to look away from the outside.

The old female blinked slowly at her. Lia glanced around the room, noting that Olwen, Flyka, and the *fake* Neve, as well as two other females, stood in the room staring at her. All were silent.

She peered back at the old giantess, who appraised her with a toothy grin.

"Our *reilleve* has blessed us with her song. I thank you." The old giantess bowed, and then straightened in her seat. Her hand squeezed Dahlia's foot once more, her claws pricking the weave. "Better?"

Lia nodded, fatigue riding her hard. She slumped back against the king, so very tired.

"Close your eyes, *reilleve*. Let yourself rest. You're safe."

She glanced out the window, watching a very large bird twirl through the sky.

Safety was an illusion was the last thought in her mind before the darkness took her.

WHEN SHE'D AWOKEN, THE KING AND HIS Haunts were gone. And her ring and necklace had been returned to her, but not the weapons. What did that mean? Did they know what she planned? Had they discovered the poison? Were they going to kill her?

They'd also left Lia with strangers.

Nonnae the healer, and her two apprentices, Lianna and Loshika.

It had been ten days since she'd seen anyone that she'd traveled with.

Ten days of healing, of fretting over the future, of concocting plans that would fail. Of worrying about Cosmos. Each day she was gone, was another her brother was on his own, in danger.

Dahlia could not see a way out of her situation.

Even if she managed to collect everything she needed

for a journey to her mother, she didn't know the land—the king and his Haunts did. They'd find her before she reached the border.

If she managed to elude them and made it to her mum, who was to say that the Giver hadn't already collected her? That thought alone made Dahlia sick.

What of the spies planted in Loriia by the crown or the Giver? Not all giants were loyal to the crown, and easily bought for a few pieces of silver. Would she be killed by one of them if she tried to escape? The only thing that gave her any comfort was that the king and his cousin were able to swap places without the Asteran monarchy knowing, which meant they hadn't managed to slip a spy into the Loriian palace.

Yet.

If she managed to poison the king, she was surrounded by his people. More Loriians arrived daily to camp outside the healer's home. Sneaking away would be next to impossible.

The hopelessness of the situation almost seemed too much.

As a visiting princess, she could have left whenever she chose.

As the wife of the king, she was trapped.

Wife.

Even now the word terrified her. While she'd spoken no vows, the king and queen had signed her life away. She was now the property of the Loriian throne—even if she was an imposter.

Nonnae had made it clear that she was bound in the Loriian custom as well. The crossing of the life-giving waters was marriage in their culture. It was why people had been leaving gifts outside the healer's home for days.

Dahlia didn't have a drop of royal blood, and yet she was married to a king. What would he do when he discovered she was a fraud? Did he already know? Was that why he'd not been by to visit? Did her legs give her away? Was he preparing her torture and execution right now?

"*Reilleve*?" Lianna called softly.

Dahlia shoved her morose thoughts aside and wiped her hands on the simple apron bound around her hips. She pushed away from the sink and smiled at the giantess who had a broken fang, making her seem somewhat endearing. "Yes?"

"Do you need a break with the washing? I can continue if you need to sit, my lady. You've been on your feet for some time."

She shook her head and leaned back against the counter, the stone pressing against the middle of her back. "I'm alright. I was just lost in my thoughts." She rotated her shoulder. It still ached now and then, but not too badly. "I just finished with the pots. What else can I help with?"

Loshika snorted, sitting near the fire and cutting strips of linen in a rocking chair. "*Lae reilleve*, you work too hard. Our king left you to heal and recuperate, not slave away like a *nonnaette*."

Lia pushed away from the counter and wound her way through tables of herbs and cots. She plopped into the oversized wooden chair next to Loshika, plucking a pair of scissors from her apron pocket. "I like keeping my hands busy. Did you really expect me to languish around and not help?"

Loshika cocked her head. "I thought I knew what to expect from humans, but it wasn't you."

"Is that a good thing or a bad thing?" she commented, taking a square of linen from the table. It was a bit of a stretch. Everything was. The house, the doors, the furniture. Everything was just a touch larger or taller. It made her feel like a tiny mouse.

Loshika scratched her pockmarked neck and shrugged. "A good thing. I've only experienced *saloes'* malice, greed, deception, and hate. From what I know of you, *reilleve*, you don't fit that description."

A twinge of guilt wriggled in her chest. Loshika had no idea the trickery Lia was involved in.

I'm here to spy, to murder.

She studied Loshika's angular profile, and the marks along her neck. "If you don't mind me asking, how did that happen?"

The giantess stopped her cutting and set her hands in her lap. "I will tell you, *lae reilleve*, but only if you tell me about your legs."

My queen.

Lianna gasped. "Loshika! How dare you ask such a thing. Apologize for your presumptuousness."

Dahlia had stiffened, holding Loshika's gaze, but not because of overstepping. No, because her whole life she'd been taught to hide her skin. To never speak about it unless she wanted to be burned as a witch.

You're not in Astera anymore.

She blew out a breath and nodded. "I'll go first." With

shaking hands, she lifted the overly long skirt until it reached her knees, the meld of patchwork skin bringing a wave of shame with it.

Lia swallowed thickly. "My mother said I was born this way. It wasn't as extensive when I was a child. It's spread over the years."

"Is it contagious?" Loshika asked. "Do all humans deal with something similar?"

"No. It's just something I deal with. I'm sure there are others who have something similar, but it is kept a secret."

"Why do you hide it?" Lianna questioned softly, moving her chair to Dahlia's other side.

"Because it's dangerous."

Lianna blinked. "Why? You said it wasn't contagious."

"Because it makes her different," Loshika replied, sharing a knowing look with Lia. "You know how our village used to treat me before *Nonnae* took me on as one of her apprentices. I was bullied, shunned, and beaten for my differences from the time I was a child."

"I'm so sorry," Dahlia whispered, feeling heat at the back of her eyes at the idea of little Loshika being beaten.

"Don't be. It made me stronger." A pause. "But I'm sure your experience was different than mine. Excuse me for speaking out of turn, *reilleve*."

"There's nothing to forgive, and our experiences are similar." *Be careful. Tell the truth but wrapped in a lie.* "My mother is a great beauty." *Truth.* "She didn't handle it well when I was born ... different." *Lie.* "She tried every cure, and then eventually had me cloistered away from the court." *Truth.* "People could whisper and start rumors all they wanted, but no one knew the truth." *Truth.* "No one but my mother, father, and nanny." *Lie.*

Lianna reached out and took Lia's hand. "I'm so sorry. That must have been lonely."

Dahlia squeezed her hand. "I found joy too. In my books. I always wanted to travel." *Truth.* Once Cosmos had been fed and put to sleep, she'd stayed up reading, living vicariously through others.

"And here you are," Loshika murmured. "Married to the Frost King. Queen of the Frost Throne."

"Here I am." *Trapped. A false queen.*

The *nonnaette* ran her fingers over her neck. "I was born near the border of Astera, between Kallere and Nieves. My parents gathered syrup for the cities. They used to tell me to sing to the trees and the syrup would be sweeter." Her smile faded. "One day, Papa got sick. He told us he was fine and went to harvest. That night he stumbled home running a fever, a strange rash all over his body. By the morning, his breathing was labored and wet. Mama did everything she could for him, and three days later he died, but not before the dots showed up on her body."

Loshika sucked in a shuddering breath. "She sent me away to my aunt's home and died alone." A pause. "My cousins got sick first. They blamed me, but I didn't have the marks. People all over our village got sick and began dying. That's when they found it."

"Found what?" Lia whispered, dread in the pit of her stomach.

"The diseased *saloes'* body in our well."

Bile burned the back of Dahlia's throat. "Was it the human from your village?"

"No." Loshika's mouth thinned, bitterness written across her face. "Humans were not allowed in our village. In fact, we'd been fighting with the human lord right over the border of Astera about who the trees belonged to. They sabotaged us, we sabotaged them. It was constant. But this ... was something altogether different. This was a battle we could not fight."

"Eventually, I got sick, but almost all of my village was gone." Tears filled her black eyes. "Then the *saloes* came. They tossed all the sick into the well and left us to die. There were three *valles* and one *vallos*. I was the only child. I only survived because they managed to toss me up high enough to climb out."

Tears tracked down Dahlia's face.

"I promised to get help, but I was sick. I climbed into a neighbor's home and managed to get a fire going. It's one of the first things we're taught—how to make a fire. I passed out and slept for some time." Loshika's voice thickened. "When I woke, my rash was fading. I ran to the well to tell them I was getting help, but they were already dead when I got there." The tears spilled over. "I was all that was left. An entire village gone."

"I'm *so* sorry." The words didn't mean enough.

Loshika shrugged and wiped her tears away. "It was a long time ago. We cannot live in the past."

Lia's stomach churned, feeling sick. "How can you even look at me without disgust? Without hate?"

The giantess held her gaze. "Because I won't villainize a whole race for the actions of a few. My *reillov* has chosen you as his *reilleve*. In our short time together, you've shown me that all humans aren't bad just because I experienced horrors at their hands."

That struck Dahlia *hard*.

Wasn't that what she'd been doing for years? Judging a whole race based on one experience? Forgetting all of the good childhood memories of Loriian friends? Only focusing on the fear?

She swallowed hard. She needed to make some changes.

"You honor me with your story," she replied. "I won't forget the lesson you've taught me."

Loshika nodded. "I've seen you try to mask your fear since you've been with us. I can imagine we look like monsters to you, but despite your fear, you've treated all of us with kindness. You're just the *reilleve* we need."

She was no queen. Dahlia was a bard masquerading as a princess. An imposter.

The door opened, letting in a burst of cold air. In stepped the king, his imposing presence filling up the space.

"Leave us." His voice was like chips of ice.

Her blood went cold.

He knew.

Chapter Twenty-Six

NEVE

NEVE NODDED TO THE *NONNAETTES*, WHO bowed to him before filing out the door behind him. It closed with a soft click, leaving him and the *valles* alone. Maybe for the first time ever. She slowly stood from the chair and faced him, her expression serene.

She dipped her chin and did a small curtsy before rising. "My lord."

He watched as she seemed to focus on his chest, not looking up into his eyes. Perhaps his gaze unnerved her as much as Dahlia's unnerved him.

Silence stretched awkwardly between them, and Neve found himself wanting to shift from foot to foot—something his *povvar* had trained out of him years ago.

Never let the enemy see you sweat.

He placed his hands behind his back and clasped them. "How are you feeling?"

She blinked, as if surprised by the question, fiddling with her ring. "I'm much better, thank you."

The healer had told him as much. *Nonnae* had expressed concern about her lungs, but it was something that could be monitored from the palace. She could travel, and that's what mattered. He needed to get home.

"It is time for us to depart. I have stayed longer than I should have." Her brow wrinkled, and he arched a brow in question. "What?"

"I did not ask you to stay, my lord. You could have left me here."

"As if I could leave my *reilleve* behind." Truly, he'd thought about it, but ultimately brushed it aside. Dahlia needed more protection than he realized. And after he'd been apprised of how delicate humans really were, well, he didn't trust her not to die while he was away.

Isn't that what you originally wanted?

"I'm not ready."

"You have to be."

The elders from the Seed had already asked him penetrating questions concerning their new queen. His people were split down the middle—half accepting her, the other hating her on principle. If he was to unite his kingdom, Neve had to dote on his little human wife so his people would accept her as their own too. Leaving her behind did not send that message.

You've never doted a day in your life.

"What about my cough?"

Neve was prepared for this. "*Nonnae* said you can travel now. She has prepared tonics to protect your lungs and aid healing." He waved a hand toward her legs. "You will ride with me sidesaddle to protect your thighs from any more damage. I have also arranged for stops each night at proper inns so you may be tended to, and warm yourself properly."

Her jaw dropped, and then snapped closed. "As generous of an offer that is, my lord, I'll ride my own *rukhal*."

He clicked his tongue, rocking back on his heels. "It is tradition that the bride ride with her husband. You will ride with me, wife."

The placid mask on her face slid away, revealing growing anger and absolute determination. "Make no mistake, *reillov*, we might be bound, but I am *not* your wife."

"Be that as it may, as you said, we are bound. There is no going back." Neve pointed to the window. "Our people have been waiting to meet you for a fortnight."

"*Your* people, my lord."

His jaw clenched. Why did she have to be so difficult? "You have made your disdain for the Loriian people abundantly clear since—"

"No." She sliced her hand through the air. "I've made my disdain for *you* clear." For some reason, her words cut. "From the moment I met you in that alcove, you've done nothing but threaten, frighten, and bully me. I don't like you, and I certainly won't stand for it any longer."

It seemed she forgot about all the things he'd done to make her life easier. The warmer clothes, food she was familiar with, the extra day at the barn so she wouldn't have to travel in the snow, the *rukhals* instead of the wide horses. He accusations made him want to act like a villain. "You have seen nothing yet, *valles*."

"Stop calling me that," she ground out. "My name is Dahlia."

"I will call you what I like." He ate up the distance between them and captured her chin, lifting until she was forced to meet his gaze. "Hate me all you want, but the outcome will not change. You are *lae niliave*, my wife. You will get on Cessa with a smile on your face as we try to figure out the mess we have both been thrown into."

Her breath sawed in and out. "And these are the words of my husband?"

"No, these are the words of your king."

For a moment, he thought she might spit in his face. Instead, he watched with wonder as she shuttered her gaze and wiped all expression from her face. Once again, a blank mask.

Neve should have felt triumphant at getting his way, but instead hated that he couldn't read the princess.

No. Your queen.

Unconsciously, he ran this thumb across her plush bottom lip, his claw skating her bowed top lip. Why was he so intrigued with her pink mouth? Why did it draw his attention?

There is something wrong with you.

Dahlia jerked out of his grip, her breaths coming a little faster. He stared at his callused fingertips, the phantom feeling of her soft skin leaving a tingling sensation behind.

Maybe she was a witch.

"I have a request," she stated.

He arched a brow. "Oh?"

Her little fists clenched at her sides, but other than that, she was a mirror of serenity. "I would like Loshika to come with us if she wishes."

"I procured a healer from the city."

"I want Loshika. She's been with me while I've been sick. She has more hands-on knowledge about my health."

Neve shrugged. If it made her more biddable, it was an easy ask. "Fine. I will send Loshika in with your clothes. She will help prepare you for the journey. You can ask her yourself."

It was only one small win, but he'd take it.

More fights were to come, he was sure.

OLWEN READIED THE *RUKHALS* AS NEVE WEAVED through the throng of people, clasping arms with warriors, blessing new marriages and newborn children as Flyka shadowed him. His face hurt from smiling, but it was a good hurt. This was what he loved, where he truly wanted to be, among the people, not sequestered in the palace playing chess against the rest of the known world.

A crescendo of cheers rose behind him, and he turned to face the healer's home.

His *loviaye* stood on the porch, once again dressed in white. Her cloak was trimmed in white fur that framed her face. She pushed back the hood, revealing her golden hair that shone a pinkish-red in the light as she stepped toward the stairs, skirts flowing around her legs. A small bud of pride unfurled in his chest at the foreign but regal presence she had.

Her hazel orbs scanned the crowd, a sweet smile curling her lips. Motion in the sky caught his attention, and cries of delight sounded in his ears as an *astrylle* landed on the pitched roof right above Dahlia. The massive bird of prey, with its white feathers trimmed in black, and gold eyes, studied the people below and hooted once.

The crowd cheered.

"You've been blessed," Flyka murmured, awe in her tone.

The *astrylle* took flight and swooped over the crowd.

Neve smiled at Dahlia, who stared wide-eyed at the departing *astrylle*.

He held his breath as a child escaped his mother and scampered up the stairs as fast as his chubby little legs could carry him. The young boy held a black lysterm flower in his pale blue hand as his mother reached the bottom of the stairs, chastising him.

Dahlia knelt on the porch and smiled at the little boy. "That's a pretty flower. I've never seen on that color."

"*Lae reilleve*," he said, placing his other hand on her knee and holding the flower out to her.

The mother made a distressed sound, and went to snatch up her son, but halted as Dahlia ducked her head to meet the wee one's gaze.

"*Jiaell vei*," she murmured softly. "It's beautiful."

Thank you. When had she learned that?

Neve watched as she took the proffered flower from

his chubby fingers and tucked the bell shaped flower into her braid. "Is it pretty?" she asked softly, ignoring all the eyes on her.

"*Sei!*" he answered. "*Mommar!*"

"*Sei,*" the mother murmured, pulling the little boy back down the stairs and into her arms. "Very pretty." The mother bowed low, and the wee one waved as they melded back into the crowd.

Dahlia waved, a genuine smile on her face.

It struck him. Neve hadn't seen that smile before. He found himself at the bottom of the steps, staring up at his wife. He held out his hand and waited, praying that she wouldn't make them both look like fools. And hoping that maybe she could turn that smile on him.

Time slowed as she stared down at him, the smile fading to serenity.

Disappointment filled him. *Stop it. Her smiles don't concern you.*

His hearts raced when she took one step, then another, and another, until her hand slipped into his own.

Relief crashed over him. Her fingers were so delicate in his grip. Everything about her made him feel like a monstrous brute.

He led her down the final steps, and the people of the village cheered. Neve led her to Cessa, and he dropped her hand, slowly reaching for her waist. Her breath hitched, and his gaze flew to her face and found no emotion, just her mask. It made him want to needle her, to cajole the *valles* until she stopped pretending.

Carefully, he lifted her up onto Cessa's back. She squirmed when her skirt hitched up, revealing her soft trousers beneath. He tugged the dress down. "All better, my lady?"

She gave him a short nod.

Good enough.

Neve sprang up, landing on Cessa's back behind Dahlia. She clutched at his forearm as he scooted forward, tugging her body into his own.

"Wave, wife. Give them a pretty smile for your king."

Her elbow dug into his stomach, but it didn't hurt. She lifted a mittened hand and waved, flashing her flat human teeth in a wide smile.

"For them I will," she said out of the corner of her mouth.

He almost smirked at her audacity.

Neve preferred her fire to the indifference.

What else could he do to break through her wall?

He couldn't wait to find out.

Chapter Twenty-Seven

Neve

They traveled north through the village, deeper into the city.

It was a slow-going procession as the crowd seemed to thicken when they neared the Seed, the homes alongside the road rising to two or three stories high.

The immense branches of the Seed cast shadows over the cheering crowd. Dahlia alternated between waving to the people and staring upward at the tree in awe.

"I've never seen something so grand," she murmured to herself. "It must have lived a very long life."

"The tree has always been part of our history."

She glanced at him quickly before her attention turned back to the Seed. "It no longer flowers?"

"No. It has long gone to sleep."

Her face fell. "How sad."

Neve shrugged. "The tree provided shelter, food, and trade for many years. Even in death it provides."

His *niliave* cocked her head. "How so?"

"Look." He leaned forward and pointed to the trunk.

She shifted in his lap and followed the direction of his claw. Her gasp of surprise made him smile.

"It's a city in a tree!"

"Yes. The center for trade and worship."

"Will we go inside?" Her voice held a touch of tempered excitement.

"Not today, *jaivelle*." Neve stiffened as the endearment flowed from his tongue. He barely managed to keep the frown off his face. Her shoulders slumped the smallest bit, but the smile never left her face. "Next time," he offered gruffly.

They approached the town square, where the area bottlenecked right before it opened up. His Haunt had formed a loose circle around them, constantly searching the crowd. Olwen was grinning and waving, playing the part while Eyri occasionally waved shyly. Then there was Flyka. Not a smile anywhere near her face, her head on a swivel.

"What did your healer say?" he asked.

"She had to pack, but she will catch up to us tonight."

"Does that please you?"

"It does."

A shrill whistle passed his ear, and screams erupted around them.

"Ambush!" Olwen shouted.

"Protect the *reillov*!" Flyka roared.

The crowd burst into motion, everyone trying to get out of the way as another volley of arrows rained down on them. The Haunts closed in on them.

Neve hunched over Dahlia and dug his heels into Cessa. The *rukhal* bolted forward, people diving out of the way. The princess tried to look around his shoulder, but he shoved her back under him. "Don't be stupid. Keep your head down."

"Where are they coming from?" she shouted over the din as they fought to get off the main road.

"Don't know."

"Give me a weapon."

"Everything I own is too bulky for you," he roared, waving an arm for the citizens to move when an arrow grazed his left forearm. He hissed and pulled his arm back, scanning the rooftops for archers.

"Where's my slingshot?"

For some reason, he'd kept the infernal thing. It looked old and well loved. He couldn't trash it.

"Strapped to my bow—what are you doing?" he snarled as she pushed at his chest.

"Move," she growled.

The *valles* deftly maneuvered herself until she faced him, her legs thrown over his thighs. He wrapped his arm around her back and held on as her fingers reached around his cloak for her slingshot.

"Stones?" she muttered in his ear.

He huffed. "Why would I carry stones?"

"Fair enough." She slid one hand down his chest, grabbed the top button of his tunic, and yanked it off. She leaned back against Cessa's neck and notched the button in the sling. "Don't let me fall," was the last thing she said before leaning to his right, completely exposed.

An arrow whizzed by her head, lodging in the ground as Cessa sped by, Olwen and Eyri by their sides.

"Got him," the princess murmured. She pulled back the slingshot and fired. "Godsteeth, I missed. Olwen, do you see him? Behind us, blue window, second story."

"I see him," Olwen growled, turning his *rukhal* around.

An assailant rushed them from an alleyway to the left. Neve yanked Dahlia upright. "Wrap your arms around me." She obeyed as he pulled a dagger from the sheath at his chest and struck, hitting the giant in the jugular.

One down.

"To the left," Eyri shouted, his spectacles fogged up. "They're trying to force us into the bottleneck."

Neve urged Cessa left, past the dead assailant. The ring of the *rukhals'* hooves against the stone cobbles echoed around them. Cessa snorted and panted hard as they continued to run. He wasn't made for sprinting but rather for endurance.

They swung around the corner and Dahlia was torn from his arms, his claws ripping right through her cloak. He yelled, and vaulted from the beast's back, a blade already in his hand. He spun and snarled at the giant dragging the *valles* by her thick braid. She held her scalp, tears in her eyes as her feet tried to find purchase against the slick stones of the alley.

"Drop her now," he bellowed, stalking toward the stranger dressed in black.

The vagabond wore the royal color. A taunt.

"I'll slit her from ear to ear if you get any closer," the giant threatened, his tattooed head on display.

Vergllos. This was one of his men.

"Release the *valles* and I'll let you go free." *A lie.* Neve would kill him.

The traitor cackled. "I know you better than that, *reillov*. Watch as she bleeds crimson."

Neve lunged as the assailant yanked Dahlia up to her feet and brought the knife to her throat. The little human sank her teeth into the fleshy part between his thumb and wrist. The giant yowled and loosened his grip, dropping his blade, but still she didn't let go.

He shoved her, her body flying through the air before tumbling over the hard ground. "I'll kill you, *bentai.*"

Neve drove his blade into the attacker's upper heart. "Me first," he barked. "Who sent you?"

The giant laughed, the sound deranged. "Your reckoning." His laugh cut off as an arrow lodged in his throat.

Neve tossed him to the ground and spun to find Flyka on the nearest roof, her crossbow in hand. "We needed information."

Eyri helped Dahlia up from the ground, and Flyka slid down a drainpipe to land silently beside Neve.

"I saw his tattoos from above. He was Vergllos, and wouldn't have given you anything." A pause. "Plus, you had already stabbed him. He wouldn't have survived."

"He threatened my *reilleve*. He deserved it."

Neve scanned his little human from head to toe as she turned to face him. Her clothes were filthy, and she had a bruise forming on her cheek, but other than that she looked fine. She spat on the ground and wiped at her mouth with her sleeve.

"Your shoulder?" he asked brusquely, crowding into her space. He crooked his finger underneath her chin and tipped her face to the side so he could see the bruise better. No blood, only the attacker's. That was something.

"It's fine."

"It seems your flat teeth do have some use."

She bared them at him and pulled back out of his reach, once again spitting on the ground. "He shouldn't have grabbed my hair." Her gaze narrowed on the tramped lysterm flower. "He ruined my gift," she snapped. "I hate bullies."

It seemed his little *valles* had some fight in her. She's survive another day.

"Olwen?" he asked, striding back to Cessa.

"Cleaning up the mess. He'll meet us at the edge of the city," Flyka answered, her eyes sweeping the ally and roofs above. "Where your soldiers await you."

Neve nodded, and held his hand out to Dahlia. "Let's be gone."

She didn't complain as he lifted her onto Cessa's back and then mounted behind her. Nor when he pulled her curvy, soft body against his own. She shook slightly, but he didn't scent fear.

"Are you alright?" he asked.

"After-fight jitters. Happens every time."

He stared down at the top of her hair. Just how many times had she gotten into fights? Just what sort of mischief had the princess gotten up to in the past?

"Was that meant for me or you?" she whispered.

His lips thinned. "Both of us."

"Should I be worried?"

"No."

He'd worry for the both of them, and pray they'd finally make it to the Glace Palace alive.

Chapter Twenty-Eight

Dahlia

Dahlia came to several conclusions as a company of soldiers joined them outside the city.

First, that she was only a prisoner if she let herself be one.

Second, until this very moment, she'd been letting fear control her. Since the Giver had handed her off to the Asteran monarchy, Lia had been helpless in their schemes, but no more. She needed to be logical in each of her decisions going forward or her fear would get her killed.

Third, she'd always prided herself on being pragmatic. To be honest, she'd never had the choice to be anything else. There was always the next town or city, the next show to be performed so they could eat, the next healer to query discreetly. Lia literally could not afford to be herself. But in the last month, she'd experienced anger, joy, sadness, and empathy, and expressed them outwardly in a way she'd never done before. It was ... *freeing*.

Fourth, Dahlia needed allies if she was to ever escape Loriia and reunite with her family. The Giver had told her once she could charm a snake, and since he was a backstabbing serpent, she figured that was true. In the icy lands, Lia was the outsider, but she'd already made a friend of Loshika. Who else could possibly help her? Her attention turned to Eyri. He was curious about humans, and he'd been nothing but kind to her. That was a start.

Fifth, she would never let anyone use her again. It would be *her* choice. Randa, Allium, and Neve all thought to manipulate her to get their way. She might be a peasant bard, but she'd never be at their mercy again. It was time to start acting like a royal.

And sixth, she was fairly certain she'd seen Jekket in the crowd near the Seed. A shiver of foreboding worked down her spine. Was he just a figment of her imagination? Or had the Giver sent him?

And seventh, the Frost King smelled of rosemary and cedar. She liked it all too much.

"You're quiet," the king rumbled.

"I'm tired." She'd held herself stiffly away from Neve for hours, and the sun was about to set. The muscles in her back twinged and she grimaced.

A heavy sigh ruffled the hair atop her head. She squeaked when the king pressed her head against his chest and shoulder. "Then *rest*. You're making Cessa nervous."

Her initial reaction was to pull away from him, but she stayed, peeking up from underneath her hood. Lia was met with the strong column of his indigo neck that led to Neve's sharp jawline.

Handsome.

She blanched, wanting to scrub the thought from her mind. He was the enemy. If he found out that she wasn't the real princess, there was no doubt in her mind that he would execute her. The thought sobered her.

Dahlia focused on the soldiers that flanked their right side, from time to time catching a warrior studying her like she was an oddity. She frowned at their large shaggy horses. None of the soldiers rode *rukhals*.

"Why do they have horses?" she found herself asking. Didn't the king say the stags did better in the deep snow?

"They are war horses bred for the deep north. They have been trained for endurance, bursts of speed, and warfare."

Lia schooled her expression as a soldier glanced her way while she was eyeing his horse. When she needed to make a break for it, she'd need one of those horses.

"They're lovely," she commented. "I like their shaggy feet. It's cute."

"Cute? They are animals of war, warriors in their own right. They are *not* cute."

His tone was so offended on behalf of the horses, a giggle snuck out. Once she started, Dahlia couldn't stop until she started coughing.

"Are you done yet?" he asked gruffly, patting her back awkwardly.

"Yes." She wheezed. "For the time being."

They lapsed into silence, and an owl-looking creature

swooped to the far south. She drifted off, dreaming about golden eyes and white feathers.

LOSHIKA CAUGHT UP TO THEM LATER THAT night.

She crept into Dahlia's room, listened to her chest, and then went to sleep on her own pallet. The next two days followed the same pattern. Ride all day in the king's arms, trading softly spoken barbs, and then sleeping in a real bed with a roaring fire.

By the last day, it had grown so cold Lia had wrapped a scarf around her nose and mouth to protect them from the icy air. The terrain grew rockier and started angling upward, forcing her back against the king. The longer they rode, the tighter his body seemed to coil, and the shorter his temper grew. Every word he spoke was sharp or cutting.

Finally, Dahlia couldn't take his suffocating ire and the cramp in her calf any longer. She didn't care how close they were to the palace. Lia needed to get away from him.

"Please stop. I need to rest."

The Frost King huffed his displeasure, but lifted his hand into the air, the company of soldiers all slowing to a stop at his signal. He slid from the *rukhal*'s back and helped her to her feet. She muttered her thanks, but he didn't reply, dismissing her immediately.

Lia grumbled under her breath and wound through

the warriors until she found Loshika. She waved at the healer and stretched her leg out, her calf muscle twisted fiercely.

The healer climbed down from her own beast and crossed her arms. "When is the last time you drank water, my lady?"

"Before we left?" She grinned behind her scarf and held out her arms innocently when Loshika scowled at her. "What?"

"You need fluids to heal, *reilleve*."

Dahlia knew that, but no one had outfitted her with a waterskin, and she didn't want to ask the king, since speaking to him had become … unpleasant. He was downright beastly today.

No, it was better to go without if it meant not having to speak to him.

Loshika dug in her bag, retrieving dried fruit, meat, and a canteen. She slapped them into Lia's mittened hands. "Now, go sit down and eat."

Lia dipped her head and padded out of the crowd of warriors. The back of her neck prickled with all the eyes that watched her, but she ignored it and picked her way through the rocks, scrub brush, pines, and snow, until she found the perfect seat.

Brushing the snow from the flat stone, she sat down and pulled her scarf from her face. The cold nipped at her cheeks, but it felt refreshing. The scarf had felt smothering in the last hour.

While Dahlia preferred the warmth of summer, she could absolutely fall in love with the beauty of winter. She plopped a hard, dried apricot into her mouth and chewed slowly, the fruit slowly warming up as she admired how the pines added a pop of color to the crisp landscape. The snow sparkled under the sun, shining like a blanket of diamonds.

A hoot above was all the warning she got before an enormous owl landed on a pointy boulder to her right. She stared at the creature with wide eyes. The bird flapped its wings before settling down. The owl had to be at least the size of a large dog with its wide wingspan.

They stared at each other, and the owl tippy-tapped on the rock, an impatient dance.

"Why, hello there," she murmured softly, hoping that her voice wouldn't scare the creature away.

The owl blinked at her and focused on her lap, particularly the food.

"Are you hungry?" Lia picked up an apricot and tossed it over to the rock. It landed with a dull thud. The bird pecked it but knocked it away with its beak. Apparently, it didn't like apricots. "Maybe some meat?" she crooned, tossing a piece of dried venison over. The owl snatched it up and gobbled it down.

Dahlia smiled. "Seems we've found something you like." She yanked a piece of venison apart, her mittened fingers struggling, and tossed one piece into her mouth, chewing. Lia watched her feathery companion watching her.

Its feathers looked so soft. What would it be like to hug such a creature? She eyed its long claws and wickedly sharp beak. Lia wouldn't be finding out any time soon.

The owl hopped closer until it was only about five feet

away. Lia stared at the bird, admiring the dark bars woven through its white feathers.

"Do you want another piece?" she asked, tossing the next strip of meat to the owl.

It snatched the meat out of the air, swallowing it whole. Wow, that was something else. The owl eyed her with round gold eyes edged in black. They almost seemed sentient. She knew all creatures were intelligent in their own way, but this was something different. It was uncanny and knowing.

"You're so beautiful," Lia murmured. She'd never seen anything so stunning.

The owl hooted, and preened as if it knew she was praising it.

"*Valles*," the low voice of the king said softly from behind her. "You need to move away from the *astrylle*." There was something in his tone that made the hair along her arms raise. "Slowly."

The owl screeched, its attention on Neve. It hunched forward, its claws flexing on the stone.

"Give me a minute," she murmured, keeping her voice level, the magical moment over.

Lia gathered up her last two pieces of meat and tossed them to the owl, who didn't even look at them. It stared at her. What the devil had she been thinking, feeding a gigantic bird of prey?

She stood and began backing away, when the owl leapt into the air and darted toward her. Lia lifted her arm over her face, waiting for those long-wicked claws to sink in, but the pain never came. Instead, a loud hoot sounded in her left ear.

Lia lowered her arm just a touch and swallowed her gasp. She was nose to nose with the bloody thing. "You don't want to eat me, do you?" she whispered.

The owl crooned, and began cleaning itself like she was of no consequence.

A large set of hands settled on her hips and yanked her away from the bird. The bloody owl didn't so much as spare a glance.

Neve lifted her and ran back to the soldiers, setting her down.

"That was stupid. Were you trying to get yourself killed?"

Lia rolled her eyes and he flinched. She didn't think he liked that. She'd remember that for later. He laced his fingers together and placed them on the top of his head, pacing back and forth.

"You fed an *astrylle*," he stated, still pacing. "An *astrylle*."

"Is that what you call the massive owl?"

He scrubbed his hand over his face. "Yes, and you could have been killed. They're notoriously bad tempered."

"He didn't seem so bad."

"*She*," Neve volleyed back. "I can't believe it," he said mostly to himself.

"What?" she asked. Lia noticed that all the warriors were staring at them—at her. "*What?*"

The king chuckled, his attention on her. "It would be you. The stars are laughing at me."

"You're not making any sense."

Neve stopped pacing and pointed to the *astrylle*. "These birds of prey are special in my culture. While they are bad tempered and volatile at times, they are fiercely loyal creatures, much like Loriians. They are often heralded as bringers of wisdom or change. And every century, a few bond with a Loriian."

"Bond?"

"Yes. *Astrylle* can sense the inner person. They only choose the best of us." He swallowed hard. "And she chose you."

Dahlia looked to the owl and back to the king. "Me?"

"You."

"All she did was take my scraps."

"They don't take food from anyone but their bonded."

Lia gaped at him. "What does that even mean? The bird was hungry."

The distance evaporated between them as he cupped the back of her head. "It means, *reilleve*, that you are more precious than I thought, and perhaps what this kingdom needs."

Chapter Twenty-Nine

Neve

An *astrylle* had bonded with his *reilleve*.

Neve could hardly believe his luck.

While his council had sided with him on his choice of taking a human bride, it had been reluctant. Dealing with assassins and dimedons was nothing compared to the tangled web of court politics that awaited him. He grimaced. A lot could change in a month.

Despite how much he hated the little games of court, he couldn't wait to get home. The Mirror Bridge gleamed just ahead of them, reflecting the sunset. Dahlia gasped, leaning forward on Cessa's neck, her bottom pressing once again against his *sorav*.

He stifled his groan, fingers flexing on her hips.

The last three days had been miserable. With the gentle rocking of the *rukhal* coupled with her plush *saloes* body, he couldn't help but react to the *valles*. No matter how much he reminded himself that he didn't find Dahlia attractive in the least, his *sorav* only understood friction and heat.

It was bloody uncomfortable.

"What is that?" she murmured. "It's *beautiful*."

The warriors within earshot chuckled at her excitement, and Neve even smiled through his discomfort and irritation.

Eyri nudged his *rukhal* closer. "It's the Mirror Bridge."

"Is it made of glass?"

"It looks that way, but it is made of something far sturdier. It is constructed of reflective crystal from the Olek Mountains to the east," Neve answered, pulling the *valles* back between his legs. "Sit back before you fall."

She snorted, and then slapped a hand over her mouth. He glanced down at Dahlia in surprise. She avoided his gaze and whipped her face forward.

"What was that sound?" he whispered in her ear, smirking that she thought to hide from him. "Was something I said amusing?"

"Only the fact that you presume to order me around."

"I am your lord and king."

She twisted, her nose almost touching his own. They shared a breath, and he found himself staring at her lips. What was so confounding about them? He inhaled her spicy ginger scent and leaned the smallest bit closer.

"You are my captor, my lord."

He blinked. "I suppose I am." Like the evil *vallos* he was... he liked the idea of being her captor.

"No apology?"

"No."

She hummed, faced forward, and Neve exhaled slowly. What was it about this *saloes* that intrigued him? One moment he wanted to throttle her, and the next he wanted to bathe in the glow of her smile...

Even with her flat teeth, they'd unfortunately began to grow on him.

They reached the top of the slope and he watched Dahlia's jaw drop. Cessa's hooves clacked against the crystal bridge, and he paused when they reached the middle.

"I have no words," she whispered reverently.

Neve straightened and stared toward the west, to the Glace Palace. He knew what Dahlia saw.

A large lake covered with a sheet of thick white ice. Majestic black mountains around the western and northern edge of the lake, blanketed in pure white snow. And nestled proudly along the water's edge stood the Glace Palace, the sprawling city around it carved into the mountains like a half-moon.

The palace shot up to the sky like shards of unforgiving ice. The sunset washed over the glass, stone, and crystal, making the palace seem like it was on fire. Sharp spires jutted from the mountains like proud sentinels. Sloping roads cascaded down to water's edges, looping in different directions, elegant in their design. Frosted pine trees hid homes and taverns, only their winking lanterns visible.

This was his home.

"What do you think?" He held his breath. He didn't

know why her answer mattered to him so much, but it did.

"It's like a fairy tale. I've never seen anything like it."

He smiled, a flush of pleasure rolling through him. Olwen wiggled his brows at Neve. He quickly quashed whatever expression adorned his face but murmured to his *niliave* all the same: "Welcome to your new home."

THE SUN HAD LONG SINCE SET WHEN THEY reached the edge of Glace City, the stars twinkling brightly above in a dark velvet sky. Slowly, they traversed the winding roads, his people stepping outside their homes to wish them well or to stare. Lanterns lined the road, a merry guide to the palace.

It would have been easier to return via the barracks' entrance, but his people needed to see their new queen. Plus, while he had chosen a human bride, that didn't mean he trusted her with kingdom secrets. There was much he didn't want her to see or to know.

The amethyst sentry spires bracketed the east *passerelle*. Neve nodded to the men as they moved onto yet another bridge.

Dahlia sucked in a sharp breath. "It drops so far down."

He glanced to his left, barely making out the flowing water below. "Not much different from your Bridge of Bones, no?"

She shuddered. "Terrifying."

"Don't worry, *reilleve*. I won't throw you over."

She glared at him over her shoulder, and it made him smile. He liked riling the little human.

They passed through the portcullis and into the main courtyard, which still teemed with people. They bowed to the procession as they passed. Neve directed Cessa through a second, narrower gate that led to the entrance.

Eira and Warrin stood amongst some of the courtiers and servants waiting for them. Neve scanned the group. No sign of his sister.

He'd have to have words with Lumi. No doubt her absence would be noted.

He stopped beside the stairs that led inside the palace. He dismounted, and then pulled his queen from Cessa, the *rukhal* blocking them from prying eyes. She slowly slid down his body, and gripped his forearms as he set her on her feet. She swallowed hard.

"I'm not sure I'm ready," she whispered, a hint of vulnerability in her voice.

He stared her down and leaned forward so he didn't tower above her so much. "You must be." The vulnerability was erased, her placid mask back. He pointed to her face. "This is your war face, *jaivelle*. Use it. Do not let them see your fear."

"I'm not afraid."

A hoot echoed through the courtyard, shocking gasps and murmurs from his court and advisors. The *astrylle* had perfect timing.

"Time to meet your court, my queen."

Chapter Thirty

Dahlia

It was an odd feeling to be the tiniest person in a group.

Dahlia hadn't really noticed it until a sea of finely dressed giants surrounded her all speaking at once—some in Loriian, others in the common tongue, still others in Fierran.

None of it made sense. It was just a jumble of words.

She just nodded and smiled as she was whisked up the stairs on the king's arm and through a set of three-story-tall arched doors. Dahlia glanced over her shoulder at the starry night, already wishing she were somewhere else.

She had felt overwhelmed and lost in Florrant, but the ice palace was something altogether different. It was wealth and opulence that Lia couldn't have imagined.

The king released her, and people surrounded her, but

she didn't hear a thing they said as she soaked in the palace's opulence.

Columns of pale blue marble supported the arched ceiling, which was threaded with silver veins. Crystal chandeliers with hundreds of flickering flames sparkled like diamonds, each casting multi-hued light. Third-story banisters appeared almost as if out of thin air on each side, and led to an impressive split staircase that was wider than most homes she'd lived in.

You don't belong here.

She glanced down at her dirty travel leathers, running her fingers over the slices Neve's claws had made when they were attacked near the Seed. What must the courtiers think of her? Did they see a grubby human girl?

False queen.

She took a shallow breath, searching the sea of faces for anyone familiar. The king was moving away from her with his entourage. She curbed the inclination to call out to him. He wasn't her friend. She needed to remember that.

A warm hand touched her elbow, and she jumped.

Loshika's face swam into view. Her forehead crinkled. "*Reilleve*? Are you alright?"

"*Sei*," she murmured, finally acknowledging all the eyes on her. She smiled warmly, trying not to be intimidated.

Don't be afraid. You've been in front of audiences all your life.

A robust giantess pushed her way through the group and gave Dahlia a crooked smile. "Welcome, *reilleve*," she said in common tongue, bowing low before rising. "I am Jaessa, the head housekeeper."

"It's lovely to meet you, Jaessa."

The housekeeper's cheeks darkened to a deeper purple, something Lia had observed was a blush. "We have been anxiously awaiting your arrival since we heard of your illness. If you are ready for a bath and to retire, I will show you to your room, where the healer will see to you."

Dahlia nodded. "Thank you, but I have my own healer." She looped her arm through Loshika's, ignoring the pointed stares at the giantess' scars. "I would like to meet your healer as well, but perhaps on the morrow."

The housekeeper dipped her chin. "As you say, *reilleve*. Follow me please."

Lia nodded to giants as she passed them. She tried not to flinch when immediate whispers in Loriian followed.

They're judging you. They know you're a liar.

The housekeeper led them up the carpeted stairs, to where it split. Reaching the third floor, Jaessa turned right, the hallway curving. The left side of the hallway was arched glass panes two stories tall that faced the lake. The moon cast an ethereal glow over the surroundings, making it picturesque.

Servants tried to mask their surprise as she passed them, dropping into deep bows or curtseys.

The housekeeper turned right to another wide staircase away from the view. They climbed two more stories, then Jaessa opened a door to the right.

"Welcome home."

Dahlia stepped inside the room, clinging to Loshika as she soaked in the opulence of the chamber.

It was enormous—like five rooms put together—a half-moon shaped bedroom. To her left, a wall cut toward the windows, a wide fireplace in the middle of the wall that Lia could stand in if she wanted. Shelves of books and trinkets bracketed each side. Two delightful chairs and a long couch were arranged around the fire, making it seem like a room of its own.

Delicate curtains draped from arched windows to the floor in dainty puddles.

Lia waded farther into the room, soaking in the view.

Another fireplace was mirrored on the opposite wall with a tall circular tub before it. She released Loshika and made her way to the washing basin, running her hand over the curtains, along the silk pillows that reclined on attractive divans.

When Dahlia finally reached the bathtub, all she did was stare. It could have fit eight people—or four giants. Who needed a bathtub that large? And how much water would the staff need to boil to fill it? She blinked at the faucet. Did they have running hot water here?

Jaessa pointed to the paneled wall to the right of the fireplace. "The wardrobe is hidden behind that door." The housekeeper bustled around the tub and opened a door to Lia's right. "The shower and toilet are in this room."

"You have plumbing?" Lia asked.

The housekeeper nodded, her lips pressed together. "Only the best, my lady."

The giantess seemed a little miffed, but hid it well. Lia offered a smile. "I meant no offense, Jaessa. I'm just surprised. Your home is quite magnificent. It's a marvel of modern science. Even Florrant can't offer a shower."

That seemed to do the trick. The housekeeper beamed.

While Dahlia was curious about the shower, she refrained from snooping around the toilet room. She finally turned around and walked to the bed that stood in the very center of the chamber.

Like everything in Loriia, it was giant sized.

Gauzy fabrics hung from the ceiling and around the bed, creating an intimate cozy space. She ran her fingertips across the silky, flawless furs that adorned the mattress. It hosted so many pillows she could have created her own mattress with them. A tasteful but raw crystal chandelier hung above the bed, adding a bit of sparkle to the space. She reached the end of the bed, her knees brushing one of the trunks from Astera.

Lia spun around and sat on the burnished wooden truck from her country and stared out the windows. It was the most striking abode she'd ever had the pleasure of visiting. She should have been excited, but all she felt was dread and exhaustion. What would happen next? How long would it be until she saw Cosmos again?

"How about a bath, my lady?" Jaessa offered. "It must have been a long, cold ride for you today."

Dahlia smiled gratefully at the housekeeper. "And use all that water for one person? I think not."

Jaessa blinked at her. "It's no problem."

Lia waved a hand at the toilet room. "I will shower later."

The housekeeper frowned. "Please allow me to get it ready for you."

It seemed the giantess would not be happy unless she helped. Dahlia heaved herself from the trunk, trying to look as ladylike as possible, with Loshika silently following her. "I would be grateful if you showed me how it works."

Jaessa nodded, and opened the door for Lia and Loshika.

The room was large, with a commode in a small separate room to the left. Raw aquamarine formed the long western wall. The floor dropped down two steps, forming a sunken rectangle. The wall to the north was covered in a crystal so flawless it could have been a mirror.

Dahlia blinked at her reflection, and then looked to the housekeeper as she pointed to two knobs on the right wall. "One controls hot water and one cold." She adjusted them and Loshika gasped as water poured down from the ceiling like heavy rain collecting in the sunken rectangle and then flowing out the drain in the center.

A giggle slipped from Lia in delight. This would be her new home. She couldn't wait to try it.

Jaessa grinned. "Everything to your liking, *reilleve*?"

"I more than like it. I love it. Thank you."

"My pleasure. I'll make sure linens are ready for your ladies in waiting."

Lia cocked her head. "My ladies?"

"Yes, the king has provided four ladies-in-waiting for you as a marriage gift."

It didn't feel like a gift. It felt like another way for him to spy on her. But that wasn't Jaessa's fault. "No need to trouble them tonight."

"I will help her," Loshika said. "I will care for our *reilleve*."

"Then I will say goodnight, *lae reilleve*." The house-keeper bowed before exiting the shower room.

The air grew warm and damp as the shower continued to rain down miraculously.

"Have you ever seen something like this, Loshika?"

"No, my lady."

"Would you like a turn?"

Loshika frowned and waved a hand at the shower. "This is not for the likes of me."

Nor for Dahlia.

Feeling a little desperate and a whole lot out of place, she grabbed the healer's hand and tugged her toward the shower. "Well, you did say you would help me..." Lia darted into the spray, towing the giantess along. She laughed and held her hands up to the spray, Loshika squinting at her.

"We're in our clothes, *reilleve*."

Lia spun in a circle. "They needed a good wash, don't you think?"

Loshika *tsk*ed, but the corner of her mouth turned up. "You are something else, my lady."

"Thank you. Now let's find some soap and get the stink of travel washed from our hair."

Chapter Thirty-One

Neve

He didn't get any sleep the night of their arrival.

Nor the next day.

"Tell us again about the *astrylle*," Beram asked, running his claws over his long gray beard.

Neve choked back a growl at the old *vallos'* question. They'd been over this several times already. "At the Seed of Loriia, an *astrylle* blessed our union. Then three days later, when we stopped for a break, the *reilleve* shared her lunch with the creature."

Eyri stopped his scratching, and lifted his head, his spectacles on the tip of his nose. "I studied the *astrylle* perched outside the castle and the markings are remarkably similar to the bird from the village blessing. I believe they are the same. I think the *astrylle* followed us."

Neve blinked at his cousin. That was new.

"Our queen must be something special to be blessed by an *astrylle*, and to survive so many harrowing ordeals in the last month." Warrin, their old battle-ax of a giant, laced his fingers over his belly and leaned back in his chair. "I look forward to meeting her."

There was a murmur of agreement that set Neve's teeth on edge. This was not how it was supposed to go. He'd planned on stowing her in the tower and continuing to rule his kingdom. He didn't need the *saloes* causing trouble. "I will introduce you once she's recovered, and I've gotten some sleep."

He stood from the simple throne and nodded to the council sitting at the rectangular table. "Goodnight."

Neve retreated out the door, with Flyka and Olwen shadowing him. "You don't need to follow me to my bed."

"With what happened near the Seed, I beg to differ," Flyka retorted. "We have guesses who sanctioned that attack, but no confirmation. It could be anyone."

He sighed but didn't argue, knowing she was right. The black stone walls wavered with the reflections of the lanterns. Neve took the left staircase, taking two stairs at a time. Their war room was deep in the castle so there was less of a chance of spies. Many floors later, he found himself in the royal wing.

Flyka sped past him and held up her hand as he reached his door. She gave him a firm look as if to say *don't move until I'm done*. Neve leaned his right shoulder against the wall and crossed his arms, waiting for her to inspect his chamber.

She stepped out, her expression blank. "It's clear, my lord."

"Thank you." He clasped her on the shoulder and nodded to Olwen. "Goodnight, my friends."

He closed the door behind him and a heavy sigh escaped him.

Finally, he was home.

The lanterns were extinguished, but a fire roared on both sides of the room, making it warmer than he normally liked. He meandered to the window and stared. There was something so peaceful about a moonlit lake.

He rolled his neck and cast a longing look at the tub. How his body ached from the last ride, trying to keep distance between himself and the *valles*, not to mention the cracked ribs that still ached with every breath he took.

Sleep, then a bath in the morning.

Neve smiled at his bed. He loved pillows. It was one of his extravagances. He could give up fine clothing, fancy food, even forgo hot water, but a soft bed with an overabundance of pillows? Never. After nearly a month of sleeping on floors, makeshift beds, and bunks, he was ready for a good night's sleep.

Prowling to the bed, he tore off his loose tunic and shirt. Next, he toed off his boots, peeled off his socks, and then unlaced his leathers, kicking them to the floor. Completely naked, he flopped onto his stomach on the mattress, hugging the nearest pillow.

He groaned. It was pure bliss.

Qov, but he loved his bed.

Neve slipped into slumber, only to wake later in the night when the fires had almost burned out. He yanked the covers back and slipped under, the cool sheets caressing his skin.

This was heaven.

NEVE WOKE IN THE EARLY MORNING, HIS *SORAV* throbbing and nestled in heat. He pressed his hips into the warmth, his hand squeezing the pillow by his side.

Ginger. His favorite scent. Had breakfast already been brought in?

A bloodcurdling scream assaulted his sensitive ears, making him jerk upright, disoriented. He blinked repeatedly at the space beside him, Dahlia's crazy eyes meeting his for a second before she lobbed a pillow at him. He bellowed and bolted out of the bed as his *niliave* rolled out the other side. Her *nonnaette* popped her head up from the floor and scurried around the bed, nodding to him once.

Olwen opened the door, took in the scene as Loshika squeezed past him, and closed the door just as fast with a wicked grin.

Bloody traitor.

Dahlia screamed again and lobbed another pillow, her hand groping for the stone vase on the side table.

"Why are you in my bed *naked*?" she screeched, seizing the vase and throwing it.

Neve ducked, the vase crashing behind him. "What are you doing in my room?" he yelled back, tossing his hands in the air.

"Godsteeth," the *valles* cursed, holding her hand up. "Cover it up!"

Neve cupped his *sorav* with both hands, shielding himself from her view. "You don't get to make demands when you sneak into *my* bed."

She glared at him. "I didn't sneak anywhere. I went to bed in *my* room last night and then this morning I find you naked in my bed groping me and thrusting against my bottom!"

He almost blushed, but shoved it down. This was his chamber, and he was no maid. "My body's reaction to you is not your problem, but you were still in *my* bed." His gaze scoured her, noting that she was wearing one of his shirts. The black fabric met her knees, but laces almost met her navel. She placed her hands on the bed and leaned forward, the collar gaping open to reveal more of her body than he suspected Dahlia wanted seen.

A flash a heat ran through him.

Neve focused on the fireplace behind her, ignoring how his body heated at the small glimpse. "*Jaivelle*, I can see your nipples."

She gasped and straightened, pinching the edges together with both of her shaking hands.

"Why are you in my shirt?" he asked tightly. The possessive part of him liked it. And that was all sorts of wrong.

"Because it was the only decent thing I could find to sleep in." Her nose wrinkled. "Everything in my trunks were lacy and see-through."

Lace and see-through sleeping attire, how very intriguing. He scowled, pushing the thought away. "Why do you think this is your room?"

"Because Jaessa brought me here two nights ago and said it was so." She stabbed a finger at the end of the bed. "Plus, my trunks are here."

He eyed the trunks, frowning. How had he not noticed those last night? Or the fact that there was a little human in his bed? He side-eyed the pillows. They betrayed him. She must have been buried underneath all the fluffiness.

There was only one person who could have orchestrated something like this.

Lumi.

His jaw tightened. His bloody sister had overseen the organizing of the princess' things when they arrived. Why did she place them here when she *knew* he wanted her in the tower?

He shuffled to his discarded clothes and yanked on his leathers, leaving the ties loosened. Neve stalked around the bed, feeling like his skin was too tight. Dahlia tracked his progress as he caged her against the bed.

"This has all been a misunderstanding. This..." He gestured to the chamber. "...is my room. You were not meant to be here. It's a mistake I will remedy. But for the time being..." He lifted her onto the bed. "...go back to sleep. It's still early."

He stormed away.

"Where are you going?"

"To shower. *Alone.*"

"How'd you get those scars?"

He cursed. *Qovving* female.

Neve slammed the bathroom door behind him and turned the water on cold. He tore off his trousers and tossed them to the ground with a disgusted slap. Unwinding his braid, he ducked under the cold water, and hissed as the icy torrent doused him. He ran his hand down his face and then tipped his head back, letting the spray fall onto his cheeks.

What a mess.

His body still throbbed with unfulfilled desire for a *saloes*. It was wrong. She was the enemy, no matter how soft and curvy she was.

He didn't want her. He didn't want her. He didn't want her.

Maybe if he thought it enough, his body would start believing him.

WHEN NEVE EXITED THE SHOWER ROOM, HE WAS a lot calmer. He paused, holding the towel around his waist. Dahlia sat on the end of the bed, her bare feet resting on the middle trunk, peeking out from beneath a gauzy gold dress. She didn't look toward him but continued to stare out at the frozen lake through the arched windows.

He pushed the false door right of the fireplace and entered his wardrobe.

Neve stopped in his tracks, noting all the gowns, both

Loriian and Asteran. They mingled with his own clothing. It was bizarre, but surprisingly not unwelcome.

Quickly dressing, he pulled a black lace gown from the rack and pushed out of the hidden wardrobe. His *reilleve* still didn't glance his way. He steeled himself for another confrontation, and walked to the end of the bed. He scanned her profile before sitting on the mattress next to Dahlia, the dress in his lap.

She peeked at him from the corner of her eye, attention dropping to the dress. "You'll look pretty in that."

He quirked a smile. "It is for you. I prefer leather to lace."

She straightened, brushing her hands along her lap. "You don't like this one?"

"No, the color is beautiful on you, but it is too Asteran. You need to wear *lysterm* black."

"In my culture, it is a color of mourning." She pulled a face. "I've never looked good in dark colors."

Odd. Didn't her people use it as a sign of nobility as well? He hadn't heard of it being used for mourning except in Fierre.

"Here it is the color of royalty." He paused. "You need to look like your new people."

She nodded, staring at her palms. His chest squeezed at the scars from the rope marring both.

"You want to make me more palatable to your court," she concluded.

"That, among other things."

His wife sighed. "What do you expect of me, my lord?"

"My lord," he *tsk*ed. "Now you use the honorific. I think we're well past that in private."

"Are we? Because you still look at me like I'm the enemy even though you orchestrated this marriage. I'm wondering just what you want from me."

"Peace. Nothing else." *A lie, his soul insisted.*

"What does that look like?"

"Today, it is meeting my council and court. Tomorrow, something else. The day after that, it is up to you."

She twisted her lips. "Is that all?"

"I won't bore you with the details, but the marriage alone gave me what I wanted. You were a means to an end."

"That's surprisingly honest."

Dahlia slid from the bed, over the trunk, and held her hand out for the dress. "Alright, let's play king and queen, shall we?"

He placed the dress over her arm. "There's jewelry in the wardrobe for you. I'll send for your ladies-in-waiting. We need you to look like a *reilleve*."

"Don't worry, *lae reillov*. I won't disappoint."

Chapter Thirty-Two

Dahlia

She'd put on a brave face when her new ladies swept into the room to help her ready for the day. They'd arrived in a flurry of silk, fur, and lace.

Luckily, she'd managed to find a pair of black leather leggings and put them on beforehand. Old habits died hard. Plus, the dress the king had chosen wasn't warm. Who the devil wore lace in the dead of winter? Or sleeveless robes with no shirt beneath it?

Loriians, that's who.

Over the course of the following two hours, she'd been lotioned and polished to perfection by Freya, Bothi, Alda, and Birgit. They'd tittered over the king's shirt, and admired Lia's strawberry-blonde hair, gently weaving the locks into a feminine masterpiece. They'd laced her into an off-the-shoulder dress, and fluffed her skirt before turning her toward the ornate silver standing mirror next to the bed.

Dahlia just stared.

She'd lost a little weight in the last few weeks, her waist nipping in more than usual. The black lace cut across her chest, dipping into a heart shape, showing a hint of her cleavage. The lace sleeves clung to her arms and ended in a point on the back of each hand. A pale nude silk lay beneath the bodice, making it seem as if she had nothing on underneath. The lace skirt faded into airy onyx fur that almost appeared as frills. While she liked rich colors with lots of vibrance, for once in her life the color didn't wash her out.

Lia smoothed her hands over her hips. It was a lovely contrast. The Loriian black, tempered with the nude color of her skin. She couldn't help but think it made a statement.

I'm human, but your reilleve.

She'd chosen a simple black teardrop pearl necklace with a gold chain and left it at that. Other than the poison ring on her finger that seemed to weigh a ton.

That's just your conscience.

She focused on the four ladies standing behind her, their varied shades of cyan skin forming a wall of giants. Dahlia spun around, lifting the voluminous skirt out of the way.

"I have a question for you all, if it's not inappropriate."

"Nothing you could ask us would be inappropriate," Birgit, the tallest of her ladies said. "You are *reilleve.*"

"I couldn't help but notice how beautiful the color of your complexion is. Are you all related?"

Brigit smiled, dainty fangs peeking out. "Yes, my lady. These are my cousins."

"How fortuitous for you all to be chosen together as my ladies-in-waiting."

"It is an honor, but it also comes with our title," Freya interjected with a shy smile. "We are second cousins to the king."

Lia nodded slowly. So, he'd stationed his family to spy on her. "Truly? How blessed am I to have gained so much family."

Alda—the one with almost white hair—stood with her lips pressed together. This one didn't like her. She could feel it.

"I know it must be difficult to accept a *saloes* in your home," Lia said, staring Alda down. "But I will do my best to honor your king. Your culture is very different than mine, but I will accept it as my own."

Alda's lips eased the tiniest bit. Lia counted it as a victory. Centuries of bad blood would not be erased in a day, but perhaps she could befriend these women and learn more about this place—and then escape.

"Then if I may, *reilleve*," Bothi added. "I must advise you to reconsider your jewelry."

"My jewelry?" She thumbed her ring.

The ladies began to nod. Bothi gestured to her long, pointed ears, that were covered in studded gems. "Piercings and jewels are an important part of our culture. You are queen, and yet you only wear one necklace and ring."

"You think that's a mistake?" Dahlia thought back to

all the Loriians she'd come across. All had their ears pierced multiple times, wore silver rings on their fingers or in their hair. She gestured to the wardrobe. "Please show me what you'd choose."

All four ladies lit up. Even Alda smiled.

Perhaps she'd made new friends already.

THE PALACE WAS COLD; SHE WAS BLOODY thankful she'd worn leggings beneath her dress. Two warriors she'd never seen before had led her from her room down a labyrinth of hallways and down many flights of stairs until they'd reached a black stone corridor with no windows.

She shivered, and her pace slowed. Why did they bring her here?

Perhaps they weren't taking her to Neve but to the dungeons instead?

Don't be stupid. Why dress you up?

That thought soothed Dahlia the tiniest bit, and relief filled her as Eyri stepped through the door with a smile on his face. Surely, he wouldn't smile at her if he was to kill her? Olwen maybe, but not Eyri. The guards took their place on either side of the door as Eyri held his arm out to her.

"Are you ready?" he whispered softly.

"For what?"

"The wolves."

She shrugged. "Can't be much worse than home."

He led her through a short hallway that opened to a chamber with rough-hewn stone walls. Her heeled boots clicked against the floor, and she kept her schooled expression in place as fifteen giants stood from the rectangular crystal table and bowed. She knew two at the table, Flyka and Olwen.

"*Reilleve*," echoed in the room.

Eyri urged her forward around the largest chair until she faced the king. Her heart pounded as she met Neve's pitch gaze. Long gone was the grumpy warrior of the road, an icy monarch in his place as hard as stone.

He sat in his carved wooden throne, regal chin held high. Chains and gems dripped from his ears, and shiny beads decorated his deep blue hair. A black brocade tunic with a row of neat silver buttons marched down his chest to his leathers. A multitude of silver rings gleamed on his fingers.

Dahlia curtsied, so thankful the ladies-in-waiting had changed her jewelry. She would have looked like a simple bumpkin beside this king. Slowly she rose, and the king held a hand out to her. Lia released Eyri and took a step closer, sliding her nerveless fingers against his. He gently tugged her between his thick, splayed thighs and urged her to sit.

Lia perched on his lap, battling a rising blush. Her back was ramrod straight as he ran his hand down the back of her neck, then spine, and eventually settled on her left hip. He scooted her farther into his lap.

Dahlia did blush this time, keeping her dismay and annoyance from showing. What in the blazes was happening? She didn't want to be anywhere near his lap after this morning. Growing up in a troupe of bards meant not a lot of privacy, so she'd seen her fair share of male appendages, but she'd never seen anything like the king's ... it was as disturbing as it was *intriguing*.

Her blush burned hotter. *Stop it.*

"Let me introduce you all to my *niliave*, Princess Dahlia of Astera."

The giants bowed again before sitting in their seats, their attention focused completely on her, assessing. Lia did the same. There were some warm smiles of familiar faces, a few thin-lipped, and then she spotted a positively stormy cloud of a giantess. She seemed to fume in place; hate seeped from her pores.

Dahlia blinked slowly. A jealous lover? A wronged Loriian?

"Lumi, aren't you going to welcome your new sister?"

The angry giantess smiled, but it was mean. *Neve's sister.* "Welcome, *reilleve.*" Her tone dripped false sweetness.

"*Jaiell vei,*" Lia returned with just as much sweetness. A family feud. How delightful.

An old woman with white hair arched a brow. "My lady speaks Loriian?"

"No, but I've picked up a few words recently. It's my hope to be fluent in the future." *A lie.* She'd be long gone before she was fluent. "What is your name?"

"Eira."

"It's lovely to meet you."

The giantess quirked a smile when a giant built like a

bull grinned at her. "We heard you're quick with a sling-shot, my lady."

How did they know this already? "I wouldn't say quick..."

"Have you been trained with other weapons?"

She pursed her lips at his question, and teetered her hand in the air. "I'm a straight shot with a bow, and have a hidden love for throwing knives, but that's the extent of my education in the art of war."

"You brought us back a little fighter," a much younger giant commented, his lavender face pensive. "What a delightful surprise."

Lia didn't like him on sight. There was something *oily* about him, about the smirk as he scanned her from head to toe. He reminded her of the Giver.

The king squeezed her hip and murmured, "It seems I have."

Dahlia almost broke when Olwen winked at her and wiggled his brows. He was a cretin, to be sure. It would be very unqueenly for her to break out into a fit of giggles at her very first meeting.

"What did you make of the *astrylle*?" an older giant asked, his long gray beard quivering. He leaned his elbows onto the table, his excitement almost palpable.

She warmed to him immediately. "I've never been more awed and terrified at once."

He smiled, all his teeth on display. "An apt description of an *astrylle* if I've ever heard one."

"What do you know of the troops gathering near the border cities of Loriia?" a particularly angular giant asked, his eyes narrowed.

Dahlia lifted her chin. "I know nothing of that."

The giant scoffed. "We've had reports—"

"Enough," the king commanded. His hard tone made Lia sit even straighter.

A volley of Loriian burst from Lumi, her anger palpable. Neve replied, the lilting words sounding firm and a touch threatening. Lia observed as the king's sister stiffened and then shut her mouth. She shot a glare at Dahlia.

Definitely wasn't making a friend there.

The discussions continued completely in Loriian.

She did her best to look like she was following, when nothing made sense. After about thirty minutes of Neve ignoring her and the council pretending she wasn't in fact perching in their king's lap, she wiggled. Her toes had long since gone numb, since they'd been hanging on his thigh.

Neve inhaled sharply and she peeked up at him from underneath her lashes. The king didn't look down at her, but his jaw had tightened. His fingers squeezed her hip in warning. Lia inwardly smirked. She liked irritating him. He bothered her just as much.

The longer she watched the council, the more she noticed. Whatever they spoke of—Warrin the old warrior, Eira the wise woman, Beram the bearded, and Olwen the naughty as she named them in her head—agreed with king. Lumi the storm cloud, Glassiv the blade, Bacti the oily, and a burly giantess named Illa, all disagreed. The rest of the council was silent, observing the proceedings like Dahlia.

She caught Eyri's eye when he lifted his head from his writings on the table. He smiled softly before going back to his scratching. He must be the scribe. Just what sort of things did he write down? Was it the highlights of the meeting? Or plans for the future? Either way ... his notes could prove useful.

Next, she studied Flyka.

The Haunt never cracked a smile or showed any emotion. She could have been a statue, except for when someone turned a little heated. Then her penetrating gaze landed on them, and suddenly those giants changed their tune.

She was the muscle—the blade of the king.

She'd treated Dahlia with kindness on their journey, and Lia had lost some of her fear of the Haunt. But now watching the other giants' reaction to Flyka was a gentle reminder that the Haunt wasn't her friend. She was there to only serve the king.

"Are we boring you, *reilleve*?" the king whispered in her ear in common tongue.

Goosebumps broke out along her arms, and she barely managed to keep from gasping. The whole room had gone silent.

"Not at all."

He pressed his other hand to her navel. "Such a patient wife."

Her stomach had the gall to growl.

Olwen snickered, and she blushed again. When was the last time she ate? Last night? After the mess of this morning, she'd totally forgone breakfast, and was now paying for it.

Neve gently slid her from his lap onto her feet. "Why don't you meet your ladies-in-waiting for some luncheon."

A clear command and dismissal. And a statement about her station. While she may have the title of queen, Lia was considered anything but.

"As you wish, *lae reillov*." She curtsied and went to step away, when he reached out and caressed the black diamond choker at her throat.

"I like this."

Her eyes widened at the heated smirk that lifted his deep navy lips. Why was she staring at his mouth?

"Thank you, my lord."

"Keep that on for dinner, would you?"

She gave him a questioning look. Just what was he about? "As you say."

Lia lifted the hem of her skirt and walked out of the room, confusion swirling inside her. Why the sudden change in attitude? It threw her off-kilter.

"I don't think you'll need to evoke the concubine edict, *reillov*," Bacti the oily said just loud enough in common tongue that she heard him. "Surely our kingdom will be blessed with heirs soon."

Dahlia's jaw dropped and her steps sped up.

There would be *no* heirs.

Even if part of her wanted to see how the king's skin tasted.

Chapter Thirty-Three

NEVE

HE LURKED IN LUMI'S BEDROOM WAITING FOR his dear sister to make her appearance.

After the council meeting had adjourned, she'd all but disappeared.

Neve swirled the spirits around in his glass and leaned back in the wingback chair his sister loved to read in. Lumi's room was full of vibrant colors and warm woods, as opposed to the cooler tones he preferred.

The door swung open and he paused, the glass perched on his lips when Lumi rushed into the room, Alda tailing her. His sister flinched when she spotted him, and Alda froze.

"Shouldn't you be helping the *reilleve* get ready for dinner?" he drawled.

"She dismissed us for the evening, *reillov*."

Interesting.

"Leave us."

Alda bowed, scurrying out of the room and closing the door behind her.

Lumi glared at him. "You didn't have to be so rude. She's our cousin."

"No, she's the granddaughter of Beltisse, who is scheming to take the throne, Lumi. She's not your friend."

"Then why station her as your *saloes'* lady-in-waiting? Hoping one of them will kill her off?"

Slowly, he placed his glass down on the small round table to his left. "No, I'm honoring their family, and keeping my eye on them in the process. Beltisse wouldn't tell me no when I asked for his granddaughters, since it is such a privilege to serve the queen. But he also knows they are within my grasp now. He wouldn't dare try anything. He might be greedy, but the *vallos* loves his family."

"You're diabolical," Lumi spat.

"That's a little hypocritical coming from the *valles* who put the *reilleve* in my chambers."

Mischief lurked on her face. "I heard about that. Apparently, your new queen didn't like you being in her bed. A vase was thrown? At least that's what the gossips are saying."

"Why, Lumi?" he growled, getting to his feet. "It was my wish for her to be in the tower."

"Because I wanted to have a little fun." An evil smile. "And I wanted you to have to look at her every day. You chose to bring the enemy into our home. You don't get to pretend it didn't happen and go on your merry way. You should suffer."

"You wanted to hurt me?"

Her smile dropped and her bottom lip wobbled. "I wanted you to know you'd made a mistake. To see that I was right."

Neve shook his head. "Lumi ... I didn't *want* this. It was what our kingdom needed. Do you really think I want a wife who can't speak our language? Who doesn't understand our culture? Or hides her flinch when I reach for her? One I've had to guard myself against every second of the last month? And now you've chained me to her!"

His sister paled. "What do you mean?"

"After you slipped away today, I met with my Haunt, Eira, and Warrin. You know they keep the pulse on our people. Loriians are uneasy with a *saloes* as their queen. They need to see me accepting her. I could have done that in public only, but now the servants know she's in my bed. If I send her away now, it will be seen as rejection, and stir uncertainty. Something we cannot afford." He ran a hand through his hair. "Dahlia is going to kill me!"

Lumi's fingers curled into fists. "Dahlia? *Dahlia?* You are calling the human by her name?"

"No." *Only in your mind.* "I know you're not happy she's here, but our enemies are many. Each decision I make must be calculated without feeling. The *reilleve* doesn't have to be your friend, but you must show her respect. Our bonding has stemmed war with the humans."

"For *now*," Lumi huffed.

He crossed the space between them and took his sister's hands in his own. "You are my flesh and blood. I need your support if we are to come out of this unscathed."

"You truly believe we are in that much danger?"

"Until I have an heir … yes. Even that can't fix everything."

Lumi squeezed her eyes shut. "I'm sorry. I let my anger get the best of me. I will try to be civil to the *saloes*."

Neve pulled her into his arms and hugged her fiercely. "A good start would be not calling her *saloes*. Her name is Lady Dahlia."

His sister pulled back, her nose crinkling. "Why do humans name their offspring after flowers? It's ridiculous. Don't they know names have power? Saddling a child with such a name marks them as weak the moment they are born."

He chuckled. "I don't know, but once you get to know the *reilleve*, you might think differently."

"How so?"

He released his sister and walked to the window of her room that formed the other side of the half-moon. He watched as the waterfall thundered down from the center of the massive cavern, gems glittering.

"She has a banked fire. Every once in a while, it will burn brightly only to be extinguished, replaced by a mask of self-control. It's as if she's at war with what she wants to do and what is proper. She's pragmatic and hardworking. As she healed in the village outside the Seed, she wouldn't just rest. She helped the *nonnae* and *nonnaette* with cooking, cleaning, and healing prep. The *reilleve* is *hard*. She traveled through conditions that are normal for us but excruciating to her people without complaint. She's not squeamish or cowardly."

He turned his back to the window and crossed his arms. "I watched her charge a dimedon with only a sling-shot and a dull little dagger. She stitched Flyka's leg up like a battle surgeon."

"It sounds as if you like the *valles*," Lumi commented, her nose once against wrinkled.

"Not like, per se. She makes me want to rip my hair out." He paused. "Dahlia's sense of duty is as strong as my own. I can respect that."

"Do you trust her so readily?"

Neve smirked. "Do I trust anyone readily? We may share being duty-bound, but her loyalties are with Astera. She might be my wife and play her part as the *reilleve*, but if push came to shove, she would oppose and stab me in the back for what she believes. Only time will tell if she has an ulterior agenda."

"Have you discovered what's wrong with her?" his sister asked, perching on the arm of a green divan.

"Her legs." He pursed his lips. "The skin is multihued tans, peaches, and browns. It's not contagious, and has no effect on her overall health, from what the *nonnae* got out of her. She holds a profound sense of shame over it."

Lumi frowned. "Why? There's nothing wrong with differences in the body."

"My thoughts exactly. I believe the queen has made her feel less-than. Plus, the religious order in that kingdom likes to burn people that are considered different. It's fear-mongering, something I believe she's been trained to believe in."

"So she's a bigot?"

"No. What I meant is that I think these beliefs have scarred her, and have been ingrained since she was a child. When she realized I knew about her condition, she panicked and tried to bolt into the snow in just a shift." Even now, he could feel the way she shook in his arms, and remembered the tears that tracked down her face as she tried to battle the panic.

"Deeply entrenched fear, then." His sister whistled. "So what you're saying is, you've been saddled with a human wife that by all appearances will not die anytime soon like you'd originally hoped?"

He winced. He didn't truly wish death on her ... just that he hadn't wanted to deal with a hypothetical human wife.

"If she isn't really sick, why do you think the king and queen of Astera went through with this treaty? Even all our coin and gems weren't worth their only daughter."

"That is my question too." Neve pulled his sister into one last hug before moving to the door. "One I intend to find the answer to."

CHAPTER THIRTY-FOUR

DAHLIA

SHE'D SAT AROUND IN HER GOWN FOR HOURS after the sun set.

The king never showed up.

Loshika had tossed her pitying looks all evening that made her hackles raise. Why was she waiting around for a *vallos* anyway? It's not as if *she'd* made any vows to care for or obey him. A swim across a river and a document with the king's signature didn't make her beholden to anyone.

She was done.

Dahlia stood up from the couch and yanked the skirt of her dress out of the way, storming to the door. Enough was enough. She was starving, and she was sure the healer was as well.

Loshika glanced up from her book, a thin pair of spectacles balanced on the tip of her slim nose. "My lady?"

Lia yanked open the door, surprising the guards

stationed outside. "It's time for dinner, Loshika." She unclipped the choker and tossed it onto the bed.

The healer closed her book and set it gently on the arm of the chair before joining Dahlia. "Where are you going?"

"We're going to rustle up some dinner. I know Jaessa gave a tour today. Surely you can show me to the kitchens, where we can find something to eat."

"I'm starving." A pause. "And you can call me Lo, if you wish my lady."

Lia grinned. Her healer was warming up to her. "Lo it is."

She stepped into the hallway, Loshika closing the door behind her.

One of the guards offered, "We can send for a plate for you, *reilleve*."

"No thank you," she murmured, stalking down the corridor. "I intend to meet the staff. No better way to do it than now." The guards started to follow at a distance, but she spun around and shook her head. "I don't need you. Please stay here where the *reillov* stationed you."

The warriors obeyed, with only a glance sliding between the two of them.

At least she knew she had some power here. She would never be able to do anything or discover any secrets if they were following her around.

Lo looped her arm through Lia's and directed her to a hidden servants' staircase. "This is the only way I know," the healer apologized.

"Don't apologize. I'm happy you showed me this. Sometimes I prefer to move unseen."

They entered the simple but clean space and descended the stairs. Eight staircases later, they branched off to the left and entered the main palace once again. A footman stumbled at the sight of her and bowed. She smiled, and they kept moving.

"You're going to have the whole place astir by the time the night is over," Loshika muttered out of the side of her mouth.

Dahlia's mouth watered as she sniffed fresh bread, savory herbs, and roasted meat.

Lo slowed and pointed to the double doors to her left. "The kitchen is in there."

"You don't want to go first?" Lia teased.

"It isn't right for someone of my station to precede royalty. In fact, I should not even be here."

Dahlia glanced up at her friend and squeezed her hand. "Just because we're surrounded by all this grandeur and in jewels does not negate the fact that you have been kind and honest with me since we met. I do not leave my friends behind for treasure or position."

Loshika's lips curled. "You're something else, *reilleve.*"

"So I've heard." She looped her arm through the healer's once again and pushed through the large doors.

It was almost comical how large the kitchen was. Sinks lined the parallel wall with a fireplace that she could fit her whole bed into at the end of the room. Four square iron stoves lined the same wall as the doors, with copper pots hanging from the ceiling. An immense rectangular butcher block—more like a table that could've sat eight people on each side—stood in the center with fruits and veggies hanging from the ceiling above it. Simple wooden benches sat under each side.

A maid spotted them first, squeaking and dropping a bowl. It clanged against the floor.

The head cook had his back to them, stirring something in a pot hanging from the hearth. He shouted something in Loriian but didn't turn away from his task. The maid curtsied and scrambled to pick up the empty copper bowl. More eyes fell upon Lia, and all productivity halted as they bowed. The cook growled something and spun around, his eyes widening a fraction.

"The first time that someone is gaping at you and not at my scars," Lo muttered, humor in her voice.

"My lady," he said in heavily accented common tongue. He sketched a low bow. "What do we owe this..." He trailed off, brow furrowing in thought. "...honor?"

She grinned at the cook and the rest of the staff. "The honor is all mine, master cook. I know the heart of every home or palace is the kitchen."

He blushed and pulled a towel from his pocket, dabbing his forehead. He waved it at the rest of the staff, who jumped back to work. The cook bustled from the far end of the room, his hands wringing the towel. "What can I assist you with, *reilleve?*"

"My healer and I have come for some dinner."

"I can send a plate to your room."

"That is kind, but I would prefer to eat my meal here and see your fine people at work, if it won't be too much of a bother."

His jaw dropped, and then he snapped it closed. "It's not a problem, my lady."

He pulled out a bench and dusted it off with his towel. Dahlia wrangled her skirt underneath the butcher block, and Loshika sat next to her. The cook started shouting directions in Loriian.

"What is he saying?" she whispered to Lo.

"To not disappoint the queen. I think he's going to bring the entire larder out for you."

That wouldn't do. "Master cook?"

He smiled at her. "Yes, *reilleve*?"

"It is late. We do not need anything fancy. You and your people have worked hard and deserve your rest. Some bread and stew will be sufficient."

"It shall be done."

In no time at all, a hearty stew was before each of them, with thick crusty bread and creamy butter.

"Thank you. And please don't pay any attention to us."

He nodded, and slowly went back to his pot in the fire.

Lia felt all the glances of the kitchen staff, but it didn't bother her. They were just curious. It was nothing malicious. They weren't looking for flaws. She drained her bowl of stew in no time and stared at the bottom in longing.

"Would you like more?" a boy of maybe fifteen asked, his voice cracking.

She grinned at him. "Yes, I would."

He refilled her bowl and placed it before her quickly. This time, Lia savored the soup, taking her time to observe the staff. There were only eight in the room, plus the cook. A skeleton crew, really. All were cleaning up for the night.

A maid scrubbed the other side of the butcher block, tossing furtive glances their way. Lia put her spoon back in the bowl. "What is your name?" she asked the girl.

The young giantess glanced around to make sure Dahlia was speaking to her. "Zadieve, but my friends call me Zadi."

"Zadi!" the cook admonished.

"—my lady," the girl tacked on.

"It's lovely to meet you, Zadi. Do you normally work in the evenings?"

The giantess tucked a lavender braid behind her ear. "Mostly. I have school during the day."

"Really? What is your favorite subject?" Lia asked, taking another bite.

"I like to draw and to read."

"I love reading as well. That's something we share in common. What kind of books do you like to read?"

That opened Zadi right up. She spoke about all the books she liked while cleaning. Others chimed in as they went about their chores. By the time Lia had finished her second bowl of stew, the anxious energy in the room had disappeared altogether.

She sopped up the broth with her last piece of bread and moaned when she popped it into her mouth. It was delicious.

"Would you like tea and something sweet to end your evening?" the cook asked, excitement on his face.

"As you would have it, I have a bit of a sweet tooth. Tell me, master cook, just what you have in store for us."

"I've been working on something new. I don't like

wasting food," he said. "So I've been experimenting with ways to use vegetables in cake."

"Truly?" She grinned at him. "It would be a marvelous invention to get children to eat their vegetables to be sure."

He hustled away from the butcher block and disappeared into the larder. He returned with a little bounce to his step and set two mini cakes on the table. They looked like ordinary spice cakes with swirling creamy frosting on top.

He handed both her and Loshika a fork. "Enjoy."

Lia stared at the cake. Even though it was a mini cake, it was still enough for at least four people. She glanced up at the cook and wiggled her brow. "I think you overestimate the size of my stomach. I couldn't eat all of this if I tried. Would you and your good people join us?"

The cook blinked repeatedly at her like he didn't understand her words. "You wish for us to eat with you, *reilleve?*"

"I wish to share cake amongst friends and compatriots of this palace. Would you do me the honor?"

The cook bowed low. "It would be our honor."

The kitchen turned into a flurry of movement as everyone got seated at the table. She scooped a morsel of cake onto her spoon and then pushed the cake to Zadi. Once everyone got a bit on their forks, she wiggled her brows. "Shall we all try it on the count of three?"

The cook translated for her, and smiles blossomed on everyone's faces.

"One, two, three!"

Dahlia shoved the cake into her mouth and her eyes

rolled back into her head. The cake was spicy and moist, with a hint of texture from the nuts. The sweet yet tangy frosting coated her palate. Lia wiggled her fork at the cook.

"You, sir, are a genius."

He beamed from ear to ear, crooked teeth displayed. "You like it, *sei*?"

"I do. Well done."

Lo nudge Lia's shoulder with elbow. "I think you just made that *vallos'* dreams come true."

Lia went in for another scoop as the kitchen staff continued to snack too. A fork war broke out between Zadi and the younger boy named Xides. The cook broke it up with a sharp word and a waved hand.

Leaning her chin in her hand, she soaked it all in. There was something so comforting to see the familiar in the unfamiliar. She'd traveled extensively with the troupe and her brother. It was a lesson she'd learned. No matter where you were, you could always find a bit of home if you searched.

The door swished open behind her and all color drained from the cook's face. The servants scrambled to their feet. Dahlia didn't even have to turn around to know who was there.

The king.

Too bad he'd missed dinner.

Chapter Thirty-Five

Neve

He'd finally made it back to his room, expecting to find a sleeping *valles*, but she was nowhere to be found. Neve had even removed all the pillows to make sure she wasn't hidden beneath them. The one thing he did find was her black diamond choker carelessly tossed onto the bed. He heard the message loud and clear. Lia wasn't pleased.

Asking the guards where the queen had disappeared to was humiliating in and of itself.

The entire walk down to the kitchen, he'd rehearsed what he'd say to her.

All of it fled his mind as he pushed open the door to find her sitting with the servants sharing cake with them like they were her friends. It was downright domestic. When was the last time he'd experienced such thing? It had been years. A thread of longing struck him. He was so tempted to sit down and join them.

Neve banished the thought.

The cook spotted him first, then all the servants bolted from the makeshift table, bowing and scraping. He nodded to them and stared at the back of his wife's head. She didn't even turn to look at him, and instead took another scoop of cake, licking at the frosting delicately like he wasn't even there.

Something about her little pink tongue flicking the white frosting caused him to snap.

He crowded into her space, catching her right wrist. He leaned over her shoulder and lifted her hand up until the piece of cake she'd been fondling neared his lips. She tipped her head back, her heavy weight settling against his chest, hazel eyes burning into him.

"My lord," she murmured, completely calm.

He wanted to ruffle her.

Neve flashed his fangs at her and stole her bite. Spice and creamy sweetness burst across his tongue. He nearly moaned. No wonder the *valles* had been eating the cake like she had. It was delicious. A wicked thought entered his mind. He flicked his black tongue out to lick her thumb.

She gasped, and he watched as the pupils of her eyes expanded.

Just what did that mean? He wanted to find out.

"Delicious," he said, holding her gaze. Pink dusted her cheeks, and she glanced away.

He'd won this round.

Releasing her hand, he stepped back and held his hand

out for Lia. "My lady, it is quite late." A politely worded command.

Her jaw tightened, but she set the fork onto the butcher block, giving the kitchen staff a brilliant but somewhat strained smile.

"Thank you for dinner and the treat. It was truly incredible."

Her healer slipped off the end of the bench, and Neve kept his polite smile firmly on his face when his wife turned her back to him and scooted down the bench in the opposite direction. He stayed where he was as she hopped off the bench and whispered something to Loshika, who firmly shook her head.

Dahlia's shoulders drooped but she recovered quickly, rounding the bench and then taking his hand. She waved to the kitchen staff while Neve tucked her petite hand into the crook of his arm. He guided her into the hallway. It was empty save a few guards stationed at the stairwells.

The silence stretched between them, and he found himself grinding his molars. Neve could *feel* how displeased she was with his presence. Even now, her fingers hardly even touched his sleeve, like she couldn't bear to touch him. It rankled.

Even so, he found himself slowing their pace and taking the long way back to the royal wing. His human was so expressive. A part of him wanted to know what she thought of his home. He cut through the Hall of Mirrors.

Her anger melted away, replaced by awe.

Neve stood a little taller, and slowed just a touch so she could absorb the beauty of the massive room. Floor-to-ceiling stained glass windows covered two walls, showing off the castle waterfall. The floor was made of large chunks of broken, antique mirror that reflected the grandeur around it. This room he reserved for gatherings for foreign delegations. While it was beautiful, it was incredibly distracting, and somewhat overwhelming for someone not used to all the reflective surfaces. It made it easy to overstimulate those who were hoping to manipulate him.

He gazed down at Lia's familiar head of rose-gold hair, and then to the ceiling, staring at their reflection. He really did look like a monster next to his little *valles*.

Beauty and the beast.

He blanched at the thought, and dropped his chin, picking up the pace. Dahlia wasn't beautiful. She was a pale-faced, fragile little human. Nothing more.

All too soon, they reached the royal wing.

He ignored the warriors stationed outside his chambers and swept inside. His *loviaye* dropped his arm like she'd been burned, and put the bed between them as he closed and locked the door.

She crossed her arms and lifted her chin.

Neve spared her one glance and meandered to the spirits on the mantel of the fireplace. He poured himself a lick and tossed it back, the alcohol burning down his throat and warming his stomach. Neve poured one more before facing Dahlia.

Dahlia hadn't moved. In fact, she looked ready for warfare.

Neve held his hand out. "Let's have it. You obviously have something on your mind."

"I'm fine."

He snorted into his glass and took another sip. It seemed females of any race seemed to use the same language when angry. "I can see it on your face, *valles*." He watched with intrigue as she wiped every bit of expression from her face. How did she do that? What good did she think it did when he'd already seen the emotion?

"You do not know me, my lord."

He chuckled and set his glass down on the round table next to the couch. Neve slung a hip against the arm and then crossed his feet at the ankles. He waved a hand at her defensive pose. "Then what is all this? You're upset with me. I would know why."

"I'm not."

"*Lies*. Do you think I haven't been studying your facial expressions and body language for the last month? Do you really think I would have let you anywhere near any of my people if I didn't feel like I understood you and your motivations at some level?" He pointed to her crossed arms. "You're standing like you're ready to go to battle. You wouldn't look at me in the kitchen, and you didn't take my hand until you *had* to. Godsteeth, *valles*, what is wrong?"

Dahlia dropped the mask, and her eyes narrowed. "You had your people dress me up like a doll and then paraded me in front of your council."

"Your ladies-in-waiting did a lovely job."

Color rushed into her face, causing the sprinkles on her nose to stand out more. "Then you all proceeded to speak in Loriian for hours while I sat on your lap!"

"Not everything is for your ears. Do you really think

we would trust a *saloes* so easily? One from our mortal enemy?" Neve shook his head. "You can't be that naïve."

She dropped her arms, and her fingers curled into fists. "I'm *not* naïve. You could have easily had the meeting without me there, but you chose to act as if you did. You didn't even grant me my own seat. It was meant as a humiliation. To show your power over your human wife."

He flinched, and pushed away from the couch. "Your own seat? I shared my throne with you!" His voice rose, and Neve bit off the angry shout. Yelling never solved anything and showed a coarse lack of self-control. "Are you really complaining about such an honor?"

She blinked at him. "An honor? What do you mean? Only children and whores sit on the laps of grown men."

Neve's jaw dropped. "You mean to tell me that *vallos* do not share their seats with their women in your culture?"

Her nose wrinkled. "Not usually. Unless it is to show the power they have over the woman, or it is a sexual act."

He pushed away from the couch and ran his hand through his hair. No wonder she was stiff the entire morning. It was like having a block of wood in his lap. "In my culture, it is a show of respect between partners—especially a king."

"Oh." She just stared at him.

"That's all you have to say?" he retorted. "Oh?"

"Yes."

The sparkling black choker caught his eye, and he picked it up from the comforter and let it dangle from his fingertips. "And this? What's this about?"

Her lips thinned. "Do you remember what you said to me this morning?"

"No. I hardly remember what I ate for luncheon."

Wrong thing to say. She tossed her hands angrily into the air and then stormed around the bed in a flurry of black silk and fur. He twisted to face her as she snatched the necklace from his grasp.

"You asked me to wear this for you at dinner. It was a very blatant command in front of your people. It's uncomfortable and heavy, but I wore the blasted thing all day. We're not friends or partners. You've been my enemy since you threatened me in that alcove, but I wanted to have a bit of peace." Her expression cracked. "Aren't you tired of fighting? So, despite you embarrassing me, I wore it as an olive branch." Neve's stomach dropped as tears filled her eyes. "You never showed up. I waited for hours. Loshika and I were starving."

"That's why you were in the kitchen."

She nodded and looked away, angrily brushing a tear off her flushed cheek.

His chest ached at the sight. He didn't like her tears. They ... bothered him. Even with all the trials they'd experienced on their travels, Dahlia had never once cried. Neve had done this. This was his fault.

"*Lo bietelle.*" I'm sorry.

"For what?"

"For causing you distress."

She glared at him. "I'm not distressed. I'm angry."

He sighed. "I'm just trying to apologize. Why are you making it so difficult?"

"Because you vex me."

He eyed his little bride. "The feeling is mutual, I assure you."

"Then why seek my hand?"

"To stop the bloodshed plaguing our nations for the last thousand years."

"Oh, is that all?" A beat of silence, and then her lips twitched.

He snickered, and she chuckled, which led to him laughing until his ribs complained. Neve wiped the corner of his eye and froze when the *valles* grinned up at him, her eyes sparkling. She'd never looked at him that way before. It stunned him. He felt like he could hardly breathe. Her laughter faded. He found himself cupping the back of her neck, his claws combing through the shiny curls draped down her back.

Once again, he fixated on her pink lips. His attention moved to her eyes. The pupils were wide once again. Neve scanned her face and leaned closer, testing a theory. He scented the air for fear.

Just a touch. And something far sweeter.

Desire.

Neve pressed closer, dropping his nose to the crook of her shoulder, following the sweetness up the column of her neck and behind her ear. His little *valles* shivered, and a wicked smile curled his lips.

Maybe the beauty favors the monster.

When did he start thinking of her as a beauty?

That thought alone had him pulling away. She blinked up at him and it took everything inside Neve not to lift her onto the bed and taste her skin. His mouth watered.

"*Qov.*" He turned his back on her and stalked to his

glass, tossing back the spirits. He faced Dahlia, hating how she'd erased every bit of softness he'd seen and felt in her body. The wall was back up.

"It's time for you to leave," she said, her voice just a touch lower.

Neve grimaced. This was what he really needed to speak to her about.

"About that ... I'm staying here, and so are you."

CHAPTER THIRTY-SIX

DAHLIA

SHE'D REFUSED.

She'd argued.

And finally, she compromised.

It was the smartest choice. Allium expected information, and Lia couldn't acquire it if the king thought she was a problem. But she couldn't give in that easily or he'd suspect something was wrong.

Dahlia slunk out of the dressing room in her leggings, wearing one of Neve's large black linen shirts. He stood before the fire on the opposite side of the room with his back to her.

She swallowed hard.

He only wore his leathers.

She paused by the bath to look at him. His shoulders were wide and muscular, leading down to a tapered waist that disappeared into the waistband of his trousers.

Bruises wrapped around his ribs, marking his velvety indigo skin. Scars marred his shoulders where his *caern'ye* used to be and cut across his chest. Someone had done their best to disfigure him, but it had the opposite effect.

He was massive, monstrous, and yet ... *appealing*.

The realization was a real problem. Lia couldn't afford to think her target was handsome.

Too bad his personality doesn't match.

She suppressed her snicker and padded over to the bed. She climbed up and sighed. Stars, the bed was the softest thing she'd ever experienced. Neve glanced over his shoulder, the gems along his tapered ears winking in the firelight.

"Heavenly, isn't it?" he murmured.

"Yes. It is." She plucked a pillow from the bed and tossed it at him. The king spun and caught it.

He looked at her in question. "What's this for?"

"For the couch." *Obviously.*

He stared at her for a beat before a low chuckle rumbled in his chest. Lia scowled as goosebumps broke out along her arms. He slowly prowled toward the bed. She knelt on the mattress, clutching a pillow to her chest like a bloody idiot.

The king tossed the pillow onto the bed and leaned closer, his palms flat against the comforter. "This is my room, *jaivelle*. I will be sleeping in *my* bed."

Her eyes widened. "No."

He grinned. "Oh yes."

"But a gentleman would give the lady the bed."

His smile turned utterly wicked. "But I'm not gentleman, am I, Dahlia? I'm the monster."

Lia swallowed hard and eyed the bed. It was enormous. There was more than enough room for the both of them, but... "Fine, but you sleep with trousers on."

He smirked. "I only ever sleep naked."

"You asked me to help you pull off this ruse." She stabbed a finger at him. "I'll pretend to be happily married to you so your people accept the match, but you sleep with pants *on*. Take it or leave it."

The insufferable male laughed at her. "Humans are such prudes. It is just skin."

"It was a whole lot more than that this morning," she blurted. Lia snapped her mouth shut and blushed.

Why would you bring that up?

Neve arched a black brow. "What was a whole lot?"

She refused to rise to the bait.

He snickered and pushed away from the bed. "Don't worry, *jaivelle*. I'll keep my *sorav* far away from you."

"*Sorav*?" she questioned, sitting on her bottom to watch him move toward the shower room.

The king paused at the door and winked at her. "Use your imagination. I'm sure you'll figure it out." He disappeared into the shower room and closed the door.

Dahlia stared to the right for the longest time. Had she really just asked him that?

Imbecile.

Lia scrambled for the pillows, burying her mortification.

SHE LAY ON HER BACK WHEN THE KING CAME OUT of the shower room. She didn't look away from the ceiling as he moved into the wardrobe. Her nerves were tightly strung. She'd never spent the night with a man.

A *vallos*, as the Loriians liked to say.

She pulled the covers up to her chin as she heard him leave the wardrobe and fiddle around with the fireplace on the right side of the room. The light grew bright, but still she didn't look. Her pulse galloped as he paused at the bottom of the bed before chuckling.

"Do you think you could make a bigger pillow wall between us?"

"I could try," she croaked.

The bed dipped, but she still refused to look away from the ceiling. Neve's head entered her vision as he leaned over the pillow wall.

"Calm down," he groused. "I'm not going to molest you in the middle of the night."

"You mean like you did this morning?"

He lifted his brows. "I didn't know you were here, and again, it's *my* bed."

She reached up and flicked his nose. "That side is yours, my lord. This side is mine."

He shook his head and disappeared from view, the mattress jiggling as he got comfortable. Lia swallowed hard and tried to calm her nerves. It wasn't as if the king found her attractive. She tipped her head and watched the flames dance behind the bathtub. Much bigger flames.

He'd stoked the fire.

"Thank you," she whispered, tracing on of the scars on her palms. It had become a habit over the last week.

"For what?"

"For adding wood to the fire."

A pause. "I now know how fragile you are. I won't have the queen getting sick because she's not warm enough."

An insult, but she'd take it if it meant she stayed warm.

Eventually, her anxiety abated, and fatigue crashed down upon her. Lia closed her eyes and slept.

SHE WAS SO BLOODY WARM.

Dahlia snuggled closer to the furnace and dozed.

Rosemary. Yum.

Her furnace snored softly, and Lia's brows furrowed. That wasn't right, was it? Slowly, she opened her eyes, blinking blearily, early morning light just outlining the indigo chest she was plastered against. She gaped at her hand, which was pressed against the king's pec, his piercing tickling the center of her palm.

Ever so slowly, she turned her neck and inwardly groaned. Somehow, she'd burrowed under the pillow wall, which was still intact, and cuddled the Frost King during the night.

Lia faced forward, noting the large bicep under her cheek. How the devil was she supposed to get out of this without waking Neve up?

Carefully.

She lifted one finger at a time from his chest and peeled her palm away from his heated skin. Next, she untangled her legs from his, freezing occasionally as his breathing changed. Lia inched her legs underneath the pillow wall until she could roll onto her belly. Sweat dotted her forehead as she stared at the king's bruised ribs.

Now all she had to do was slither away.

It took an eternity to wiggle her way back to her side of the bed.

Heart pounding, she stared at the ceiling, feeling sick. What if he'd woken up to her plastered to his side? She wouldn't have lived it down. Neve snorted in his sleep, and she peeked over the pillow wall. He rolled toward the door, his back to her.

There was no way she'd be able to go back to sleep.

Lia slipped out of bed and crept to the shower room.

She'd take this to her grave.

Chapter Thirty-Seven

Dahlia

It had been three weeks since that first night.

And she was no closer to escape.

No closer to seeing her brother or saving her mum.

Each morning since, Lia found herself on the wrong side of the pillow wall and had to sneak her way back to her own side. Luckily for her, the king was a deep sleeper, and she'd become an expert in slithering away undetected.

Their campaign of wooing the people had a rocky start.

The first town they visited, the clan leader's daughter had dropped a dish of live eels into her lap. Lia had not taken it well, much to the amusement of the giants around her. She'd launched up from her chair, tossing eels in all directions.

At least she'd been able to laugh about it after the fact,

even though she knew the giantess had done it on purpose. Dahlia had known many mean-spirited women in her life; she could spot them in the crowd. By the sultry looks the giantess sent the king all night, Dahlia wondered if she'd been a lover, or just plain jealous.

Either way, it led to eels in her lap, but it could have been a dagger to the back, so she took it as a success.

Her time in the palace was spent carefully questioning her ladies-in-waiting to gather information on the king, his sister, the council members, high-ranking warriors. Very quickly, she noticed the areas of the palace the warriors kept her away from. They didn't want her venturing to the deep below, but that was negated by using the servants' passages.

Whenever she could, Lia slipped away and made friends with the staff, feeling more at home with them than any of the highborn. Already, she'd made friends that she truly cherished, and trusted. No one had ratted about her exploration even if they'd seen her. They sent the warriors in all sorts of directions.

One thing she learned quickly, gossip was currency.

She learned all sorts of sordid details from the servants that would have her ladies-in-waiting blushing. Dahlia wrote to the queen weekly in a way that a daughter would to a mother. She knew the letters were being read. She hadn't had one missive from Allium as of yet. Perhaps the Haunt weren't even allowing them to be sent. Still, she waited for the help the queen had promised.

Lia tried not to worry herself sick. She'd penned a letter to Cosmos but had no way to get it to him. She needed to find a courier outside of the palace, and that could take some time. Plus, even if it got to him, there was no way to guarantee he'd have the funds to get something back to her.

Even though the palace was impossibly large, it felt like the walls were shrinking in on her each day. Her only reprieve was when she went to the markets. Her *astrylle* always waited outside, large golden eyes calm and soothing.

She'd named her beastie Serenity.

She always brought treats for the massive snow owl. The owl had even begun to allow Lia to pet her head and scratch her beneath the beak.

Serenity soared through the air like a silent protector as Lia walked through the streets, her guards trailing behind her. At first, they'd bothered her, but she'd gotten used to their presence. She waved to the cobbler, whose craggy face cracked into a grin as she passed.

The market felt like home. At first, everyone had been stiff, but now they accepted her. All it had taken was a few compliments and genuine questions about their craft. It was amazing what personal interest could do.

Yeasty bread perfumed the air, haggling merchants argued with customers over prices, and colorful fabrics waved gently. She paused near the tanner as a familiar tune caught her attention. Dahlia cocked her head and pushed down her fur-lined cloak, scanning the area for the musicians. She couldn't spot them through the crowd.

She wove through the people, smiling as she went until she found the troupe. A group of five giants sang a jaunty tune that she remembered as a child. Lia clapped with the crowd until they finished. The shortest giant strummed a soft ballad on his *rombye*, which looked much like a guitar but had a deeper sound. He began to sing, and Dahlia closed her eyes, savoring the song. She lost herself to the music, tears pricking her eyes, the harmony vibrating through her whole body.

When she at last opened her eyes, the giant playing knelt before her.

"*Lae reilleve*, you bless us with your music."

She snapped her mouth closed, heat rushing to her wet cheeks as she realized she'd been singing with him. All eyes were on her.

"Excuse me for my presumptuousness," she replied, feeling all the eyes on her keenly. She wasn't shy when it came to performing for a crowd, but this wasn't her performance. She'd interrupted their music.

He shook his head. "The song spoke to you. It reached out and touched your soul. Music is to be shared, no?"

She smiled and pulled coins out of her pocket. She dropped them into the open case at the troupe's feet. "Thank you for sharing your song with me. It is I who is blessed."

"Will you sing one more with us?" he asked.

Dahlia almost said yes, but paused when she swore she saw Jekket move through the crowd. She shook her head no and moved toward where she'd seen the Giver's second in command. He was nowhere to be found.

Had she imagined him?

SHE WAS LIGHTER THAN SHE'D BEEN IN DAYS.

Lia practically skipped through the palace. She'd lost her guards somewhere along the way and had snuck into the nearest servants' staircase. Once she'd hit the laundry, Dahlia had stripped out of her finery and dressed in her leathers, linen shirt, vest, and boots. All she had to do was bring a few treats from the kitchen, and a few of Serenity's discarded feathers, and the laundry staff kept her secret.

Tonight, she was getting to the lower levels.

She'd heard that the training grounds were below, along with the stables. She still hadn't abandoned her plan of escape, but she needed a war horse.

Getting down to the lower levels was tricky.

The security tightened, but no one was looking for a small woman. It was easy to go unseen.

That was until the last checkpoint, where it opened onto the waterfall and the endless staircase. At least, that's what she'd heard.

Lia lurked in the shadow of a column, watching for warriors stationed at the entry point to the cavern. There wasn't any way to go about it but to just walk through. She was the *reilleve*. They had no reason to detain her, and Neve was dealing with a skirmish and was out of the city. They wouldn't be able to stop her.

She exhaled, and then stepped into view.

Immediately the warriors spotted her. They waited as she sauntered toward them, a smile on her face.

"Hello," she said. "I hope you *vallos* have a good evening."

As she went to step past them, a spear blocked her way. She stared at the iron weapon, before drawing herself up to her full height to glare at the warrior who dared block her. He blinked slowly at her, but didn't relent.

"Get out of my way, warrior."

He held firm.

"Are you denying your *reilleve*?" she asked softly.

He wavered, and the guard behind him shot off in Loriian. It sounded like a warning.

The warrior withdrew his spear and bowed low.

"Good choice."

Heart pounding, she strode past them, trying not to sprint away lest they drag her back. The thunder of rushing water grew louder and the light brighter. She slowed as she reached the end of the raw stone corridor and gaped like the peasant bard she was.

It was a massive cavern that seemed like it had no end. Weak sunlight peeked in from above, the gems sparkled in the light and prisms reflected off the waterfall that flowed down like an icy sheet in the center. A stone staircase was carved into the walls, wide enough to fit twenty giants shoulder to shoulder.

Lia stepped onto the stairs, keeping close to the wall as she descended. She shivered at the cold air that cut through her linen shirt, but kept moving. When would she get another chance like this? She couldn't even understand how the architecture worked, but it was a wonder that took her breath away.

She picked up her speed as she passed an exit with several more guards stationed there. She glimpsed several surprised faces as she jogged down the stairs. Word would be teeming in the palace about her little adventure soon enough. She wanted to get closer to the edge and look down, but there was no railing, and the idea of falling wasn't one she relished.

A prickling started between her shoulder blades, and she glanced over her shoulder.

No one was there.

Her calves burned but she kept on, air sawing in and out of her lungs. Just as she was covered in sweat and about to give up, she spotted the bottom. The great waterfall thundered into a massive round pool at the bottom. She leaned against the wall and caught her breath for a few moments, watching the water.

It didn't rise.

An underground river?

That was the only thing that made sense.

She shuddered as she thought about the frozen lake outside. No doubt this waterfall fed the lake. If someone fell in, they were dead. There was no coming back from that.

The feeling of being watched once against assaulted her.

She glanced up and down, seeing no one.

Dahlia pushed away from the wall, her sights set on the light shining through the waterfall on the other side.

The last exit. What lay beyond? What was hiding down there?

A hand wrapped around her bicep and yanked her backward. Dahlia cursed as she spun to face her attacker. Lumi stood over her, her face a mask of rage.

"Spying as soon as my brother turns his back!"

Oh no.

Her fight-or-flight instinct kicked in, and she'd always been scrappy. Lia slammed her fist into Lumi's stomach, surprising the giantess. She grunted, releasing Dahlia, doubling over as Lia shook her hand out. It was like punching a wall.

"Just exploring," she grunted.

Get out of here while she's distracted.

She leapt down two stairs at a time. The hair raised along her arms as a growl sounded right behind her. She wasn't going to make it. The exit was still too far away.

Lumi grabbed her braid and yanked. Dahlia yelled as pain assaulted her scalp, and grabbed at the back of her head.

"I'm not done with you," Lumi growled.

Get the higher ground.

Instead of pulling away, Dahlia spun and whipped around the giantess. Lumi backhanded her across the face. Pain exploded behind her eyes. The world tilted, but she fell backward onto the stairs, her braid still in Lumi's grip.

The waterfall thundered in her ears, the edge way too close.

Run.

As if the giantess heard her thoughts, she grinned and yanked Lia by the hair toward the edge.

No.

Dahlia yanked the blade she'd stolen from the kitchen from inside her shirt, sliced off the end of her braid, and kicked the giantess in the knee. Lumi stumbled backward, holding four inches of her braid. Her stomach dropped as the giantess teetered on the edge, her black eyes round.

Don't let her die.

Lia lunged forward and grabbed the front of Lumi's dress and hauled her forward, away from the edge. The giantess dropped to her knees, and Dahlia scrambled back until her spine met the curved stone wall. She held the blade out in front of her. They both panted for breath as shouts below finally registered. Warriors sprinted up the stairs, but Lia didn't look for them. She didn't dare tear her watering eyes from Lumi.

The giantess slowly lifted her head and locked eyes with Lia. "Why?"

"Because you're not my enemy."

Lumi stared hard, and Lia tensed, ready to sprint down the stairwell despite how the world was still tilting and it felt like she'd throw up at any moment.

"*Reilleve! Reilleve?*" A warrior knelt next to her, his faced creased in concern. His hand hovered over her, like he didn't want to touch her. "What can I do?"

"Help me up," she slurred.

He reached for her knife, but she pulled it away from his grasp and shakily shoved it back into the sheath she'd made to sit inside her breast band.

Lia spared a glance at Lumi before she took the warrior's arm and he helped her descend. Her right eye had already swollen closed, and throbbed painfully. They entered the last illuminated corridor. The guards looked horrified, but she nodded to them, and smiled despite how much it hurt.

"We'll send someone for your healer," the warrior said, the words heavily accented.

The short stone hallway opened up to another immense cavern. Lia grinned when the scent of horseflesh, hay, and fresh air teased her nose.

She'd finally found it.

To her left, war horses pranced in their paddocks. Toward the mouth of the cavern were *rukhals* grazing out in the open. To her right, warriors were training. Giants stopped their tasks and gaped.

"There's a place to sit over here."

"No," she muttered. "I want to see the horses."

A long pause. "As you wish, *reilleve*."

It was a short wobbly walk to the paddock, but worth it, especially when Lia spotted a familiar coat.

"Anwen!" she called.

The warrior whistled, the sound about splitting her head, but it worked. The war horse lifted his head, ears twitching, before the great beast spotted her. Dahlia tried to whistle as he raced toward her, tail lifted in the air.

She released the warrior and climbed up the first rung of the paddock fence, wobbling slightly.

"I don't know about this, *reilleve*. You're bleeding."

"Am I?" She wrapped one arm around the beam, and gingerly touched her face where it hurt the most. She pulled her fingers away and stared at all the blood on her fingers. That wasn't good.

Anwen slowed almost to a stop, just out of reach. She

switched arms, holding on with her right and holding her left hand out flat. "Hello, beautiful," she murmured, the words feeling garbled in her mouth. "Did you miss me?"

The horse snuffled her hand before nudging her palm with his downy nose. This was exactly the break she'd needed. Stealing a trained warhorse wasn't the best idea, but neither was fist-fighting a giantess, and she'd survived that.

Barely.

He pressed his head into her chest and she scratched his ear, smiling when he nosed her pocket.

"How did you know?" she whispered. Lia pulled her arm back and slipped a mangled carrot from her leathers and held it out to him, clinging to the fence as the world tilted again. "Sorry it's not much."

He took the vegetable, crunching on it happily.

"You know he's trained to snap your fingers off, right?" a familiar female voice drawled.

Dahlia closed her eyes. *Lumi.*

"I'm not sure you should be here, my lady," the warrior practically growled.

Lia slowly turned her head to see her sister-in-law out of her good eye. Lumi limped, leaning heavily on another warrior.

"What do you want?" she sniped, petting Anwen, her head feeling like it was about to crack open.

Lumi already cracked you open.

A delirious laugh caught in her throat.

The giantess slumped against the fence, sweat coating her forehead.

Lia waited for the spew of hatred, but it never came.

"He likes you." A perplexed statement.

"Anwen likes my treats."

Lumi frowned. "You shouldn't spoil him. He needs to be in top shape."

Dahlia hugged his face, pressing a kiss onto the tan star between his eyes. "One carrot won't hurt him."

Lumi huffed, but kept silent.

Lia hated the tension between them. She didn't understand why the giantess hated her so much. She'd hardly had any contact with her.

Be brave. Show no fear.

"Why do you hate me?" she asked outright, fighting to keep her good eye open.

Lumi chuckled and turned her attention on the rest of the herd. "Because you represent all that is evil in the world."

"That's a little dramatic, don't you think?"

The giantess snarled, her black gaze seeming to be on fire. "*You* are the reason I've lost both parents. *You* are the reason my brother is maimed. *You* are the reason our people have suffered. *Saloes* are the blight on this world."

Dahlia let the vicious words slide away. They weren't really meant for her. They were the culmination of Lumi's pain. "And what about you?"

Lumi frowned. "What?"

"What have your people done to mine?" She swallowed hard as old memories surfaced past the pain. "When something goes wrong, do you know who is always blamed first along your borders? The *saloes*. Do you know who gets beaten to death for the smallest crime while giants are given only a reprimand? Humans. You are not the only one to have suffered pain and loss at the hands of hate and prejudice. Stop acting like it."

Her heart raced as the giantess growled, glaring at her. It would be so easy for Lumi to break her neck.

"You speak as if you've experienced these pains yourself."

Lia's pulse leapt, but she shrugged, petting the horse. "I feel what my people feel."

Lumi swung her leg over the fence and *tsk*ed. "That's not really an answer, *saloes*."

"Do you want to tell me about your loss?" The giantess snapped her mouth shut. "That's what I thought."

"I could have pushed you over the edge," Lumi whispered.

"You were going to." Her heart lurched at the thought. "I saw it on your face."

"I would have died if you hadn't pulled me back." The giantess met her gaze steadily. "I was convinced you were causing mischief, spying for our enemy, and you were what? Just trying to visit your horse?"

Her heart leapt. That was exactly what she was doing. "Something like that," Lia muttered.

Lumi swallowed hard, her black eyes seeming glassy. "You brought the beast a bloody carrot. I am a fool. I almost committed a crime I could never come back from. You kept me from that. I deserve to have fallen."

Lia didn't answer. It wasn't her place to condemn the giantess. The world tilted again, and Lia closed her good eye and hung on to the fence.

"You saved me. I owe you my life." A pause. "Don't go to sleep."

Lia opened her eye at Lumi's sharp tone. "My head hurts."

"I should say so. You hit your head on the stairs. Your blood is ... garish."

"Yeah? How's your knee?" she slurred again, Lumi swimming in and out of focus.

"It's still swelling as we speak. You've crippled me. You have more fight than I anticipated."

"Is that a good thing or bad thing?" Stars, all Lia wanted was a nap. Her head was so heavy.

"Good. You can't be weak if you're the queen of the Frost Throne. I didn't smell fear on you once."

Lia laid her throbbing cheek against her arm, ignoring Anwen's little nudges, or how he nibbled at her damp shirt. A chill ran through her body, and she shrugged her left shoulder. "Fear wakes me up. At some point, you must decide if you're going to let fear rule you. You can run, but the problems and fear will just follow you. Better to meet it head on so it's not a surprise." She rubbed the tip of Anwen's nose with the tip of her pointer finger. "Will we ever have to do this again?"

The giantess grunted. "No."

"Why?"

"Does the why matter?"

"Yes."

Lumi sighed. "Because as much as I hate the thought of you here in my home, I would not hurt my brother. And now I owe you a life debt."

Lia scoffed. "He hates me as well."

"Maybe, maybe not. Either way, you were his choice, and I will not undermine him. There are many who already do. I won't allow it to be me *ever* again."

"He's lucky to have such devotion."

The giantess eyed her. "And who are you loyal to?"

Lumi is trying to interrogate you. Tread carefully. "I'm loyal to peace and my family." *Truths.*

"What if it comes down to one over the other?"

"Then I would have to choose peace, wouldn't I?"

Lumi pursed her lips. "That easy?"

Dahlia shrugged again. "It's never that easy."

Chapter Thirty-Eight

Neve

The palace was full of whispers, and he didn't like it one bit.

As he moved through the hallways of his courtiers, Bacti peeled away from the wall and fell in beside him, ignoring the look Flyka sent him.

"Back so soon, my lord?" he asked.

Neve grunted, glancing at the *vallos*. He was almost as tall as Neve, with light lilac-colored skin. Bacti was *pretty*, and annoying most days, but he was useful. His ties to the northern clans were important. "It was a land squabble. Easily handled."

"Good." Bacti laced his hands behind his back. "Both you and our *reilleve* have succeeded today."

Our *reilleve*. For some reason, Neve did not like the way he said it.

"What are you getting at?" Flyka asked, irritated.

"Only that she's proved herself your equal." Bacti bowed and walked away.

Neve glanced over his shoulder at the *vallos*, and then to Flyka. "What the *qov* is he talking about?"

"I don't know, and I don't like it," Flyka muttered.

He flat-out ignored the courtiers trying to get his attention. Neve picked up his speed, feeling that something was wrong. He practically bounded up the stairs to the royal wing, and growled when ten warriors milled about outside his chamber.

They bowed immediately, and Olwen stepped out of the crowd and touched Neve's shoulder. A slithering sort of fear curled in his gut and wound its way up into his chest.

"What's happened?" he snapped, feeling like he was about to come out of his skin. "An assassination attempt on the *reilleve*?" They'd already avoided two in the last three weeks.

Olwen sighed. "Dahlia is fine."

"But?"

His best friend winced, the scar on his face pinching. "She's been wounded."

Neve took one step forward, and Olwen's hand slipped to his chest, holding him in place. "What?"

"She's rough and concussed. It's a head wound, so it's bled a lot."

He pushed past his friend, through the group of warriors, and into their chambers. He stopped in his tracks, his stomach bottoming out. Dahlia sat at the foot of the bed, her legs dangling over the edge. Her left eye was completely swollen shut, and blood dripped from her right temple, down her cheek, chin, and neck. There was so much crimson. Loshika was stitching the wound, muttering softly when his wife's ladies-in-waiting murmured about fainting.

He wanted to break something.

Flyka stepped to his side and hissed. "Godsteeth, she took a beating."

Dahlia popped open her good eye and locked on to Flyka. "I thought I heard you," she slurred.

Neve moved to the side of the bed, staring down at the healer, who was tying a last stitch. "How bad is it?" he asked gruffly.

"Laceration to the head, black eye, possible fractured cheekbone, split lip, and a concussion." Loshika cut the thread and dropped the scissors and needle into an empty wooden bowl on the bed.

He scowled, and stepped between his wife's knees when the healer moved out of the way. Gently, he slipped his finger under her chin and tilted her face to the side to glare at her swollen eye that was a garish black, blue, and red. Humans were ugly when beaten.

"What happened?" he demanded.

She flinched. "Not so loud. My head feels like it's going to crack open."

He glanced over his shoulder at her ladies-in-waiting. "Were any of you there when this happened?"

All four shook their heads no.

Loshika pressed in on his left side and began cleaning the blood off her neck.

"And you?"

The healer didn't spare him a glance. "No, my lord."

He growled. "Can anyone tell me what the *qov* happened to my wife?"

Dahlia blinked her one open eye at him, her pupil blown wide. He frowned. She didn't smell of fear or desire. Why was her eye like that?

"Her pupil," he murmured.

"A side effect of the concussion, I believe," Loshika said softly.

"You believe?"

"I've been studying about *saloes* since she asked me to travel with her. It's not my specialty, my lord."

Fair, but frustrating.

Dahlia's head lolled back for a moment. "The light hurts."

"Dampen the lanterns," he commanded to his cousins.

They rushed to the lanterns, turning them down. His *valles* sighed, a half-smile on her swollen face.

"I want to sleep," she whispered, wavering slightly.

"No sleep," Loshika said sternly. "I don't know what will happen if she sleeps. If she's anything like our people, it can be dangerous." She finished cleaning up the blood. "I'll stay here for the night to care for her."

"I'm going to..."

Dahlia turned green a moment before she leaned forward and vomited all over his chest and down his trousers. Neve stared over the top of her head, trying not to breathe. His *niliave* continued to heave, emptying the contents of her stomach. He cupped the back of her neck and ran his thumb back and forth, not moving as she clutched his hips.

"It hurts," his wife moaned.

"Did you give her something for the pain?" he asked the healer.

"As much as I dare." Genuine worry and fear crossed the healer's face. "She's not well."

Dahlia began to shudder and lifted her head, wiping her mouth with the back of her arm. Tears dipped down her cheeks. "I just want a shower. I need the darkness. I want to be warm."

"I'm going to kill whoever did this," he promised, hating how vulnerable his *valles* was.

"Ha! Can't do that. You love her too much," Dahlia slurred.

Neve leaned down to stare at her one good eye. "Who do I love too much?"

"I can do it, my lord." Loshika set her rag down and made like she was going to push Neve out of the way.

He shook his head and carefully scooped up the *valles*. She moaned and clung to his soiled shirt. His questions would have to wait. Neve stepped over the puddle of vomit and strode to the shower room, kicking the door shut with his boot. He used his elbow to turn on the water. He waited a minute for the water to heat up and then carefully stepped into the spray.

The *valles* sagged against his chest. "My ears are ringing."

"A side effect of the concussion, I presume." He sat on one of the steps, the water soaking his clothes and dripping down his face. Neve stared down at the top of her head and just held her. She shivered and cuddled closer.

He didn't know how long they sat there, but time stretched on, rain falling around them.

She stirred, face creasing. "I feel sick."

He managed to help her sit up on his knee, before she leaned over his arm and heaved once again. He pulled her loose braid over her shoulder and snarled. It was four inches shorter, the ends all jagged. Neve swallowed hard and ran his claws over the end of her hair and rubbed her back gently.

Someone had mangled her hair. While Dahlia was an oddity, her hair had always been exotic and stunning. One of the things he found beautiful about her bizarre form.

"It's fine," she rasped, as if she could feel his anger.

Neve glared over her head at the wall. It was *not* fine.

"I did it myself."

His eyes widened as she sat up and leaned her good cheek against his shoulder. "What do you mean, *jaivelle*?"

"She grabbed my braid and dragged me toward the waterfall. I had to cut it."

A chill ran down his spine. Bile burned the back of his throat. He was going to be sick. Neve closed his eyes and breathed through his mouth. They were going to toss her over the ledge. It was a heinous death only meant for the worst of traitors.

Remorse and loathing weighed heavily on his shoulders. "*Lo bietelle. So* sorry." While he hadn't wanted her in his life, he hadn't wished for her to be attacked and almost pitched into the waterfall and drowned.

"It's not your fault. Your sister and I figured it out."

He stiffened, her words echoing in his ears. "What did you just say?"

Dahlia sighed. "She's okay. Don't worry."

Neve began to shake. His own flesh and blood had done this.

His *niliave* leaned back in his arms, her head resting in the crook of his right elbow. She reached up, trailing her fingers along his clenched jawline until she could cup his cheek. Her one good eye focused on him.

"I'm not sorry I damaged her knee."

He blinked at her, and then burst out laughing. It was the last thing he'd expected her to say. She winced as his laughter jiggled her body. He tried to push it down, and leaned away from her. Neve tipped his head back, her fingers sliding from his cheek. Immediately, he missed her touch.

A lump rose in his throat at the realization.

This wasn't supposed to happen.

He glanced away from the *valles*, closing his eyes and focusing on the water dripping down his face. Neve could not allow these feelings to grow. Dahlia was just a pawn to secure his kingdom. Nothing more.

Steeling himself, he shoved the feelings away. While he knew she was at the waterfall, he didn't know *how* she got there. Had his sister coerced Dahlia there? Or was she sneaking around the palace in his absence? Either option disturbed him. He couldn't trust anyone.

"We need to get you out of these filthy clothes," he said woodenly. "You stink."

"True."

Despite her modesty, his little *saloes* didn't complain when he sliced the clothes from her body instead of trying to wrangle the wet material from her skin. He eyed the makeshift sheath and blade strapped between her breasts. He reached for the knife, but Dahlia closed her fingers around it.

"It's *mine*."

He scanned her swollen face and nodded. She could have it if it made her feel safe. Not that it would be able to do much damage. He'd have to get her a proper blade...

Neve gently laid her on the wide stone stair that served as a bench before unwinding the rest of her braid. She leaned her cheek on her arms, the expanse of her back on display. He worked soap into a rag and began cleaning her hands. Silver blood and dirt had caked beneath her torn fingernails. He passed over the emerald ring she always wore and he frowned.

Had a lover given her the trinket? Had she left behind someone who was the world to her? Was that why she wore it day in and out?

Unease and a thread of jealousy wormed its way around in his gut.

Why did he care if she wore a ring from another man?

Because you want her for yourself.

Neve banished the thought and set the rag down. He laved soap into her hair and let the water rinse it away. Purple bruises dotted her creamy skin, and he ground his back molars. All he wanted was to press kisses to each and every one.

Get yourself together.

"Stay there," he muttered.

She huffed. "Not moving."

He quickly stripped his own filthy clothing from his body and threw it out of the shower with a wet slap. He scrubbed the lingering scent of vomit from his body, his gaze latched on to Dahlia's back, particularly the dimples right above her buttocks.

Why did she stir him? Why did he want to lave every hollow and divot with his tongue?

Neve glanced away, feeling disgusted with himself.

She's hurt, you lout.

He stormed out of the shower, dripping water everywhere, and yanked a towel from the shelf in the toilet room. He wrapped it around his waist, grabbed another towel for the *valles*, and then stomped over to the water controls, turning the shower off.

Reaching the *saloes*, he gently helped her stand, swaddled her in the fluffy towel, and carried her out of the room. Flyka, Olwen, and Loshika all sat near the fire across the room. The healer hopped up as he prowled to Dahlia's side of the bed. Loshika pulled back the covers and Neve gently laid her down, pulling the covers up to her chin.

She blinked up at him and he moved to step away when she caught his hand. He stared down at his *niliave*.

"Don't leave me."

Her simple plea struck him right in the chest.

His mouth went dry, and he could feel all eyes on him. "I won't," he muttered.

Neve couldn't have left her even if he tried.

Chapter Thirty-Nine

Neve

He cracked his eyes open.

The sun hadn't yet risen and there was a warm body snuggled next to him.

Neve rolled his head to the right and stared down at Dahlia pressed to the right side of his body. She'd healed slower than he'd liked in the last week, but at least the swelling had gone down around her eye, so she had her vision back. The skin beneath her eye was an ugly yellow-green, but the *valles* had assured him it was normal.

Her assurance had plagued him. How did she know how quickly a black eye healed? It's not as if she was a street urchin looking for fights. He had a feeling it had something to do with her brute of a father.

Who hurt you?

He rolled his head back to the middle of his pillow and closed his eyes. This was his favorite part of the day.

He had always been an early riser, the complete opposite to the *valles*, not that she knew that. Every day for the past month, he'd pretended to be sleeping when she awoke and slunk away in shame.

He understood her feelings. If you didn't acknowledge it, then it wasn't real.

Liar, liar.

Neve's eyes popped open, and he stared down at his *niliave*, his hand playing with the tips of her soft rose-gold hair. The bloody fact of it all was that he liked waking up with her in his arms. In sleep, she was soft and pliant—not on guard like she was all the time. Sure, she'd softened since she'd left Florrant, but it wasn't enough.

He wanted ... more.

And yet, how could he take more when he didn't trust her?

Dahlia hadn't done anything outright dangerous, but she was always going missing and coming up somewhere she wasn't supposed to be. She'd made loyal friends all over his castle, servants and highborn alike, but she kept him at a distance...

Except in her sleep.

Even now, her right hand rested over his upper heart as if she were seeking to be closer to him.

She stirred, her lips falling open as she pressed her cold toes against his calf. Neve wrinkled his nose. That was one thing about humans he'd learned rather quickly. Their hands and toes were *always* cold. At least Dahlia's were.

He sighed, hoping she didn't wake soon.

Once his wife was out of bed, it meant he'd have to endure the day.

It was Lumi's judgment day.

As soon as Neve could leave Dahlia once it was safe for her to sleep, he had gone straight to his sister. She had been laid up in bed with a knee so swollen it looked fake. Lumi hadn't begged or cried when he told her she was to be locked in her room until judgment could be passed on her behavior.

Lumi had admitted everything to him outright, no embellishments.

His sister had almost killed the *reilleve* and Dahlia had saved her anyway.

Today, his sister would be punished.

His breath sped up and his hearts began to race. Neve closed his eyes and tried to calm down. Lumi was his closest family member. For her crime, she could be executed or banished. Despite how difficult she was at times, he still loved her.

The fingers on his chest flexed, and the feeling of being watched washed over him. He cracked open his right eye and Dahlia stared up at him, expression sleepy but serious. She didn't say anything for a long moment, nor did she scuttle away like she normally did.

Instead, she began to hum and then sing.

Neve closed his eyes and listened to her song. His hearts slowed and so did his breathing. The tension fled his body, and he opened his eyes. His *niliave* stared up at the ceiling, lost to her song. He watched her face as she sang the haunting melody. The last note hovered in the air, and he kept silent for a minute longer, not wanting to break the spell.

"Lovely," he whispered.

Her attention darted to his face and her cheeks pinked. "My mother used to sing it."

He had a hard time imagining Allium comforting any child, but he was happy that Dahlia had received that much from her mother at least. She tried to wiggle away, but he settled his right hand around her back and on her hip, keeping her in place.

"What are you doing?" she asked, her voice a little higher.

"Resting, *jaivelle*. Lie here and watch the sun rise over the lake with me."

She huffed, but stayed in place. "I'm sorry for sleeping on you. I promise not to do it again."

He arched a brow. "Dahlia, let's stop pretending you haven't been sneaking away from my side of the bed for the last several fortnights, shall we?"

Her eyes rounded comically, showing more of the white. "You knew?"

Neve grinned. "I'm an early morning riser."

Her cheeks turned a bright red. She looked up at him sheepishly. "I'm sorry."

"Don't be. If I had minded, I would have deposited you on the couch."

The sun crested the mountains behind the palace, the ice and snow shimmering and sparkling outside. The majesty of his kingdom still took his breath away.

"It's magical," Dahlia whispered.

He looked down at the *valles* and couldn't help but agree. She caught his look and stared. His gaze lazily trailed the slope of her nose, the curve of her cheek, the winged bow of her upper lip. She licked her bottom lip, and heat curled low in his belly.

"Can I touch your face?" he whispered, giving into his longing.

She blinked slowly but nodded. Neve rolled toward her slightly and cupped her face. His palm covered her entire cheek, temple, and ear. He ran his fingers through her wavy hair, tracing a nail along the rounded shell of her ear devoid of any piercings. She shivered, and he paused. What was that? Neve did it again, smiling when goosebumps broke out along her arms. His little *niliave* had sensitive ears like Loriians.

Next, he sketched her arched brows and along the slope of her nose. He twitched when she inhaled sharply as he brushed his thumb along her bottom lip. Why the devil did he want to bite it? His people didn't mate with their mouths like *saloes*. The idea should have disgusted him, but all he wanted was to press his lips against hers. To *kiss* her.

A rumble started in his chest, and she placed a hand over his upper heart. He glanced down at it as her fingers flexed. Was she trying to hold him back or urge him closer? The heat of desire grew inside him as his attention moved back to her lips.

He wanted, no *needed*, to taste her there. *Now.*

Neve leaned closer, and just before his lips touched her own, she placed her fingertips over his lips. He froze as she stared up at him without a shred of emotion. His chest seized, embarrassment crashing over him. Neve was acting like a youth coming into his first heat.

"I know today won't be easy for you," she whispered,

her eyes darting across his face. "I'm your friend, Neve." He closed his eyes, loving the way she said his name. "Trials can make people do things they wouldn't normally do."

His eyes snapped open. She thought he was trying to mate her mouth because he was worried about his sister and needed a distraction.

She's given you an out. Take it.

"You're right," he rasped.

He leaned away and flopped onto his back, tossing an arm over his eyes. *Qov*, he was an idiot. Why in godsteeth would he react in such a way by touching her like that?

Because you want your valles.

The covers rustled and he trapped the snarl in his throat as Dahlia scooted away, leaving his side cold. She cleared her throat, and he lifted his arm to find her sitting cross-legged next to him.

"What, Dahlia?"

She brushed a lock of hair behind her ear. "I was wondering if I could ask you a few questions." She puffed out her cheeks. "And my friends call me Lia."

Neve dropped his arm. *Lia*. He liked the way that sounded. "Of course, *Lia*."

"Why do you have so many piercings?" she blurted.

He sat up and scooted backward until his back hit the headboard. "In my culture, piercings represent many things." He touched the piercing toward the top of his long, tapered ear. "The flesh here is painful to pierce and takes a long time to heal. We can choose to pierce our ears there when we lose our parents, siblings, a mate, or children. It reflects our pain and the time it takes to heal from loss. These are permanent. We never take them out."

Neve touched the bottom stone. "Some celebrate accomplishments. The stones have different meanings. My largest black diamond is for when I became a warrior."

Lia nodded and gestured to his chest. "And those?"

"These are reserved for married *vallos*."

Her mouth dropped open and she swallowed hard. "Do married women have to get those too?"

He grinned, knowing exactly where her mind went. "No. Some *valles* choose to pierce their nose as a sign of being married."

She visibly wilted in relief. "So those are new? Did they hurt?"

"Not as badly as my mourning piercings."

Her attention returned to his ears. He could see her counting how many he had. Her lips turned downward. "Five?" she croaked.

"Yes. Three siblings and two parents." Each day he felt their loss. He had turned his emotions off to function. Lumi had raged at the world, drowning in her feelings.

She shuddered, understanding and empathy filling her face. "I'm so sorry. I know how painful that can be."

He cocked his head and really looked at his little human. Both of her parents were alive, and she was the only heir, and yet he could see that she felt his pain. Who had his *valles* lost?

"Next question," he finally said.

Lia nodded. "Do you have pupils like me?"

He smiled. "Yes. If you look close enough, you can see a slight difference in my eyes."

His *niliave* popped onto her knees and shuffled closer, leaning in. He widened his eyes and tried not to blink.

"I can see it." Her attention moved to his ears, but he was eyeing her freckles. Did they serve a purpose? Or were they there just to draw his eyes to her face?

"Can you see better in the dark?"

"Better than you, *sei*."

"Can I touch your ear?"

"Sure," he muttered without thinking. Just how many spots were there? It was like brown sugar had been baked onto her cheeks.

He jerked when she brushed the tip of his ear. Lia flinched and gaped at him.

"Did I hurt you?"

"No," he drawled, ignoring the heat flaring in his chest at her innocent touches. Just when he thought he'd break, she stopped fondling his ears and sat back with her hands on her knees.

He sighed. "Can I ask you a question?"

"Yes."

He tapped a claw on her legging-covered legs. "Why do you still cover yourself up? I know you're still wearing hose underneath your dresses."

She scowled. "How the blazes would you know that?"

"Because there is always a pair in the basket that the laundry maids collect."

Dahlia crossed her arms and glanced away toward the windows. "I don't know."

"It's just skin," he stated bluntly.

She frowned. "No, it's not. It's what has separated me from everyone else for years. It's what has made me undesirable to men, repugnant to my own queen, something to be scoffed at, and put me in danger. It's made me into a monster, not human."

"Like me."

"You're not a ... monster."

He arched a brow at her. "Am I not? By all accounts, since I look different than you, that makes me flawed."

Lia pursed her lips and hung her head. "I just want to be free of this curse."

"You can't change who you are. But you can learn to accept and love it. That is the only way you will ever be free."

"And your scars?" she volleyed back. "The ones you refuse to talk about. Are you free from them?"

He ground his back molars. She had a point.

She blew out a breath when he stayed silent. "We should probably get out of bed, no?"

His *valles* was shutting him out, but it was his fault.

Neve nodded. He'd let it go. And figure out how to talk about his scars somehow.

"I do have one more question for you."

He eyed her. "What?"

"Will you pierce my ear?"

CHAPTER FORTY

DAHLIA

THE TOP OF HER LEFT EAR THROBBED WICKEDLY.

Dahlia hadn't cried, but godsteeth it hurt to have it pierced for her mum, and yet it felt right. While her mum still breathed, she died that day of the Haunt attack. Her mind and body were broken and utterly irreparable. Some days, Lia wondered if it would have been easier to lose her mum altogether that day than to watch her fade into nothing – a shell with a spirit.

Her ladies-in-waiting had *ooh*ed over the simple amethyst stud on her ear as they dressed her for the judgment. They chose a black lace gown that hugged her curves, with lavender silk peeking out. A crown of black diamonds and amethyst was set upon her head that was so heavy it felt like it would fall off any second.

Despite the healing black eye, she looked like a proper queen.

What are you doing?

Playing queen wasn't going to save her mother.

She needed to kill the king. Dahlia fiddled with the ring on her middle finger.

Lia placed a hand over her belly, nausea rising at the thought. Neve wasn't good, but he wasn't evil either. The longer she stayed in this place, the more confusing everything got.

"Nerves, my lady?" Lo asked from the couch. "I have a tonic for that."

Dahlia shook her head and turned from the mirror. "No." *Just guilt.*

She ran her damp palms over her hips and padded over to the couch, leaning on the back of it, watching Brigit, Freya, and Alda embroider or knit. It was all so very domestic. Loshika glanced up from her book, a thin pair of spectacles on the tip of her nose.

"You're stalling, *reilleve.*"

Her friend knew her well. Over the last month they'd bonded over being the oddities among the Loriian court. Sometimes, she felt as if Loshika was the only one she could really trust.

"I know." She pushed away from the couch and faced the door. "I will see you when it is all done."

"Be strong, my lady."

Dahlia nodded once and strode to the door. She stepped into the hallway and was met with Eyri's endearing face. Some of her worry faded away at his small smile. He held out his bare arm and she took it, thankful to have a friend escort her to the throne room. It was one of the few places she still hadn't been.

"The king?" she asked.

"Already there." He squeezed her arm, leading her down the first staircase to the hallway of frosted windows, his long robe brushing her skirts. "You will need to walk through the *jaivelle* arch to start the proceedings. The king will welcome you to share his throne."

Her mind latched onto *jaivelle* arch. "What is a *jaivelle*?" she asked, nodding to familiar servants as they passed.

"Rough translation is something like a singing stone. If you run your fingers over the stone just right, it sings for you. The *jaivelle* is iridescent and looks delicate, but it's one of the strongest stones. Our people revere it as holy."

Dahlia swallowed past the lump in her throat. How many times had Neve called her that over the last month? Did he really mean it? Or was it a pet name Loriians used?

Eyri escorted her down several more sets of hallways until they reached the entry. She still hadn't gotten over the lavish columns and arched ceilings. He showed her to the right hallway, moving toward the mountains. The floor sloped downward and ended in a wide staircase.

She stumbled as a flashback of her fight with Lumi pushed to the forefront of her mind. Irrational fear tightened around her lungs.

"Are you alright?"

Swallowing hard, she nodded, and let Eyri pull her down the staircase. They reached the bottom, and it opened up into a narrow but tall cavern. Her jaw dropped as she stared at its beauty. A meandering onyx pathway wound upward through the center of the cavern, leading to an archway held up by ancient-looking marble columns. Iridescent crystals grew from the ground, the walls, and ceiling. They covered the archway, casting rainbows around the dim room from the skylight high above.

Flickering lanterns hung from some of the crystals, looking like fireflies.

It was raw, powerful, and otherworldly.

"Are you ready, *reilleve*?"

She nodded and squeezed his arm. "Just Lia to you."

They walked slowly along the black stone pathway through the *jaivelle* crystals. She longed to reach out and touch one to hear what it sounded like, but didn't dare. Even so, she could hear how their steps echoed around the room off the crystals. It was tinkling like bells.

A few lone notes slipped from between her lips, bouncing around the room in a melody. What would it be like to sing in a such a place? She imagined it would be better than performing in some of the best cathedrals.

She held her breath as they stepped up to the archway. Stone closed around them, forming a short hallway. Lia locked her expression in place as murmurs reached her. The short corridor ended and once again opened into a cavern, one that had been carved by Loriians. Shiny black stone with a view of *jaivelle* were carved into the starry sky above.

Hundreds of Loriians parted, and she swallowed at the amount of people watching her. Lia kept her head held high as she spotted Neve sitting on the great amethyst throne. He looked every bit the king with his royal black garb, deep blue-black hair woven into intricate braids and pulled back from his strong jaw. He sat tall with his legs braced apart, not a single emotion on his face. He was once again the cold king.

Dahlia wanted to turn tail and run.

He was fearsome. And he wasn't going to like what she had to say.

She glanced away from him, locking eyes with Lumi, who knelt before the dais.

The giantess dipped her chin, no malice but resignation on her face.

Lumi expects to die.

Eyri released Lia and bowed. "This is where I leave you, *reilleve.*" He left her at the bottom of the dais, and she stood there, not knowing what to do.

"Come, *lae reilleve,*" the king called.

So apparently she did need an invitation. Dahlia lifted the hem of her dress and ascended the five stairs to stand before Neve. He held out his hand and she took it. His warm touch curled over her shaking fingers and tugged gently. She let him reel her in and pull her onto his lap.

He leaned close, and brushed his lips along the junction between her shoulder and neck. "Lean back and relax, Lia," he breathed onto her skin.

Her body tingled, and she tried not to shift on his lap, but did what she was told. He lifted her legs behind her knees, and draped her legs over the arm of his throne. The whole affair felt too informal and scandalous, but she didn't fight him.

Her nerves ratcheted up a notch and she inhaled deeply through her nose, taking comfort in Neve's cedar scent.

Hundreds of eyes were on her, but she didn't buckle.

Sweat dripped down the back of her neck as a well-dressed warrior addressed the crowd and listed off Lumi's crimes.

"For these crimes against our crown and *reilleve*, Lumi, sister to the Blade of the Frost Throne, is sentenced to death or exile amongst the *saloes*. Unless someone speaks up on her behalf."

You could have heard a pin drop.

No one spoke up.

Lia waited for Neve to speak, and he said nothing.

This is wrong. You must speak up.

Dahlia waited one second longer before saying, "I'll speak on her behalf."

The king's thighs stiffened beneath her, but other than that, he didn't react. The warrior turned to the throne. "You wish to speak on behalf of your attacker, my lady?"

Swallowing hard, she found her voice. "Yes. Our dear Lumi has suffered much at the hands of *saloes*. My people caused this. I do not fault her for her rage and hurt. I don't believe violence is the answer to such problems, but sometimes it controls us, not the other way around. The punishment does not fit her crime."

Neve could have been a stone behind her.

"What would you wish upon her, *reilleve*?" the warrior asked.

She locked gazes with Lumi. "First, I wish for her to find peace." Murmurs broke out among the people. "Secondly," she continued over the whispers, "I wish for her to work along the southern borders, harvesting with the humans."

The crowd fell silent.

"Hard labor instead of execution or banishment, my lady?" the warrior questioned.

"Banishment to Astera is a death of its own. I want Lumi to learn how to control her pain and anger through hard work. But I also want her to see that not all *saloes* are evil."

The warrior bowed. "Very wise. What say you, *reillov*?"

Neve clicked his nails along the throne's armrest. "I support my *reilleve* in this decision. Let it be done."

The warrior picked Lumi off her knees and helped her limp through the crowd.

Lia watched her go, feeling no joy in her punishment. She prayed the king wouldn't rip her head off for sending his only family away. She scanned the people, looking for anyone who was disgruntled, and froze as she spotted a familiar face.

You.

Jekket—the Giver's right-hand man, stood in the crowd, staring straight at her. Her pulse galloped when he didn't look away, and a slow smile spread across his face. Either Allium or the Giver had finally sent the *help* they'd promised. She hadn't imagined him shadowing her journey.

The monsters had truly arrived.

And they were there for her.

Chapter Forty-One

SHE'D SPARED HIS SISTER.

Neve had been fully prepared to let the punishment take its course.

It had made him sick, but he couldn't play favorites.

The moment Lumi had been escorted out of the judgment chamber, he'd taken Lia and fled. As soon as they were away from prying eyes, he'd rounded on her.

Flyka and Olwen followed behind from a distance.

"Why did you do that?" he snapped.

She looked at him with shock written all over her face. "What?"

"Why? She deserved it."

Dahlia shook her head. "Do you hear yourself? That is the last of your family. How could you say such a thing?"

He stabbed a finger toward her eye. "Because of the marks that still cover your body. She told me everything. If you hadn't fought so fiercely, she would have murdered you." He ran a hand through his braids.

"It didn't come to that. We're both fine."

"Really?" he growled. "Because I've heard your nightmares, Lia." She snapped her open mouth closed and looked away. "Your body is healing, but what about your mind? You've hardly explored this week. Since you've arrived at the palace, there hasn't been a day you haven't poked around."

"Why are you angry at *me*? I saved her for *you*!"

He pressed into her space, his hand tangling in the hair at the nape of her neck. "I didn't ask you for that."

"But you wanted it all the same." She glared up into his face, defiant even when he glowered at her. "I would never part you with another family member." She reached up and touched the mourning piercing he'd given her earlier. "I found another solution. One where your sister can heal and become a better person. Where you don't have to say goodbye forever."

Emotion surged inside him, and he broke.

He grasped her chin and pressed his lips against her own. Hard.

It was foreign and felt wrong, but he didn't regret it. He stared wide-eyed at her. He didn't know what to do from here. All he knew was that he'd been obsessed with her lips from the first moment he'd taken one look at them.

She didn't move for a moment, and he pulled back, panting. "Show me," he rasped desperately. "*Seittae.*" Please.

Her eyes darted all over his face, before she grabbed a

handful of his tunic and lifted onto her toes, pressing her soft lips against his, sliding them back and forth in a teasing caress.

Pure bliss crashed over him. This was what he'd been missing. What he'd been craving for weeks. Neve shuddered, wanting to drown in the sensation. He threaded his fingers through her curls as one of her hands wandered down his chest.

It was heaven. It was hell. It was *everything*.

Her lips parted and she bit his bottom lip. Heat surged in his chest, and he released her chin, cursing and slamming his shaking left hand against the wall. She was so bloody soft it made him lose himself. It would be so easy to be too rough. She bit at him again and he growled.

Everything about Dahlia was delicate, but her little bitty bite? It stung and he *loved* it.

Neve tilted his head and nipped gently at her bottom lip, minding his fangs. A spark shot through him, thrilling at the way her breath stuttered and how she pulled him closer.

But when she opened her mouth and licked at him? He lost all sense.

She tasted like perfection. Ginger, and something sweet.

He pulled on her locks, dipping her head back against the wall. His left hand curled around her thigh, and somehow he found himself with her legs around his waist.

He blazed a path of kisses down the delicate column of her throat and laved her pulse with his tongue. Madness swirled in his mind; he wanted to lick every inch of her. She grabbed a handful of his braids and pulled him back to her sweet mouth. The heat of her body melded into his own and he shuddered when she flicked her tongue along his fang. He tipped her head farther back, tangling his rough tongue with her smooth one.

His left hand clenched on her thigh, his claws pricking the delicate material.

It would be so easy to tear the fabric from her body and claim her right here.

The thought was like a bucket of icy water.

He flinched, and pulled back with all the self-control he possessed.

Dahlia opened her eyes, her pupils wide. He inhaled deeply, and groaned at the sweetness of his *jaivelle*. Her crown was askew, her lips puffy, her cheeks flushed. He'd done that and it made him feel like a *qovving* king.

Her chest rose in deep breaths as they shared the silence. He stared into her foreign eyes, noticing flecks of gold in those green depths. He'd never thought *saloes'* eyes were anything but bizarre. But's Lia's? They were beautiful.

Slowly, lucidity returned to her gaze, and with it the scent of regret.

"Let me down, my lord."

His jaw flexed as she locked herself away, the placid mask sliding back into place. "Don't do that," he whispered gutturally. "Don't you dare retreat."

She released his braids, her gaze sliding to the side. "Please put me down."

Lia was shutting him out. He studied her for a second before staring down at her legs wrapped around his hips. He wasn't sure how all mouth matings worked, but she'd been an enthusiastic participant. Maybe she needed a moment to process what they'd done. He could give her that.

Neve wrapped his fingers around her nipped-in waist and stepped away from the wall. Her legs unwrapped from his hips, and he set her on the ground. His hand lingered until she found her footing and stepped away from him.

She adjusted her crown, straightened her dress, and then dabbed at her lips with the back of her hand.

Erasing all evidence of your touch.

A cleared throat had him glancing over his shoulder. Olwen and Flyka had stepped back into the corridor. His best friend arched his brows, and Neve huffed. He'd forgotten all about their audience.

Turning back to his *niliave,* he scowled and then cursed. She'd taken off and was already turning the corner ahead. Every part of him wanted to hunt her down and take her mouth again, but he curbed the impulse. Neither one of them had expected to have attraction to the other, much less some degree of affection. All he needed to do now was be patient.

A grim smile curled his lips. Patience was one thing he excelled at.

His little wife did everything in her power to avoid him the next three days.

The first night he came to bed, he'd found her sleeping on the couch. It had felt like she'd slashed open his chest. A clear rejection.

He hadn't let it slide.

Neve had gathered her up and tucked her into her side of the bed, making sure to build the pillow wall.

The next morning, he'd woken up and she'd vanished.

No one knew where the queen had gone.

When she'd finally shown up back in their chambers late that night, he'd been furious. She'd given him an explanation about charity work and time with Serenity, her *astrylle*, and then locked him out of the shower room. The icing on the cake had been that she'd worn his shirt to bed, walked right past the mattress and to the couch. He'd fumed in the stifling silence. It had taken her hours to fall asleep, but as soon as she begun to snore, he'd moved her back into the bed.

The second morning had gone much the same.

He had woken up alone.

Neve hated it, but he didn't have time to search for her when a message had come in about raiders to the southeast. He'd had to leave without a word from his elusive queen. When they'd arrived at the village, they were met with more than a raid. It was almost a whole bloody battalion of mercenaries.

It had been bloody, harrowing, and disheartening.

By the time he'd returned home two days later, he'd buried too many bodies and sported a few more scars. Beram was the first to welcome him home, his lips set in thin line beneath his gray beard. They'd discovered who'd sanctioned the act.

It seemed as if the attack had been sanctioned by the Asterans, but they'd used Loriian mercenaries.

"Where's the *reilleve*?"

"On her way to the midwinter festival, I believe, as is all of your court."

Qov. He'd forgotten all about the bloody festival.

He stalked through the palace, servants and courtiers alike scurrying out of his way. He cleaned up, donning simple black leathers and boots, and a sleeveless black brocade robe, leaving his chest bared. Olwen awaited him as he left his chambers. His friend took one look at the scowl on his face and fell in step beside him.

"How bad is it?" Olwen asked.

"I buried *children*," he growled, his stomach swirling with sickness.

This was what *saloes* did.

"Why would they risk an attack?" His friend asked. "You've a treaty. You're married to their daughter."

"That is the question of the hour, isn't it? I think we should ask my dear wife."

They reached the ballroom that faced the lake, clear windows so high and wide that the stars seemed to reflect off the floor, making it seem as if the people were dancing in the jewel-studded sky.

He paused in the doorway, observing the celebration. Luxurious tables laden with decorations and food lined the edges of the ballroom, framing the dance floor. He scanned the room for a familiar head of rose-gold hair as he moved to the refreshment table. A servant handed him a goblet of spiced wine, which he tossed back.

Just where was his little wife?

He caught sight of her on the dance floor in the arms of Bacti, one hand near his *caern'ye*.

Wearing the color of *Frost*.

Pale blues seemed to swirl on the flowy skirts as she floated across the dance floor. The edges of her bodice swooped up at the shoulders, creating jeweled *caern'ye*. Tonight, she looked like a Frost Queen.

And yet another *vallos* held her.

Neve took another goblet from a tray and watched as the *valles* tipped her head back and laughed at something the pretty giant said. Neve growled and sipped his wine, ignoring how Olwen was watching him from the corner of his eye.

The dance ended and Dahlia still hadn't seen him. She was too wrapped up in Bacti. A growl rumbled in his throat when the giant placed his hand on her lower back, pulling her a little closer to his body. The hair along his arms rose as Bacti kissed the back of her hand and gave Lia a sultry look. Pink filled her cheeks, and she glanced away coyly.

"Today has been a rough day," Olwen said softly. "It was just a dance."

"She's smiling at him," he gritted out. And the bastard was staring at her lips. Did he want to lick and bite them too? His fingers tightened on the silver cup. He wouldn't take any more of this. Neve tossed back the wine and handed the goblet to his friend. "It's time to retrieve my *niliave*."

Chapter Forty-Two

DAHLIA

JEKKET HAD GIVEN HER FIVE DAYS TO KILL THE king before her ruse was revealed.

Tomorrow would be day five. Nausea rose up. The poison ring felt heavy upon her hand.

Bacti smirked at her. "It was a pleasure to dance with you, my lady."

She glanced away from him, hiding her discomfort behind a smile. "Thank you."

Neve entered her line of sight, stalking toward her, black robes flowing around his legs, chest bare. He looked like some sort of pagan god. Her breath hitched as he drew closer, his attention completely focused on her.

The Frost King ignored Bacti and held his hand out. "*Lae reilleve.*" *My queen.* "Shall we dance?"

She pulled her hand from the giant's and placed it in Neve's. He'd come to save her. The king cut through the crowd and spun her until her back pressed against his abdomen. He held her arms out to both sides and curled his fingers around her wrists, like giant shackles.

"You wear the color of *Frost*," he whispered in her ear. "Why?"

"Because I knew it was a midwinter festival. I am trying to fit in."

A low chuckle escaped him that caused a shiver to run down her spine. "You will always stand out, *valles*. Especially when you wear the color of fertility in public. One that is a symbol to all you are ready for a child."

She gasped, blushing bright red. No wonder her lady-in-waiting, Alda, had snickered when she'd picked out the Asteran gown.

The music started off achingly slow, and the king directed her effortlessly around the floor. He lifted their hands above her head and then draped them by his shoulders, before pressing a large warm palm over her midriff and leading them through the next steps. It was a bit of a stretch, but she popped up onto her toes, trying to follow as the music raced to a crescendo.

Her mind raced as she ran over all the titters, stares, and odd conversations she'd had during the night. They all thought she was a baby-making trollop.

"I'll change."

"Now, now, do not be hasty. That is why I took a human bride after all. Peace through marriage, and an heir."

She craned her neck to stare up at Neve, whose eyes glittered dangerously. What the devil had gotten into him tonight? Was this still about her sneaking from their bed?

She'd never planned on getting close to the king, but the more time she spent with him, the more she liked him. The kiss was never supposed to happen, and yet she couldn't stop thinking about it, even if she didn't have any right.

She was the traitor. The deceiver. The one tasked to kill him.

Neve was rough around the edges, but he cared for her, and he didn't deserve it.

"Then I'll leave."

His grip tightened on her a moment before he spun her around. She caught her breath as his hands settled on her hips, before he threw her into the air, catching her around the thighs. She glanced at the other dancers, who all held their partners in a similar hold.

He spun in a slow circle, his grip loosening a touch, so she began to slide down his hard body. A riot of emotions swirled in her gut as her feet finally touched the floor, the song ending at last. Neve took her right hand and bent over it, kissing the back, in the very same place Bacti had.

Understanding clicked into place.

He was *jealous*.

His tongue slipped out, licking one knuckle, and she shuddered. He was playing games with her.

The audience broke out in applause, breaking the moment, and the king straightened, pulling her toward their table. He moved to his silver chair that was so big it was really a throne, and sat. He tumbled her into his lap, tossing her legs over the arm of the chair. She grabbed the sides of his robe and stared up at his flexing jawline.

"Bad day, *niliov*?" *Husband*. It was the first time she'd used the word.

All his attention focused on her face. "I am husband to you now? Even though you creep from our bed each morning?"

Dahlia winced. "I had to think." He turned away from her, but she reached up and cupped his cheek, forcing him to stare down at her. "I wasn't prepared for you, for this life. I'm doing the best I can."

Neve swallowed, a touch of softness around his eyes, but it disappeared in an instant. "You run my from touches and yet you invite *Bacti*'s." His accent thickened. "You wear another's jewelry."

Lia shook her head, caressing his jawline. He thought her ring was from another suitor? "I did not. I'm not sure what you saw..."

"You smiled at him."

"I hid my unease beneath a smile." She gave him a firm look. "If you'd been paying attention to me and not the giant you're jealous of, maybe you would have seen that. And as for the ring, it was one of the few gifts from my mother." *A truth and a lie.*

Lia really looked at him. There were shadows underneath his eyes, and a new cut at the base of his neck that the collar of his robe covered. She dropped her hand to gently touch the very edge. "What happened?"

His lips thinned. "An act of war."

She jerked. "What do you mean?"

He glared down at her like he knew her deep dark secrets. "Your family set mercenaries on a fishing village. Ten out of fifty survived."

"I'm so sorry." Why would Allium and Randa do such a thing?

"You do not refute what I've said?" The words held a challenge.

"No matter who ordered the attack, it is still sad."

"Why are you here?" he hissed.

"Because you bought me." *A truth.*

He caught her chin. "Can I trust you, *valles*?"

"As much as I can trust you."

The king scoffed, leaning so close that his lips almost touched her own. Her breath hitched, and tempered interest carved a smirk onto his face.

"I don't think you're as innocent as you pretend to be."

"And I don't think you're as cruel as you think you are," she retorted.

"You and I are bound." He sighed. "But we are also doomed."

Two truths.

Both of which she didn't want to acknowledge.

THE FESTIVAL PROGRESSED LATE INTO THE night, until finally Dahlia snuck away, intending to seek her bed. She gave a sleepy smile to a few of their people as she wandered out of the ballroom and into the immense hallway leading to the entryway.

As she passed a shadowed alcove, a hand wrapped

around her wrist and yanked her into the space. Her back slammed against the freezing window, stealing the air from her lungs. She clawed at Bacti's lavender hand, barely able to breathe.

He leaned into her space, and she turned her face away from him as he ran his nose along her cheek. "It's time you and I had a conversation, *valles*. How fragile you are." The giant gave her throat one more squeeze. "Keep your mouth shut and I won't take your life right now."

She nodded and he relaxed his grip. Lia coughed, eyes watering as she stared up into Bacti's terrible face. "What do you want?" she rasped, dropping her shaking hands from his wrist to the top of her dress. If she played this right, she could get to her knife.

"What everyone wants, little *saloes*. Power."

"How do you expect to get that from me?" she said, leaning heavily against the window; her pointer finger dipped into the top of her dress, just brushing the pommel of her blade.

Just a little more.

"You have been a thorn in my side since you arrived. You're everywhere, and yet no useful information has been shared about this palace."

Dahlia's jaw dropped. The lavender giant gave her a smug smile.

"Did you really think you were going to be sent here without any supervision?" He cocked his head, licking his lips. "You've had two jobs, and yet you've failed on all fronts." She froze as he glanced down her body and then back up. "Your queen made a mistake sending a common whore."

"How dare you speak to me in such a manner," she snapped, fear tightening in her gut.

"Yes, *valles*, keep playing your part." He pressed her harder against the window and crowded over her. "You have one day before I spill your secrets to the *reillov*. One day before I send word to have your mother executed." She flinched as he ran his tongue along the rounded shell of her ear. "And don't worry, we're very close to finding your brother."

"I've done everything the queen asked except commit regicide." Tears blurred her eyes. "The king gave Astera everything they wanted for peace. Why?"

Bacti grinned, but it sent a shiver down her spine. "Because we don't want peace. Mixing our people is unnatural. Imagine how our people will react when the human queen murders their fearless ruler. They will band together and eviscerate you."

"What do you get out of this? What did Allium promise you?"

He pressed a soft kiss to her cheekbone. "I can't spill all of my secrets." Bacti released her neck and stepped back as she doubled over, catching her breath. "Tick-tock, *valles*."

The giant winked at her and backed away, swagger in his step. Dahlia tilted her head back against the window and blinked away her tears.

There was no way out.

Either the people she loved died or she did.

CHAPTER FORTY-THREE

NEVE

HE STROLLED THROUGH THE QUIET HALLWAYS OF the palace.

Tonight, he had been out of line.

Pain, distrust, and jealousy had gotten the best of him.

He trudged up the stairs to the royal wing, Flyka following behind him. Neve paused on the top stair and waited for his friend to catch up.

She arched a brow at him. "What is on your mind, *reillov?*"

"She wore the color of *Frost.*"

Flyka whistled. "That she did."

"She didn't know what it meant."

"And yet..." Flyka drawled.

"I wanted it to be true," he admitted. His *jaivelle* had been stunning tonight. More than one gaze appraised her with appreciation.

"Why do you sound so ashamed?"

"Because an heir is a duty." He shouldn't want his human as much as he did. Especially since he still didn't know where her loyalties lay.

Flyka grinned. "Can it not also be fun?"

"She is my enemy."

"Could have fooled me. For our enemy, she's constantly helping our people."

"And if it's all an act?"

"If it was, wouldn't you have already taken her to bed or locked her away?"

That was a fair point.

Flyka sighed. "Stop being a coward and claim your *reilleve*."

"She could refuse me."

"She could, but she won't." Flyka waved at him and began jogging down the stairs. "Be gone with you."

Neve steeled himself and took the last step toward the royal wing. He entered their chambers and closed the door behind him with a soft click. Dahlia sat in their bed, wearing his black shirt, swirling a cup of tea.

Without her leggings.

He stared at her bared legs for a beat, and then dragged his gaze to her face. She was watching him, the shadows playing about her face.

"No hose?"

She set the cup on the side table next to the bed. "You were right. It is time to stop hiding."

He sat on the edge of the bed, twisting to face her. "I was harsh tonight. You didn't deserve my ire. Forgive me."

"There's nothing to forgive. We all make mistakes."

She sighed, glancing at the window. "I'm so tired. It won't be long until the sun rises."

Neve stood from the bed and closed all the curtains. He kicked off his boots and tossed his robe over the back of the couch. "Do you want me to stoke the fire?"

"I'm okay," she called.

He returned to the bed and watched as she tossed some pillows off the bed and snuggled in. Neve pulled the coverlet back and climbed in. "No pillow wall?"

She rolled onto her side, hands tucked underneath her cheek, a small smile on her lips. "What's the point when I just slip underneath them and molest you in the night for your heat?"

He grinned at her. "I didn't mind much."

Her smile disappeared slowly, and she reached out a hand toward him. He stared at her hand, and then laced his fingers with hers. He loved the stark contrast their complexions made.

"Can I ask you a favor?" she whispered into the darkness.

"What is it?"

She swallowed hard. "Would you ... hold me?"

He pulled her toward him immediately, until she was curled against the side of his body. Neve's hearts pounded like crazy, and he closed his eyes, savoring the way she felt. This was peace. Bliss.

His brows furrowed as he ran his thumb over her wrist, feeling her pulse racing. "What's wrong, *jaivelle*?"

"Everything." She shivered and pressed her cold nose against his arm. "Why is life *so* hard? I'm just so tired of it all. Don't you ever want to just run away?"

He lifted his left hand and rotated toward her slightly so he could run his fingers through her hair. "Sometimes, but then I think about all the people that need me."

"Have you ever had to do something horrible to protect others?" she whispered.

Neve nodded. "Yes. Does that make me a monster?" He looked down at her.

She peered up at him. "I don't know. There's not always a right or wrong, is there?"

"No, there's not."

"I'm sorry."

"For what?"

"The pain my people have wreaked on you and your family."

"It wasn't your fault."

"I'm still a *saloes*. That will never change."

Neve shrugged. "You can't help what you are any more than I can. Best just accept that about each other, no?" He leaned down and brushed his lips across her forehead. "Get some sleep."

"Goodnight, *niliov*."

"Goodnight, wife."

AT SOME POINT DURING THE NIGHT, HE'D curled himself around Lia. She wiggled and he groaned, tightening his arm around her waist. *Just a few minutes*

more. He pressed his nose into her hair and tried to slip back into sleep.

His little human wiggled again, shifting in the bed. He lifted his hand slightly and she rolled toward him. Neve settled his hand on her hip and pulled her closer as she slung her leg over his own. He caught the crook of her bare knee and hiked it over his hip. She sighed, and he smiled sleepily, brushing his fingertips up her bare thigh over the edge of her shift, and pulled her body into his own. She was so warm and soft.

She sighed, her breath brushing his lips. Neve cracked his eyes open. Dahlia lay entangled in his arms, her expression one of complete peace, lips slightly parted. Heat surged in his belly and longing crashed into Neve. When was the last time someone had trusted him enough to sleep in his arms?

He froze as her eyes blinked open; his hearts stuttered as she offered him a beatific smile. *Stunning*. She might be human and different, but she slayed him all the same. Would she scream once reality set in? Or curse him out with that wicked mouth?

Neither happened.

Instead, his little wife snuggled closer, cold nose touching his chest, and went back to sleep, her breath evening out once again.

His fingers flexed against her back as he settled against the pillow. She was a dangerous creature that would break him if he wasn't careful. But it was worth the risk.

Sleep tugged at him, and he followed its call with his wife sleeping in his arms.

It felt like mere moments had passed when he registered Lia's touch along his jaw. He kept his eyes closed, savoring the soft caresses that ventured to his sensitive ears and down his neck. His body burned and ached for the *valles* as she explored. His right arm tightened around her, and he blinked open his blurry eyes.

Dahlia stared up at him, pulling back her hand, the shadows in the room casting her features in hues of blue and gray. He caught her fingers and pressed a kiss to her knuckles and whispered, "Don't stop."

Having her touch was one of the best feelings he'd ever experienced. Neve didn't know what power she possessed over him, but he liked it and *craved* it. He placed her palm on his cheek and then draped his hand lazily over her tiny waist and waited.

Seittae. *Please touch me.*

His hearts clenched as she traced his lips, and longing struck him hard. All he wanted was to taste her again. The memory of their kiss had haunted him for days. His hand wandered over her back, kneading muscles and drawing circles over her thin garment.

Her little fingers slipped underneath his hair and cupped the back of his neck. He watched as emotion flickered across her face before she settled into resignation.

"What?" he murmured.

"Just this once," she breathed as she applied pressure to the back of his neck, urging him closer.

Neve leaned down and kissed his little wife. He'd never been interested in humans as a whole, especially in their mating rituals, but in the days since Neve had tasted Lia's lips, he'd managed to find a few books on it in the library—kissing in particular. And he *loved* it.

He threaded his fingers into her hair and cradled her face. The bones beneath her skin were so delicate, and he didn't want to hurt her. Her fingers brushed the skin of his jaw with tenderness. This kiss wasn't anything like the one he'd given her in frustration and pent-up desire. It was gentle, tantalizing, and so bloody soft that he could drown. When had anyone ever touched him like this?

Never.

He wanted all of it.

Chapter Forty-Four

It was selfish.

To kiss him. To want more. Especially with what she planned.

Dahlia pushed the thought away and threw herself into the kiss, her lips parting his own. He made a small noise in the back of his throat that sounded like want and surprise and need all in one. She gasped as his hand moved to her bottom and hauled her against him as he took possession of the kiss.

It was as if all his restraint had crumbled, leaving raw need behind.

He kissed her with fervor, pressing closer until his bare indigo chest rubbed against her shift-covered one. She held on to his hair, her tongue tangling with his. It was everything she needed and everything she shouldn't want.

The king rolled her onto her back, kneeling between her legs. Cool air kissed her bare thighs.

Embarrassment flooded her cheeks at how exposed she was, wishing now more than ever she'd worn something underneath her shift.

She trembled as he broke the kiss, his massive blue body caging her in. He skated his warm lips down her collarbone, tugging the shift out of the way so he could lave her collarbone with that wicked black tongue. Her embarrassment fled as a powerful wave of desire crashed over her. There was no shame here. Imposter bride or not, she was still married to him.

And he wanted her.

Lia closed her eyes and sank her fingers into his blue-black hair, tilting her neck so he had better access. Slowly, she ran her shaking right hand down his chest and taut abdomen to the waistband of his trousers. She tugged on the laces and they loosened immediately, threatening to spill his *sorav* into her hand.

Neve lifted his head, and she opened her eyes as he stared down at her, brow furrowed.

"What?" she rasped.

He reached for her right hand and lifted it to his mouth, kissing her palm. "You're shaking, *jaivelle*."

"It's nothing," she whispered, leaning up for another kiss. She could do this.

The king brushed his lips along hers tenderly. "You're afraid."

"No." She wanted him, but she also knew what she must do.

He pulled back, really studying her. She blushed at how high her shift had ridden up, exposing all of her body save her breasts. He leaned back on his heels, and she jerked when he skimmed his warm palms down her thick thighs to her rounded lower belly, his thumbs resting dangerously close to her core. The silence stretched on as he soaked her in.

Lia's breath fled her as he lifted her left leg and pressed a kiss to the inside of her knee. Tears blurred her eyes as he proceeded to pepper the patterns on her legs with kisses. Each touch felt like acceptance, as if he were healing her kiss by kiss.

She didn't deserve it.

"Stop," she cried softly.

"Never." He pressed kisses to the scars on her inner thighs. His gaze lifted to hers. "I'm sorry for these."

She shook her head, a sob lodging in her throat. "Not your fault."

The king hunched over and kissed the swell of her lower belly, flicking out his tongue to create a pattern around her bellybutton that had her panting. Neve worked his way up, kissing each freckle and mole along the way. When he reached the edge of her shift, he carefully caught the hem and pulled it down until she was covered once again.

"You don't want..."

Neve pulled her upright and into his lap as he leaned back onto his heels. Her legs straddled his hips. The proof of his desire pressed insistently against her, and her shocked gaze flew to his tender eyes as she blushed.

"I do, but not like this." He pressed his forehead to

her own. "You and I have only just begun to know each other. You've seen the worst in me, and I've yet to show you the best. Dark days are ahead of us, and tough decisions will need to be made by both you and I. An heir is expected."

She glanced away, feeling sick. He'd never get an heir from her. Only betrayal.

The king crooked an indigo finger beneath her chin and directed her attention back to his face. "This is not the life you were promised by your family. I've known for quite some time that I would have a human bride, and it has taken me this long to soften. I don't expect you to want me as I want you. And I don't want you to surrender to me out of duty."

"I'm not."

He arched a brow. "I've watched you. You give of yourself to everyone around you, and take nothing for yourself. You didn't rail against me when I told you I was the king and you'd been promised to me, nor when I embarrassed you with my council, or when I asked you to play the obedient bride for my kingdom. I can see what it has cost you. This..." He kissed each of her cheeks. "...is yours to command."

Tears spilled from her eyes as she stared up at the monster who'd become something much more dear. She was the monster, not Neve.

You're not worthy of him.

"No need to cry, *niliave*. I'm here."

Wife. She didn't deserve that title.

That was the problem. He was being too sweet. Why couldn't he be completely evil? Be the cold king that came out to play from time to time? It would make her decision that much easier. She hugged him close, pressing her face into the crook of his neck. He held her, running his hands through her hair and down her back in soothing strokes.

Dahlia closed her eyes and spun the ring the queen had given her. She flicked open the top, and pulled back to crush her lips to Neve's, tears pouring down her cheeks. He responded with a full-body shudder. Lia stabbed the thin needle into the back of his neck and bit his bottom lip, hard, holding on. She needed it in for ten seconds.

The king jerked, dislodging her.

That was not ten seconds. Lia would be lucky if it was five.

He frowned and reached for the back of his neck. "*Jaivelle*, what...?"

Neve swayed and then toppled backward. Lia scrambled off him and ran her hands over his face. He blinked at her, disoriented.

"I'm so sorry," she wept, tasting salty tears. "I don't have a choice. *Lo bietelle.*"

His eyes cleared for a moment and then hardened. Dahlia flinched and jerked back, staring into the dark pits that were his eyes. All traces of Neve were gone—only the Frost King remained. She'd done that.

No time for sentiment. You need to flee.

His lips moved but she heard no sound. Dahlia leaned closer as his eyes began to close, her ear near his lips.

"*Run*," he whispered.

She scrambled off the bed and sprinted for her things. He'd only said one word, but it held a wealth of meaning.

Run, because if he survived he'd hunt her down.

Run, because he was vengeance itself.

Run, because there would be no mercy or escape.

Run, because she'd created a monster and broken his heart.

Continue the series with:
Scorched Wings

COMING SOON

SCORCHED WINGS

BLOOD BEFORE LOVE

About the Author

Thank you for reading FROST BOUND.
I hope you enjoyed it!

FROST KAY is a USA Today bestselling author and a certified book dragon with an excessive TBR.

She adores telling stories of strong women, diverse cultures, and epic fantasy worlds filled with relatable characters and true love. She lives in the United States and when not immersed in her newest book, you can find her free diving in her mermaid tail, rock climbing, camping, or soaking up the sun with her cat.

If you'd like to know more about Frost, her books, or to connect with Frost online, you can visit her webpage https://www.frostkay.net/ or join her facebook group FROST FIENDS!

Afterword

Every single time I try to write one of these my brain short circuits. I have so many people to thank after I finish each book, and Frost Bound is no exception.

As you all know, I'm a huge fan of slow-burn in romantic fantasy. Neve and Dahlia are so very different in ALL the ways and there was a huge cultural bridge to gap between the two. Especially when it came to attraction. Thank you to my lovely friends who let me talk out my character's trauma and backgrounds until it felt just right.

All my love to Emma Hamm, Natalia Jaster, Hanna Sandvig, Annette Marie, and Jamie Dalton for your input when it came to blurbs, titles, and covers. Y'all know how much I hate writing synopsis and you really helped me get it just right.

And to Heather Renee, Casey L. Bond, Olivia Wildenstein, and Jesikah Sundin you've been amazing when I need to bounce ideas off of someone. Being in the indie pub business can feel isolating at times, but thanks to your friendship I've never felt that way. All the hugs to you.

To my editors and proofreaders... you all know how I struggle with deadlines. Thank you for putting up with me when I decide to rewrite half the stories two weeks before the appointment. Your patience is so very appreciated as is your constructive criticism and insight. I promise to be on time the next go around (knocks on wood).

Dear betas, proofreaders, and ARC readers, I wouldn't have been able to publish a single book without you. You're very much loved.

To the love of my life - your constant support, cheerleading, and willingness to wrangle the wee ones anytime inspiration strikes is invaluable. Our late night chats about characters and cocktail therapy sessions over tricky story-lines are the best. You are my favorite person.

My lovely readers... Thank you for sticking with me over all the years. Each time I start a new series, I'm terrified no one will like it or read it. You always prove me wrong in the best way.

xo,

Frost

Also By Frost Kay

THE AERMIAN FEUDS

(Dark Epic Fantasy)

Rebel's Blade

Crown's Shield

Siren's Lure

Enemy's Queen

King's Warrior

Warlord's Shadow

Spy's Mask

Court's Fool

Prince's Poison

THE BANISHED QUEEN SAGA

(Dark Romantic Fantasy)

Traitor of the Tides (2025)

THE TWISTED KINGDOMS

(Epic Fantasy/Fairytale Retelling)

The Hunt

The Rook

The Heir

The Beast

The Hood

The Wolf

DRAGON ISLE WARS

(Epic Fantasy)

Court of Dragons

Queen of Legends

Throne of Serpents

ENTANGLED WITH TRICKERY

(Romantic Fantasy/ Monster Romance)

Frost Bound

Scorched Wings